a Shelter of Hope

WESTWARD CHRONICLES

TRACIE
PETERSON

a Shelter of Hope

BETHANY HOUSE PUBLISHERS

Minneapolis, Minnesota

2005 edition

Cover print/photograph credit: Library of Congress, Prints and Photographs Division, Detroit Publishing Company Collection
Cover design by Melinda Schumacher

Published by Bethany House Publishers
11400 Hampshire Avenue South
Bloomington, Minnesota 55438

Bethany House Publishers is a division of
Baker Publishing Group, Grand Rapids, Michigan.

Printed in the United States of America

ISBN 978-0-7642-0048-9

Library of Congress has cataloged the original edition as follows:

Peterson, Tracie.
A shelter of hope / by Tracie Peterson.
p. cm. — (Westward chronicles ; 1)
ISBN 0-7642-2112-4 (pbk.)
1. Women pioneers—Fiction. 2. Waitressess—Fiction. 3. Wyoming—Fiction. I. Title.
II. Series: Peterson, Tracie. Westward chronicles ; 1.
PS3566.E7717 S54 1998
813'.54—dc21 00-503040
CIP

Dedicated to my son

Erik

God gave you to bless me,
to teach me trust,
to open my imagination and
show me a new way of seeing things.

But most of all,
God knew that as my last born,
you would complete our family
in a very special kind of love.

I'll love you forever.

Books by Tracie Peterson

www.traciepeterson.com

A Slender Thread • *I Can't Do It All!***
What She Left for Me • *Where My Heart Belongs*

ALASKAN QUEST
Summer of the Midnight Sun
Under the Northern Lights • *Whispers of Winter*

THE BRIDES OF GALLATIN COUNTY
A Promise to Believe In

THE BROADMOOR LEGACY*
A Daughter's Inheritance • *An Unexpected Love*

BELLS OF LOWELL*
Daughter of the Loom • *A Fragile Design*
These Tangled Threads

Bells of Lowell (3 in 1)

LIGHTS OF LOWELL*
A Tapestry of Hope • *A Love Woven True*
The Pattern of Her Heart

DESERT ROSES
Shadows of the Canyon • *Across the Years*
Beneath a Harvest Sky

HEIRS OF MONTANA
Land of My Heart • *The Coming Storm*
To Dream Anew • *The Hope Within*

LADIES OF LIBERTY
A Lady of High Regard • *A Lady of Hidden Intent*
A Lady of Secret Devotion

WESTWARD CHRONICLES
A Shelter of Hope • *Hidden in a Whisper*
A Veiled Reflection

YUKON QUEST
Treasures of the North • *Ashes and Ice*
Rivers of Gold

*with Judith Miller **with Allison Bottke and Dianne O'Brian

TRACIE PETERSON is a popular speaker and bestselling author who has written more than sixty books, both historical and contemporary fiction. Tracie and her family make their home in Montana.

PART ONE

ONE

Wyoming Territory 1883

DARKNESS ENGULFED Simon Dumas like a protective blanket, cobwebs clinging to her hair and skin. Normally the ten-year-old would have been fearful of such things, but not now. Retreating farther into the embrace of blackness under the rope-tied bed of her parents, Simone listened to the sounds that filled the otherwise silent April night.

Sounds of pain. Sounds of misery and anguish.

A scream tore through the air, and Simone threw her hands over her mouth to stifle her own cry. Silently she prayed that God would put an end to the hideous nightmare.

"You are a miserable excuse for a wife," a man's voice bellowed.

"But, Louis," the woman pleaded, "the baby needed my attention. I'll have your supper in but a moment's time."

A loud crash left Simone little doubt that her father was hurling furniture at her mother. Even her hands, tightly clutched over her ears, could not block out the sounds of his drunken attack. Her mind sought to remember the French fairy tales her mother often told, but it did little good. She even tried drawing to memory the Bible verses her mother had helped her learn in her studies.

"'I am the way . . . the life . . . the truth . . .'" Simone's recitation fell silent as the unmistakable sound of her mother's crying blended with that of the howling screams of her baby brother. Simone stifled a cough, lest her father hear her. She was barely over a bout of measles, and it had taken all of her strength to simply crawl beneath the bed.

"If you can't make that brat be quiet," her father yelled over the din, "I'll tie him to a papoose board and hang him from the nearest tree." Simone could not understand why the baby's cries made her father so furious. He was, after all, so very little. Crying just seemed a natural thing.

"You'll not take my child into the woods," Winifred Dumas screamed back, and Simone could hear the sounds of scuffling.

"I ain't taking lip from my woman. You'll do as I say," her father demanded.

"Leave the baby alone!" her mother screamed, and Simone cowered back as far as the log wall would allow. Now would come the worst fighting of all. Her father would remove his belt and whip her mother repeatedly until only a heap of torn clothing and bloody wounds remained. And when her father was done with her mother, he would no doubt come looking for Simone.

It was no less than a weekly ritual, much like the concerts her mother had told her of from her girlhood days back East. Only *these* were demonic concerts. Symphonies of desperation and destruction. Simone had never known a time when her father had not acted this way. Her mother tried to explain that it was because so many women in his life had hurt him when he was young. His grandmother had been severe, his mother a woman of loose morals, and even his sisters were vicious and cruel to the only boy in the household.

But in Simone's ten-year-old mind, it seemed that such treatment would make her father desire peace and kindness. Her mother was a gentle person. Surely her father would prefer that to the ugliness he'd known growing up. It was just too much to understand.

Simone now wept bitter tears and bit her fist so hard she drew blood. She could taste the salty warmth against her still-swollen lips. Yesterday her clumsy attempt at cleaning one of the oil lamps had reduced the lamp to broken shards of glass, and Simone's efforts were rewarded with a beating. Louis Dumas had cared little that her measles blisters were barely healed or that Simone had dropped the lamp because of her weakened condition. His backhanded slap across her face had resulted in a split lip and bruised cheek.

But the physical wounds would heal. The wounds within, however, ran much deeper. He had told her she was a bad child, an ungrateful wretch that would never bring anyone anything but pain and sorrow. His words pierced her heart even now.

"I wish you had died at birth like the others," he had told her. Her own father wished her dead.

Remembering her own pain helped Simone focus on something other than the gruesome scene before her. She wanted to run to her mother's aid, but she was too afraid. What good could it do anyway? She was only ten years old. She couldn't defend *herself* against the man's tirades, much less help her mother. Her father was a monster, and every night Simone prayed that God would take her father far away and never let him come home again. But as of tonight, her prayers went unheard. Or so it seemed.

Sometime amidst the argument, Simone had mercifully drifted into a light sleep. It was hours, or at least it seemed like hours, later when she woke up to find the house silent. But it wasn't entirely silent. She could make out the mournful sobs of her mother and knew that her father had either left the cabin or passed out. Either way, Simone knew the respite would be brief.

Slowly, in absolute stealth, Simone pulled herself forward. She could feel the rough planks beneath her bite into her tender flesh as her skirts shifted away and her petticoats inched their way up her legs.

The sound of someone moving about caused Simone to freeze in place. Was it her father? She drew a silent breath and held it. The sound came again, but this time Simone knew it wasn't of her father's doing. It was the sound of her brother nursing. Exhaling, Simone felt a sense of grave reservation. Perhaps if she remained in hiding they would all forget about her. Maybe God would take her and her mother and brother to heaven and they would never have to be hurt by her father again. Maybe.

She regathered her courage and moved out from beneath the bed. "Mama?" she called softly.

"Simone? My poor baby, come to me," Winifred Dumas encouraged.

Simone saw her and burst into tears at the sight of her mother's bruised face. Her right arm dangled rather oddly at her side, while her left one cradled baby John.

"Shhh," her mother tried to comfort as Simone drew herself gently against her wounded body. "He's gone for now."

"Gone?" Simone barely choked out the word.

"Oui, ma petite cherie."

Her mother's French calmed her in a way that English words had never done. Her mother always spoke French when tucking Simone into bed at night and when studying the Bible and whispering prayers. There was comfort in the sharing of such a sweet language, and that was why Simone easily switched into it to ask, "When will he be back?"

"I don't know," her mother admitted. "But you and I, we must speak before he returns."

Simone nodded, wondering fearfully what her mother would say. There was an odd expression on her face that Simone had never seen before. It almost gave her hope that the nightmare would soon end.

"I must try to get to safety," Winifred told her daughter. "If I can get to Uniontown, I may be able to get help from the lawmen I've told you about."

"Will they really help us?" Simone questioned, snuffing back tears and wiping her face with the edge of her tattered skirt.

"Oui. I believe they will."

"Can we go now?"

"*We* cannot go. I must do this without you or I'll never make it."

Simone felt the shock of her mother's words hit her like the back of her father's hand. "You're leaving me?" Her voice raised in obvious fear.

"Simone, please listen to me. I must sneak away when I know your father will not be able to stop me. I will lash John to my back and travel very quickly, but you are too weak. You are barely out of your sickbed. Because of this, I will leave you here and return with the lawmen."

"No!" Simone screamed, mindless that her father might well be within listening distance. "Don't leave me, Mama!"

Winifred's eyes filled with tears. She shifted her now sleeping son awkwardly, her right arm useless as she gently placed him in the cradle. "Come, Simone," she motioned, and with her left arm, she embraced the child close. "My arm is broken. I cannot take the gun with me to shoot when the wild animals come. I must run all the way. At least as far as Naniko's cabin." The old woman's cabin was a well-known resting-place between the Dumas cabin and Uniontown.

"I can shoot the gun, Mama," Simone promised, although she'd never tried.

"It won't take very long," Winifred said, refusing to change her plans. "If you are very quiet and stay out of sight, he won't hurt you, and I can be back with help before he knows I have gone."

"I won't stay here," Simone said with sudden determination.

"If you don't," Winifred replied, "you may be hurt beyond my care. You are still so very frail, Simone. The sickness has left you weak and incapable of the long journey. And the mountains are fierce—the snow too deep. You know very well how the storms come without warning." Simone nodded, knowing that her mother spoke the truth. "If I had a horse, I could take all of us out at one time and ride quickly to Uniontown or even south to the trading post on the river. But your father has the horse, and he keeps him guarded more carefully than he does any other possession. If I am to escape, I will have to do it quickly. He's gone now to check the lines to the east. That will give me only a couple of hours."

Simone knew her mother's determination. She knew it as well as she knew that she would be obedient to her mother's wishes. The country around her was cruel. Cruel and harsh and deadly. The mountains were unforgiving of intrusions, yet Louis Dumas had long ago carved his scars upon their face and proclaimed his right to land that refused to be settled. Simone had always feared that this land might one day swallow her whole, and now it felt as if that day had come.

"Please let me come," she begged her mother one final time. In her heart she knew what her mother's answer would be, but nevertheless she asked the question. "I promise I will be strong and run fast."

"Non, ma petite angée," Winifred whispered and tightened her hold. "It would be the death of you. I feel it in my bones."

Simone pulled away. Anger began to harden her heart. Her mother was deserting her, leaving her to fend for herself against the very monster that *she* was fleeing. A deep sense of betrayal saturated her soul. The only person she had ever trusted to remain faithful was now abandoning her.

"You won't ever come back," Simone said flatly.

"But of course I will," her mother insisted. "Simone, please come here."

But Simone refused to listen and continued to back away. "You don't love me, or you wouldn't go away and leave me behind. You only want John, and so you are taking John with you. Not me."

She saw the pained expression on her mother's face. Noted the longing in her eyes and the outstretched arm. And in that moment it became quite clear to Simone that she could never again allow someone to desert her in such a fashion. "I'm glad you're going," she lied. "I don't want you to be my mama anymore."

"Simone, don't say such things. I love you, my sweet."

"If you loved me, you would not leave me. Nobody leaves people behind when they love them. If I had a little girl, I would never leave her behind."

Winifred broke down at Simone's declaration. "You will see, Simone. I will be back for you. You will be safe."

Simone shook her head. "You won't come back. I know you won't." She turned and ran out the front door, mindless of the cold air and her lack of something warm to shelter her from the biting wind. Panting and barely able to find the energy to make her body move, Simone sought the comfort of solitude. She made her way to the pelt shed, and as she had done so many times before, she buried herself deep into the pile of pelts and sobbed silently so as not to draw attention to herself. For reasons beyond her youthful understanding, Simone felt certain she would never again see her mother or her brother. They seemed forever lost to her.

Simone desperately wanted to run back to the house and beg her mother's forgiveness. She was the only one who had ever shown

Simone tenderness and love. How would she ever be able to live without her? Simone began to tremble at the thought of her father's rage. *He will be so mad when he learns what she's done.*

Why was God letting this happen? Mama had always said God was good. It was too much to comprehend that God could be both good and let bad things happen to a person at the same time.

Simone reasoned at that point that God must not care. She was probably the horrible child her father had declared her to be, and this was all her fault. They had all betrayed her. Betrayed her love. First her father, then her mother, and over all—God.

Curling into a ball, she sucked her thumb, something she only did when truly troubled or hurt. Her last wakeful thought was of the smell of death surrounding her. Death in the pelts that her father had taken that winter. Death in severing herself from her mother's love. And death that Simone felt somehow certain was soon to visit itself upon her mother and brother.

TWO

Wyoming Territory 1885

AUTUMN IN THE TERRITORY was something glorious to behold. The tall lodgepole pines remained fixed as green sentinels, but the aspen and cottonwood washed the landscape in molten gold. Simone, now a spindly twelve, liked autumn best. Autumn meant that cold weather would descend down the mountains, and soon the valleys would be covered in thick blankets of snow. Snow meant what few animals remained in the area would grow thicker, richer pelts, and her father would leave her and go to tend to his traps.

Trudging through the dry, brown grass, Simone paused beside a standing of mountain ash and watched as several birds feasted off the shiny red berries of the tree. The red leaves and berries made a pleasant contrast to the golds and greens painted across the landscape. Simone sighed and lifted the water buckets once again. Just beyond the ash trees their main source of water melodiously danced across the rocks, ever rushing away from the place Simone called home.

How many times had she wanted to join in on the journey? She'd often longed to simply wade into the stream and follow it until she was far, far away. But she always chose to stay, for what reasons she still could not truly understand. Maybe it was that even after nearly two and a half years, Simone was still waiting for her mother to come back for her.

But her mother wasn't coming back. She was never coming back.

Her mother was dead.

Simone tried not to think about it as she filled the wooden buckets from the icy mountain stream. Her mother had never made it to the freedom she sought. Her father had tracked Winifred down and killed her and Simone's little brother. He had returned to Simone that night and gloated his victory, reveling in giving the helpless child the complete details of his actions. She could still remember his face. Still hear his rage that anyone should dare defy Louis Dumas. But mostly, she remembered the way he had threatened to revisit the same horrors on Simone should she ever contemplate running away from him. Maybe that was why Simone stayed. After all, where could she go that he would not follow?

Her fingers felt numb from the icy flow of the creek. It served to remind her that her heart, too, was numb—from grief and from the betrayal of those who should have loved her. Numbness was her only defense, and memories of her mother did not serve to maintain the strong wall she had erected.

With the buckets now filled, she tried to shake off the cold along with her thoughts. Her mother had chosen her path, and now Simone would have to seek her own way. Staying, quite frankly, was easier than leaving. Doing nothing seemed safer than striking out against the only remaining family member she had. True, her father's hatred was quite evident in his actions toward her, but he was all that was left to her.

Struggling under her load, Simone contemplated whether or not it might be more to her advantage if he, too, went away and never returned. She used to pray for such a thing, but not any longer—mostly because she no longer prayed. She found it difficult at best to believe in the loving God her mother had trained her to know. If He were truly so good and so loving, He would never have allowed her to endure the miseries she knew as her life. For what fairness—what love—lay in allowing a small child to suffer such pain? How could God expect her to accept such a life?

A sudden cramp in her stomach nearly doubled her over. Simone paused, set the buckets down, and rubbed her aching abdomen. It had been like this off and on since yesterday, but she dared not show her father the slightest complaint. Once, when she had fallen from a tree and sprained her foot, her father refused to acknowledge her injury. Since she was stupid enough, he had said, to climb up there in the first place, she should bear her punishment in silence.

It wasn't the only punishment she took in that manner. When she had been small, her father had seemed to take irrational pleasure in beating her until she cried out. One day she simply forgot to cry, and it was then that she realized the beatings would end much sooner when she remained silent. Her father's pleasure could not be found in the stoic behavior of his child. At first, this had angered him even more and in turn he had beaten her even more severely. But then, when she was nearly unconscious, he had stopped. He'd looked at her oddly, threw down the blood-smeared stick he'd been using, and trudged off as if to contemplate what had just occurred. After that, Simone never cried.

Simone straightened gingerly and the pain returned, and with it a very necessary urge to relieve herself. She wandered over to the seclusion of some thick shrubs and when she pulled up her skirts, she noticed blood on her inner thigh. Frantically, her mind raced to consider what harm she might have done herself. Had some insect bitten her? Had she somehow injured herself without knowing what had happened?

She forgot everything, including the water buckets, and raced toward the cabin. She had little desire to confront her father with this news, but there was no one else to ask. And what if she were dying? Surely even her father would want to know that.

"Papa?" she called, coming up to the pelt shed.

"What do you want?" His harsh tone assured her this would be no easy matter.

"Papa, I don't know what is wrong," she said, panting to draw breath.

"Wrong? What are you talkin' about, girl?" Louis Dumas questioned, coming through the opening of the shed. He held a long filleting blade in one hand, and his hands were covered in blood and bits of fur. The blood seemed a poignant reminder of her own condition.

"Papa, I am bleeding."

"You mindless twit. What've you done?" His gaze showed nothing but the abject disgust he felt for her. His weatherworn face scowled at her from behind his heavy black beard.

"I don't know," Simone replied honestly. "I went for the water—"

"And where is it?" He roared the question, looking around her for some sign of the buckets.

"I left them by the stream. I was afraid," she admitted, not really understanding why she had opened herself up to an attack by admitting her fear.

"Afraid?" he laughed and rolled his eyes. "Because of blood?"

"But, Papa, I don't know why I am bleeding. I don't remember hurting myself, but there are pains in my stomach." She touched her abdomen as if to reinforce the truth of the matter. "And when I raised my skirts, I found blood on my legs."

Dumas looked at her dumbly for a moment before he roared into a laughter so hideously unfeeling that Simone actually backed away in fear. "Stupid, stupid girl. Did your mother not teach you anything? You have the woman's curse, that's all. Yer cursed like all your kind, and it won't go away till you marry."

"I don't understand," Simone said, barely finding the strength to challenge his reply.

Dumas waved her away. "It's a woman's curse, I tell you. Every month you bleed—just like you bleed the hearts and souls of the poor, unsuspectin' men around you. Now get me my water. You'll be lucky if I don't beat you for such stupidity."

Simone swallowed back the lump in her throat. Her humiliation was made complete as her father turned to go and laughed again, muttering to himself about how God could not have cursed him with a more dim-witted child.

"A woman's curse," she whispered, moving back along the path toward the stream. Why had her mother not told her? Why had her mother not told her a great many things? she wondered bitterly.

She retrieved the buckets, still wondering what it all meant—what the curse was about and why she should bleed in such a way. Her only hope of learning more than what her father told her was to seek out the old Indian woman who lived several miles away. Naniko would tell her what the curse was about. Until then, she would simply have to suffer in silence.

Slipping away to Naniko's cabin proved easier than Simone had imagined. She went on the full instruction of her father to seek out the old woman and trade her food for the animals she'd managed to trap in her crude fashion. Simone had watched Naniko capture animals many a time with little more than a hand-dug pit carefully concealed by fragile branches and straw. Naniko, drawing upon her Indian and French heritage, knew the ways of the land and had carefully imparted her knowledge to Simone on more than one occasion. Now, Simone hoped, Naniko would tell her the mystery of the woman's curse . . . and Simone would no longer be stupid.

Louis Dumas stared in open wonder as Simone made her way down the wooded path to the Indian woman's cabin. He couldn't help but try to calculate her years. Was she eleven? Twelve? It seemed impossible that she should already be that age, but the fact that the curse was upon her was reason enough for him to see her in a new light. She was nearly a woman grown. Nearly old enough to marry and bear children of her own.

This idea seemed too startling to accept without great consideration. Simone was nearly grown. Nearly old enough to leave him as her mother, in all her unfaithfulness, had left him. Old enough to treat him as ruthlessly as every other woman in his life.

His own mother, a prostitute who kept his lazy father in liquor and gambling money, had long ago taught him that women were not to be trusted. Just when he had needed her the most, she had run away with a peddler, leaving his grandmother and sisters to raise him. Even now he could feel the rod against his back as his grandmother sought to beat the evil out of him.

Growling at the memory, Louis threw himself back into his work. Work! If Simone left him, who would work for him? Who would serve his needs?

He could take another wife—he'd often thought of it. He'd even contemplated going north into Canada since the fur trade was played out in this area. It was only stubborn determination and an aversion to the responsibility of packing for the move that kept Louis Dumas in the area. Wyoming was a changed sort of land from the place he'd come to so long ago. The railroad ran stripes across the territory, and the Indians had been rounded up and moved onto government land. There remained a wild element to the vast, high desert plains and rugged pinnacles of the mountain ranges, but it wasn't enough to make Louis a rich man. He'd considered mining the area, hearing wild tales from other folks about the richness of the untapped resources, but mining was hard work. Much harder, in his estimation, than trapping. No, perhaps Canada was the answer. And if not Canada, then somewhere else.

He could go down to Denver and get himself another wife, then trek off to the north country. And if he didn't need to concern himself with Simone, he might well find that a very pleasurable journey. He thought long and hard on the situation. Perhaps there would be someone in the territory to whom he could sell Simone. After all, short of her ability to work around the cabin, she meant nothing to him. Yes, that might be the answer. He could sell her over to someone else before the brat up and got the idea to desert him. Let her run away from someone else. Let his purse be filled with coins before the wretched creature betrayed him as the others had.

It gave him a great deal to ponder.

That night, Simone lay awake in her bed for a long time. She thought on what Naniko had told her and marveled at the changes in her body. She was becoming a woman, Naniko had said, and it wasn't a curse—it was a good thing. Simone believed her, not because she felt any real bond to the woman, but because she didn't trust her father to be honest with her for any reason.

Sitting up, Simone hugged her knees to her chest and watched the dancing flames in the fireplace. Her father was leaving tomorrow for Uniontown, and after that it would not be much longer before he was gone for several weeks, maybe even months, in order to work his traplines and hunt. She'd heard him say that the area was worked out. Very little remained in the way of real food or support for their needs. And as if to prove his point, each year Louis seemed to venture away for longer periods of time. Not that Simone minded.

She remembered the first year he had taken off after her mother had gone. She had only been ten years old, but she had learned quickly to survive on her own. Her father had called her stupid, but Simone knew that stupid people didn't survive in the mountains. Stupid people died.

That thought brought to mind her mother, and although Simone tried to push it aside, the hazy image of her mother's smiling face haunted her. She could remember her voice better than her features, and sometimes it seemed that she whispered to Simone in her dreams. Despite her determination to harden herself to any sensation or feeling, Simone couldn't deny the warmth that spread over her at the memory of her mother's embrace. She thought of the hours spent learning to read and write, all under her mother's tender tutelage. She remembered the stories and the way her mother read from the Bible and explained the meaning of the words Simone could not understand, though she understood a great deal. She had begun to read at the age of three, and by the time she was seven, the Bible didn't seem such a difficult book to master. Of course, reading and understanding the meanings were two different things, her mother had often told her.

Simone shuddered and hugged her legs tighter. She tried to imagine strong arms hugging her in return, but the feeling was fleeting and the emptiness it left in its place was almost unbearable. *No more memories*, she demanded of her mind. Memories caused pain. And pain was simply too high a price to pay.

But her mind refused to listen to reason as her gaze fell upon her mother's Bible and prayer book. When Simone discovered that her mother had quickly fallen through with her plan to escape on that day so long ago, the only things Winifred left behind to remind her daughter to hope for her return were her Bible and prayer book. Simone remembered the carefully penned note her mother had left inside the front cover of the Bible. They were to be her mother's last words to Simone, and even now, try as she might to forget, Simone could still remember them:

Darling Daughter,

I love you more dearly than my life, and I would gladly give it to save you from harm. Look for me, I am coming back for you, just as Jesus promised He, too, would come back for us one day.

Mama

Simone refused to believe her mother's words, just as she refused to believe the other words in that book. God could not possibly be who her mother claimed Him to be—a Father of mercy and love. There was no mercy in Simone's life. There was no love. And therefore, there could be no God.

She had wanted to burn the Bible and prayer book, but even as she stood over the fireplace on many an occasion, Simone could never bring herself to deposit the books into the fiery mouth. Something made her hold back. She tried not to think of it, but her mind was her enemy as far as Simone was concerned. No matter how hard she tried to keep those vivid memories from returning, she couldn't forget.

A tear slid down her cheek, and Simone angrily wiped it away, refusing to allow any others to follow. There was no room for such things in her life. No room for tears *or* smiles. She simply couldn't allow herself the luxury of feelings. And if there truly was a God, she would have asked Him most sincerely to rid her of the ability to ever feel anything again.

THREE

May 1890

SCOWLING AND MUTTERING CURSES, Louis Dumas led his horse down the muddy streets—if they could be called streets—of Uniontown. The furs he'd brought in from his winter traps were hardly the best, and therefore the amount of money in his pocket did little to lift his spirits. His boredom drove him to Uniontown nearly a month before any real warmth would come to the area. And while the cold weather should still be able to provide him with thick pelted furs, Louis knew enough to realize there were problems. The area appeared to be trapped out. Too civilized. The animals had gotten wise to him and the hordes of others who had come to settle the land and had moved deeper into the protection of the mountains. He tried not to think of what the months ahead might have in store. He could scarcely imagine the money lasting him the summer, much less grubstaking him for the winter months after that. He hated the thought of pulling up stakes and moving. Not that Uniontown held any real hold on him, but moving was a chore he'd rather not have to deal with.

"Ho, there, Louis," a man called to him from a bench in front of a battered-looking structure. "Comin' in for a haircut and bath?"

"Not hardly," Dumas replied. He'd certainly not waste his time or his money paying someone to cut his hair when he could just as soon have his daughter see to the matter for free. No doubt Old Man Murphy needed the money as much as he did, and Louis couldn't fault him for trying. "Might play a game of poker or two. You comin' over to the Slipper?"

Murphy grew thoughtful. "I jes' might."

Louis nodded and, being intent on his purpose, walked on. He needed a drink. A strong one. And he needed to think about his finances. Thankfully, he could do both at the Red Slipper Saloon. Tying his mangy beast to a crude hitching post outside the saloon, Louis spit a brown stream of tobacco and saliva, then reached up to retrieve his rifle.

"Louis Dumas," a haggard but clearly female voice called out. "Ain't you a sight for sore eyes."

He took his time acknowledging the town's only prostitute. "Ada. See you didn't freeze out this winter."

"Same for you, Louis," she replied.

He looked up and nodded. Standing there smiling, two front teeth missing and sporting a scar that ran down the side of her left cheek, Ada could hardly be counted as the town's welcoming committee. Nevertheless, Louis threw her a grin. After all, she was the only white woman around these parts, with the exception of his daughter.

"Comin' in for a drink?" she asked as if she didn't know his intentions.

"That and some cards," Louis told her as he climbed up on the boardwalk.

"There's quite a game of poker going on. Has been most of the day," Ada replied and toyed with the cuff of her serviceable brown dress.

"Who's playin'?" Louis asked before stepping into the establishment.

"Mostly regulars. Gus, Dave, Flatnose," she began listing. "Oh, and a new guy. Been here about a week and seems to have plenty of money to burn. Garvey Davis is the name."

Louis thought a moment on the name, then decided it meant nothing to him. "Any good?"

"You mean at cards?" she asked, giving him another gap-toothed grin. "He holds his own."

Louis nodded. "Go pour me a drink, Ada. A good, tall whiskey, and bring it to the table."

"Will I see you later?" she asked, unmistakably hopeful.

Louis laughed, slapped her on the bottom, and pushed her aside. "You might. Just depends on gettin' my other business tended to first."

He didn't wait for her reply but instead walked into the dimly lit saloon, rifle cradled in his arms. There were four tables in the establishment and just about the same number of chairs. Regular bar fights kept the chairs down to a minimum, and even though Ada had everyone's pledge to replace the objects they'd destroyed, few of the men had honored their word where the chairs were concerned.

As his eyes adjusted to the lack of light, Louis gave the room a once-over. At one of the corner tables, Louis located the gathering of card players and wondered—almost daring himself to hope—that he might boost his earnings with a few intense games.

On the opposite side of the room a makeshift bar lined the wall. The long, wooden structure ran about ten feet in length, with extended planks on either side that had been set atop kegs in order to give more drinking space to the customers. Uniontown didn't boast a big population. In fact, there were probably no more than fifty people in a twenty-mile radius, and forty some of those were men. But every last man depended on the Red Slipper Saloon to show him a good time. And Ada hated to disappoint anyone.

Seeing the woman already at work pouring him a drink, Louis ambled over to the card table, doing his best to appear completely disinterested in the game.

"Louis, how's the furs this year?" one man asked.

Louis shrugged. "Same as always."

Just then Ada came to him with the drink, and before answering anything more, Louis downed a good portion of the whiskey and smiled. "Ahhh, 'tis mother's milk."

The men and Ada laughed while Louis finished the glass and motioned for Ada to bring him another.

"You gonna join us, Louis? Spend a little of that wealth you made on furs?"

Again Louis shrugged. "Don't know as I should take the time, Gus."

Gus laughed. "What else do you need to be doing? Get a chair and sit down."

"He can have mine," Ada called from the bar. "I've got work to do. Dave, you still going to Laramie?"

"Yup. Day after," the man replied.

"Don't head out without my supply list," Ada reminded.

"Wouldn't dream of it, darlin'."

Louis took this in, all the while studying the stranger who sat staring at his cards. The man seemed deceptively quiet. *It never pays to turn your back on the quiet ones*, Louis thought, pulling up a chair. The man clearly had the winning take on the table, and Louis couldn't help but wonder if he held a talent for cards or a gift for cheating.

"This here's Garvey Davis," Gus told Louis. "Jes' up from the silver and gold mines of Colorado and itchin' to spend his fortune."

Louis nodded as the stocky redheaded man looked up and grunted. Davis appeared to be somewhere in his forties, but Louis couldn't be sure. Hard life aged a man, and it was clear that Davis had known his share of bad times. The large hooked nose appeared to have been broken more than once, and even from across the table, Louis could smell the rancid odor of the man. To just look at him, one would never have guessed the man to have money, and maybe that was exactly as Davis planned it. A man looking as he did was less likely to be robbed on his travels.

Raising bushy eyebrows over pale brown eyes, Davis said, "You gonna play or talk?"

Louis gave a grin. "Depends on what we're playin'."

Gus laughed. "Well, it started out poker, but Davis is playin' a mean hand, and now we're mostly just handin' our money over to him."

Louis allowed his eyes to lock onto Davis's weatherworn face. *Here*, he thought, *is a worthy opponent. Here is a man who has clearly come with a purpose.*

"Ain't hardly fair of me to leave the man so burdened," Louis replied. The other men laughed, but not Garvey Davis. So with nothing else said, Louis gave a disinterested shrug and fished out a few of his precious coins.

Three hours later, the others had given up and only Davis and Dumas remained. Louis had caught on early to Davis's style of cheating, and without ever revealing the man's secret, he played along, matching him card for card. Louis now sat with a healthy pot of cash, intrigued by the man's deadly calm but even more so by the talk of Colorado streams so full of gold that a man had only to dip his pan into the water to make himself a fortune.

"Iffen there's such a fortune to be made, why'd you leave it?" Dumas asked seriously. "Seems downright ignorant to walk away from a meal ticket."

Davis stuffed a wad of tobacco into his mouth and made a pretense of rearranging his cards. "Money's good, but I needed a change. Thought to settle down in a place of my own."

Dumas saw the possibilities of a new life for himself and pursued the situation. "I've got a trapline about twelve miles from here. House, pelt shed, and the tools a man would need to make it all work. I could sell it to you."

Davis looked up at this and met Louis's stare. "Trapping, eh?" He scratched his chin through the matted red beard. "Tell me more."

They sat there another hour discussing the land and the business of trapping. Davis had experience in trapping elsewhere, but Louis felt it important to explain the benefits of working this particular area. He artfully left out the fact that most of the game had been depleted years ago and instead focused on the benefits of having a trapline already established and a cabin to live in.

"I was kind of figurin' to get me a wife," Davis finally said. "Don't appear to be no white women I'd wanna hitch up with in these parts."

Louis had already been contemplating the complication of Simone. It'd be hard to get himself another woman with Simone underfoot. She'd no doubt cause all manner of problems and be difficult at best to keep under control. He felt certain the only reason he'd managed her thus far was the isolation of their home. Simone seldom went any farther than Naniko's cabin and had only been to Uniontown a handful of times.

"I got me a daughter," Louis said, thinking through the idea as he spoke. "I could include her in the package."

"White?" Davis questioned.

" 'Course she's white. Her ma was a full-blooded Frenchy. Met her in Denver."

Davis threw him a suspicious look. "Why in tarnation would a man sell his own kid to the likes of me?"

"She's just now come to the age of needin' a man. I've figured on findin' me another wife," Dumas explained. "The girl would be in the way."

"She ugly?"

Gus overheard the men talking and brought his drink back to the table. "She's got a face like an angel, and she's all curvy and round. Why, the last time Louis brought her to town, must have been a whole line of us fellows askin' after her. Talks real purty, too. Kinda like one of those uppity women down in Laramie."

Dumas frowned. Gus spoke the truth, although he never really considered the matter. Simone worked for him, and to consider giving her in marriage to one of the Uniontown losers wouldn't have served him any purpose. But this . . . this was different.

"How come none of you ended up with her?" Davis asked, now quite serious about the discussion.

"I needed her, plain and simple," Louis replied. "She's a hard worker, and she knows the fur business. Smart too. Talks and writes French and English, reads just about anything she can get her hands on. She talks good 'cause her ma thought she should. Can't figure why the woman saw it as useful out here, but what with her comin' from a good family and all, guess her ma figured it was only right. Simone can cook with little of nothing and make it taste like a feast, and as Gus pointed out, she'll do a nice job of warming a man's bed."

"How much?" Davis questioned, apparently having heard enough of the sales pitch.

"I don't rightly know," Louis admitted. "Ain't never considered the matter before now." He spit on the floor, then leaned back in his chair. "I wouldn't want to clean you out, but I'd have to make back what I've invested. And by your own admission, there ain't another white woman in the area—lessen you count Ada."

Davis nodded. "Don't mean I couldn't go find me one."

"Yes, but this one already knows the business you plan to set your hand to. Seems kinda foolish to pass up on a gal who's got both looks and experience. Besides, ain't gonna be too many women what are willin' to come out here and be so isolated."

Davis's expression told Louis that he saw the sense in the matter. "And would your daughter also be willing to this arrangement?"

"She's only seventeen. She'll do what I say. She's had the whip laid to her on occasion, so she knows the price of disobedience." He didn't want Davis to think her a troublesome wench, so he quickly continued. "Iffen you think this is somethin' you'd like, come on back with me to the cabin. You can check out the lines and the cabin—and check her out, too. I might add one other thing . . . she's never been with a man. I wouldn't allow it. You'd be getting yourself something mighty special."

"I still don't understand why you'd be willing to just sell her out like that," Davis remarked. "Probably plenty of fellows elsewhere that could give you better money than me. Why, some of those mine owners would probably pay a pretty penny to have her there to keep the miners happy."

Louis shrugged. The thought had never crossed his mind before Davis mentioned it. He supposed he should think the thing through more clearly. He'd never seen Simone as an asset before. Still, he thought of the pelt business and how summer would find him half crazed and bored. "Suppose I could take her with me," Louis replied, "but I'd rather not be slowed down." He sighed and made up his mind right there and then. If Davis wanted her and agreed to his price, he'd do the deal and be done with it. "Look, she has to marry someone. At least you'd have the house and trade, and she'd be comfortable. Who knows? Maybe she'll give you a few sons to help keep you in your old age. And with Simone off my hands, I can tend to my own needs—get me a wife, maybe have a few sons of my own. After all, I'm not much older than you."

Garvey took all of this in and became so fascinated by the idea that he forgot to cheat at the game and Louis threw down the winning hand. "I've had enough of cards. What say we make our way to your place?" Davis suggested hopefully.

Louis eyed the stack of money in front of him. His winnings nearly doubled what he'd started out with, and if he could somehow sell off his place and daughter, he might well triple it. "Let's go," he told the man. He hoisted the rifle, which had lain across his lap the entire duration of his stay at the Red Slipper, and threw a gold coin to Ada. "I'll be back to collect on the change," he told her with a wry grin.

Simone had taken the event of her father's absence from the house as a reason for celebration. Her first order of business came in the form of a rare treat—a hot bath. She went to the pelt shed and took down the largest tub she could find, then dragged it back to the house. Next, she drew water and ice from the stream and spent nearly three quarters of an hour getting enough of the liquid heated over the hearth to fill the tub. It took a lot of effort, but it was definitely worth the time and trouble. Sinking into the steaming water, Simone couldn't remember when anything had ever felt this good.

Using hard lye soap, she did her best to wash her long black hair. Many times she had no other recourse but to use cornstarch to rid the ebony mass of oil and dirt, but most of the time her hair simply went dirty and unkempt.

After her bath Simone tied an ancient robe around her body, stoked up the fire in the hearth, and heated another kettle of water. Her clothes were next to go into the tub. With only two outfits to her name, both having belonged to her mother, Simone had to be careful to keep them as serviceable as possible. They usually went days—sometimes weeks—without a good washing, and yet Simone often worried that if she washed them too much, the poor things might fall completely apart.

She finished the task quickly, then spread them out in front of the fire. With this accomplished she emptied the tub, braving the cold temperatures to walk back across the yard to the pelt shed. The cold wind whipped up under the robe, stinging her legs. Picking up her pace, Simone didn't even take the time to appreciate the beauty of the day before her. She longed only for the security and solitude that came from the closed door of her cabin. A sigh escaped her as she closed the door and sought out the warmth of the fireplace once again. She readjusted the clothes, then began to comb out her hair, drying it by the heat of the hearth.

If only it could be like this always, she thought. *If only he would stay away and leave me be. I could live quite happily without ever seeing another human being, if only my father would disappear from the face of the earth.*

Simone always found herself hopeful that her father might one day forget to come back to the little cabin. She didn't go so far as to pray for this because she had firmly convinced herself that prayer was little more than mutterings and utterances from weaklings and cowards. But she did wish for it and often imagined her life without Louis Dumas. In fact, this became her favorite pastime.

She pictured herself living quietly on the side of the mountain. No one coming or going. No one to even know of her existence. She also considered the idea of loading up the things that were important to her and trekking off across the rugged mountains to parts unknown. She wouldn't go to Uniontown, however. The men made her uncomfortable there, and the women, mostly mixed race, were quiet and kept to themselves. Naniko told her that it wasn't good to be alone so much of the time, but Simone thought it the lesser of the two evils in her world. To be alone simply meant the absence of her father, and that cherished state of living held far greater interest to Simone than his companionship.

When her clothes and hair had dried, Simone dressed and went to work preparing a simple stew. Her father could very well spend the night in Uniontown, but it was also a possibility that he would return. And if he did so and found nothing in the way of supper, Simone knew his rage would be endless. Opening several cans of vegetables and cutting up the last of a hindquarter from a bighorn sheep, Simone had the stew simmering in a matter of minutes. She loved canned vegetables. It seemed so little would grow for her here in her mountain habitat. And why should she labor over the poor soil when someone had already gone to the trouble to package the necessary article in a can of tin? Her father, too, seemed pleased with the convenience and never balked at the purchase.

Of course, bread was another matter. Simone didn't really mind putting her hand to baking. In fact, of all her tasks she rather enjoyed this one. A person could work out a great deal of anxiety and frustration on a lump of dough, she had decided. And she found she had a knack for producing light, fluffy biscuits and golden, crusty loaves of bread that made one's mouth water just catching a whiff of the aroma in the air.

Simone thought for a moment, then reached for some flour. They would have biscuits tonight. She liked to cut them out and float them atop the stew to bake and brown as the stew cooked. It made a tasty treat that both warmed the body and stuck to the ribs. And it required very little attention on Simone's part.

Leaning against the single window in their cabin, Simone stared out on the landscape and wondered if her life would ever be different. She found it easy to maintain a stoic reserve in regard to her welfare. She knew nothing else, although she'd heard stories of cities in other places and of people in beautiful clothes riding in carriages. But Simone had done such a good job of keeping her emotions in check that she couldn't even muster enough imagination to contemplate the possibilities of such a life. Her one and only concession was to consider Naniko's suggestion that being alone wasn't good for anyone. But even here, Simone kept a close guard on her heart. Naniko's friendship had been a welcomed and wonderful thing when Simone's mother had first left her, but Simone was no fool. She saw the aged woman's health begin to fail and knew that death would not be far behind. Realizing that, Simone had begun a systematic effort to wean her affections away from Naniko. She never again wanted to feel the pain of losing someone she cared about, and the only way to accomplish that feat seemed to be simple: Don't care about anyone.

She started to turn from the window but movement in the trees caught her attention. Far down the path that led to the Dumas cabin, Simone could make out the figures of two men on horseback. One was clearly her father, but the other man was a stranger. Simone watched for a moment longer, then gave a shudder. They'd no doubt drink and carry on until all hours of the night, leaving Simone little choice but to seek solace in the pelt shed. The only problem was, her father had just sold off his pelts. The shed would be cold and comfortless.

Thinking on this, Simone went quickly to a small trunk and pulled out her one pair of woolen stockings. They had been darned and mended many times, but they were still warm. Pulling these on and securing them with a garter, Simone dug into the trunk again and pulled out pantalets. They had once belonged to her mother and Simone seldom found a need to wear them, but thinking of the freezing temperatures and a night in the pelt shed, Simone pulled them on as well and relished the added warmth. She slipped on her knee-high moccasins and was just finishing up the laces when she heard her father's voice in the yard outside the cabin.

"You can see for yourself," he said in his bellowing way, "the shed is there. Just beyond is a creek with clear water and plenty of fish. Oh, and berries so juicy you'll thank the Maker for such sweetness."

Simone wondered at this tour of the property. Her father seemed quite happy, and yet she knew he'd left in a fit of frustration and anger. The pelts were substandard, he had told her, and he was certain to be cheated out of a fair price. Simone had fully expected him to drink himself into oblivion and sleep it off in Uniontown. Maybe even stay with Ada at the Red Slipper Saloon. Yet here he stood, waving his arms in different directions, preaching of the merits of his land and holdings. What could it mean?

Simone went again to the window and, without revealing herself to the men outside, peeked out. They both still sat astride their horses and, to her relief, faced away from the house. The man with her father was a shorter, stockier man with a grizzled look to him. She watched as the men walked their horses in a lazy circle around the yard before returning to the house. Simone could clearly see the stranger now. His face, half hidden by a bushy beard and moustache, seemed leathery and worn. His nose bent to one side before hooking down like an eagle's beak, and his eyes were deep set and pale. Simone thought him the ugliest man she'd ever seen. Even uglier than Flat Nose, a man in Uniontown whose nose, it was rumored, had been cut off by the Indians some forty years earlier.

The men began to dismount, and Simone, not wishing to be caught watching them, hurried to the fireplace to check on the stew. It appeared to be thickening nicely and already the biscuits were rising amidst the bubbling broth. She straightened up just as the door latch lifted, and with spoon still in hand, she waited to see what might happen next.

Her father came in first, with the stranger close upon his heel. They both just stood and stared at her for a moment, almost as if they hadn't expected her to be there. Then her father started to laugh and gave the stranger a hearty slap on the back.

"Well, tell me, Davis. Did I lie? Ain't she a beauty?"

Simone felt nauseous as the man called Davis leered at her and licked his thick lower lip. "That she is. I'll happily pay your price."

"What price?" Simone couldn't help but ask.

Louis Dumas ignored her and went about the room, gathering up first one article and then another while Davis counted out several gold coins.

"What's going on?" Simone asked, her voice tremoring. Placing the spoon on the mantel, she braved her father's wrath and went to him. "What are you doing?"

"I'm leaving."

"Leaving?" she asked, swallowing hard. "Where are we going?"

"*We* ain't goin' anywhere. I am goin' to Colorado to seek a fortune and get me a new wife. You," he said, stopping long enough to motion in Davis's direction, "are staying with him."

Simone felt a chill descend upon her body and began to tremble. It was akin to reliving her mother's desertion all over again. She had no lost love for her father, but at least he was familiar and she knew how to live with him. "What do you mean I'm staying with him? I don't know this man."

Louis Dumas laughed and pushed his daughter in the direction of the stranger. "You'll know him soon enough. He's your new husband."

"Husband?" Simone stepped to the side and rounded the table where Davis still counted out coins. Terror seemed to rise from her stomach and choke her. She could scarcely breathe.

Her father joined the man and nodded as he tested each coin to see if they were real. "Garvey Davis is his name. He's buyin' the place, the traps, and . . ." he paused to look at her, as if to ascertain whether she was listening, then added, "you."

"I don't understand. I don't want to marry this man. In fact, there isn't a preacher around here for miles," Simone protested. "Mother told me you needed a preacher to marry folks."

Dumas laughed. "It isn't the way of the wilds, girl. Folks round here live as married. When the preacher gets around, they do it right—or not. Davis here is your husband now, and you'll answer to him." He finished checking the coins, then threw them into a pouch. "Good luck, Davis."

"To you as well," the gravelly voice called back.

"You can't just leave me here," Simone protested, unable to keep the fear from her voice. Her breath came in rapid, shallow draws. The last thing she wanted to do was allow him to see how afraid she really felt. Her father might be an oppressive beast of a man, but at least he was a beast she knew and halfway understood.

"I can and I am," Dumas replied. "He owns you now, same as this place. Do what he says, or it's my bet you'll get a worse beatin' than anything I ever gave you."

And with that, Louis Dumas walked through the door and out of her life. Simone could scarcely believe what was happening. On one hand, she'd just been given her wish. Her father would never again need to be a part of her life. On the other hand, the leering stranger he'd left in his place was a completely unacceptable and frightening alternative.

꧁ FOUR ꧂

AFTER AN ETERNITY of heavy silence, Garvey Davis decided to get down to matters. "What you got cookin' over there?" he asked, wiping his filthy sleeve across his mouth.

Simone, still staring at the closed door, turned to face the man. "What?" she asked in confusion. It seemed so incomprehensible that the man was simply standing there, acting as though nothing out of the ordinary had just taken place. Simone remembered times when her father had spoken of someone trading their daughter for a sack of flour. And once, he'd carried on long into the night about a man selling off his children to the highest bidder and all because they were worthless, ungrateful children. Simone had never believed the farfetched tales. Now, however, she had to admit that perhaps the stories held more truth than she'd given them credit for.

Davis threw his saddle pack to the floor and pulled a filthy fur cap from his head. "I'm hungry, woman. I asked what you got to feed me."

"Stew," Simone said simply, unable to think clearly. Surely this man didn't think she'd just willingly remain behind to be his wife. He couldn't be that ignorant, could he?

"Dish me up some," Garvey ordered.

"I don't think," Simone began uncomfortably, "I understand this situation."

Davis shrugged out of his coat. "What's to understand? I bought your pa's land and house. He threw you in on the deal, seein's how I needed a wife and all." He sized her up and nodded approvingly. "Seems a right good deal."

Simone felt her heart racing inside her chest. She had tried so hard to be void of feelings and emotions for the better part of her life, but this matter couldn't be dealt with in the same manner as the others. She not only felt rage and frustration with her father's actions, but genuine fear. Fear that edged on panic.

"You gonna stand there starin' at me like that or are you gonna feed me?" Davis questioned, looking none too happy to have to repeat his request for food.

Simone did as he asked. She needed time to think the matter through, and with Davis preoccupied with eating, maybe she could figure out what her options were. She couldn't stay here—that much seemed clear. Davis expected a wife, and from her talks with Naniko, Simone knew basically what that would entail and found the whole idea completely unacceptable. She didn't want intimacy with this man. He looked hideous with his barrel-like midsection and thick, stocky legs. He reminded Simone of the trolls in her childhood fairy tales. Evil, hideous creatures who preyed upon the weak. *Well, he won't prey upon me*, Simone thought as she lifted the lid from the kettle.

With her hand shaking so hard she could hardly grip the ladle, Simone filled a wooden bowl with the stew and biscuits, grabbed up a spoon, then put them both down on the table and went to retrieve the pot of coffee that could always be found sitting at the corner of the hearth. It would grow as thick as mud after a day of sitting on the coals, but her father never seemed to mind it that way. Simone could only hope that Davis felt the same way.

They didn't exchange another word until Davis took his seat at the table. He looked at the stew, then grabbed the spoon Simone had brought him and tasted it.

"Ain't half bad. Guess your pa didn't lie when he said you could cook."

Simone stood beside the fireplace wondering what she should do or say. She found she could not quell the mixture of fear and anger that was building inside of her. She watched Davis pick up the bowl and begin to shovel in the food as though he'd been weeks without a good meal. Coherent thought evaded Simone, and she hadn't even begun to formulate a plan when he grunted at her and extended the bowl for a second helping.

Simone could feel Garvey Davis's stare as she refilled his bowl. It made her uncomfortable, especially knowing that he considered himself her husband now. She had to think. Had to do something to help herself—but what? What could she do? Where could she go to be safe? And why, at seventeen years of age, did these have to be the questions that had haunted her all of her life?

"You're a mighty purty woman, Simone," Davis said with a leer when she brought the bowl of food. Her name on his lips came out sounding like *See-moan*, but it was the intensity of his gaze upon her body that made Simone feel ill. "Yessir, I'm gonna like bein' a husband," Davis said before beginning the entire shoveling action again.

Simone had heard enough. She quietly crossed the room to where the beds were partitioned off from the rest of the house. Spreading out a blanket, she put her change of clothes atop it, then retrieved her mother's Bible and prayer book. She didn't know why they were so important to her, but she couldn't imagine leaving them behind with Garvey Davis. But neither did she know what to do with either one. Her mother had always encouraged her to read the Bible daily, and while Simone had very nearly read the entire thing cover to cover out of boredom, she refused to hold the words in esteem. God hadn't seen fit to keep her mother alive, and neither had He rescued Simone from a fate worse than death.

She toyed for a moment with the well-worn cover of the Bible before adding it and the prayer book to the articles of clothing. Next, she went to her trunk and pulled out a small leather pouch that Naniko had made for her. Inside she had two coins, both of which she'd stolen from her father during one of his drunken stupors. She had no idea what they would buy her, but they might possibly be useful to her journey and she couldn't leave them behind. Lastly, she reached back into the trunk and pulled out two pelts. For more than three years she had managed to keep these pelts hidden from her father. They were choice pieces and would bring in a tidy sum of money, and that was exactly the reason Simone had hidden them there. Caressing the soft fur and touching it to her face, Simone could only hope they would bring her freedom and safety.

Binding everything together in her blanket and securing it with strips of rawhide, Simone drew a deep breath. In a matter of moments she would have to face Garvey Davis and explain her actions to him. With any luck, he'd be too happy with what he already possessed to worry about whether or not she stayed. Or maybe he'd actually care that she was not a willing participant. Simone could only hope to find some thread of compassion in this stranger. She had just turned to retrieve her threadbare coat when Garvey Davis pushed back the curtain.

"Well, well. You're an anxious little thing, ain't ya? Figured I'd have to drag you in here."

Simone froze in place. She could tell by the look on Garvey Davis's filth-smudged face that he had now turned his attention from food. Mustering up courage amidst her anger, Simone tightly hugged her coat to her body. "I'm leaving," she told him flatly.

"Beg your pardon?" He seemed momentarily taken aback by her words.

Simone felt a tingling charge resonate through her body. "I don't figure on being your wife or anyone else's. I realize, however, that my father has sold this property to you and that I no longer have a home here. Therefore, I'm leaving."

He stared at her a moment longer, then broke into a hearty laugh that shook his frame like a pine tree in the wind. "You do talk real good. Your pa said you had a way with talkin'—something about your Frenchy ma teachin' you proper-like. But you ain't goin' nowhere. I paid good money for you, and I intend to get my money's worth."

He moved toward her, but Simone darted around him. "No!" She moved to the bed to get her things, but Davis shadowed her.

"We're goin' to have a good time, missy. Sooner you settle yourself down to the idea, the better."

Simone grabbed her pack and tried to edge down along the side of the bed. "I'm sorry if my father gave you the wrong impression. You can't expect me to just up and marry you without knowing anything about you, and you can't expect me to cooperate with what you have in mind."

Davis laughed and lunged for her, knocking the pack and coat from her hands. His beefy fingers caught her thick braid, and he yanked her head back painfully. Simone fought against him, knowing—fearing—what was to come as his free arm wrapped around her to force her body against his.

"Leave me alone!" she screamed, pushing and straining to free herself.

Davis threw her backward down across the bed, but Simone moved quickly to the side and avoided being pinned down by the man. She jumped up, stumbling back against the washbasin. For a stocky man, Davis moved with lightning speed, and before Simone could gather her things and escape, he had already reached out to take hold of her again.

Screaming and kicking, Simone slammed back against the washbasin as Garvey grabbed and fumbled at trying to remove her clothes. "Don't make me hit you, girl," Davis bellowed out in anger. "Just settle yourself down. We can do this the hard way or the easy way. It's up to you."

Simone had no idea what the hard or easy way might entail, but either way, she had no desire for anything that included Garvey Davis. Trying to steady herself against the attack, Simone's hand grazed the cold porcelain of her mother's basin and pitcher. Without giving it a second thought, Simone turned and took hold of the pitcher. Then, without warning, she whirled back around, bringing the pitcher down on Garvey Davis's head.

For a moment, nothing happened. The man stood weaving in place for several seconds, looking at her with such an expression of disbelief that Simone almost felt sorry for him. Almost, but not quite.

Then in a flash, everything changed. Blood began pouring down the side of Garvey's face and the man's knees buckled. With a loud, resounding crash, Davis fell in a heap at her feet, leaving Simone to now stare in disbelief.

She nudged at his body with her moccasined foot. He didn't move. Blood continued to pour from the head wound, and instantly Simone became aware of what she'd done.

"I've murdered him!" she declared in horror.

Instantly she recalled a story related to her in Uniontown of a cantankerous old man who had taken a half-breed woman to be his wife. The woman, fed up with being beaten on a nightly basis, had poisoned his food and killed him. They had her strung up and hanged before twenty-four hours had passed, and all for the murder of a ruthless man that nobody much cared for.

"And now I've done my own murdering," Simone murmured. Terrified at what it all might mean, she quickly gathered her things and headed for the door. She had to get away before someone found out what she'd done. She pulled on her coat and tried to steady her nerves.

"What should I do?" she questioned, as if someone might give her the answer.

She glanced around the room and shook her head. Hunger gnawed at her stomach, but she couldn't take time out to eat. Instead, she went quickly to the kettle and skimmed off three of the biscuits and wrapped them in a dish towel. This accomplished, she grabbed her bedroll and hurried out of the cabin.

The first thing that met her eye was Davis's horse and gear. He'd not even bothered to unsaddle the beast, and now that he lay dead in her house, Simone believed it a much lesser crime to consider stealing his horse and saddle. She tied her bedroll to the back of the saddle, then went to take up the reins from the post. The horse whinnied softly as if questioning her actions, but the mare seemed otherwise unconcerned as Simone hurried to mount.

Struggling against the cumbersome skirt and the heaviness of her coat, Simone finally righted herself atop the horse. The cold leather of the saddle pervaded the thin material of her pantalets, causing Simone to shift uncomfortably in the seat. It was only then that she noticed the gun belt slung over the horn of the saddle. Reaching down, Simone fingered the butt of the revolver and found the piece gave her added courage. With a gun, she could protect herself. She could also hunt for food.

She suddenly realized by the fading light that night would soon be upon her. It wasn't wise to travel the area after dark, but Simone felt desperation quickly overcoming her sensibility. A man lay dead in her cabin, and she certainly couldn't stay the night with him. She had the gun and she had a horse; surely she could make it to safety somewhere. She thought of Naniko, then realized that would probably be the first place they'd look for her. She couldn't risk it.

Glancing again at the cabin, Simone felt a strange sense of separation. She knew no other home, and yet she held no great affection for this crude arrangement of logs and chinking. Still, this had been the home where her mother had lived and loved her. This place had seen her brother's birth and the birth and death of other siblings she had never known. There had been happy times here, she allowed herself to acknowledge. But they were so long ago and so faded from her memory that Simone could not get a clear picture of the past. Bitterness had built a wall between her and the remembrances that might have warmed her icy heart.

The skies to the west were turning rosy and orange in twilight, and the chilled air of evening blew down from the mountaintops and whipped at the edges of her coat. The elements seemed to beckon her to forget her nostalgic reflections and flee.

Simone took one last look around her and knew that the time had come. As much as she feared what lay in the unknown before her, she feared her past even more. Her father had deserted her, her mother was dead, and she had killed the man who was meant to be her husband. Accident or not, they would surely hang her for her actions, and there would be no one left to mourn her passing.

Taking a deep breath, she kicked at the sides of the horse and turned him toward the narrow, rocky path. She'd made her choice, and now she would have to find a way to live with it.

FIVE

LOUIS DUMAS LIKED the weight of gold coins in his pocket. He also liked the feeling of freedom that had come in ridding himself of the responsibilities of the trapline and of Simone. The girl reminded him more and more of her mother, and that only served to remind him of things he'd just as soon forget.

He'd never once gotten a thing in his life without taking it or forcing it. It just seemed to be his lot. He'd taken Winifred in her moment of weakness and desperation and shown her that her only hope was to become his wife. Then he'd thought by putting her away in the hills, away from folk and the pretty things she'd grown up with, that he could somehow make her forget that such things existed. But he hadn't.

He shook his head and spit. Women were more trouble than they were worth. They were sharp-tongued in an argument and then, without batting an eyelash, could turn on the sweetness and deception without warning. They were born to deceive men, as far as Louis was concerned, and there wasn't a single example in his own life that had proved otherwise.

After stocking up on a few things he'd need for his journey to Colorado, Dumas decided to have one last round of drinks at the Red Slipper. It seemed strange to consider leaving the area after having given so much of his life to the place. He'd come to this territory to escape the Civil War. That and the death sentence on his head for desertion during battle. Trapping was something he'd learned from his father, a Canadian who had married a backwoods New York girl and built a house on the border of both countries. Trapping seemed a good way to lose himself and his identity to the rest of the world, and the territory had been good to him. Now, as he considered mining and what the future might hold in store, Louis couldn't help but wonder if he'd made a mistake in selling out to Davis. Perhaps his original plan of moving north to further his trapping efforts was the wiser choice after all. With the Indian population rounded up and housed on government reservations, there would be all manner of animal to harvest. He'd heard stories about the riches of the Canadian Rockies that made him itch to go and see for himself.

Securing his horse outside the saloon, Louis took hold of his rifle and went inside. The dilemma of what to do and where to go continued to battle inside him. There didn't seem much sense in going over what was already done, and yet a nagging doubt remained in the back of his mind. Maybe after a few drinks it would all make sense enough.

"Louis, you've come back to share some of your wealth," Gus called from the far end of the bar.

"Came back for a last drink, if that's what you mean," Dumas grunted.

Ada came in from the stock room and beamed Louis one of her smiles. "I hoped you'd come back to at least say good-bye."

"Hey, Louis," two men called in unison as they entered the Slipper. "Saw you head in here and thought we might get a game going."

"Jervis, Butterfield," Louis acknowledged. "Don't rightly know as I have time for a game."

The men laughed. "When have you ever been too busy to relieve us of our money?" Jervis asked.

"Lessen you're afraid you've lost your touch," Gus joined in.

Ada snickered at the challenge and poured Louis a tall whiskey. "You can't let 'em get away with talkin' to you like that, Louis."

Louis downed the whiskey and pushed the glass forward for a refill. "All right, since you seem so all-fired impatient to lose your money. I already spent one night in town, don't hardly seem a problem to spend another." Gus and Jervis gave a whoop.

By this time, several more men had entered the bar, and they joined in the cheering as they realized the intent of the men at the bar. Boredom could only be relieved in one of several ways: fighting, loving, drinking, gambling, or working. Since most men were single, loving wasn't often an option. Fighting could occur as the evening wore on, but it was usually an added bonus to either drinking or gambling. And working . . . well, that was clearly not an option on this fine day.

"Come on," Louis said, tucking the bottle under his arm. He took up his glass in one hand and his rifle in the other and motioned to the tables. "If we're all gonna play, you'd best push 'em together."

"I'll go get Harley's bench at the dry goods store. He won't mind us borrowing it so long as we don't split it into kindlin'," Gus said, heading out the door with great enthusiasm.

Louis felt a thread of amusement as he observed the actions around him. These men were starved for entertainment and socializing. Some had just now come to town, having lived out the winter in solitary seclusion. Others were up from Laramie, their pockets full of coins from their latest job or trade.

"River's thawed," Butterfield offered, pulling up one of the free chairs. "My pa says the signs point to a warm spring."

"I don't trust it," Jervis said, as if anyone cared about his thoughts on the matter. "I've seen it like this before. Just about the time you figure on things warmin' up, along comes a blizzard to freeze you to the bone."

Louis looked at the man and nodded. He chose for himself a seat that placed his back against the wall. *"Never put your back to any man,"* his father had told him, and Louis knew he was alive to this day because of heeding that advice. "He's right, ya know. Never makes sense to rush the elements. I saw signs in the clouds that speak of another good snow. That's one of the reasons I'm moving down out of the mountains before the weather turns sour."

"So you're really gonna do it?" Butterfield asked.

"I'm here, ain't I?"

"Heard tell you sold off your kid," Jervis said, throwing himself down on a roughly hewn stool.

"Sold it all off," Louis said, balancing the rifle across his lap. He liked the security of its weight. The barrel was wrapped in a piece of beaded, fringed buckskin casing. The design of the piece showed intricate artistry, but there wasn't a man in Uniontown who didn't realize Louis would just as soon blow a hole out the end of the casing as to take the time to release the rifle should any man challenge his authority.

Gus lumbered in with the bench balanced on one shoulder, and behind him Harley Burkett, the dry goods owner, followed with another two chairs.

"Heard Gus say there's gonna be quite a game," Harley said. "Didn't rightly figure on missin' out."

"Come on in," Louis told the man. "The more of you there is, the more money I can win. But I ain't wastin' too much time. There'll be another snow inside of a day or my name ain't Louis Dumas."

"Louis was just tellin' how he sold off his land and traps," Butterfield said, scooting his chair over to make room for Harley.

"Sold his kid, too," Gus added, positioning the bench. "Wished I'd had enough money to buy her from ya. That Simone is a looker for sure."

"You sold her to Davis?" Harley questioned, as though Louis had lost his mind. "What about your friends, man?"

Louis shrugged. "Ain't a one of you that ever came to me posin' such a question."

"For fear you would have kilt one of us," Jervis interjected. "We all saw the way you decked old Flatnose last time she was in town and he dared to try to talk to her."

"Talkin' wasn't what Flatnose had in mind," Louis replied matter-of-factly. This brought a hearty round of laughter from the table, which by now was filling up with additional men.

"With a looker like your daughter," Gus dared to say what every other man was thinking, "talkin' wouldn't have been my first choice, either."

Louis had never felt any real concern for Simone's reputation or purity. What he had resented from the men at this table was the threat they had posed to his own security. To lose Simone to one of them would have meant losing his housekeeper, cook, laundress, pelt-skinner, and anything else Louis needed from his well-trained daughter. Now that he had plans to take himself to Colorado, Simone seemed to be a liability more than an asset.

"Davis probably didn't pay half what some folks might have been willing to give you," Butterfield chimed in, while Harley took it upon himself to shuffle the cards.

"Yeah, for one as purty as Simone and with the fact that she was still not knowin' a man and all," Gus said, "you probably could've got a real fortune for her."

"Sure," Jervis added, nodding. "Could've taken her with you to the mining town and sold her there."

"Could've sold her a buncha times," another man said seriously. "I mean, look at Ada . . . and she ain't near the looker your daughter is."

Louis let the men ramble on without saying much. In truth, their words disturbed him greatly. He hadn't thought about the possibilities of Simone being of value to him outside of working around the house. It had never once dawned on him to sell her to his friends for their ongoing pleasure. In truth, before Jervis had mentioned her value as entertainment in the mining communities, Louis had never allowed his imagination to wander in that direction. He supposed it was because of the bitter memories he harbored of his mother. His father had put her to work selling her favors for whatever money it earned him, and Louis couldn't know for sure, but he suspected there wasn't a single one of the Dumas children who had the same father.

Now as Louis began to contemplate the notion of selling Simone into prostitution, he found he feared he had committed a grievous error in judgment. The whole situation was beginning to wear Louis down.

Ada sashayed across the floor, bringing drinks and smiles to the men. Louis could imagine Simone bringing a much higher class of clientele, with her mother's petite but well-rounded figure and smoldering blue eyes. If they set themselves up in the right place, Simone might well be able to make upward to fifty dollars a night, maybe more. Somewhere deep down inside him, Louis knew that the idea of such a thing should be repulsive to him. But it wasn't. What repulsed him was the idea of having lost a small fortune.

"Yeah, it's just too bad that Garvey Davis is enjoying her instead of one of us," someone said.

Louis began to think about the situation, and the more he thought about it, the more ideas came into his head. He could take Simone with him. Maybe he wouldn't have to work if he did things right. He could set up a place for Simone to work instead. His father had done it, and it had certainly served him well enough—until his mother had run away. It wasn't anything new. In fact, it was practically the oldest profession known to woman—and to man.

Maybe Simone had already given Davis enough trouble to make him gladly turn her back over to Louis. Maybe he could just show up at the cabin and find the man desperate to be rid of Simone. Maybe, but not likely. Louis tried to concentrate on the cards being dealt him, but in truth, the idea of recovering Simone and taking her with him to Colorado had overrun his thoughts. He lost four straight hands in a row before realizing that he needed to make a choice. Either play cards or contemplate what to do about the girl. He couldn't do both.

He turned his mind back to the game and won a couple of hands before the ideas started churning once again. *Think of the money to be made*, he told himself. *The girl isn't just pretty, she's a real beauty.*

Of course, she'd fetch more money if he saw to it that she was taken care of. He could give her a nice place to stay to conduct her business. He could even see to it that she had nice clothes so as to attract a better-paying customer. The thought of sitting pretty in a city house with plenty of food on the table, maybe a servant or two, so captivated Louis that he again lost a round of cards.

"You don't hardly seem yourself tonight, Louis," Harley said as he took the pot.

"Well, you know how it goes, Harley. There's a lot to think about when a man is making a new life for hisself," Jervis commented before picking up the cards to deal the next hand. "Throw in if you're a-playin' this hand."

The clink of coins on the wooden table caught Louis's attention, but only long enough to make him throw his own coin in.

"I heard tell that some city feller found gold not far from here in one of those old abandoned mines," Jervis continued to chatter. "Says he believes the whole mountain to be full of gold. Maybe that land of yours was a gold mine and you didn't even know it, Louis."

"Shut up, Jervis," Louis growled, feeling ever more the fool.

He scarcely even noticed when Ada laid her hands on his shoulders and began to knead his knotted muscles. Gold in these mountains seemed unlikely, but the golden opportunity Simone represented was another issue entirely. With her looks, she could be his ticket to ease and comfort, and yet he'd thrown her away for a mere pittance of what he might've been able to make.

It was this point that settled the matter in his mind. He'd just go to Davis and take her back. He'd plead hindsight or some other notion, but he would persuade the man to see things his way. Of course, the man might need more than words to persuade him. It could very well take a good deal of the money Louis had in his pocket to settle the deal. Then again, maybe Davis could be convinced to see things Louis's way without ever having to discuss money.

Louis smiled and absentmindedly studied the cards in his hands. Why barter at all? Simone belonged to him, and she was underage. He'd just go and reclaim her whether Davis liked it or not. He'd blame it on the whiskey and challenge Davis to see it otherwise. If the man gave him too much trouble, he'd simply give him a beating he'd not soon forget. And if that didn't do the trick, he'd kill him. After all, Davis was a stranger to these parts. Who'd even give a second thought if the man came up missing?

Throwing in his cards, Louis got to his feet. "I've had enough of this. Don't seem to be able to concentrate on cards."

"You've lost a fair bit of money," Gus commented. "You sure you don't want a chance to earn it back?"

"I'll figure another way to earn my money," Louis replied, then nodded to Ada. For the second night in a row he was going to reject her offerings. Somehow it just didn't hold the same intrigue anymore. Simone could clearly create a new future for him . . . and that was far more interesting.

~ SIX ~

SIMONE COUNTED TEN NIGHTS since departing her childhood home. She felt hopelessly overwhelmed by the vast territory she'd already covered. Especially given the fact that nothing of civilization seemed to present itself to her.

Aching and sore, Simone stretched beneath her blanket and moaned. Never had she been forced to sleep on the ground outdoors. Her father never took her anywhere that required them to be gone from the cabin overnight, so she had always enjoyed the modest comfort of her own bed or the furry softness of the pelt shed. Now, more than ever, she questioned the sanity of her choice.

Forcing her body to obey, Simone slipped out from beneath the warmth of her blanket and met the morning chill. The sun barely touched the morning sky, fading the blackness of night into a dull, gunpowder gray. Simone couldn't help but sigh. She'd seen skies like this before, and usually they meant snow. Shuddering beneath her coat, Simone rubbed her hands together in a desperate attempt to keep warm. She longed for a roaring fire and a decent meal, but neither were to be had in the Wyoming wilderness.

Glancing around at the scenery, Simone felt little comfort. There simply appeared to be no sign of a town or village anywhere. Her stomach rumbled and ached in a way that made her feel sick. She'd had very little to eat in the past week and a half. After the biscuits were gone, she'd turned to nature for food. She managed to shoot a rabbit but had no way to cook it. After contemplating the horror of eating the meat raw or going hungry, Simone had forced herself to eat part of the animal. She'd also skinned the scrawny thing and used the pelt to form a makeshift cap for herself.

She knew she looked a fright. Upon gazing into the icy waters of the river she'd followed for the past three days she saw her reflection, where she appeared as a hodgepodge of cultural contrasts. Indian moccasins. Woolen skirt and faded calico shirtwaist, both handmade in a previous decade. And a coat so old and threadbare that it did little to cut the harsh cold of the mountain air. Simone had taken the beautiful fox and wolf pelts she'd stolen from her father and slipped them between the lining and outer material of her coat. She thought them better used there as they helped to ward off the biting wind. She'd even taken to wearing both sets of her clothes and wrapping the blanket around her coat for extra protection. It helped, but not much. The elements were simply too harsh and unyielding. The earth didn't care if she died in a rocky crevice or was swallowed up in an ice-packed river. The earth didn't care, and neither did any of mankind. She was the ultimate orphan. Abandoned and forgotten by all.

She hoped she was forgotten—at least by the people of Uniontown. She could only cling to the possibility that no one knew of her father's actions, and that even if they did, no one would attempt to strike up a bosom companionship with Garvey Davis. No one ever bothered to come to the cabin, and with any luck no one ever would. It might be months before anyone thought to wonder what had become of Davis and Simone.

Reaching down to scoop up a handful of water, Simone grimaced at the thought of Davis. She again wondered how she could possibly live with the nightmarish images in her mind. She had condemned her father for murdering her mother and brother, and now she found herself no better. *But maybe Davis isn't dead*, she reasoned with herself. Maybe the blow had only rendered him unconscious.

She closed her eyes, shaking her head. It seemed foolish to hope that Garvey Davis was still alive. There had been too much blood. Even now she could see it pooling on the floor of the bedroom. She could still remember the stunned expression on his face. It even haunted her in her sleep, so that the past few nights she awoke screaming—fighting off invisible intruders. Shuddering uncontrollably, Simone forced the images from her mind. There had to be something better to dwell on.

The sun peeked through the gray, and for a moment the rays seemed to touch Simone. Lifting her face to catch the warmth, she caught sight of the mountain range she'd gradually been making her way down. Her mind instantly went to the Psalms.

"I will lift up mine eyes unto the hills, from whence cometh my help."

The one hundred and twenty-first chapter of Psalms had been one of her mother's favorites. Why she should remember such a thing at a time like this was beyond Simone. She wanted no part of remembering her mother or the God her mother had served. She wanted complete separation from anything that would remotely allow her to feel. Her heart was like stone, and Simone wanted it that way.

Oh, her heart still possessed an element of fear; Simone thought fear to be a healthy thing, however. Fear kept you always searching—always looking over your shoulder. Fear kept you from becoming too comfortable. Comfort, Simone had learned, caused a cascading effect on the soul. Comfort inevitably stimulated pleasure, and pleasure brought about true happiness. And if a person were happy, they could also be made sad—and Simone wanted no part of that.

But where is your well-being, Simone? an inaudible voice seemed to question.

Simone went back to her bed of pine boughs and gathered up her things. *I won't give in to such thinking. I won't believe the lies that my mind would tell me.* But deep down, Simone knew that it was very possible that the words she had heard within her own soul might not be lies. She wanted them to be, because if they were, she could more easily stand back and point a finger at yet another way her upbringing had failed her.

Her mother's faith would have her believe that God spoke to a person's heart in order to offer them guidance and comfort. But Simone refused that nonsense. She knew her mother had cherished the psalmist's declaration that his help came from the Lord who made heaven and earth. The Psalms shared words of comfort, with clear examples of times when the author had faced adversity and loneliness and had turned to God for help.

"But I won't turn to God," Simone declared, looking heavenward. "Because I don't believe you really care. I don't believe you even see me here, all alone. I don't believe you've ever really seen me—otherwise, how could you have allowed me to suffer? How could you have left me alone with a man who would sell me to another?" Simone suddenly realized how her words very nearly sounded like a prayer. It startled her to realize she'd spoken the words aloud. Was she going mad?

Again she gazed up at the mountain peaks. She thought of Naniko and a portion of an old Ute saying. "My help is in the mountains where I take myself to heal the earthly wounds that people give to me." Naniko believed healing came from the elements. The earth. The winds. The waters. Simone thought of how the Psalms and the Ute message shared a common interest. The mountains seemed to represent a fortress of strength. A haven from harm. The psalmist, however, knew his strength came from the One who made the mountains, while the Ute legend looked to the mountain itself. But these mountains seemed anything but helpful to Simone. In fact, she feared they might be her undoing.

The horse whinnied from where she'd staked him out. He pawed at the ground, as if impatient for them to be on their way. No doubt he was just as hungry as Simone. Gathering up her things, Simone resaddled the animal and led him to the water's edge. She tried not to be discouraged by the fact that the sun had gone back under the blanket of clouds. The gloomy gray better fit her disposition anyway.

By the time Simone mounted her horse, a light snow had started to fall and the wind had picked up. It seemed futile to complain or even to shake a fist at the sky. Her surroundings wouldn't heed her even if she pleaded her case, and neither would God. Shrugging down under her blanket, Simone urged the horse forward.

They headed downriver, seeking to put the mountains behind them. Simone believed that if she could get to flat ground, she would more easily be able to discern directions and other signs of life. She noticed the slightest warming of the temperature as the horse picked his way down the trail. The farther they traveled from the higher altitude of the snow-capped mountains, the more signs of spring emerged. Surely they weren't far from a trading post or town.

When they came through a clearing of trees, Simone was shocked to realize they had come to the edge of a rocky drop. The horse nervously pranced and backed a few feet, sending bits of rock tumbling over the ledge. They could clearly go no farther. The ledge revealed no path that might allow Simone to navigate the steep incline. The view down below, however, held her attention in greater capacity than the obstacle of the ledge. Far in the distance, nearly beyond her field of vision, Simone made out the lazy rise of smoke. The snow had stopped, and now, looking out across the open valley, Simone possessed hope for the first time since leaving home. Smoke could only mean some manner of civilization.

She glanced around, trying to figure out how they might conquer the drop. It appeared that if she made her way back to the river and crossed over to the other side, they would have an easier path down into the valley. Of course, that meant getting wet, and Simone had no idea how deep the river might be. She could easily risk her life and that of her mount. But it was either that or waste time exploring in the opposite direction. Her reasoning told her the river would be a better way, and without giving it another thought, Simone urged the horse to retrace their steps.

She navigated the river with little difficulty. The place where they came back out of the woods revealed a shallow bank and water that only came up to the horse's hocks. Simone nudged the horse with her heels and set out into the icy stream. The mare protested by nickering softly, but in a matter of minutes the obstacle lay behind them and no longer concerned the horse. Simone rubbed her stomach as it once again gave off a growl. She'd been existing on buried roots and pine—and very little else. It hardly satisfied her need, and weakness gradually overtook her.

"Just a little farther," she encouraged the horse. She knew she was really encouraging herself, but it seemed completely proper to issue the words.

She tried to imagine what the town would be like. She wondered if it held very many people, and whether those people would think her queer for making a trek down from the mountains. Then it dawned on her that someone was bound to question her arrival. What should she say? What kind of story could she make up that would sound believable?

She'd tell them that her parents were dead. As far as she was concerned, that much was true. But how could she explain her sudden appearance in their town? She didn't even know where she was, much less a reason for coming to this particular place.

With a heavy sigh, Simone watched her breath turn to steam in the chilled morning air. She simply wouldn't answer their questions. She'd tell them only what she had to and leave it at that. She'd attempt to sell the pelts and see if someone would sell her some basic supplies, then she'd get out of there on the double. Towns meant lawmen—or at least citizens—who sought to uphold some form of justice and order. She remembered her mother telling her that much. She couldn't stay there and hope to keep her identity a secret for long. Sooner or later, someone would find Garvey Davis's lifeless body, and then they'd come after her.

These thoughts consumed Simone while the horse moved ever closer to the town. She could now make out several plumes of smoke, as well as the outline of multiple structures. Here in the valley, the snow lay in sporadic clumps, giving the land a patchwork appearance. Dry needle grass was interlaced with delicate shoots of green, suggesting that a false thaw had come several weeks earlier to this portion of the territory. Of course, the past winter had been nothing compared to the winter of '86. Simone remembered the heavy snows and bitter cold. Many folks had suffered, or so she'd been told. However, she hadn't suffered—not overmuch. In fact, Simone remembered the time as rather pleasant. Her father had been caught unaware when a blizzard had come upon him, and he had to take refuge for several weeks in Uniontown. This winter, though irritatingly slow in its departure, had been very mild in comparison. The sun once again broke through the clouds and beamed down upon her. How wonderful it felt! Perhaps spring really would come.

The warmth invigorated Simone. She urged the horse to pick up his pace, knowing he had to be near collapse. They would make it. She could see that now. But whether she could hold her own and manage to keep from being further harmed was another question.

Remembering her appearance, Simone reached up a hand and untied the rawhide strips that held the rabbit pelt to her head. She tucked the pelt inside her coat, where the other two were doing a remarkable job of keeping her upper body warm. There seemed little hope of making herself look presentable, but Simone fretted over the idea anyway. It wasn't that she cared much for her looks or for making much ado over her appearance, but the last thing she wanted to do was draw attention to herself.

She laughed, and the sound came out hollow and without feeling. "As if a stranger—a woman alone, no less—coming down from the mountains won't create its own scandal."

The horse whinnied as if to agree. "It doesn't matter," she told him in reply. "I have no other choice. *We* have no other choice."

SEVEN

THE CRUDE SIGN at the edge of town had seen better days. Simone tilted her head first one way and then the other, as if this would help her to get a better look at the ancient letters on the beaten and faded sign. She could only suppose the sign represented the name of the strange little gathering of businesses and homes. She studied the collection, disappointed to find it so small, but nevertheless grateful to have found any form of civilization. Somewhere a dog barked, and Simone found she could recognize a mixture of sounds that represented hope to her. The clanging of an anvil, the lowing of cattle—all manner of sounds that meant people occupied the tiny dwellings. If only she could find someone willing to help her by buying the furs. That would be the real trick. She needed money to help her on her way. Wherever that way might lead.

She slowed the horse and gazed around her. The buildings were for the most part unpainted and well worn. The harsh weathering elements had taken their toll, but the buildings remained, nevertheless. Simone spotted the dry goods mercantile and decided this might be the best place to start. She dismounted, quickly glancing up and down the rutted road to see if anyone had stopped to pay her any mind. But no one seemed the least bit interested in her. Mainly because there was no one on the street to take an interest.

Simone tied the horse to the hitching post and felt her knees start to buckle as she took a step. Her vision swam before her for a moment, and she knew if she didn't get something to eat soon, she'd probably faint dead away. Pulling the leather pouch from her bedroll, Simone hoped the coins might be enough to purchase some form of nourishment. If not that, then she would try to sell the pelts and hope luck was with her in getting a decent trade.

The bell on the front door jingled as Simone entered the tiny establishment. She gave the place a quick assessment. Bolts of cloth and sacks of seed and flour were propped against one wall. There were also bags of other provisions and tins of who-knew-what. Simone felt her stomach twist uncomfortably and pressed forward to the counter.

"I thought I heard someone out here," a man told her, emerging through a curtained doorway. "Well, you're new to town, ain't ya?" He looked Simone over as though trying to decide whether she merited his attention.

"Yes," she said softly. "I need to buy some food. Maybe crackers or jerky. Do you have jerky?"

"Sure," the man told her and pulled a jar up from behind the counter. He pulled out a large stick and put it on the counter. "Two cents."

Simone took out her coins and held them up. "Will these do?"

He frowned at her ignorance and took hold of the coins. "They'll do."

Simone sighed and grabbed the piece of meat and began to tear at it. Now was no time to worry about how this stranger perceived her.

"Whereabout you from?" the clerk asked her.

"Lived in the mountains," Simone managed to say before swallowing.

"You here by yourself?" The man craned his neck to look out through the store's solitary front window.

"Yes," Simone responded cautiously. She forced herself to slow her rapid devouring of the jerky and turned to raise her question regarding the pelts. "I have two pelts with me, and I wondered if you or someone else in this town might be interested in buying them."

She put the jerky in her pocket and unbuttoned her coat. She worked to dislodge the pelts as the bell on the door jingled once again.

"Ah, Reverend," the storekeeper called out. "Good to see you. What can I do for you today?"

Simone managed a quick glance at the older man. He appeared to be in his sixties, with gray hair and bushy eyebrows. He stood short and round, and from the looks of the smile on his face, he appeared to be very happy. "Mornin', Tom. Gladdy sent me to pick up a few things. She's putting lunch together just now and ran out of salt."

"No problem," the clerk replied and reached once again behind his counter. He produced a five-pound bag of salt and waited to see what else the reverend would need.

Just then Simone finally managed to free the fox pelt. "I have this one, as well as a fine wolf pelt," she told the man, placing the fur on the counter.

"Don't rightly have any reason to buy either one," the man told her. He ran his hand over the fur and smiled. "It is a nice piece. Guess I could give you somethin'."

The silvery wolf pelt soon joined the fox piece. "Ah, now, that is a beaut," the man said, eagerly studying the fur.

"I need money enough to buy some supplies. And I need some directions. I'm not sure where I am," Simone replied.

"Why, child, are you lost?" the reverend asked.

Simone nodded. "I suppose so. I'm making my way to . . ." She thought for a moment. Where could she go? The only city name that came to mind was one she remembered her father spouting off about, and that was Laramie. "I'm going to Laramie."

"Well, you're in a good place for that. Stage will be heading through in about two weeks. You could catch it and it'll take you straight there."

"No," Simone said, shaking her head. "I'll ride my horse. He's just outside. I need to get us some feed, but then we'll be on our way."

The older man stepped forward. "I'm Reverend Elias Canton," he told her. "Who might you be, child?"

Simone bit her lip for a moment. She wanted so much to be calm and collected about the entire encounter, but her heart was racing and her stomach was hardly satisfied with her meager offering of jerky. She felt weak, even to the point of collapse, but she couldn't allow that to happen in front of these strangers.

"My name is Simone." She made a quick decision about continuing. Perhaps if she told the man her story, he'd leave her in peace. "My folks died this winter. They left me without anything but these pelts." She felt uncomfortable in the lie but forced herself to hold steady with her story.

"Do you have family in Laramie? Is that why you're making your way there?" Elias Canton questioned.

"Ah . . . yes," Simone said, nodding. "I've come down from the mountains."

"How long have you been traveling?"

"Almost two weeks. I got lost," Simone said by way of explanation. "I'm still not even sure which direction I've come from."

"Well, no matter now. You are now among those who can help you find your way," Elias said with a laugh. "Tom, I'll buy those furs." He reached into his pocket and counted out the coins for the salt, then turned to Simone and handed her several coins. "There's more than enough here to buy your supplies and a ticket on the stage. You could come and stay with my wife and me until the road clears enough for them to make it over from Laramie."

"No," Simone replied adamantly. "I'll just get what I need and go."

She turned to the man at the counter. "I need matches, jerked beef—lots of it—and crackers, if you have them." She thought for a moment and added, "I'll also need another blanket and a canteen." The man looked rather blankly at her for a moment, then nodded and went to retrieve what she'd asked for.

"At least come share dinner with us. I know my Gladdy would be furious if I let you go without a hot meal to warm you."

"No. Thank you anyway," Simone answered and waited until the clerk returned with the requested articles.

"Tom, you wrap her a good portion of those dried apples, as well," Elias commanded. "The fruit will taste mighty good to you on the road," he told her.

Simone nodded, not knowing how to take his kindness. The clerk wrapped everything up in the new blanket, then turned to Simone.

"That'll be three dollars and twenty-five cents."

Simone looked at the money in her hand. She knew her numbers and could add and subtract, even multiply and divide, but she'd never been given a reason to handle money. Frustrated, she looked to Elias Canton, not quite trusting either man to be honest with her.

He smiled kindly and reached out to her open hand. "These are quarter eagles," he told her. "They're each worth two dollars and fifty cents. This here is an eagle. It's worth ten dollars. This is a dime and these are nickels. They're only worth cents. Ten cents to a dime. Five cents to a nickel."

"Thank you," Simone replied and studied the money for a moment before handing the two quarter eagles to the storekeeper. "That's four dollars and one hundred cents," she told him proudly.

"One hundred cents equals a dollar," Elias explained to her in a gentle voice while the clerk went to retrieve her change.

Simone took this information as gospel and committed it to memory. "So that's five dollars. I'll get back a dollar and seventy-five cents," she said, looking to Elias to make sure of her numbers.

"You're right good at figures," the man behind the counter commented.

"You certainly are. I can see that your mother and father cared enough to educate you before going home to be with the Lord. Do you read, as well?"

"I read," Simone replied. "I've been reading since forever."

Elias smiled. "Probably not a great many books up there in the mountains."

"I had my mother's Bible and prayer book," she told him, not able to keep the words from spilling out. She felt so starved for conversation that she couldn't help herself. She didn't want to tell this gentle-looking old man her life's story, but he put her at ease in such a way that she couldn't seem to do anything else.

"Many a young'un has been taught to read by the Good Book," the clerk replied, handing her the change.

"Indeed," Elias replied and went to pick up his salt and the two pelts. "Simone, I'd really appreciate it if you would reconsider joining us for dinner. I could stable your horse and see to it that he can eat his fill, as well. Doesn't hardly seem Christian for me to send you off on your way without seeing first to your most basic needs."

Simone looked at the man and felt uncomfortable at the kindness she read in his expression. No one had ever treated her in this manner but her mother. She grabbed up her bundle and shook her head. "No, I'd better be going."

She hurried for the door and had just stepped outside when a robust woman appeared from around the corner of the store. Not realizing Elias Canton had followed her outside, Simone was startled when the woman said in mocking disgust, "There you are. Thought you'd had to go mine the salt yourself."

Simone froze in place, uncertain as to what she should say or do.

"Now, Gladys," Elias's warm voice sounded from behind Simone. "I met this young traveler and invited her to eat with us."

The woman stopped in her tracks, her face rosy from the chill of the air. Her smile sent her cheeks into round little balls on either side of her face. "Well, you're most welcome to come and eat with us."

"No, really," Simone replied, edging toward her horse. "I couldn't impose."

"Ain't hardly an imposition. We don't get too many strangers in these parts," Gladys answered. " 'Sides, lunch is ready. Or it will be as soon as I can salt the soup. You might as well come share a bowl with us. I've got fried ham and apple cobbler, too."

The thought of fried ham caused Simone to reconsider. It had been a long time since she'd had anything hot to eat, and even longer since she'd had pork. The very thought of a thick piece of ham caused her mouth to water and her stomach to growl loudly. But any delay could prove hazardous to her well-being. What if someone had found Garvey Davis?

"We wouldn't detain you for long," Elias whispered, as if knowing her thoughts. "You would still have plenty of time to make for Laramie. In fact, I could tell you a place you might spend the night on your way."

Simone realized she was losing the battle. She nodded. "I'd be grateful for a hot meal," she told them both.

"Well, then, come on with me," Gladys said, taking hold of

Simone's arm. "Elias, you bring that beast."

Simone glanced over her shoulder at the gray-haired man in surprise. Elias laughed. "Don't fret, Simone. It's just her way. She means you only the very best."

Simone nodded as Gladys pulled her along and around the corner of the mercantile. "We've got a little place right over there," the woman told Simone. "Snug and cozy with two bedrooms, a kitchen, and a front room. I think you'll like it."

Simone didn't know what to say. The cabin looked much like any other cabin, with the exception that a three-foot cross had been nailed to the right side of the front door. *What in the world have I gotten myself into?* The cross seemed to burn its image into her soul. *Why won't you just leave me alone?* she questioned, glancing heavenward. *Just leave me alone and let me be.*

EIGHT

SIMONE MANAGED TO ignore the cross as she entered the house. The warmth of the room immediately made her glad she'd come. It seemed like forever since she had stood in front of a fire—since she'd really been warm. Going to the hearth, Simone put her bundle of supplies on the floor and extended her hands toward the flames. How good it felt.

"Simone has been traveling for nearly a fortnight," Elias announced. "Her folks died and left her alone. She's made her way down from the mountains and is headed to meet up with family in Laramie."

"A fortnight in the mountains? You must be near froze to the bone," Gladys said, her voice registering disbelief. "Goodness, child. All alone in the wilderness." She continued to chatter without taking a breath. "Imagine, and you just a wee thing! Well, thanks be to Jesus, you're safe and sound now."

Simone could barely take it all in at once. Gladys's continued statements, Elias's gentle smile and tender actions. No one had ever cared whether she lived or died. Well, at least not since her mother had left her to fend for herself. Kindness seemed a foreign, almost uncomfortable condition to deal with.

Simone glanced around to find Gladys bustling from one room to the next. She brought a rocking chair and two heavy quilts to where

Simone stood. "You take off that old coat and wrap up in these."

Simone looked at the woman warily. She wanted to maintain her rock-hard wall of indifference, but the genuineness Gladys displayed softened her resolve. Not having bothered to rebutton her coat when she'd left the mercantile, Simone shrugged out of it and allowed Gladys to take it. Simone watched a moment while Gladys hung the coat on a peg by the door. It wasn't that she believed the woman would steal the mangy thing, but she didn't want it too far out of her sight.

"Here now," Gladys said, unfolding one of the quilts. "Let's get you wrapped up good and warm, then I'll finish fixing our dinner."

Simone reached out and took the blanket, surprised at the toasty warmth. "It feels like it's been sitting in the sun all day," she murmured and without thinking, smiled up at the woman.

"I keep 'em in a stack by the kitchen stove. Never know when someone takes a chill and needs to be warmed up. Around here it's mighty easy to freeze to death. You're one blessed little gal to not have done so in the mountains. God is good to look after us in our hour of need." She paused to look at Simone as if trying to figure out how the girl could have existed so long on her own. "Jesus is truly good," she finally said, shaking her head.

Simone said nothing. She pulled the quilt around her, then waited patiently while Gladys unfolded the second quilt and draped it over the first.

"Now," Gladys said, leading Simone to the rocker, "you just sit here and rest while I tend to dinner."

Something in her actions reminded Simone of her mother's tenderness. Her mind had blocked out the loving memories for so long, and even thinking of them now caused an ache to grow deep within her.

Simone didn't argue. She felt terribly weak and horribly tired, and the added warmth and comfort of the Canton cabin produced an overwhelming desire to sleep. Unable to fight the feeling any longer, Simone closed her eyes and allowed the heat of the fire and blankets to penetrate her body. Even Garvey Davis's wounded image wasn't able to haunt her at that moment. Relaxing slowly, she let herself descend into nothingness.

"Simone?" Elias Canton softly called her name. Simone jerked awake with a start.

Blinking several times, as if doing so might help her remember her whereabouts, Simone finally cleared the clouded images from her mind and replied, "Sorry. I must have dozed off." She sighed, a foreign feeling of safety and contentment washing over her.

Elias laughed. "You've been asleep for over two hours. Gladys and I just went ahead and ate without you, but I figured since you were concerned about moving on to Laramie that perhaps I should wake you. Are you sure you wouldn't like to just spend the night? We have an extra room. Used to belong to our daughter, but she married and moved away. You're certainly welcome to sleep in her bed and take your leave in the morning."

The idea sounded wonderful, but Simone knew that delay might risk the possibility of being caught. "No. I'm sorry for falling asleep on you." She got up, casting off the quilts. "It was kind of you to take me in."

"Well, come on, then, and have some dinner. We've kept it warm for you," Elias replied. He led the way to the back section of the house, where Gladys was just now pulling golden brown loaves of bread from the oven.

"Oh, I told him to let you sleep, but he said you were in some all-fired hurry to get to Laramie. It doesn't hardly seem fitting that a young woman like you should travel alone. There's all manner of wild beast out there just waiting to do you in."

"Yes," Elias agreed, "and not all of them are the four-legged type."

Simone nodded. She knew full well what the Cantons were insinuating. "I'll be careful. I have a gun."

"So does everybody else in the territory," Elias countered in a somewhat amused tone. "Look, why don't I ride with you a ways. I could make sure you stayed on the right road and—"

"No!" Simone declared, a little more emphatically than she'd intended. Elias pulled out a chair for her, and without looking him in the eye, she sat down. "Thank you," she murmured.

Gladys scurried forward with a platter of fried ham and biscuits. "These ought to fill you up a sight better than jerky." She went back to the stove and took the lid off a large kettle. Taking up a bowl, Gladys ladled a liberal portion of steaming soup. "This will finish warming your insides, if there's any chill left in you." She laughed and brought the soup to the table. "At least the color has returned to your cheeks."

Simone put a hand to her face absentmindedly. Both Elias and Gladys were looking at her as if they expected her to do or say something, but Simone wasn't sure what it was they expected. Nervously she thanked them for their generosity, then dug into the food.

It tasted like nothing she'd ever had before. The ham steak cut easily with her fork, the succulent juices running out across her plate. Simone tried not to show too much delight in the meal, but in truth, she felt as though she had stumbled upon a kingly feast. She tried the soup next and found it seasoned in a way that she couldn't recognize. Had she felt more comfortable, she might have asked Gladys for the recipe.

"So you have kin in Laramie?" Elias asked again.

Simone only nodded and continued eating. She didn't want to have to answer Elias Canton's questions. She didn't want to lie to this kindly man with his generous, chatty wife. These folks had been mighty good to her, and while that had never been a privilege Simone could remember, she didn't want to just out-and-out lie to them. Thinking like this startled Simone. She understood how to handle harsh, angry people. People with grudges or vendettas. Men who approached her with suggestive thoughts that Simone would just as soon never be a part of. But to have someone care about her needs, see to it that she was warm and fed . . . well, that was another story. It chiseled away at her defenses, and while Simone had always considered herself capable of facing most anything, she felt helpless in dealing with these people. Maybe it wouldn't be so bad to return their openness.

Still, she reminded herself that remaining aloof and silent would afford her a protection she might well need in the days to come. The less they knew about her, the better. Knowing too much about her and about what she'd done might actually cause them a great deal of grief, and that was certainly no way to pay back a kindness.

"Here, child," Gladys said, coming forward with a steaming cup. "I just made this tea. I hope you like tea."

"Tea's fine," Simone murmured and accepted the cup.

Gladys sat down in the chair beside her and shook her head again. "You look like you could stand a few days of rest. I sure wish you would change your mind and stay on with us. I miss my own girl so much that it would be pure pleasure to spend time with another young woman."

Simone tried not to think about the woman's aching heart, not wanting to imagine the misery of a daughter so far away from home. Simone took a large bite of the fluffy biscuit and tried not to think of anything but the food. *Don't be a fool*, she reminded herself. *The Cantons are nothing to you. Don't get caught up in who they are and what they want. Don't feel for them. Don't care about them.*

"I'm afraid that Gladdy misses our Eliza a sight more than some mothers might. She's our only child, you see," Elias told Simone. He smiled proudly. "She was even named after me, in a roundabout way."

Simone dared to look up at the man and found only loving approval in his eyes. She swallowed hard and took a long sip of tea from the mug. The lump in her throat refused to move. No one had ever loved her the way these people clearly loved their child. Of course, their child had most likely not committed murder. That thought shattered Simone's feelings of comfort in their presence.

"I thank you for your kindness," she said uneasily, "but I really should be on my way."

"I wish you would at least stay and have a bath," Gladys said. "Your clothes could use a good scrubbing, and I'd be right happy to see to it for you."

"Your horse looks pretty well shot," Elias added. "I've put him in the barn. Gave him feed and water, but he could use with a rest, as well."

He reached out to touch Simone's arm, but she drew back sharply. Having never known a touch by a man that wasn't intended for harm, Simone stood up abruptly, knocking the chair over backward. "I'm sorry," she said, suddenly realizing her reaction. "I can . . . cannot stay."

Elias's expression registered surprise. "I meant you no harm, child."

Simone realized how awkward the situation had become. "I'm sorry. I thank you for the meal. Thank you, too, for buying my pelts. But I've got to go now!" Her feelings were starting to frighten her. She longed for nothing more than to stay with these kind, gentle folk, but she couldn't—she was a murderess and a thief, and nothing good could ever come to her again.

She moved away from the table, casting one last regretful glance at the uneaten portion on her plate. Gladys seemed to understand this and hurried to remedy the situation.

"At least take some of this with you," she told Simone. "I'll wrap up the rest of the ham and biscuits. They ought to travel well. Oh, and you can take one of these loaves of bread. That ought to do you for a couple of days and by then you'll be to Laramie."

"Thank you," Simone replied, not knowing quite what to do. She wanted to reject the offer, but it seemed foolish to do so and her practical mind wouldn't hear of it. She went to the door, retrieved her coat from the peg, and waited until Gladys and Elias approached with the cloth-wrapped food.

Elias pulled on his own coat and smiled. "I'll help you saddle the horse."

"That's not necessary," Simone replied, but he'd hear nothing of her argument.

"Now, you be careful on the trail," Gladys told her. "I'll be praying for a legion of angels to surround you and keep you from harm."

Simone stared at her strangely. How odd this woman was with her prayers and her generosity. Simone had a tremendous urge to embrace the older woman, but she fought it with the only defense she had: indifference. It seemed natural for Gladys to act as she did. No doubt it was her nature, but Simone could not allow that nature to influence her own actions. She wanted nothing more from the couple, and she certainly didn't want for them to desire anything from her.

"Oh, don't forget this," Gladys said, retrieving Simone's earlier-purchased supplies from the floor in front of the fireplace.

"Thanks again," she murmured, accepting the goods. She reached out for the door handle but found Elias had already opened the door.

He smiled at her and motioned her to go ahead of him. "I'll be back in a few minutes, Gladdy."

Simone kept moving toward the side of the house, uncertain as to which way offered her the quickest path to the barn. She glanced around and felt a sense of relief when Elias pointed the way.

"Barn's over there."

Simone nodded and followed him to a small stable. The run-down building hardly looked sturdy enough to stand, but inside it was surprisingly warm. Elias immediately set to work saddling her horse while Simone tried to rearrange the pack she'd made out of the extra blanket. She added Gladys's generous offerings to her supplies and felt rather confident in the abundance she now had in her possession. Food, matches, and water. *Water*. She suddenly remembered the empty canteen.

"Could I fill my canteen before I go?" she questioned Elias.

"Sure," he answered, reaching out to take the object from her. "I'll just go do it for you. You go ahead and finish what you're doing there."

Again, Simone stared after the man in dumbfounded silence. She was used to being a servant, waiting on others—not the other way around. That this man should go after water on her account was beyond Simone's understanding, and when he returned she barely managed to acknowledge his actions.

"If you stay on the main road and head back in the direction you came, you'll go straight to Laramie. It'll take you two, maybe three days. There's a run-down shack about ten miles from here. You could stay the night there. It's not much, but a sight better than sleeping out in the open."

Simone nodded but said nothing. She hated the way this man made her feel helpless and needy. She longed to escape his vigilant concern and once again be on her own with no one but herself to count on.

"Have I offended you?" Elias asked her softly.

Apparently her discomfort was evident, and Simone instantly wished she'd been born a better liar. "I just don't know why you're being so nice to me," she said, wrapping the canteen strap around the horn of the saddle.

"The Bible says that we should love one another. Jesus said, 'Thou shalt love thy neighbour as thyself.' I'd certainly hope you'd do the same for me if I begged a cup of water."

"It also says, 'Trust ye not in a friend, put ye not confidence in a guide,'" she muttered.

Elias looked at her strangely. "Where does it say that, child?"

Simone shrugged. "Micah, seventh chapter." She grew uncomfortable and turned away, unable to face him. She secured the remaining supplies on the rump of the horse and tied them down tight.

Elias, however, wasn't a man to be easily put off. "Simone, it seems to me that you have not known much kindness in your life. You can't simply pull one verse out of context and pattern an entire life around it. The Bible is a book full of wisdom and hope."

Simone had heard more than enough. The last thing she wanted to do was find herself in a discussion on the Bible and its meaning. She took up the horse's reins and started to lead him from the barn.

Elias walked out after her and watched the whole time as she remounted the horse. Awkwardly, Simone shifted to dislodge her skirts until she felt comfortable in how they lay around her. She looked down upon the preacher and felt a strange desire to seek his wisdom for a better understanding of many things. So many questions went unanswered in her life. She wondered how it would be to share her fears and her concerns with this man and see what he might have to say about them. But the face of Garvey Davis disrupted this pleasant thought.

She was still too close to home. There still remained the fearful possibility that someone would connect her to Davis's death and come after her. She couldn't afford to trust her life to Elias Canton.

"Child, I know your heart is heavy," Elias commented softly. He came to stand beside the horse and took hold of the halter. "I just want you to know that no deed, no fear, no sorrow is too big for the Lord to deal with. You have apparently acquainted yourself with God's Word—therefore, it is my prayer that you would acquaint yourself with the Father himself. He is a loving, protective Father."

"He is also a judge and punisher of wrongdoings, is He not?" Simone replied quite seriously. A part of her longed to believe the old man was right—that God was loving and giving. That He cared about her. But if she allowed herself to believe that, then she would have to believe other things. Painful things. She would have to feel again, and the misery might well be the death of her.

"For those who refuse to confess their sins and turn from evil, yes."

Simone nodded solemnly and pulled the reins to the right in order to free the halter from Elias's grip. The old man easily released his hold. "Again, thanks for buying the pelts." She gave the horse a solid nudge in the side and urged the animal forward. She had no desire to listen to more of Elias's preaching.

But to her surprise, the man said nothing more. He didn't call after her, and for that Simone was grateful. She slapped the reins hard against the horse's neck and relished the briskness of the wind in her face. It helped her to corral her feelings and, by doing so, to feel less vulnerable. Vulnerability was deadly, she reminded herself, paying no heed to the single tear that escaped her eye.

NINE

IT WAS OFTEN SAID that Zack Matthews was the spitting image of his father. Tall and beefy with thick, muscular legs and broad shoulders, Zack stood six feet three without boots. His face had been called handsome by some of the local women, but Zack didn't brook concern with such nonsense. He devoted himself to working alongside his father, George Matthews, and it was Zack's intention to make his father proud. Lawmen seemed to fall into two categories in Wyoming: corrupt and more corrupt. George Matthews held his position as sheriff to be a very serious matter. Zack held his position as deputy no less seriously, and both hoped to see the office receive the respect of the citizens.

Respect was an important issue to Zack. The respect of the citizens and the respect of his father. So when George Matthews received word that a man had been murdered in the area of Uniontown, Zack volunteered to take care of the matter. Zack felt this to be as good a time as any to prove his mettle. At twenty-seven and as the youngest in the family, Zack very much desired his father's approval. His older brothers Ben and Harold had already proven themselves in law and cattle ranching, and his only sister, Emmaline, had married well-to-do. Now Zack felt as though they were all waiting collectively for him to prove his ability, ensuring the family's pride and name.

He looked around the small cabin just outside Uniontown and

wondered at the now departed occupants. The place appeared to have been well kept. But there lacked any sense of pleasantries or feminine touches.

"You say Dumas lived here with his daughter?" Zack asked the old trapper at his side.

"That's right. Louis and I used to trap together a long time ago. He up and brought him back a wife from Denver one year and that put an end to that."

"But the wife no longer lived here?" Zack again questioned.

"No," the man said shaking his head. "Some say she died, some say that she left. I don't rightly know. All I do know is that the dead man we just drug outside isn't Dumas."

"Do you have any idea who that man is, Mr.—" Zack couldn't remember what the man had called himself.

"Just call me Pike, everybody does. And to answer your question, no, I don't rightly know who that man is, but the folks in town might have a better idea."

"I plan to ride back over there this afternoon, but first things first," Zack answered, beginning to poke around the kitchen. He saw the spoiled remains of a stew, still positioned over the now cold hearth. Dirty dishes sat unattended on the counter nearby, and for all intents and purposes it looked as though the occupants had simply forgotten about them and the meal they were apparently participating in.

"Why was it you came to the Dumas cabin?" Zack questioned Pike.

"Cabin fever, I guess. I live on up the mountain a ways off. I figured on spending some time in town. I brought my own pelts down and stopped here on the way."

"And what did you find when you got here?" Zack questioned, still taking a visual inventory of the main room of the cabin. He stopped long enough to study the grizzled character. He stood at least a foot shorter than Zack and smelled as though it had been a month of Sundays since he'd seen a bath.

Pike shrugged. "Didn't find much of anything, 'ceptin' that dead man."

"Nobody else was around?" Zack pressed.

"Nope. Not even the girl."

"This girl," Zack questioned, moving again to the hearth. "How old is she?" Pike didn't answer, causing Zack to pause in his duties. "Well? Don't you have any idea how old she is?"

"I was just figurin' it up," Pike replied. "Best as I can figure she's seventeen, maybe eighteen."

"And this wife of Louis Dumas," Zack continued, checking the mantel for anything that might shed light on the situation, "you say she died?"

"That's what I'd heard. Died or run off. This country's mighty hard on women."

"But if she'd run off, wouldn't she have taken the girl?"

Pike shrugged. "I don't rightly know. The Dumases kept to themselves. Louis and I played cards and trapped together in the early years, but that was it. We wasn't much for socializin'."

Zack nodded. "Yet you came here first before going on over to Uniontown."

Again Pike shrugged. It seemed to be a habit of his. "Like I said, it's been a while since I'd seen another human being. I figured Dumas would be about as much in need of whiskey as me. Not to mention a good game of cards. Sure couldn't get that stuck here all by yourself—even if you had a child with you."

Zack halted his questioning while he peered into the bedroom area of the cabin. Two crude homemade beds were the main occupants of the room. A nightstand stood beside the smaller of the two beds and a trunk marked the foot of the same. On the far side of the room, Zack noted a small handmade wooden bench. It looked like the kind used for storage, so Zack crossed the room and lifted the seat.

Inside there was a hodgepodge of articles. Blankets lined the top, and under these were several pieces of clothing that clearly belonged to a baby. A silver-handled brush and comb, several pieces of paper that spoke of operas in Denver, and other feminine memorabilia were buried beneath these. At least they offered proof that a woman had actually lived in this cabin at one time. Seeing nothing noteworthy, Zack went to the trunk at the end of the small bed. It was empty.

Straightening up, Zack pulled out his pocket watch and noted the time. "My guess is that it'll be dark in another couple of hours: I think we'd best get that man buried and head over to Uniontown."

Pike, who'd continued to watch Matthews from the cloth partition, gave his typical shrug. "It's hard work burying a man."

Zack nodded. "But we can't leave him out there, and I see no reason to drag him back in here. The sooner we get to it, the better. Why don't you go scout around in that shed outside and see if you can scare up a shovel."

Zack waited for Pike to shrug, but the man merely turned and walked away. Zack hoped he intended to give him a hand with the necessary duties, but if he didn't, it wouldn't be the first time Zack had found himself facing an unpleasant duty alone.

Walking outside, Zack went to the body and frowned. The man had bled to death from injuries to the head, and from the looks of the body, it appeared to have taken place the better part of a month ago. That would have put it at the early part of May, and he found it hard to identify the man's features. It was this reason, and the overwhelming stench, that caused Zack to forego hauling the man into Uniontown. Death was neither welcoming in sight nor smell, and in this case the latter was far more oppressive than the first. Reaching a hand inside the man's pockets, Zack came up empty. Whoever had done the man in had robbed him, as well.

"I found this here shovel," Pike announced. "There's a plot of ground round back of the pelt shed that looks to have been part of a garden. Guess that'd be our best bet for burying him."

"All right. You start digging, and I'll get the body ready," Zack told Pike.

Pike seemed accepting of this arrangement and took off back in the direction of the shed. Zack shook his head, still puzzled about the entire matter. He wanted very much to return to Laramie with the killer in hand and a confession bubbling from his lips. But there weren't even enough clues to figure out who might have wanted the stranger dead.

Zack retrieved a sheet from the larger of the two beds and rolled the dead man inside. This helped considerably to cut down on the stench, although everything around him seemed to be saturated with the smell of death. Zack reasoned that it couldn't be helped, but it didn't stop his stomach from churning.

Once he had the man wrapped and tied inside the sheet, Zack hoisted the body to his shoulder and made his way past the shed. Pike had already dug a fair-sized hole and stood knee-deep in the dirt.

"You want me to take over?" Zack questioned, sliding the body to the ground.

"Suit yourself. Don't reckon to dig it full size. We're gonna lose the sun in another hour and that'll put us on the trail after dark. Ain't friendly to be on the road at night in these parts."

Zack nodded. "Looks deep enough. I guess if we can put some rocks on top of it, we'll have done our part."

This met with Pike's approval and the man half rolled, half stepped from the hole. He ambled over to Zack and helped to take hold of one end of the man while Zack grabbed the other. They lowered the body into the hole, then Zack took up the shovel and began covering it with dirt.

He contemplated all he had seen at the cabin and realized there was nothing more to be done here. He would return to Uniontown and ask questions of the locals. Surely someone would know who the man was and whether or not he had any enemies. If not, then perhaps they would know what had become of Louis Dumas and his daughter.

Later that night, Zack sat down to a bowl of watery stew and rock-hard biscuits. The only place to get a meal or a room to sleep in was at the Red Slipper Saloon, and while Zack wasn't given to frequenting bars, he figured it the best place to get some answers.

"I'm Ada. Pike says you buried a man up at the Dumas place," a woman said frankly as she placed a cup of black coffee in front of Matthews.

"That's right. I'm here to check into the man's murder. Did you know him?" Zack sized up the woman, realizing her occupation immediately. She wore a low-cut gown of yellow satin that had obviously seen better days, and more makeup adorned her face than was decent for a woman to wear.

"Well, from the description Pike gave, I'd say it would have to be Garvey Davis. He and Dumas did some bartering right before Louis took off. He bought Louis out."

"Bought him out?" Zack questioned, finally believing he was getting the necessary answers to his questions.

"Louis owned a fair-sized trapline. He also owned that cabin you saw today. He was in here one day and he and Davis played cards. Davis told him about gold in Colorado, and since he was tossing quite a bit of money around, Dumas listened with real interest."

"You seem to know quite a bit about this whole affair. Would you mind sitting down and telling me the rest?" Zack questioned.

Ada looked around her for a moment. "Seems like everyone is lookin' out for themselves. Guess I could talk for a spell." She pulled out the chair and motioned to Zack's bowl. "You'd best eat up, however. That stuff ain't hardly fit for man after it gets cold."

Zack nodded and picked up his spoon. "So Louis Dumas sold his cabin and traplines to Garvey Davis. What about his daughter? Pike says he had a daughter who would have been seventeen or so. Did she go with Dumas?"

Ada laughed. "No. Louis couldn't see saddlin' himself with the girl. He sold her to Davis, too."

Zack had just taken a mouthful of the stew, and at this news spit most of it back out. "What?" he sputtered and coughed. For a moment, he had a hard time getting his breath, and it wasn't until he managed to swallow down some coffee that he managed to stop coughing. "He sold his daughter?"

"Things ain't quite as refined up here as they are in the city," Ada said as though the matter was unimportant. "Simone was the only other white woman in the Uniontown area. Men fancied the way she looked, and I figure Garvey Davis was no exception."

"But to sell your own child?" Horrified at the idea, Zack could only contemplate what manner of man would strike a deal that included his own flesh and blood.

Ada's expression told him that she didn't find the matter at all offensive. "Louis did what he thought best. Both for him and the girl. Weren't hardly practical that he should drag her over the mountains to

Colorado. Simone needed to be gettin' a husband anyway. She was full-growed."

"But Davis wasn't a husband, he was a purchaser," Zack countered.

"Louis figured Simone to be given to Davis in marriage. I don't much think it mattered to him that the man paid out money for her. Men have been either payin' or gettin' paid to take women off other folks' hands for forever and a day. These parts ain't likely to see a preacher very often, so most folks just count themselves married."

Zack shook his head. For all his years growing up on the western frontier, this idea had never been one promoted in his home life. "So Davis and Dumas struck a bargain that included Simone. Then what?"

"Then they rode out of town and headed over to Louis's cabin. Heard him suggest Davis look everything over—includin' Simone—before makin' up his mind. Later Louis returned to Uniontown, said the deed was done, and took a good deal of grief from the menfolk for havin' sold Simone so cheap."

Zack's eyes narrowed. "Dumas and Davis both have their own horses?"

"Sure," Ada said with a nod.

Zack realized that there had been no sign of a horse at the cabin. Whoever had robbed the dead man had obviously taken his horse and gear, as well. Zack ate in silence for several minutes. Ada had given him the answers to a great many questions in his mind, but that still didn't answer his concerns about Simone Dumas. Had someone also done her the same harm they'd done Garvey Davis?

"Is anybody else missing from these parts?" Zack finally asked the woman.

"It's hard to say. Men come and go, and now that spring is upon us, they'll be goin' down to Denver or over to Cheyenne or Laramie for supplies and such."

"What about Simone Dumas?" Zack questioned. He found he was rapidly becoming obsessed with the young woman's welfare.

"I can't say what might have happened to Simone. Whoever done Garvey in might have taken her. She's a handsome woman." Ada paused as if the truth had cost her considerably. "Then again, she might have done Garvey in herself."

"What?" Zack wasn't sure he'd heard her right.

"Hey, Ada," a man called from the bar, "you gonna talk all night or serve me some whiskey?"

"Be right there, Jake," she replied, then turned to Zack apologetically. "Sorry."

"Wait a minute," Zack said, reaching out to take hold of her arm. "Do you have some reason to believe Simone capable of killing Garvey Davis on her own?"

"Not unless you count bein' unwillin' to be sold a reason. 'Course, I have no reason to believe she was unwillin'," Ada said, smiling. "Now, why don't you stop worryin' about business. Maybe we could talk again . . . later." She gave him a smile, and Zack was instantly aware of the gaping hole where teeth should have been.

He nodded but said nothing. He knew she intended him to be interested in something more than talk, but he was on a mission to prove himself, and nothing but the truth and Garvey Davis's killer would put his mind at rest. And if that weren't enough, Zack knew better than to ever entangle himself with a woman like Ada. His mother hadn't raised him to take part in immoral activities, whether it helped his investigation or not.

Sitting in silence, Zack finished his meal and contemplated what to do next. He had already secured the bed in the back of the storeroom for his night's rest, and weariness was setting in. With a yawn, he decided that he might be able to think more clearly after a good night's sleep. Maybe then he could figure out who had killed Garvey Davis and where Simone Dumas had run off to.

TEN

LIFE HAD BECOME one adventure after another for Simone Dumas. After her uneventful arrival in Laramie, she found her courage bolstered and determined that there was nothing she couldn't do. Still, the ominous weight of her past crowded in on the hopefulness of her future. Constant fears plagued her. Would someone learn of her deed? Would they come after her? Laramie hardly seemed far enough to run once she arrived in the busy town.

The town itself seemed far larger than anything Simone had ever encountered. She gave the horse a loose rein and stared around her in open amazement at the bustle of activity that greeted her. Buildings stretched out for blocks, and people appeared and disappeared inside the confines without seeming to even consider those around them. Realizing the horse had stopped, Simone stared down to see what obstacle had caught his attention. Both she and the horse quizzically considered the dull silver rails that crossed their path. She studied the rails, wondering what it meant and how it worked when a loud blasting whistle sounded just to the east of her. Simone fought to keep the horse under control as a massive black contraption moved along the rail. It came nearer and nearer, and finally Simone turned the horse away and put some distance between her and the great beast.

The whistle sounded again, and looking up, Simone found a man waving down from a small platform at the back of the steam-belching machine. What in the world was this?

Waiting for the entire thing to snake past her, Simone couldn't help but be amazed by the object. Watching with great curiosity, Simone nearly gasped aloud as she found windows on what appeared to be small boxed houses on wheels. People looked out to her from the windows and some even waved. What could it all mean? It was as if someone had taken a wagon and stretched it out to hold hundreds of people. She would have to find out what in the world it was she'd just witnessed, because within moments the black beast and its many cars were completely out of sight. A person could certainly put a great deal of distance between him and whatever else he wanted to get away from by riding on one of those things, Simone reasoned.

And it was with this thought in mind that Simone found herself convinced to leave Laramie behind and try a new mode of travel. The locomotive. Trains were said to be the rage, and the stationmaster told her that within a matter of days Simone could find herself completely across the country with hundreds of miles to separate her from the Wyoming Territory. It was the idea of such a great separation between her and Garvey Davis's dead body that finally convinced Simone. She needed distance.

Days later, Simone sat glued to the window in complete amazement as the landscape seemed to be literally eaten up. She'd managed to sell Garvey's horse and gear, and before she knew it, Simone found herself headed for a place called Omaha. After that there was a change of trains, and she would journey on to what the conductor promised her was an entirely different world called Chicago. Without telling him her desires to be lost and forgotten, Simone had listened to him tell of massive buildings and throngs of people. And, he had added with a wink, stores aplenty to strike at the heart of any young woman. But it was only after he added sympathetically that the trip was still a good distance away and included several changes of train that Simone made up her mind. Surely this would guarantee her safety.

"You travel much?" a matronly woman at her side questioned. The woman's traveling attire seemed ill fitted, and given the heat of the day, she appeared very uncomfortable.

Simone shrugged. "When I can." She thought this the safest answer. With her trip drawing quickly to a close, the hard wooden seat and close quarters were beginning to irritate Simone.

"I can't abide these things," the woman continued, "but they're the only way to cross a great deal of country in a short while. Don't you agree?"

At the woman's attempt to draw her into a conversation, Simone nodded but said nothing as she continued to stare out the window. She felt overwhelmed with the reality of what she'd done. She knew nothing about the cities she'd passed through except that they were large and heavily populated. Compared to Uniontown, they appeared to be the kind of place where a person could easily be forgotten. But while she'd considered debarking the train before her scheduled stop in Chicago, Simone remained. The conductor had stated that a man might live there his entire life and never cover the entire area of the city. Simone liked that idea, and while it was difficult to imagine such a place, she took the man's word as gospel.

"I've got two daughters living in Denver," the woman told her proudly. "Why they've chosen to live there is beyond me. The scenery is pretty enough, but it's in the middle of nowhere. Now, Chicago suits me just fine. It's close enough to get just about anywhere you want to go."

Simone let the woman rattle on about Chicago, hoping she would offer up some meaningful information in the course of her conversation.

"We have a house near the lake," the woman announced as though it should mean something to Simone. "Well, it's not right on the lake. In fact," the woman added with some hesitation, "it's several blocks away, but near enough.

"It's a good time for you to come to the city," she continued. "Not too hot yet, and most of the heavy rains have already been spent." She leaned closer to Simone and added, "We're a proud people in Chicago. Proud of our city and our heritage. You should see us celebrate the Fourth of July." Simone struggled to remember what significance that day held over others. "Yes, indeed," the woman continued, "celebrating the independence of America is something we don't intend to let our children forget."

Simone nodded, suddenly remembering lessons her mother had taught her about the history of America. *Of course*, she thought, *the Fourth of July is the day the Declaration of Independence was signed.* The history lesson came back to her in bits and pieces, the phrase "Life, liberty and the pursuit of happiness" coming to mind. How she'd like to believe that those qualities were extended to her, as well.

When the woman halted the conversation long enough to retrieve something to eat from her bag, Simone took the opportunity to lean back against the seat and close her eyes. She was a solitary pilgrim on a journey that would lead her into a foreign land. She thought of stories she had read about Abraham in the Bible. He, too, had gone into a foreign land without any idea of what he would find.

"Next stop, Shee-cog-go," the conductor announced, coming through the car. "All off for Shee-cog-go."

Simone bolted awake and her heart begin to race.

"You fell asleep," her traveling companion announced. "Although how you did it with the heat mounting and all the ash from the smokestack making the air unbreathable, I'll never know. We'll be pulling into the station within a matter of minutes." The woman turned her attention to tidying her appearance.

Simone felt a sensation of panic build inside her. What would she do? Where could she go? Suddenly the stranger sitting next to her seemed very important. "Excuse me," she said, turning to the woman.

The woman looked up in surprise and halted her attempt to button the too-tight jacket. "Yes?"

"Well . . . that is," Simone paused uncomfortably, "I just wondered where I could go to get a place to stay."

The woman's expression grew sympathetic. "You don't have kin in Chicago?"

"No," Simone said, shaking her head. "My family is dead."

"I'm so sorry. Oh dear, a young woman on her own," the matron muttered and appeared to consider the matter a moment. "I have an old acquaintance who runs a small boardinghouse. She lives a good distance from the station, but you can get there on foot. I'll give you the directions and write a note of introduction. Elvira Taylor won't allow just anyone to take a room at her house." The woman paused for a moment, then added, "You can read, can't you?"

"Yes, and I'm obliged for the help," Simone replied. From somewhere in the recesses of her memory, Simone remembered her mother saying that courteous behavior would take you far. Experiencing the helpfulness of strangers had caused her to soften her thoughts on humanity.

While she waited for her letter of introduction, Simone turned her attention to the window. The world outside fascinated her in a way that she could not even begin to explain. There were such things, such wonders she had never even considered possible. She remembered her mother talking about huge multi-story buildings of brick and stone, but until she had seen them for herself, it had been hard to believe.

She noticed the drastic change of scenery outside her window as such buildings broke the pattern of vast stretches of farm and grazing land that had accompanied her across the plains.

A suppressed strain of excitement fluttered to life inside of Simone. Perhaps her new life in Chicago would bring her safety and hope. Surely in a city as large as this one, no one would pay any attention to her. With any luck at all, Simone would simply assimilate into the town and become just one more citizen. She timidly smiled at this idea. To simply drift into anonymity without a care in the world. Now, there was a thought.

The woman at her side signaled the conductor and insisted he allow her to borrow his pencil. The man grumbled and seemed none too willing but nevertheless handed the article over and waited while the woman jotted her note. Upon finishing, she thanked the man and passed the note to Simone. "This should give you an open door. Elvira doesn't have a fancy place, but she tries to be careful with her tenants."

"Thank you," Simone said, taking the paper in hand. The train had already begun to slow, and Simone felt her nervous anticipation build. "How do I get there?"

The stranger spent the next few minutes explaining the intricate walk to the Taylor boardinghouse. "Of course, you could just hire a hack," the woman told Simone seriously.

"A hack?" Simone questioned in confusion.

The woman seemed not to hear her question. "But they cost a good sum, and for a healthy girl like you, a walk shouldn't prove too harmful. Don't talk to strange men, however. They're never up to any good, and a woman unaccompanied is oftentimes mistaken for being of lesser quality and character. If you get my meaning."

Simone nodded. She did indeed "get her meaning." She knew full well the consequences of paying too much attention to men. She knew better than to look a man in the eye lest he think her being forward and suggestive, and she knew better than to allow herself to become indebted to any of them. Men had strange ideas when it came to paying back favors.

"Oh, and since this is your first visit to Chicago, I'd suggest you stick with me until we're outside the depot."

"Depot," Simone repeated the word solemnly.

"The station is usually absolute bedlam, and I wouldn't want a wee thing like yourself to be swallowed up in the rush."

Simone started to protest, then thought better of it. If this woman wanted to take responsibility for getting her through a serious situation, then Simone had sense enough to yield to the idea. It wasn't like the woman could hold her against her will should something go amiss. Besides, Simone was quickly coming to realize that not everyone desired to hurt her. Her father had been an evil and hideous man, but his ways were not the ways of the world, she had learned. Still, there was no need to get out of line over the whole thing. Simone didn't want the past to keep her from finding peace in the future.

When the train finally came to a halt in Chicago, Simone found herself caught up in the sea of people hurrying to depart. With the carpetbag she'd purchased after selling Garvey's horse, Simone followed her traveling companion. It was all so overwhelming—the noises, the people, the bustle of activities. Simone had never experienced anything like it in her life. She actually found herself moving closer to the woman who had so kindly offered her help.

"It doesn't profit a soul to stand still in this place," the woman told her while quickly maneuvering Simone through a group of men and women who seemed equally intent on boarding the train that Simone was leaving.

Finally, after a series of twists and turns, Simone found herself outside the grand station house. It appeared no less chaotic here, however, than inside the depot. The streets were overrun with carriages and wagons of all manner. Simone felt overwhelmed by a complete sense of confusion. What manner of place had she come to?

"Now, over there is the street I told you about," the woman said, pushing Simone along. "You head across that intersection and right up that way for three blocks. Then turn right and head six blocks up and . . ." She continued with the instructions as Simone tried to take it all in. How would she ever find her way in such a place?

"You'll have to find work if you're going to survive in this town," the woman was saying as Simone once again forced herself to focus on the words. "There's jobs aplenty, but some of them aren't for the likes of proper women. You'd do well to get yourself fixed up, get some different clothes. Of course, a lot of folks will expect letters of reference, so you may find yourself limited in what you can and can't apply for."

Simone had never thought about a job. She had very few job skills outside skinning and preparing furs for market. Perhaps there was someone in this town who worked in the pelt business. She thought to ask the woman, then changed her mind.

"Thank you for your help," Simone replied, keeping her fears and concerns to herself. One way or another, she would survive in this town. It certainly couldn't be any worse than what had awaited her in Uniontown.

And then Simone was alone. Alone in a city with thousands and thousands of people. She had never seen so many people! Standing in the middle of the rushing throngs, Simone felt shaken and wondered if she should take what little money she had left and get back on the train. At least some of the other towns she'd passed through didn't seem half so big. She glanced upward, looking beyond the street corner. Tall buildings, just as her mother had described, rose around her and spread out in the distance. Chicago!

"Out of the way, girl," a harsh voice called.

Simone glanced up to find a matronly woman pushing her way through the crowd. Following her were three young girls, all who were dressed in such lavish finery that Simone could do nothing but stare. Their gowns were pale pink and trimmed in lovely spidery webs of lace and shimmering ribbon. They reminded Simone of a gown her mother had once shown her. The dress had been something Simone's mother had owned before marrying Louis Dumas. She had hoped to save it for Simone, but Louis had burned it in a fit of rage one night. Lovely dreams disintegrated in the greedy flames.

The girls bobbed by in perfect order, from tallest to shortest, following in confident silence. Their faces were turned upward, as if to acknowledge that nothing but the heavens deserved their attention. Simone could only glance down in disgust at her own miserable attire and shake her head.

After being bumped and jostled by the passing crowds, Simone forced her mind to concentrate on the instructions she'd been given. Moments later, she made her way up the street and finally felt her confidence begin to return. She emphatically reminded herself that she had lived in the rugged mountains of Wyoming. She had spent weeks traveling on her own through unfamiliar territory. She had trapped and hunted for her food, had made shelter for herself and havens of safety. For more years than she cared to remember, she had been required to take care of herself. Why should this big city be any more of a challenge than the wilderness had been?

The people around her hardly gave her a moment's notice, and for the most part were too busy scurrying for carriages or hacks to give Simone any notice. For this, she was grateful. As she drew farther away from the station, Simone found fewer people, but the activities were still considerable. As was the noise. Such noise!

Wyoming had been a tomb of silence compared to Chicago. She found it impossible to take everything in at once as bells, animals, and traffic noise blended in a chaotic rhythm. Then, too, the smell amazed and overwhelmed Simone. The stench of industrial smokestacks mingled with the smoke from the trains was only a fraction of the odors emitted by this strange city. And wrapped around the smells came the ever-present shouts and cries of the street vendors.

Grateful that her trek took her even deeper into what appeared to be a lower-class neighborhood, Simone no longer felt quite so self-conscious. Here she found women dressed similarly to herself. Simple cotton skirts and blouses, usually accompanied by aprons and children, revealed that these women were more her equals than many of the passengers aboard the train into town.

The closer she drew to her appointed destination, the more comfortable Simone grew. Debris and trash lined the streets, while shoddy-looking characters called out from two-wheeled carts.

"Fresh fish! Get 'em fresh!" a man called from behind her, while another vendor with fruits and vegetables volleyed for customers' attention.

The wind began to pick up again, as it had off and on since she started her journey from the depot. The woman on the train had told her that Chicago was well-known for its windy temperament, telling of a fire that occurred nearly twenty years earlier that had wiped out most of the town. The woman had blamed the winds for adding to the problem, citing that this, along with the poor response of the fire brigade, had rendered Chicago helpless. It didn't appear to Simone that the city had suffered overly from that destruction. She'd never seen so many buildings in one place.

A woman scurried past, clutching a newspaper-wrapped article in her arms. The two small boys at her side also juggled packages, and when one of them tripped and began to cry, the woman halted and fussed over the child in motherly fashion. Simone froze in her steps not four feet away. Something about the mother's tenderness brought poignant memories of her own mother.

"There, now," the woman cooed, "you're all right. Let's get home to Granny and fix us a fine feast before Papa gets home." The boy, his lower lip still quivering, nodded and reached back down for his bundle.

A piece of the newsprint had come free from the boy's package and blew back against Simone's skirts. She reached down to retrieve the piece and thought to offer it up to the woman, but when she straightened, the woman had already moved off. Glancing down at the newspaper, a boxed advertisement caught her attention.

> WANTED: Young women. 18–30 years of age, of good moral character, attractive and intelligent as waitress in Harvey Eating Houses on the Santa Fe Railroad in the West. Wages 17.50 per month with room and board. Liberal tips customary. Experience not necessary. Apply at the Harvey Employment Office, Eighteenth and Wentworth.

"Experience not necessary," Simone murmured, wondering about this Harvey Eating House and its other requirements. She wasn't yet the required age, but while she was small in stature, Simone figured she could easily pass for eighteen. Still, it would be a lie to say she met the standards when she didn't. And she wasn't all that sure she could convince anyone that she was "of good moral character, attractive and intelligent." But she had to try. After all, it required no experience, and the pay seemed very good. It offered her room and board, plus it promised to place her somewhere in the West on the Santa Fe Railroad. She wasn't at all familiar with where that might lead her, but it was at least worthy of consideration. Perhaps Mrs. Taylor would know something of this Harvey House matter.

ELEVEN

ELVIRA TAYLOR GREETED her with stilted reserve until Simone produced the letter of reference. The woman eyed the note for a moment, then studied Simone intently.

"You came in on the train with Grace, eh?"

Simone hadn't realized her traveling companion's name but nodded in affirmation. "She thought you might have a room I could rent."

Mrs. Taylor nodded. "I have one room left. Ain't much to look at, that's for sure, but it's warm and dry. It'll cost you fifty cents a day. You got that kind of money?"

Simone nodded. "I'm not sure how long I'll need it. I plan to apply for a job with the Harvey Eating House. Do you know anything about them?"

The woman's face lit up. "Do I! My own daughter Rachel is housemother to a passel of Harvey Girls in Topeka, Kansas. They train 'em there, you know."

Simone shook her head. "I really don't know much at all about them. What is this Santa Fe Railroad, and where does it go?" she asked, glancing down at the advertisement.

"Oh, the Santa Fe is a line that goes south across Kansas and down along the south way of the nation. They go clear to California, on the edge of the ocean. 'Course, most of the stops are completely removed from civilization, and my Rachel says that some women would rather not find themselves stuck out there with nobody but railroad folk to talk to."

"Doesn't sound half bad to me," Simone murmured, having no idea where these places might be.

"Well, you'll have to clean up a sight better than this," Elvira chided her. "You need to look your best when you go to the employment office. Do you have something nicer to wear?"

Simone looked down at her patched wool skirt. "No."

"Well, if you have extra money, I'd suggest you go up the street to Handerman's Used Clothing Store. They have some good bargains there, and the clothes are really nice. He takes in the stuff the well-to-do folks get rid of."

Simone nodded. "All right, I'll do that. Whereabout is Eighteenth and Wentworth? That's the address on this piece of paper."

"I'll draw you a bit of a map when you're set to go. Right now let me show you the room. I require cash up front for at least a week's stay."

The train ticket had taken a good bit of her money, and Simone felt reluctant to part with yet another large amount. "Does that include meals?"

"Sure does," Elvira said, grabbing up a key and motioning Simone to follow her upstairs. "Three meals a day and a hot bath. We've got electric lights and running water. That's why I have to charge full price for rooms."

Simone glanced up at the electric light at the top of the stairs. It fascinated her the way the thing illuminated the hall around them. There seemed to be so much more in this world than she had ever known back in Uniontown.

"Whereabouts you from?" Elvira asked as she paused to insert the key in a nearby door.

"Wyoming Territory," Simone answered honestly, then thought better of it.

"Ain't a territory no more. Leastwise, it won't be. I read in the newspaper that they're making it a state." She reached to the wall and immediately the room was flooded in light.

Simone had no knowledge of this and even less understanding as to why it should matter. However, the light fascinated her.

"How did you make the lights come on?"

Elivira eyed her strangely, then showed her the workings of the switch before pointing out the rest of the room. "Like I said, it ain't much."

Simone noted the small iron bed and washbasin. At the foot of the bed was a small dresser, but otherwise the room was bare, a single tiny window offering the only view.

"Don't use the light unless you have to. And turn it off if you leave the room," Elvira told her. "I'll take your money now."

Simone counted out three dollars and fifty cents, then asked for directions to the clothing store. The way she saw it, there was no time to be lost on idleness.

The next morning Simone felt—and looked—like a new woman. She had taken a hot bath in Elvira's thoroughly modern bathing room, then donned her new suit of blue serge. The suit and blouse had cost her plenty, and because of this, Simone had opted not to purchase shoes to go along with the outfit. She knew her moccasins were hardly considered proper, but she figured she could hide them well enough beneath her skirts. She had no plans to hire a carriage, so there would be no need to expose her feet as she climbed up to take a seat, and should she have to negotiate stairs, she would simply be mindful of her condition and take extra care.

Her hair worried her. She had seen the intricate and fascinating coiffures of the Chicago ladies at the train station. Here at Mrs. Taylor's boardinghouse she was equally fascinated by the neat and tidy buns sported by her landlady and by the spinster schoolteacher who had the room next to hers. She tried to imitate what they had done but found it impossible, so she finally settled on braiding her clean ebony hair down the back.

Joining the others at breakfast, Simone was relieved to find only a portion of the group she'd dined with the night before. The spinster chattered on with Mrs. Taylor while an elderly gentleman Simone knew only as Mr. Zimmerman checked his pocket watch and downed his coffee.

"Are you off to apply for the Harvey House job?" Mrs. Taylor questioned. "You'll make a good impression on them looking like that." Simone felt her cheeks grow hot and concentrated on her breakfast while her landlady spoke in great praises of her daughter in Kansas. Hearing the woman speak with such love and pride about her child caused Simone's heart to ache. Was this how people really lived? Were children really esteemed and counted as a blessing?

"I have a little map for you," Elvira continued. "Drew it out myself last night." She proudly displayed the piece of paper and handed it over to the schoolteacher, who readily approved her work.

"She should have no chance of getting lost with this. This is a fine job, Mrs. Taylor. I wish my students could do half so well."

Mrs. Taylor relished the praise with a smiling nod. She placed the map beside Simone and pointed. "You can see that we are here. Wentworth is this street over here."

Simone eyed the map carefully and nodded. The distance would be considerable, but it couldn't be helped. Her only real concern was whether or not she'd be able to maintain her orderly appearance. Tucking the map away, Simone ate in silence, thinking about the ordeal to come and considering the snatches of conversation between Mrs. Taylor and the schoolteacher.

Once breakfast was completed, Simone stepped from the boardinghouse into a warm June morning. Again, the unending clamor of the city assaulted her. She was amazed to find such a large congregation of people, all in one place, seemingly interested in doing a hundred different things. Thinking of her mountain cabin and Uniontown, Simone shook her head. Folks back there would find Chicago an intrusive place that disrupts their peace of mind.

Taking out the map, Simone made her way down the street. Mrs. Taylor's directions were easy to follow, and because the weather appeared so fine and mild, Simone found herself standing in front of the address before she knew it. Daintily climbing the stairs lest she reveal her moccasins, Simone opened the door of the establishment and walked in.

"May I help you?" a stern-faced matron questioned.

Simone nodded. "I'd like to apply for this position." She took out the advertisement, now trimmed from the piece of newsprint, and offered it to the woman.

"You may set up an appointment," the woman said, her serious expression never changing.

"An appointment?" Simone questioned. "What do I do, then?"

"You wait until we can see you," the woman said rather haughtily. "Interviews are by appointment only."

"But I had hoped to see someone today. I—"

"It simply isn't done that way, miss."

"Mrs. Blevins is a tough taskmaster," a male voice called from behind Simone.

Turning, Simone found the owner of the voice leaning casually against the doorjamb. His eyes were a warm chocolate brown and seemed to be illuminated with pure amusement. His lips curled into a smile as he met Simone's thorough study of him. "I'm Jeffery O'Donnell. I'm in charge here. Leastwise, when Mrs. Blevins allows me to be."

The older woman grunted something inaudible as Jeffery clearly took over the situation.

"So to what do I owe the pleasure?"

"I, uh . . ." Simone stammered, feeling quite nervous. "I came about the job with the Harvey Eating House."

"They all do," Jeffery replied. "That's what I do here. I hire young women of good moral character to be Harvey Girls for Fred Harvey's eating establishments. Would that one of them should just show up to see me for myself."

"I told her she needed to make an appointment," Mrs. Blevins added.

"Nonsense, Mrs. Blevins. We are rather desperate for help at the moment. I'll see her without an appointment." He extended his arm and motioned to Simone. "If you'll step right this way."

Simone heard the old woman clicking her tongue at his decision, but she refused to look back. She walked through the massive wood doorway and felt only slight discomfort when Jeffery closed it behind her.

"Have a seat there," Jeffery pointed to one of two leather chairs positioned in front of his desk. "I'll need to get information about your background. We thoroughly investigate our young ladies. Mr. Harvey wants only those of the highest character working for him."

Simone felt a wave of nausea pass through her. She couldn't help but think of Garvey Davis and wondered how Mr. Harvey would perceive a murderess as one of his employees. An extensive investigation would surely reveal her past, and that would surely put an end to any ideas she had of being a Harvey Girl.

"First of all, I need a name," Jeffery said, looking up to meet her gaze. He smiled again and raised his eyebrows as if they were posing the question for him.

Simone instantly felt overwhelmed by his attentive interest. He didn't leer at her like so many other men had, but rather, his expression was one that seemed a cross between delight and concern. She found herself drawn to him despite her resolve to care nothing for the people who crossed her path. His entire countenance suggested kindness and honesty, and he was clearly the handsomest man she'd ever seen. She let her gaze linger a moment longer on his face before finally replying, "My name is Simone."

"What an unusual name," he said, taking up a pen to write. "What's your last name?"

Simone realized that she had painted herself into a corner. Folks in Uniontown knew her, and if the law came looking, they'd be seeking her under the name Simone Dumas. Glancing nervously around the room, she spied a book by Washington Irving.

"Irving. Simone Irving."

"All right. Your age?"

"Eighteen," Simone lied.

Jeffery continued writing, not in the least concerned as to whether or not she was telling the truth. "Where are you from?"

Simone felt hesitant. She didn't know how to answer the man's question. She certainly didn't want to bring the authorities down on her head. "Chicago," she finally managed to squeak out.

"Lived here long?" he questioned, returning her hesitant gaze with a smile.

"No," Simone replied. "My parents died. I came here after that."

Jeffery frowned. "I am sorry. What a terrible burden to put on the shoulders of one so young and beautiful."

Simone lowered her head, feeling her cheeks flame with heat. This man's words did something to disturb her sense of comfort. Either that or it was the lies she told him.

"I'm sorry to make you sad," Jeffery continued. Simone instantly realized that he presumed her to be upset, maybe even crying. She took advantage of it and kept her head bowed. "Where did you grow up?" Jeffery asked.

Simone took a deep breath and sighed, hoping he would mistake it for a sign of grief. He did.

"I'm sorry. Perhaps you'd rather not talk about it, what with your folks and all."

Simone nodded, still keeping her face from view.

"I completely understand. Look, we usually do a very detailed review of our employees, but the truth is, I need someone right away. In fact, I could use about ten someones, but I'll start with you."

"What kind of job are you offering?" Simone summoned the courage to meet his gaze.

Jeffery laughed. "I'm offering to make you a Harvey Girl. It's one of the sweetest jobs you will ever know. Fred Harvey is quite a man. He came to this country from England, and after doing an odd assortment of jobs, he came up with the idea to run restaurants on the Santa Fe Railroad line. Of course, these aren't just any restaurants. The Harvey House eating establishments have become internationally known for their fine cuisine, impeccable dining rooms, and friendly service."

"And what would I do?"

"The Harvey Girls serve the meals and see to the customers' needs. There's basically only twenty to thirty minutes to serve the passengers from any given train. That isn't a great deal of time, but Mr. Harvey has worked out a complicated yet effective system in which everyone's meal is ready and awaiting their arrival."

Simone tried to imagine it all, but having nothing to base it on, she merely nodded and waited for the man to continue.

"Can you begin work immediately? As in leave Chicago tomorrow morning?"

"Leave?" Simone questioned.

"Yes," Jeffery replied. "The training is in Topeka, Kansas. It's a lengthy trip, but by train the time passes rather quickly. The scenery is lovely this time of year with fertile green farmlands and quaint prairie towns. Topeka itself sits on the Kaw River. There isn't as much boat traffic on the Kaw as you'll see on the Missouri or the Mississippi Rivers, but it's a busy town nevertheless." He continued speaking as if Simone had asked him a bevy of questions. "There are several railroads who make Topeka their home. The Union Pacific is our biggest competition. They own a depot on the north side of the river, and their major route will take you straightway to Denver."

"I see," Simone replied, not fully understanding but unsure as to what else she should say.

"I don't usually accompany the girls to Topeka, but it just so happens that I'm to make an employee inspection of the line and meet with Mr. Harvey. Hopefully, I'll even get a chance to recruit a few more women for the job. But, that aside, I think it would only be right that I help you along your way. Especially given the fact that things are so hard on you just now."

Simone swallowed the lump in her throat and nodded. "That's very kind of you. I can leave in the morning."

Jeffery seemed quite pleased with this response and got to his feet. "Good. Then if you'll give me your current address, I'll pick you up at seven. Oh, and don't worry about bringing a lot of things with you. It isn't allowed. You'll be clothed and given items for grooming by the Harvey House. The less you bring, the less you have to ship back—" He paused, as if realizing Simone probably didn't have any place to ship things back to. "Just bring the essentials."

Simone gave a pretense of gathering her strength. She squared her shoulders, then got to her feet. "Thank you, Mr. O'Donnell. I appreciate that you would take a chance on me."

"Not at all, Miss Irving. You seem the honest sort."

Simone turned away to keep Jeffery from seeing the grimace that instantly marred her expression. *I'm anything but honest*, she thought, and it deeply grieved her to have deceived so nice a man.

"Seven o'clock sharp. Don't forget," he called after her.

"I won't," Simone assured him. "You can believe me on that."

PART TWO

TWELVE

June 1890

AFTER A WEARYING RIDE on what Jeffery assured Simone was one of the Atchison, Topeka, and Santa Fe's finest passenger trains, Simone was grateful when the conductor at last called out the name "Topeka." She'd hardly known a moment's peace since their journey from Chicago had begun, and by this time she was questioning the sanity of her move. Jeffery O'Donnell, she discovered, was quite a force to be reckoned with. He insisted on being her personal chaperone whenever she wanted to move about the train, and when the locomotive made passenger stops, he had constantly been at her side offering her a brief walk or bite to eat. He also asked a lot of prying questions that made Simone very uncomfortable. She found herself continually having to lie or simply put him off, and it was beginning to wear on her nerves.

"Topeka is nowhere near as big as Chicago," Mr. O'Donnell explained. "It's a funny little town. Kind of a mix of other small towns with a strong twist of government thrown in just to make things interesting. Most of the folks living outside the city are farmers, and the rest tend to be in business for themselves. That is, unless they work for the Santa Fe." Simone said nothing as he reached up to help her from the train. She shied away momentarily, then allowed his hand to close around hers. "And Topeka is thoroughly modern. They have telephones and electric lighting. Why, there are five electric plants just to keep the place supplied with electricity."

"How interesting," Simone murmured, allowing him to continue pointing out the oddities and interests of the town.

"And you will positively adore Miss Taylor. She is a saint and a woman of such kindness and generosity that she shames everyone else around her," Jeffery said lightly.

Simone could hardly imagine what it would be like to meet the woman in person. Her mother had praised her, and now Mr. O'Donnell spoke of her as though she held a special place in his heart. The woman must truly be wondrous.

They took a short walk along the platform and paused in front of an unassuming entryway. "Well, here we are," O'Donnell announced. "The Santa Fe has corporate offices across town, but this is where the real heart of the action is. The Harvey Eating House and Depot."

Simone nodded but found that fear bound the words in her throat. *They'll know I'm a fraud*, she thought. *They'll know I'm not good enough to be here with them. To be one of Fred Harvey's "Girls."* Still, she had to try. She had nothing left to lose.

Jeffery opened the door and ushered her inside. Simone stood in amazement at the bustling activity and sea of churning people. Within seconds, however, she was equally impressed by the way the crowds were seated in the dining room.

"Remember the breakfast order we put in this morning?"

Simone's stomach rumbled as if to answer Jeffery's question. "I remember it well."

Jeffery led her to their assigned table and helped to seat her. "The order was wired ahead. The cook has everything already prepared, and the girls have just under thirty minutes to see to everyone's comfort and happiness. Watch carefully, and you'll get a feel for what you have to look forward to." The corners of his lips turned up ever so slightly and his brown eyes twinkled mischievously as he added, "Of course, you can't change your mind and desert me if you decide it looks too challenging."

She quickly looked away, too nervous at the thought of having her past discovered to concern herself with how hard the work might be under Mr. Harvey's employment. The ever-efficient Harvey Girls moved swiftly and smoothly through the room. The tables were immaculately set with fine tablecloths, beautiful dishes, and gleaming silver that had been shined to perfection. Simone reached out to gently touch the cup and saucer. "It's all so lovely."

"What would you like to drink?" a young woman suddenly asked Simone. "We have coffee, hot tea, iced tea, and milk."

"Coffee, please," Simone replied. She turned to watch the woman. Dressed in a black shirtwaist gown and white bibbed apron, the Harvey Girl nodded and left Simone's empty cup upright in the saucer. "And for you, sir?"

Jeffery smiled. "I'd like hot tea."

At this, the girl positioned his cup upside down in the saucer and moved rapidly on to the next person seated at their table. Simone watched in fascination as the young woman continued questioning what the people desired for their beverage, all the while smiling and repositioning the cup or leaving it upright in the saucer. It was only moments before two other young women, dressed and groomed almost identically to the first, appeared with pitchers in hand. They smiled and chatted and proceeded to fill the cups without ever asking the customers at the table what it was they had ordered.

Simone quickly realized the code left to these women by the earlier Harvey Girl. Upright cups meant coffee. Upside down in the saucer, hot tea. There happened to be one child at their table, and for this the Harvey Girl had positioned the cup upside down on the table, away from the saucer. Simone watched as a small glass of milk was placed within the child's reach.

"Have they completely amazed you?" Jeffery asked, appearing to be amused with her study of the place.

Simone opened her mouth to speak, but just then the food began to arrive at their table. The aroma of eggs, thick beefsteaks, and biscuits filled the air, causing Simone to feel even more hungry. Seeing the others begin to dig into their food, Simone did likewise, taking a forkful of scrambled eggs. She sighed as the buttery flavor filled her mouth. The taste made a delightful contrast to the food she'd endured during her journey from Wyoming to Chicago. The feast even topped the meals she'd shared with Mr. O'Donnell on their way down to

Topeka. She tried the steak next, pleased to find it fresh and cooked to perfection.

Simone continued to eat with relish until the delicately beautiful plate sat empty and a Harvey girl appeared to ask them if they would like apple pie to top off their breakfast.

"Oh no, thank you," Simone replied. She found it hard to imagine that anyone could put another morsel of food into their mouths after experiencing the Harvey House breakfast, but several of the men at her table did just that.

In another five minutes a gonging sound echoed through the dining room. A black man clad in a white coat appeared. "No need to rush, folks. You have fifteen minutes before the train is scheduled to leave."

Jeffery leaned over. "They do that again in ten minutes and then in five. Mr. Harvey doesn't want people to feel they have to hurry through their meal, but neither does he want time to get away from them."

"I see."

Simone watched as some people began gathering up their things. Others lingered at the table, finishing their meals and sharing conversation about the trip to come.

"We'll wait until the dining room empties of passengers, then I'll call Miss Taylor to speak with us."

"Do the townsfolk eat here, too?" Simone questioned.

"Sure, but train passengers have first priority and since the schedule is fairly fixed, folks know to stay clear until the rush is fed." He paused, glancing around, and added, "Rush usually lasts about an hour with the northbound train coming in earlier and now the southbound. The northbound passengers left Topeka about seven this morning and townsfolk either ate before then or they'll straggle in here now. In another half hour or so, they'll shut down breakfast and start preparing for lunch."

True to what Mr. O'Donnell had told her, the gong rang five minutes later and again five minutes after that. In a matter of minutes the dining room emptied, leaving Jeffery, Simone, and a bevy of black-and-white-clad Harvey Girls to an awkward silence.

"And that, Miss Irving, is Fred Harvey's system at its best."

Simone startled at the unfamiliar name but remained calmly under control. For a moment she'd very nearly forgotten who she was and why she'd come to Topeka in the first place. The name Irving was a painful reminder, and the memory of her deception caused Simone to feel a great deal of sadness.

"Ah, there's Miss Taylor," Jeffery said, getting to his feet.

Simone looked up to find a buxom redhead in deep discussion with several of the Harvey Girls. *So this is Elvira Taylor's daughter*, Simone deduced. She appeared as a simple motherly figure with her surrogate daughters all clamoring for attention. She pointed first in one direction and then another, continuing her discussion amidst the girls' nods and questions. She didn't, in Simone's opinion, appear superhuman by any means.

"Miss Taylor?" Jeffery called.

She looked up, as if concerned that anyone should address her besides her beloved girls. "Mr. O'Donnell." She whispered something to the girl at her right, then left the circle of young women and came to Jeffery's table. "I heard you were here. I had a bit of trouble this morning with a couple of my newer staff members. The men were not being very cordial in their behavior. I'm afraid one poor girl was frightened to tears."

Jeffery's eyes narrowed. "You did see to the problem, did you not?"

Miss Taylor laughed. "Do you doubt it? No one speaks disrepectfully to my girls, much less handles them. I threw them out on their ears."

Simone stared in amazement at the woman. Her protective nature toward the Harvey Girls made an instant impression on Simone. The words that followed struck Simone with their simple sincerity.

"The safety and happiness of my girls will always come first."

"That's quite understandable," Jeffery replied. "I called you over to introduce you to Miss Simone Irving. Miss Irving is here to sign the contract and begin working for Mr. Harvey."

Miss Taylor's face lit up. "How wonderful! We can certainly use the help. I've had to fill another three positions from girls here on my staff. The minute they finish training, I have no other choice but to put them out there on the line. I do realize we're a training house, Mr. O'Donnell, but often I find us short-staffed. I've spoken with the house manager about it, but his hands are tied, as you well know."

"I have some other new recruits en route from back East, but it will be several days before they get here," Jeffery announced. "But Miss Irving came into my office just as I was preparing to make my way here to Topeka. I figured with the desperation of our need, I should bring her on board immediately."

"I do appreciate that, Mr. O'Donnell. Miss Irving, it is a pleasure to meet you. I'm Rachel Taylor, the housemother here. I'm in charge of all Harvey Girl training and for seeing that nothing goes amiss at mealtime."

An inner sense told Simone she'd find shelter and tender care with this woman. It was easy to see why she was so highly spoken of—her entire demeanor seemed nothing but sincere and honest. She spoke with a gentle tone, and her ruddy complexion and red hair made her green eyes appear bright and cheery. Fred Harvey might dress his girls in black-and-white monotones, but Rachel Taylor brought her own color to the uniform.

"I'm glad to meet you. I met your mother in Chicago," Simone offered.

"You did?" Rachel's voice revealed her pure delight. "We will have to find a quiet moment later when you can tell me all about her."

Simone had nearly forgotten the hastily written letter that Elvira Taylor had tucked in her hand along with a refund for part of her rent. "I have a letter for you," Simone replied and looked around for her carpetbag.

"I had our bags moved to your office, Miss Taylor," Jeffery said, seeming to understand Simone's concern.

"Well, this is a particular pleasure." Miss Taylor gave a quick glance to the watch she'd just taken out of her pocket. "Why don't we move to my office and discuss the matter in detail."

Simone followed them from the dining room and down a narrow corridor. She could still hear the clamor of the staff clearing away the tables but forced herself to concentrate on the conversation taking place in her company. It was difficult to understand, but almost against her will she was relaxing and realizing that there was something good in this place. Something of healing and hope.

Miss Taylor opened a glass-windowed door and ushered them inside. "We can conduct business in here without interruption."

"I've been explaining some of the details surrounding the job," Jeffery offered. "Miss Irving—"

"Please call me Simone," she told them with a pleading in her voice. Every time she heard that name, Simone couldn't help but feel guilty.

Jeffery smiled warmly at her. "I would be delighted."

"We do address each other rather informally," Miss Taylor replied in a serious tone. "But never around customers. Just keep that in mind."

"I will. I promise," Simone answered. Jeffery offered her a chair, then brought the worn carpetbag to Simone. She instantly procured the letter and handed it across to Rachel. "Miss Taylor, this is from your mother."

The woman reached out to take the small envelope. "Thank you so much, and please call me Rachel. All the girls do." She set the letter aside, then opened the drawer of her small desk and pulled out a piece of paper. "This is our standard contract. If you'll read it over . . ." She paused and looked once again at Simone. "You do read, don't you?"

"Yes. I read quite well," Simone assured her.

Rachel appeared relieved. "Good. Then read this over." She handed the paper to Simone. "You'll note that there is no pay for the first month and that you have to sign for either six or nine months of service."

"Six or nine months?" Simone questioned, scanning the paper.

"And you also agree not to marry during that time," Rachel explained. "Most girls sign for the shorter amount of time because, frankly, it's one of the hardest parts of the contract to adhere to. After all, most of the Harvey Houses are in remote areas of the country where women of quality are hard to come by. There used to be a saying that's held pretty true. 'There are no ladies west of Dodge City and no women west of Albuquerque.' Fred Harvey has changed all of that, and men out that way seem to consider Mr. Harvey their own private source for spouses. But if you break your contract to marry, you must forfeit half your wages and be expected to pay them back to the Harvey Company."

"That isn't a problem, I assure you," Simone said quietly.

"I disagree," Jeffery commented under his breath.

Simone met his expression of amusement with knitted brows. "What do you mean?"

"Given the fact that you are a beautiful young woman, Simone, there will be more than the average number of men lining up to play suitor to you."

A knock sounded at the door before Simone could reply. Rachel excused herself and went to take care of the problem while Jeffery remained seated, a look of challenge on his face.

"I'll sign for nine months," Simone finally answered.

"I don't think that's wise," Jeffery teased.

Simone chose to ignore him. "If I don't get paid for a month, what do I do about uniforms and such?"

"Everything is furnished," Jeffery replied. "When Rachel takes you upstairs, you'll be assigned a room and given uniforms and anything else you need. Even the laundry is taken care of for you. The uniforms are sent down to Newton, Kansas."

Simone, who had been responsible for her own laundry ever since her mother's desertion, stared at him in open surprise.

"Ah, I see I have managed to impress you at last."

"Do I understand correctly that I am to be given room, board, and uniforms, and I will be paid seventeen dollars and fifty cents a month?" Simone questioned in disbelief.

Jeffery laughed and leaned toward her. "Yes, but you cannot get married during those long nine months. Are you certain you wouldn't rather just sign for six?"

Simone shook her head and reached for the pen.

"Besides," Jeffery replied, sobering a bit, "the work is hard. You aren't just handed that money without a great deal expected in return. You'll work six- and seven-day weeks, ten to twelve hours a day."

"Hard work doesn't frighten me, Mr. O'Donnell. I've worked hard all my life and received little or nothing in return."

Just then a commotion sounded outside the office door, and Jeffery rose to see what the problem might be. Simone instantly came to attention when the door burst open and Rachel came in with a short man clad all in white. The man complained that his room was too small and that he had no place in the kitchen for all of his equipment.

Simone found his animated expressions and hand gestures completely captivating. She watched for a moment, amused by the man's grandiose display.

"I'm sorry, Mr. Flaubert," Rachel replied. "I don't understand a word you're saying." She turned to Jeffery. "I brought him here hoping that perhaps you speak his language."

Jeffery shook his head. "No, I don't speak French."

Simone suddenly realized that the man was indeed speaking her mother's native tongue. When the other three fell silent to stare in confusion at each other, Simone questioned the man as to his problem and rather enjoyed the surprised expressions on everyone's faces.

"Simone! You speak French?" Jeffery questioned.

An expression of utter delight came over the old man's face, while one of relief washed over Rachel's countenance.

"My mother was French," Simone answered simply. Then turning to the old man, she repeated her question. "What is it that you wish them to know?"

"Ah, you are an answer to prayer," the man told her. "There is no way I can stay in that tiny room. I must have space. And the kitchen is a disgrace. There is no room to work. I must have more room."

Simone turned to Rachel. "He's unhappy with his living arrangements. He says there isn't enough space in his room or in the kitchen."

"Is that all?" Rachel declared more than questioned.

Simone took it as a serious question, however, and asked the man, "Is there anything else?"

"Non," the man replied. "It is enough."

Simone smiled and turned back to Rachel. "He said that's enough."

"Tell him we'll do whatever we can to make the accommodations acceptable."

Simone translated the information and felt a certain amount of gratification to see the man grow calmer.

"I am blessed," he told her, reaching out to shake her hand, "to know you. This woman is quite good to me, but she knows nothing of my native tongue."

Simone nodded, nervous at the touch of a stranger. "I know how it feels—being so new to something and no one seeming to understand you."

The man still grasped her hand and patted it gently. "From what little I have observed, I have found it a good house to work for and live in. Except that the rooms are too small," he said with a laugh. Then realizing the time, he dropped his hold and hurried for the door. "My soup will boil over!" he declared and rushed from the room.

"He has soup boiling," Simone related to her stunned companions.

"Simone, I had no idea you could speak French," Jeffery said in complete amazement.

"You didn't ask."

"Simone, I would like for you to be Mr. Flaubert's translator. There's supposed to be an interpreter coming to help, but until then I'd appreciate it if you would act in this capacity for us. Of course, you'll continue to be trained as a Harvey Girl," Rachel said and added, "I'm so glad you've come to us. Why, without you we might never have known what the problem was, and we would have risked losing a wonderful chef for our restaurant. What a brilliant young woman you are."

Rachel Taylor seemed genuinely thankful, and it gave Simone a sense of worth and value that she couldn't remember ever having felt before. No one had ever praised her in such a manner. She felt awkward and uncertain as to what she should say.

"I'll be happy to help in whatever way I can," she finally told Rachel. "Just tell me what you need from me."

"I need you to sign that contract," Rachel said with a laugh. "I don't want there to be any chance of you getting away from us."

"I don't intend to leave," Simone replied. And within her heart she thought perhaps she might never want to leave. Someone actually valued her for the help she could give. It created an entirely new sensation of feelings inside her. Dipping the pen in the ink, Simone put the paper on Rachel's desk and began to sign her name.

"Nine months is a long time," Jeffery whispered under his breath.

Simone smiled to herself. After what she'd spent a lifetime enduring, nine months didn't sound like much time at all. In fact, nine months sounded like just the right amount of time to polish off the rough edges of her isolated childhood and establish herself as a refined and well-bred lady.

THIRTEEN

JEFFERY O'DONNELL checked his watch and realized he only had another half hour before the southbound was due in. He finished going over Rachel Taylor's employee records and jotted down several bits of information before blotting the ink and closing the book. He stretched and felt twinges of pain in his shoulders—ample payback for his long hours bent over the desk.

He'd hardly managed to see Simone since their arrival in Topeka two days earlier. When he had seen her she was intently listening to the instructions of a dark-haired woman whom Jeffery knew to be the head waitress. And from what Miss Taylor had told him, Simone was one of her quickest and brightest students.

But she was also a mystery. Jeffery had little to go on for her background information, and even though he'd given Miss Taylor company funds to telegraph her mother for further details on Simone's history, Rachel had come up empty-handed. Mrs. Taylor knew little more than they did. It appeared that her friend Grace had ridden with Simone on the train from Cheyenne to Chicago. Grace, however, had no idea how long the girl had been on the train prior to that, but Elvira Taylor confided that Simone was more than a little worn from her ordeal. Her appearance had been frightfully unkempt, and she was so pale that Mrs. Taylor had feared her to be diseased in some manner.

Jeffery shook his head. Who was Simone Irving? For all intents and purposes it was as if she had dropped into the real world from out of nowhere. He thought of her haunting face, the deep set of her blue eyes, and the soft ebony hair that cascaded down her back and begged his touch. She had appeared a petite, delicate flower when she'd first graced his doorstep, but the Harvey uniform made her look even smaller, maybe even younger, and that, too, was a worry to him. Harvey Girls applicants often found it necessary to lie about their ages. After all, many of the women came to him out of sheer necessity. There weren't many honorable jobs for women in the 1890s. They could teach, be a nursemaid or nanny, or put their time in at one factory or another, but even those jobs were limited. Just last year Jeffery had met a woman physician who wanted to work on the Santa Fe line. The superintendent had put an end to that idea, even though the woman came highly recommended and was willing to relocate to the farthest reaches on the line. There simply were limited places where women could find acceptance and respect.

Women of Simone's beauty usually married young and were well on their way to motherhood by the time there was any need to consider earning a living. They passed from their father's care to positions as social matrons with husbands and children of their own. Simone had admitted to coming in from the Wyoming Territory, a place where women were sure to be at a premium, but still she remained single. Perhaps her parents were very protective, and when they died, Simone had no one on which to rely. She appeared, like many others, to have fallen on hard times.

Once again, Jeffery felt the overwhelming urge to find Simone. He longed to know her full story. To hear from her own lips what had happened to bring such misery upon her. He laughed at himself for acting so out of character. His own stoic mother would find his behavior uncalled for. She had raised him to be socially acceptable and gainfully employed. She also had in mind the kind of woman he needed for a wife. A woman of Simone's meager background wouldn't qualify to act as a chambermaid in the O'Donnell lakeside home in Chicago, much less as a suitable mate for her son.

But Jeffery's real dilemma came in the circumstances of Simone's employment. He was responsible for the women he employed and answerable to Fred Harvey for the choices he made. He also knew that it was expected that he know the detailed background of each girl hired, and up until he'd accepted Simone for employment, he had. If Mr. Harvey found him shirking his responsibility in keeping track of the moral character of his Harvey Girls, Jeffery knew there would be consequences to face.

Getting to his feet, Jeffery shook the lint from his brown serge coat and straightened his tie. He intended to find Simone and at least speak to her for a moment. Given the busyness of the Harvey House a half hour before the train arrival, Jeffery knew he was expecting a lot, but nevertheless, it was business. He needed more information on her for his investigation. At least that's what he told himself.

The dining room down the hall was bustling with Harvey Girls. He smiled when he saw Rachel pick up a china plate for inspection, then shake her head. Fred Harvey had declared that even the slightest chip or crack would render the plate unusable for Harvey Eating Establishments. This was also true of torn linen, whether it be the tablecloths or the oversized napkins that the restaurant had become known for. Fred Harvey would hear of nothing but the best for his businesses, and even the furniture had been imported to meet this high standard. It was part of the allure of the Harvey House.

Not finding Simone among the uniformed trainees, Jeffery made his way across the dining room and into the kitchen. The interpreter had still not arrived to assist the chef, and it seemed logical that Simone might be here among the cooks, bakers, and food preparation staff.

The aroma of Monsieur Flaubert's succulent pork roast greeted Jeffery. Flaubert was a genius in the kitchen, and Jeffery had made it his business to try most everything the man had created. As usual, Fred Harvey's choice of chefs was to be applauded.

Jeffery nodded approvingly at the action inside the busy kitchen. Various preparation staff bustled up and down the extended counter, where salads were being given the final touches before the passengers' arrival. Jeffery leaned down and pretended to inspect the salad nearest him. Lush avocado quarters, fresh from California, lay on a bed of lettuce with brilliant red tomato wedges as garnish for effect. It appeared both artistically aesthetic and appetizing. He smiled his approval to a nearby worker, then looked beyond the counter for some sign of Simone.

She stood with her back to him, completely engrossed in the rapid-fire French conversation of Monsieur Flaubert. Moving closer, Jeffery heard her timid response grow more intent, and while he had no idea what they might be discussing, he felt confident that Simone's words were in contrast to the opinion of the older gentleman.

"Simone?"

She jumped, startled by his unknown presence. Turning to face him, Jeffery saw an edge of fearfulness in her eyes. Why did she always look as though she'd just been caught in the act of some heinous crime?

"You were looking for me?"

Jeffery nodded. "I'd like very much to speak with you for a moment. You see, I'm catching the southbound after dinner, and there won't be another chance for us to talk for a couple of weeks. I have to go south on the line and inspect the houses on the way."

"I see," Simone said, lowering her gaze to the floor. "What did you need to speak to me about?"

"For one, you might tell me what the overly excitable Monsieur Flaubert is complaining about this time," Jeffery began, hoping to ease her discomfort. For all the time they had spent together, Simone Irving still remained as skittish as one of his father's high-spirited Arabian stallions.

"Oh, he . . ." She paused to look over to where Henri Flaubert had turned his attention back to an oven full of baked veal pies. Simone twisted her hands nervously and glanced back to Jeffery. "It's nothing, really."

"If it's nothing," he said with a grin, "then why not tell me?"

"He doesn't care for Topeka," she replied. "He says it's too backward, and their regular opera singers screech like cats with their necks being wrung."

Jeffery laughed out loud at this. "Tell him I wholeheartedly agree, and I admire his ability to make a journey to the opera so soon after his arrival in Topeka."

Simone's lips curled upward ever so slightly, and Jeffery relished the sight. A smile from Simone was quite rare indeed, but when she looked as she did just now, with a hint of amusement in her expression, she was incredibly beautiful.

Simone tapped the chef on the shoulder and rattled off an exchange of words to which the older man glanced over at Jeffery and burst out laughing. He acknowledged Jeffery's words with a nod before catching sight of some employee offense that set him off in raised tones of anger.

"Now what?" Jeffery asked as he watched Flaubert move to one of the other stoves.

"The Bordelaise sauce," Simone answered simply. "He's protesting that the assistant cook has put in the wrong kind of wine."

"What's the sauce used for?" Jeffery questioned. Flaubert was in rare form, flailing the ladle and bellowing at the top of his lungs.

"It's for the Beef Steak Frascati, and Henri says it is ruined and will have to be thrown out." About that time, Henri picked up the pot and headed for the back door. Simone shrugged. "He knows what he's talking about. I've never tasted anything like the food he prepares."

"So you were used to simpler fare, eh?" Jeffery said, hoping the conversation would lead to more details.

"Very simple fare indeed."

When she said nothing more, Jeffery checked his watch. "We still have a few minutes and there are some questions I have to ask you. Mr. Harvey will expect me to conduct a thorough investigation of you." At this, he saw the color drain from her face, and even though the kitchen temperature was overwhelmingly warm, Simone trembled as if suddenly chilled.

Jeffery took hold of her arm and led her from the kitchen back into the dining room. Pulling her to one corner, he continued to grasp her arm. "Simone, are you feeling ill?"

"No," she said, shaking her head. "I don't know what you need to know, but there isn't much to tell."

"I could use some references. You know, folks I could notify and question concerning your character."

"There's no one," Simone said seriously. "We lived too far into the mountains. There was no one else. Just my father and mother, and now they're dead."

"Surely someone can vouch for your character."

She bit at her lip and shook her head. "No, there's no one. If you have to fire me, I understand, but I can't tell you anything more. I lived in the Wyoming Territory, and I'm not even sure what part I came from."

Jeffery felt an uneasiness about her declaration. Surely it wasn't possible in this day and age of modern conveniences and improved transportation for a young woman to be so clearly uncertain as to where she grew up. It also seemed highly unlikely that no one could vouch one way or the other for her character. Still, she appeared to be well-mannered and intelligent, although Miss Taylor had spoken of her lack of knowledge when it came to many of the things other girls took for granted. She maintained a fascination with indoor plumbing and electric lighting, and Rachel had told of Simone being completely intrigued by a sewing machine stationed in one of the upstairs rooms.

These things, added to what bits and pieces Jeffery had been able to gather from his earlier conversations with Simone, seemed to point to a very secluded existence.

"Simone, you needn't allow this to upset you. I have no intention of firing you. I simply have a job to do, and investigating all of our girls is a part of that job. Mr. Harvey will expect me to account for each one of you."

She nodded. "I understand, but—"

Just then the sound of the train whistle could be heard. "One-mile warning!" someone called out, and Simone pulled away from Jeffery.

"I have to get to work."

"I understand," he said, watching her hurry off to join her Harvey sisters in carrying salads to the tables.

"Well," he chided himself, "you're no better off now than when you started."

He took a seat at the table just as the dinner gong sounded. Once again the rush of patrons and staff overwhelmed the once quiet little dining room. His table quickly filled up with other men. Some were well dressed and obviously from a more refined background, while several were clearly cowboys, no doubt bound for the western ranches along the line. One thing marked them as alike, however, and that was the fact that each man wore a suit coat either from his own wardrobe or from Fred Harvey's supply of dark alpaca coats. No man was allowed to dine in the Harvey House without a coat because Mr. Harvey insisted that this small bit of civilization was necessary to have a companionable and refined dinner. He had also confided that men tended to be less inclined to fight when wearing their Sunday best—or someone else's Sunday best, for that matter.

Simone approached their table warily and questioned each man about their choice of drinks. Many asked for liquor, which wasn't on the menu. Even if it had been, Kansas was an adamantly dry state, at least on paper. They settled for coffee when Simone made it clear that beer and whiskey weren't an option. Jeffery watched her work in the dining hall and felt good about his choice to hire her. He might know next to nothing about her background, but her ability to learn and the quiet manner in which she conducted herself spoke for itself.

"Now, she's sure a looker," one man told his traveling companion.

"You're tellin' me. Old man Harvey knows how to pick 'em. Even if he does dress 'em like nuns."

"Say, darlin', wouldn't you like to marry me and go west?"

Simone ignored their teasing, and only once, when a man reached out to touch her, did she flinch and act the slightest bit disturbed. Jeffery said nothing, but the scene only confirmed his earlier thoughts that Simone would most likely not fulfill her full nine-month contract. Her features bordered on angelic, and her figure, even hidden in the black shirtwaist gown and high-necked white apron, made most of the men at his table sit up and take notice.

Before he knew it, the fifteen-minute warning sounded. Jeffery finished off his pie and coffee and excused himself from his remaining dining companions. He retrieved his papers and satchel, and by the time he'd returned to the dining room, most of the passengers had made their way back to the train.

With his brown derby in hand, Jeffery approached Simone as he headed for the door. "You did a good job, Simone. You're a quick learner."

She looked away from him and stared at the floor. Flattery apparently made her uncomfortable, but for the life of him Jeffery couldn't figure out why. Most women enjoyed hearing they looked pretty or had done a good job, but not Simone. It only seemed to create an air of tension between them.

"I'm still willing to bet you break that contract," he said, deciding that teasing her was the only way to lighten the moment.

At this, Simone lifted her face to meet his gaze. "What are you willing to bet?"

He looked deep into eyes so dark and blue that they almost appeared black. Her beauty seemed to heighten with each passing day, yet Simone clearly had no confidence in her looks. Had no one ever told her she was pretty? Had no one ever courted and wooed her in hopes of winning her hand? Jeffery found this so hard to believe that he happily threw out the challenge. "I'll bet a month's worth of pay that you marry before the contract is up."

"Seventeen dollars and fifty cents?" Simone questioned, her face contorting anxiously in consideration of his announcement.

"Precisely. If you marry before your contract is up, you will pay me exactly that amount. If you manage to hold out, which I don't think will happen," he said with a teasing grin, "then I will pay *you* a month's salary. What do you say?"

Simone seemed to think on the matter for several moments, and it wasn't until the conductor came into the dining hall to make sure all passengers for the southbound were on board that Simone nodded.

"I'll take your challenge, Mr. O'Donnell," she said softly. "But you'll lose."

"Will I?" he said, grinning as he stepped outside and popped the derby on his head. "I suppose only time will tell."

FOURTEEN

LOUIS DUMAS SMILED at the ticket agent and nodded. "Yeah, that sounds like my daughter. Could you by any chance remember where she was headed?"

The man scratched his head for a moment. "Seems she was headed to Chicago. I remember her saying that someone had told her about Chicago. She was short on the price of a ticket, but I suggested that she sell the horse she rode up on."

"I guessed it might be somethin' like that. I just talked to the liveryman and learned that he had her horse and gear," Louis replied. "So then she returned here and headed out for Chicago?"

"As best I can remember," the man replied. "She came back on foot with the price of the ticket in hand. She bought her ticket, but I can't say that I know for sure that she got on board the train. Doesn't seem likely she wouldn't, though. Not after having spent the money and all. Still, even if she got on the train, ain't no guarantee she stayed on it."

Louis ignored the man's thoughts on the matter. Simone would probably be too frightened to get off before the assigned town. "When was that?"

"Oh, pert near a week ago. Maybe more. Say, you gonna buy a train ticket? Eastbound's due inside of thirty minutes."

Louis shrugged. "Perhaps. I need to do some thinking first."

At this, the ticket agent lost all interest in Louis and turned his attention to a stack of papers. Louis thought to question the man further but realized he'd already provided the bulk of necessary information. Leaving the depot, he looked up the street, first one direction and then another, finally deciding that what he needed was a drink.

She couldn't have gotten far on her own, Louis decided. Of course, he hadn't planned on her being quite so enterprising. So far she'd managed to keep herself just a few paces ahead of him, and it was only by the grace of the modern steam locomotive that she managed to separate herself in any real manner from her father's diligent search.

Uncertainty and doubt plagued his mind. He'd already expended more energy and time on Simone than he'd intended. The fool girl had wandered in circles in the mountains, consuming days—even the better part of a week. Louis had easily picked up her tracks, then not so easily covered up both his and her markings to keep anyone else from following after them. But was it worth the cost of following her to Chicago? After all, his money was starting to run low. Panning for gold awaited him in Colorado, and that was only a couple of days journey to the south. He could easily lose himself in one of the many mining communities and forget about Simone and everything else that had happened to him in the past few weeks. Or . . .

"She's worth a fortune," he muttered. He remembered the enthusiastic suggestions from his companions in Uniontown. They had lusted after her in a way that evidenced the possibility of making easy money. "I could put her to work in the mining camps, and even at the cheapest rates she would bring in a profit. Why allow her to go her own way?" It was, after all, a matter of pride and an issue of obedience. He had given her over to Davis, and she had gone against his wishes. With Davis dead, she was once again Louis's responsibility . . . and property.

Approaching the nearest saloon, Louis paused long enough to take heed of two lawmen already congregated by the hitching post outside the poorly constructed building.

"I have a description of the man's horse," the younger of the two men said. "I sent Billy down to the livery to check out if old Bailey has seen anything of a sorrel mare with two white socks on the front and a white blaze on the forehead. I figured Laramie is the closest town of any real size, and since the Union Pacific is here, it would be the logical place to head. Then, too, if a fellow was making his way on the run, it would be a good place to load up on supplies before trekking out across the mountains or the plains. One way or another, he'd probably stop to see the horse fed and cared for before setting off again."

"Possibly," the man replied. "But other than the description of the horse and the dead man, Garvey Davis—"

Louis barely heard anything else. *So they know Garvey Davis is dead.* That could be a problem. He hadn't figured on anyone finding out so soon. What could have happened? He knew for a fact that Simone hadn't gone into Uniontown. Was it possible that someone from town had come out to check up on Davis and Simone? Possibly. He knew he had to learn whatever else they might know, but to hang around the men with no real purpose might appear out of line. Glancing down, Louis spotted horse droppings and purposefully stepped in the pile. No one would question his need to pause and clean off his boots. Cursing and putting on a show of disgust, he walked right past the two lawmen to a place four or five feet away before pausing to sit down on the planked boardwalk.

"Zack, are you sure no one in the town knew where this Dumas man and his daughter had gone off to?"

Louis had just picked up a stick and had proceeded to clean his boot when his name was mentioned. He felt his heart begin a rapid beat.

"No, sir, I already told you. Dumas was last known to be headed for Colorado, but nobody knows much of anything else. I've asked in all the saloons around town, but no one fitting his description has been seen over the last couple of weeks. Of course, I don't have that good of a description to go on, but Dumas would have naturally passed by this way if he was headed south. The daughter was supposed to be given to Davis for a wife, and while I have a good description of her, nobody remembers seeing anything of her in the local stores. I thought I'd best check things out with the depot stationmaster to see if he's seen either one of them. They can't just have disappeared."

Louis heard exasperation tinge the young man's words. He almost sounded anxious, as if the entire matter were of the utmost importance to him. But why should it be? So what if an old drifter was dead? It happened all the time, and in these parts, it wasn't at all unusual to be bushwhacked by one person or another. Hardly seemed necessary to include a sheriff on the matter, but it was evident that this was the case. He picked at the boot and waited for something more to be said. Surely now that there was little or nothing to be gained in the way of information, the man would just let the matter drop.

"Zack, I know you did your best," the man began saying. "Frankly, it's just good to have you back safe and sound."

The younger man quickly interjected, "Dad, I feel sure that I'm on the verge of putting it all together."

Ah, so they are father and son, Louis thought. Perhaps this accounted for the younger man's anxiety. Zack continued speaking, and Louis forced himself to pay close attention to the details.

"There are just too many things that don't add up. Dumas seemed rather anxious to sell off and get out of Uniontown. At least according to the folks I talked to."

Good-for-nothings, Louis thought. There was a time when he would have killed a man for opening his mouth to bear witness against him.

"No one seemed to think much of the idea that Dumas had sold his daughter. Seems quite a few of the men in the area fancied themselves as potential suitors for Simone Dumas. To hear them tell it, she was quite a beauty."

"Was?"

"Is or was," Zack replied. "I have no way of knowing if she's still alive. I searched the area and didn't find any signs of a body or anything else that would give an indication to her whereabouts. There wasn't much in the cabin to suggest that any female had ever lived there. I did find a few dodads and notions in an old trunk, but nothing else. If Simone Dumas lived there, she did so without much in the way to call her own."

"Or she took it all with her," Zack's father suggested.

"That hardly seems likely. If she's like most females with their baubles and clothes, she couldn't have crated the stuff out in two wagons, much less on foot or horseback. Even the few things I did find seemed more likely to have belonged to her mother."

"Most likely they were too poor to have much in the way of niceties."

Louis would have laughed out loud had he not known it would draw attention to himself. Niceties, indeed. What did a girl like Simone need anyway? A roof over her head, food on the table, and the clothes on her back. Why should he have provided more? He had given her mother plenty, and look where that got him.

"I'm afraid that whoever killed Garvey Davis might have taken Simone with them."

"What if the girl did the deed?" the older man questioned.

"That is possible," Zack answered.

More than possible, Louis thought, remembering the mess he'd found when he'd come back to the cabin.

"But you don't sound convinced that she's to blame."

"Mr. Matthews! Zack!" a boy of about fifteen or sixteen yelled, waving and hollering as if someone had set fire to his backside.

"What is it, Billy?" Zack questioned, stepping down from the boardwalk to meet the boy in the street.

"Bailey has her!"

"Has who?"

Louis looked up just enough to get a good view of the man and boy. The older man joined his son.

"Davis's mare!"

Zack looked to his father and back to the boy. "Are you sure?"

"Positive. Says a young girl with dark black hair and the face of an angel brought her in last week. Both were pert near worn to death, but she asked Bailey to buy the horse and seemed in an all-fired hurry to get the matter settled. Sold him the horse and gear, and he never saw her agin."

"A girl, you say?" the older man questioned.

"She fits the description of Simone Dumas," Zack muttered. "I have to admit it looks like the field of suspects has just narrowed significantly."

"And it makes sense as to why you didn't find any of her things. Apparently Miss Dumas loaded her things up and took off on Davis's horse. Apparently she didn't think much of being given over to Davis.

Of course, it doesn't mean that Louis Dumas wasn't in on it. Could have been a bit of father-daughter teamwork. Sell off to the man and get most of his money, then leave the girl to do him in and get the rest of it. They could have had plans for her to join up with her father elsewhere. Let's go check out the livery and see this animal for ourselves," Zack's father suggested. "Maybe we'll manage to figure out what to do from there. Bailey know which way she was headed?"

"I didn't ask," Billy replied.

The three took off down the street, leaving Louis Dumas to stare after them. He frowned, wondering what he should do. He heard the train whistle in the distance and remembered the ticket agent saying that it would be only a matter of half an hour until the eastbound would be pulling into Laramie. Perhaps he would do well to be on it when it headed east. After all, he'd asked questions of the liveryman concerning Simone. When this Zack fellow began asking his own questions, the man would no doubt remember Louis's inquiries and make comment on another man looking for the petite, black-haired girl. Then, instead of blaming Simone for Davis's murder, the law just might come looking for him.

Louis got to his feet in a hasty manner and threw the stick away. He had his own horse and gear still hitched in front of the station. He could just book passage for himself and leave before the lawmen had a chance to come back and check matters out. At least, he hoped it would work that way.

One thing was certain, though. He couldn't stay in Laramie.

"So you don't remember the girl telling you where she was headed?" Zack Matthews asked Joe Bailey.

The man glanced up from his work. He was backed up against the rump of a horse, the mare's rear leg bent upward between his own legs. He stood short and wiry, but his arms revealed the raw strength and muscles necessary for his trade. "Nope. Figured maybe she was here to stay. Elsewise my guess is she took the train and didn't want to have to bother with the horse. She didn't say much, and I didn't ask." He turned his attention back to cleaning the mare's hoof.

"We could ask the stationmaster," Zack told his father. He felt a rush of excitement with this first real lead he'd had on this case.

"That's what I suggested to that other feller," Bailey offered to no one in particular.

"What other fellow?" Zack and George Matthews questioned in unison.

Bailey looked up and shrugged. "A rough-looking fellow who was in here this morning. Said he was looking for a girl and described her. I told him what I just told you, and he took off out of here."

"Who was he?" George asked.

Bailey shook his head and continued his work. "I don't know. He was dark-headed, had a full face of whiskers, and was built a little heavier than you, but about the same height."

"Sounds like Louis Dumas," Zack said, completely baffled by this new twist. He'd received only the briefest descriptions of Dumas from the folks in Uniontown. It seemed the group was rather clannish in protection of their own.

"Could you describe him enough for Zack to sketch out a picture?"

"I suppose so," the wiry man replied. "He wern't hardly here long enough to get too good a look. Now, the girl, well, she'd be a different story."

"I'd like to sketch her out, too," Zack replied, pulling a small book from his back pocket. He opened the book to reveal an empty page and stub of a pencil marking the spot where he'd left off. For as long as he could remember, he'd loved to draw anything and everything. He'd tried desperately to get sketches of the Dumases in Uniontown and felt like a complete failure to come away empty-handed. And even now his father had been the one to ask about the possibility of Bailey giving the descriptions to Zack.

"You think them there pictures will help you?" Bailey questioned, dropping the horse's leg. He finally seemed intrigued enough to give the Matthews men his undivided attention. Even Billy seemed excited by the idea of Zack's work.

"They've helped before," George stated seriously. "Zack makes some of the best Wanted posters around these parts. Can't help but work to our advantage."

"Well, I always figure on helping the law where I can," Bailey said, putting down the hoof-pick. "What do you want to know?"

Twenty minutes later, Zack held up the book to reveal sketches of Louis and Simone Dumas. "Is this pretty close?"

"For sure on the girl. The man . . . well . . . like I said, I didn't pay him much attention."

"That's all right, Bailey," George Matthews said, nodding approvingly at his son. "This will take us quite a ways."

FIFTEEN

SIMONE WAS TOTALLY unprepared for the kindness she found in her Harvey House sisters. Given the experiences she'd shared since leaving Uniontown and her father, Simone was quickly coming to realize that the rest of the world operated in a much different manner than Louis Dumas.

Her roommate in the upstairs dormitory of the Harvey House was Una Lundstrom. Una, a big-boned Swedish girl, was a fair-haired contrast to the petite frame and ebony tresses that Simone possessed. Una spoke perfect English, but the long letters she wrote home to her family in Lindsborg, Kansas, were generally written in Swedish. Una had explained that it was important to her family that she be an American, as was her birthright. And while many of her relatives were unable to boast that privilege, Una explained that being American was very important to her family. They eagerly clung to and took on for themselves the coveted title of their children's American heritage.

Simone thought little on the matter. Being an American had never been much of an issue in her home. Her father was American, but her mother had been Canadian by birth. Winifred had moved with her family to Denver, Colorado, shortly before her fifteenth birthday, but by that time her French heritage and cultural background had been clearly instilled. Simone had grown up with flavoring from both American and French ancestry and had never given the matter much consideration. Una made it clear, however, that while she was proud of her Swedish heritage, she was prouder still of her American birthright.

Night after night, once the rigors of the daily routine had passed, Una could be found sitting at the tiny desk in their shared room laboring over a letter of love. Simone wondered what it would be like to have a family who cared about her and missed her. She had never known that family could be so concerned and considerate of one another. She remembered her mother's love but buried it down deep within so that it couldn't hurt her with the painful reminder of how love had departed from her life. Kansas and Fred Harvey's business were her future. It did little good to dwell on the past and what she had lost. The girls here were friendly and eager to strike up conversations and companionships, which should have made it easy to set aside her nightmarish childhood.

Simone, however, remained wary. Who could be trusted? What if someone hurt her again? Worse still, what if someone learned about her past and knew her secret? She couldn't afford to get close to anyone, although it greatly appealed to her in a way that she couldn't argue or fight. She watched with envy and frustration as she observed the closeness of some of her Harvey sisters. Perhaps it was just as well that Una preferred spending her time writing letters and focusing on family rather than on Simone.

"Are you going to walk uptown today?" Una asked one morning.

Simone yawned and stretched before answering. It was her day off and, with the last bit of money she had managed to hold back, Simone was determined to buy herself material for a day dress to wear when she wasn't required to be in uniform.

"I'm going shopping," she finally admitted.

"It's going to be a hot one," Una said, the cadence of her voice clearly betraying her Swedish background.

"I've never known heat like what Kansas has," Simone said, forcing herself out of bed. Even with the window open, the room was stifling, and sweat left her nightgown sticking to her most uncomfortably.

"This is nothing," Una said with a brief smile. "Some humid days make you feel like you just stepped into a laundry house. Only you can't step out into someplace cooler and drier."

Simone nodded and scowled at the thought of donning cotton stockings and petticoats. She thought of the dry mountain air she'd grown up with—thought, too, of her simpler life without concern for stockings and shoes.

"Makes a body want to find a shade tree and sit until it cools off," Una added.

"Just remember, heat or no heat, you promised to show me how to run the sewing machine. I'm going to buy material for my dress today, and then I'll have something to work on while you write your letters home."

Una nodded. "*Ja*, I'll show you." Una glanced at the clock. "I'll have to hurry. I've got the front station, and there's a lot of work to be done. Rachel said we needed to go over all the china. She's been finding chips in the plates and says that if Mr. Harvey shows up and sees them, he'll throw the things across the room."

Simone nodded. "I heard that, too. Still, you can't fault the man for wanting things nice. I've never seen the likes of such elegance. I sure never knew you could have matched sets of dishes like the ones on our tables. We were lucky to have a cup and a plate to call our own."

"Ja," Una said with a laugh. "I have ten brothers and sisters, and most of the time we shared plates between us."

"Ten brothers and sisters," Simone said, trying to imagine what it might be like to have so many siblings. She remembered baby John and how much he had cried. Beyond that, she had the tiniest recollection that there had been twins born to her mother, but they had died very young, when Simone herself hadn't been very old.

Una seemed not to realize the effect her discussion had on Simone. She hurried around the room, dressing as she went, then finally came to Simone in order to have her do up the buttons on the back of her dress.

"I'll see you later. Don't forget the thread," Una admonished and then was gone.

Simone smiled. It was something she was now given to doing from time to time, and in spite of her fears, smiling felt good. The comfort of the Harvey House routine and the kindness of the people she worked with were beginning to soften the hard encasement she'd wrapped her heart in. For the first time in years, Simone was pushing aside her shield . . . and truly *feeling*.

Dressing quickly, Simone pulled on her blue serge skirt and a worn white shirtwaist that Una had given her. She had long since learned the secrets of tending her heavy black hair and quickly and efficiently wound it into a coil and pinned it high atop her head. The weeks at the Harvey House had been good for her. She had learned much and would continue to learn if given the chance. She felt an eagerness inside to absorb as much as possible—as quickly as possible, for fear that it might one day soon be taken away from her. She had listened to the girls share secrets about their lives, watched and accepted lessons on embroidery, cooking, and etiquette, and found it all so very fascinating.

Topeka was much smaller than Chicago but more stately and populated than Laramie. It boasted the honor of being the state capital, and even though the capitol building was still under construction, government made its mark on the growing town. Walking from the Topeka depot west to Kansas Avenue, Simone tried to take in everything at once. She wanted to experience this city and know the meaning of belonging to a community. She had spent so much of her life in a solitary existence that she felt like a new creature just come to life.

Rachel had told her about the opera house and the theater, as well as the various parks, where all manner of entertainment could be enjoyed. There were even plans in the works for several of the Harvey Girls to journey across the river and enjoy Fourth of July festivities at Garfield Park. Marshall's Military Band would provide hours of music for their enjoyment, the natatorium would be open for swimming, and boats could be rented for rides up and down Soldier Creek. It all sounded so very charming to Simone, and she found herself looking forward to the day with great enthusiasm—at least on the inside. On the outside, she was still given to guarding her feelings and keeping her reactions in check. It would do little good to set herself up for further pain and disappointment. Especially now when the nightmares had stopped and the memories were fading into a numb blur.

Of course, Jeffery O'Donnell's return to Topeka on the second of July brought a new realm of emotions to Simone. She tried not to think about his arrival as she walked with a determined purpose toward the busier parts of town. Jeffery might well be her undoing, and Simone knew she would have to be particularly careful when it came to him.

Thoughts of the mild-mannered man caused Simone to quiver. The image of Jeffery's sincere face and dark brown eyes invaded her mind. He was one of the first men who had ever looked at her without leering, and even though she knew he found her attractive, Simone was aware of the respect he had for her and wasn't offended by his attention. On the contrary, she felt overwhelmed by his interest and open desire to seek out her company. She had tried to convince herself that this interest was simply a part of Jeffery doing his job, but several of the girls had told her otherwise. They thought it wonderful that the clearly well-to-do Mr. O'Donnell should have an eye for a lowly Harvey Girl. Most of the girls married into the railroad family by acquiring husbands from the pool of hardworking rail shop and yard workers or various other employees who occupied positions on the Santa Fe payroll. But that Simone should have the attention of a man in Jeffery O'Donnell's position seemed a fairy tale come true.

"Simone!" a voice called out from behind her just as Simone reached Kansas Avenue. Turning, she found Rachel Taylor hurrying to catch up with her. "Do you mind if I join you?"

Simone shook her head. "Not at all. If I'd known you were planning to come to town, I would have waited for you." And she meant it. Simone liked Rachel and appreciated the kindness the older woman had shown her.

"I wasn't sure I could find the time to slip away, so I didn't say anything," Rachel managed to say between huffing and puffing for breath. "This humidity surely does a body in."

"Yes," Simone agreed. She glanced upward to the billowing white clouds set against a rich sapphire blue. "But the day certainly looks pleasant enough."

"It does indeed. Where are you headed?" Rachel questioned.

"I'm going to buy dress material. I've been wanting to make something else to wear," Simone said, frowning as she looked down at her well-worn outfit. "Una said we could probably manage to put it together in time for the celebration."

"Hmm, that gives you till Friday. Four days. That ought to be enough time. Say, I know just the place. Crosby Brothers is up the next block."

"And you think they'll have a good selection?" Simone questioned hopefully.

"Absolutely. And better yet, the prices will be reasonable."

Simone smiled. Rachel Taylor was a fair-minded woman with a keen sense of organization, and she kept a watchful eye on her girls like any good mother would.

They walked up the avenue in companionable silence, and only after crossing Fifth Street did Rachel point to the building marked *Crosby Brothers*. "Here we are," she said, taking Simone by the arm.

They passed the day in girlish laughter and amiable friendship. Simone had never known a time when she had enjoyed herself more. It still amazed her that people could be so openly friendly and pleasant. When lunchtime came Rachel insisted on buying Simone a treat, and together the women sat down and continued to share about their lives.

"I wish you wouldn't have spent so much on lunch," Simone said, thoroughly enjoying her fruit salad. It wasn't as good as Henri's, but it would do.

"You needn't worry about that," Rachel told her with a smile that reinforced her sincerity. "You won't get paid for another week, and I know you've already spent most of your money."

"It wouldn't have been so bad if I hadn't needed to buy black shoes when I first arrived here," Simone commented, remembering her mad dash around town to find an inexpensive pair of shoes that would meet the Harvey House demands.

"But everything else has been pretty much taken care of," Rachel countered. "You can't say that Mr. Harvey doesn't know how to take care of his people."

"That's true enough."

Rachel polished off a piece of sponge cake and sat back to study

Simone. "You are a good worker, Simone. I've been very pleased with your performance, and in a short time you'll no doubt be leaving us."

"Leaving?" Simone felt her chest tighten. She was just becoming comfortable with her surroundings, and now Rachel talked of her leaving.

"Most of the girls move on. After all, Topeka is a training house. Still, I do manage to keep a few regulars. Maybe you'll want to be one of them."

"I'd very much like to stay," Simone replied. "I've heard some of the girls talking about other places, but honestly I'd rather not go."

"Some want to be nearer to their family. Isn't there someone you'd like to live closer to? Perhaps a grandmother or aunt?"

Simone panicked. She hadn't expected the conversation to take this turn. "There's no one. I have no family," she answered quietly.

"If you don't want to talk about it, I'll understand," Rachel began, "but I wondered if you might tell me how your parents died?"

Simone felt the joy of the day leave her in the wake of this prying question. "I'd rather not talk about it."

"I know how it is to lose someone you love," Rachel stated softly.

Simone choked on her iced lemonade. Loved? Well, in truth, she had loved her mother and brother. But her father was another matter entirely. She had never loved him and had never known love from him.

Rachel patted her back. "I'm sorry if I upset you. I just want you to know that I understand. I lost my father shortly before coming to Topeka. He was killed in a rail yard accident. I don't think I'll ever stop missing him. We were very close."

"You were?" Simone asked as though it was an uncommon thing.

Rachel smiled and her eyes took on a faraway look. "Yes. I was an only daughter and he doted upon me as most fathers might. He spoiled me terribly—always buying me little gifts and letting me do things my mother would have never allowed."

Simone felt sick inside. The lemonade seemed to sour in her stomach and spoil the contents of her lovely lunch. She put her hand to her abdomen and tried hard not to appear in the least bit upset.

"Are you all right, Simone?"

"It's just this heat."

Rachel pulled out her pocket watch. "We should be making our way back. No sense getting sunstroke. I've already spent longer away than I should have. Come on. If you need to, you can lean on me."

Simone shook her head. "I'm not that bad off." She picked up her brown paper package and smiled. "Thank you for a lovely day and thank you, too, for the lace. I would never have considered spending the money . . . not that I had it to spend."

Rachel laughed. "A girl needs to look pretty for special occasions. Hopefully you and Una will be able to whip that dress into shape in time for the celebration. And who knows, Mr. O'Donnell might even stick around to attend the festivities with us." She grinned knowingly.

Simone nodded and waited until Rachel turned to lead the way back to the Harvey House before letting out her breath. How many more times could she manage to avoid talking about her parents and what had happened? But as she had done since first leaving her cabin, Simone pushed her fears aside and barricaded them away where they couldn't hurt her. She liked the peace and contentment she experienced here, and she didn't want to do anything to jeopardize her position with Fred Harvey's company.

Later that night, Simone lay in bed rethinking the events of the day. She felt a comfort that she could never remember having known before. Was this what it was like to be happy? She thought of her life and of the horrors that had once haunted and confronted her on a daily basis. In the security that surrounded her at the Harvey House, the memories were slowly fading from her mind, and even the ordeal of Garvey Davis didn't seem quite so intimidating. She felt responsible for what must surely have been his death, but she also knew it was self-defense. At least, that was how she was choosing to view the deed. Davis would have forced himself upon her, and while her father considered them married, Simone could not accept that this man would take her to be a wife when she neither loved him nor had the benefit of a proper ceremony.

She glanced across the room to where Una sat, faithfully writing to her mother. *What joy it must be to have that kind of love between mother and child*, Simone thought. Her gaze passed to the bedstand and the old Bible that had once belonged to Winifred Dumas. For reasons beyond her understanding she had placed it there upon arriving in Topeka, and there it had sat until this moment.

"I will always love you, Simone," she could nearly hear her mother saying. *"I will come back for you. You will see."* How badly she had wanted to believe that promise.

But her mother hadn't come back. She would never come back. With a sigh Simone closed her eyes and allowed sleep to drift over her. Life seemed such a contradictory existence. Some people had all the good things—love, family, friendship—while others knew only sorrow and misery. She'd already spent seventeen years in the latter group, and now Simone longed to embrace the other side . . . the happier group. The group where children were cared for in love and tenderness, where people did not hurt each other and set out to destroy all hope.

SIXTEEN

JULY SECOND DAWNED muggy and warm with the promise of even higher temperatures to come that afternoon. Simone joined her Harvey sisters on the floor of the dining room, serving first one customer and then another. The black uniform was unbearably warm, and the high-necked apron felt as though it were tightening around her neck. Longing for a breeze to offer the slightest bit of ease, Simone lingered for several moments by the open window. But it was to no avail. The air hung heavy and still. She thought of the crisp mountain air and the home she'd grown up in. She'd always taken for granted that everyone lived in a climate such as hers. But even the mountains with their cool, refreshing breezes couldn't make Simone wish to go back to what had once been.

Moving around her station, Simone tried to forget how warm it was. "Do you need anything else?" she sweetly asked a young mother, burying her thoughts of Wyoming.

The woman shook her head, glancing from the plate of one child and then another. "No, I believe we're just fine. My husband would probably enjoy more coffee," she added. "He just stepped outside for a moment."

Simone nodded. "Of course. I'll have it right here." She turned to the four men who sat opposite the woman. "And what about you gentlemen? Will there be anything else?"

"Are you by any chance on the menu?" one scrawny-looking man asked. He reminded Simone of a man she'd known in Uniontown, and the thought made her stiffen.

"I assure you that I'm not," she stated coolly. She felt uneasiness mingle with the beginnings of a headache.

"I told you that you weren't her type, Gabe," another man joined in. "She's my type." The men laughed as though sharing a great joke.

When no one suggested needing anything else, Simone left them to continue with their comments and went to retrieve the coffeepot. Her head began to pound in earnest, and she didn't know if it was the heat or her taut nerves that caused the pain. She loved working at the Harvey House, except when rowdy characters, such as the two customers she'd just dealt with, showed up. Usually the house manager kept those types under control, but by the time Simone reported it, the train would be ready to depart and the unruly men would be on board.

"Are you feeling all right?" Una asked her softly. "You look kind of flushed."

Simone picked up the pot of coffee. "I'm fine. Just dealt with a couple of lewd characters."

"Ja, there surely seems to be a lot of them."

Simone nodded and returned to the table with a fixed purpose. She wouldn't let the men and their comments destroy her peace of mind. She just couldn't allow that. Men had been pushing her around and dominating her life for as long as she could remember. Perhaps it was the reason she refused to deal with them, along with God. God had always been spoken of as her heavenly Father. Well, she didn't think much about the word *father* in either its earthly or heavenly form. Maybe this carried over into her feelings toward men in general. Men were demanding. They always expected something of her, and it was always something directed at bettering their own lives or pleasuring themselves. Only Jeffery seemed to show any signs of being different.

Refilling the coffee cups of those who asked for more, Simone felt extremely relieved when the fifteen-minute warning was issued. And then, before she could focus on any further comments, the room emptied and the train pulled out of the depot, taking her crude customers with it.

After that, some of the townsfolk came for breakfast, as well as a good number of railroad men. Simone cleared her tables quickly and efficiently, replacing dirty linen tablecloths with freshly cleaned and pressed ones. This was the rule for customers in the dining room, whether they were railroad workers or bank presidents like Cyrus K. Holliday, the founding father of the Santa Fe. Simone liked the idea of everyone receiving equal treatment. Even the lowliest person could find themselves respected and honored in Fred Harvey's eating establishments.

The day wore on, and just as it had been foreseen by more than one person, the temperatures rose to an unbearable high. At first, Simone thought she might faint from the heat. She found herself polishing silver by an open window and, finding little relief, thought she might collapse. Then, just when she thought she could stand no more, Henri called for her to come to the kitchen.

If the dining room had been hot, then the kitchen was a veritable inferno. Simone picked up a china plate and actually used it to fan herself. Not that it helped.

"The orders were just brought to me for the luncheon group," Henri told her. "We are going to need another table set up in the dining room. There are more people than we can fit."

Simone massaged her aching temples with one hand while fanning herself with the other. "Why so many?"

Henri shrugged. "Ah, who can say? Perhaps your American holiday has them hurrying home to celebrate?"

Simone smiled. "Perhaps just as many will travel by rail on Bastille Day, no?"

Henri laughed and motioned her to the door. "Hurry now. It won't be long before the whistle will sound."

Simone nodded and put down the plate to go in search of Rachel. She found her easily enough, conversing with the head waitress about a mismanaged station.

"Miss Taylor," Simone began, "Monsieur Flaubert tells me that the telegraph has indicated additional passengers who will be taking their meal in the dining room. He suggests we make room for an extra table or two."

"That's just what we need," Rachel said, clearly irritated. "Grace! Olive! You two go fetch a couple of the boys in the kitchen and have them bring in the sewing room table." The girls moved quickly to do her bidding. She turned back, nearly running into Simone, who once again stood rubbing her temples. "Well, don't just lollygag around, Miss Irving. I suggest you get to work!"

Simone's head snapped up at this. It wasn't like Rachel to be so cross. "I'm sorry," she whispered.

Rachel's angry expression softened. "No, Simone," she said, reaching out, "I'm the one who's sorry."

Simone dodged her hand and instantly regretted it. She could see by the look on Rachel's face that her reaction hadn't been lost on the woman.

Rachel pulled back and smiled. "I guess this heat has made me irritable. I had no call to screech like that. Please forgive me."

Once again, Simone witnessed how people often grew angry yet managed their differences without resorting to violence. Her father's treatment had made her believe that all the world resolved their differences with force. She had dodged Rachel's touch for fear of it being meant for harm, but this woman had shown her nothing but kindness. Nearly everyone had been kind, with the exception of a couple of the other girls whose jealousy over Rachel's treatment of Simone had caused them to snub her. Simone hardly concerned herself with such snobbery. She certainly hadn't come to Kansas to make friends.

By this time Olive and Grace had returned and were directing the boys as to where the table should be positioned. Rachel sighed in exasperation and called out, "No, wait. We'll need to move some of the other tables closer together."

Simone swayed on her feet and felt panicked for a moment when her vision seemed to blur. It passed quickly, and taking a deep breath, she hurried back to the linen closet to procure additional linens for the new table. A bit of a breeze touched her cheeks, but it didn't seem to help much. She longed for a cool bath and a chance to lie down, but she knew better than to expect that for a long time to come. Her regular shift would run the course of twelve hours, and then she would still have the finishing touches to put on her new gown of red gingham.

The one-mile whistle sounded and the girls quickly scattered to their stations. Simone thought she felt a bit better. At least she didn't notice the heat as much. In fact, she was no longer perspiring at all. She hurried to set herself up at her own station. The salads wouldn't be brought to the table until the customers had arrived. The warmer temperatures would only spoil them or cause them to wilt, and Harvey rules dictated that the food be at a premium both in looks and taste. The salads safely sat on ice in the back room, and Simone thought how wonderful that sounded. She couldn't help but smile at the idea of joining them.

It wasn't until the gong sounded, announcing the train's arrival, that Simone remembered this would be the train on which Jeffery O'Donnell would make his return. She felt a nervous fluttering in her stomach. She faced his return with mixed emotions. Would he come demanding more answers, or would he, as several of the girls had suggested, come seeking Simone's companionship for other purposes?

The rush of passengers flooded the dining room, and only for a moment did Simone feel disappointment at not seeing Jeffery among them. Without time to give the matter any serious consideration, she quickly set out to learn the menu choices of her guests.

"I've changed my mind," one man told her. "I don't want any salad, I want soup."

"I want something cold to drink immediately," a plump matronly woman demanded.

Simone smiled and nodded, positioning their cups in order for the beverage girls to meet their desires. She went in search of the salads and soup, all the while feeling herself grow weaker and weaker. Her heart pounded a throbbing cadence in her head, yet there was nothing she could do to ease her misery. Perhaps when this group of customers had gone she would beg Rachel for a short time to bathe and nap. She could always offer to work extra time later.

She stumbled twice in the kitchen and both times managed to catch herself before dropping her tray. Simone knew something wasn't right. It was more than just being a little overheated. But for the life of her,

Simone had no idea what was wrong. Serving the salads as best she could, Simone still saw no sign of Jeffery in the dining room. *Perhaps he's been further delayed*, she reasoned, then put the thought from her mind. Concentrating on her duties required every bit of strength she could muster.

"What's the matter, Simone?" Carrie asked sarcastically. "Working too hard?"

Carrie never said anything to Simone unless it was to criticize or condemn. The girl had worked here longer than anyone else and had taken it as a personal assault when someone else had been appointed head waitress. Then when Simone began to receive more than her fair share of attention, Carrie and her constant companion, Betsy, formed an alliance against the newcomer. Una had warned Simone of their whispered rumors of Simone being more than what she seemed. It worried Simone to think they might actually stumble upon the truth.

Struggling to regain a bit of strength, Simone threw Carrie a look of indifference and refused to take the bait. Rachel had severely reprimanded other girls for arguing, and Simone knew Carrie would love nothing more than to draw her into a fight. And now, feeling as she did, Simone knew she had to conserve every ounce of strength for her duties.

She approached Henri and relayed the dictates of the man at her table. The temperamental chef was livid that the man should change his order, but Simone calmly reminded him that Fred Harvey's first rule of business was to please the customers. Henri was unimpressed and continued to mutter about the change, even while he dipped up his famous cold, creamed *vichyssoise*.

He handed Simone the bowl, and for a moment she stood blinking at it in confusion. What was she supposed to do now? Her thoughts seemed all jumbled and fuzzy. She had just told Henri something about customers and now she couldn't think of what she was supposed to do. Fearful that someone should question her, Simone turned away from Henri and headed back to the door of the dining room.

Soup. I have a bowl of soup in my hands, she reminded herself. Someone wants soup. Oh yes. The man at the rear table. He didn't want salad. He wanted soup. She breathed a sigh of relief and headed toward the back of the dining room. The room tilted a bit to the right and Simone tilted with it, sloshing the soup on her hand. She steadied herself against the back of one customer's chair and tried to appear as if nothing were amiss.

Placing the soup in front of her customer, Simone again found it difficult to remember what she was supposed to do next. She glanced at one table and then another, hoping that something would trigger her memory. The images of the people swam before her eyes, and Simone knew she was fighting a futile attempt to stay on her feet.

"Where's the rest of our food?" the demanding matron questioned.

Food. "Yes, I need to bring their food," Simone muttered to herself.

She turned back toward the kitchen and again the room shifted first one way and then another. *I have to get back to the kitchen. I have to go lie down.* Forcing herself to cross the distance, she had no sooner made it to the kitchen door when Carrie came through with a tray of steaming food.

"Watch out!" Carrie snapped, and Simone quickly backed away.

"Sorry," she whispered.

"Are you all right?" Una asked, pausing to glance back over her shoulder from several feet away.

"No, but I will be," Simone assured her, hoping that somehow the words would convince herself, as well.

Her legs felt like rubber, and Simone knew that if only she could make it to the kitchen, Henri or one of the cooks would be able to help her. She pushed open the door and, biting her lip to keep conscious, stepped through the portal and into the arms of Jeffery O'Donnell.

"I must say, Simone, this is a pleasant surprise," he said, laughing.

He stepped back to release her, but by this time Simone's strength had given out. "Help me," she whispered, collapsing against him.

"Simone!" He easily lifted her into his arms. "Simone, what is it?"

"Hot. So hot," she murmured. His worried expression was the last thing she remembered before the room went black.

Jeffery stared down in stunned silence at the woman in his arms. Simone's face was flushed red and her body felt on fire with fever. Rachel came through the door and stopped in her tracks at the sight.

"She fainted," Jeffery told the woman. "I think it might be the heat."

"Henri, get some ice," Rachel called to the worried chef.

"Come up the back way," she told Jeffery, "we'll get her to bed." She grabbed up the ice as she passed by Henri and led the way up the back stairs.

"Una thought she looked sick, and I was just coming to check on her," Rachel explained. "She hasn't handled the heat very well. I don't suppose she's used to it."

"No, I don't suppose she is," Jeffery replied, carefully negotiating the stairway.

An odd feeling of despair washed over him. He had looked forward to his return to Topeka with great relish. He had already planned to join the Harvey Girls as they attended the Fourth of July celebration and had even plotted as to how he might have a private moment or two with Simone Irving. Now she lay so lifeless in his arms that he worried she might not recover at all, much less in time for the Independence Day festivities.

"This is her room. Bring her in here," Rachel ordered.

Jeffery barely heard the words. He couldn't believe how frail and tiny Simone felt. *Why, she couldn't weigh much more than a hundred pounds*, he thought. Jeffrey had known from the first moment the train had pulled out of the Topeka station that he'd be unable to keep her from his thoughts. Now he felt only despair and misery in his concern for her well-being.

"Put her on this bed."

He did as he was told and watched as Rachel rolled the small woman over and began unbuttoning her uniform.

"Mr. O'Donnell, you'll have to leave us. Men aren't allowed on the dormitory floors, and you know that better than anyone else. Go for the doctor and feel free to wait in my office. I'll let you know the minute I learn anything regarding her condition."

Jeffery stared at her for several moments before realizing there was nothing else to be done. "I'll get the doctor and send one of the girls up to help you."

"No, there are too many customers to take care of. I have this ice, and if you would move the washbasin over here and pour some water before you go, I'll have everything I need."

Jeffery quickly complied and turned to go. He hesitated at the door, glancing back one final time as Rachel slipped the apron from Simone's body. "She will be all right, won't she?" he asked.

Rachel looked up, and the seriousness of her expression spoke volumes. "Just get the doctor quickly."

SEVENTEEN

RACHEL STRUGGLED TO get Simone out of the heavy black Harvey uniform. Why hadn't she been more attentive to the poor girl's condition? As housemother, it was her place to see to their well-being, and now she had failed. She tugged at the sleeves of the dress and was finally rewarded for her efforts when the gown separated from Simone's body. Pulling the dress forward, Rachel gently rolled Simone to one side and pushed the uniform off without any further hindrance.

Placing the ice in the washbasin, Rachel allowed the water to grow cold before dipping the washcloth. She began by systematically rubbing the cool cloth over Simone's burning body, hoping and praying that the girl was merely overcome and not suffering from a heat stroke, as Jeffery had suggested.

Drawing the cloth over Simone's silky white arms, Rachel felt double guilt for having snapped at her young charge earlier in the day. The heat was difficult for everyone. Rolling Simone forward so that she could wash her back, Rachel gasped at the scars that peeked out from beneath the girl's chemise.

"What in the world has this poor child endured?" Rachel whispered, pulling the chemise down as far as she could. Ugly pink scars stretched from one shoulder to the other, revealing the unquestionable mark of multiple beatings. In fact, Simone's entire back was a crisscross pattern of scars, both old and new. Some were thin-lined and white with age, while others were still pink and raised, maybe no more than a month or two old.

Rachel calculated the three weeks Simone had been on the Harvey payroll and realized that the girl must have left her abuse and fled directly to Chicago. *No wonder she was on the train*, Rachel thought. And no wonder she hesitated to talk about her past. Was it possible that Simone had been placed in the care of heavy-handed relatives and now wished to forget them and what they'd done? Could it be that her parents weren't really dead after all but, rather, were abusive in their actions? Questions flooded Rachel's mind, refusing to be ignored.

"How does one so young endure such beatings?" Rachel murmured. "Oh, Lord, help this child. Whatever her past, no one deserves to be dealt with in such a manner."

A knock sounded at the door, and Rachel quickly drew the sheet over Simone's body and got up to see who it might be. Finding the familiar face of a local physician, Rachel ushered him in with grave concern.

"Dr. Hill, I'm afraid one of my girls succumbed to the heat."

"Mr. O'Donnell told me all about it. Let's have a look," the short, stocky man said, handing his bowler hat to Rachel.

"There's something else," Rachel said hesitantly. "I mean . . . that is . . ."

"Well, speak up, Miss Taylor. I've never known you to be at a loss for words."

"I've never found myself dealing with this situation before," she replied and motioned him to Simone's bed. Pulling back the sheet, she pointed to Simone's back. "She's clearly endured years of unthinkable punishment."

The doctor sat down on the bedside and examined the scars for himself. "Yes, she has. And not so long ago, by the look of these marks atop her shoulders. Although they've healed, it's quite clear that they aren't that old."

"That's what first drew my attention," Rachel replied. "She's only been with us for about three weeks. I know very little about her, but this came as a complete shock."

The doctor eyed the marks critically for a moment, then rolled

Simone onto her back. "There's nothing I can do for them now. The more immediate concern is her fever."

Rachel nodded. "I need to go speak with Mr. O'Donnell, but I'll be right back." The doctor nodded and opened his black bag.

Rachel hurried from the room, unsure of what she should tell Jeffery. Obviously there was more to Simone than met the eye, but Rachel had no way of knowing what the vicious scars indicated in Simone's past. Perhaps Jeffery had been able to learn something more about Simone while on his trip. He would have little trouble getting information back and forth from Chicago, and knowing his persistence to fully examine each of the Harvey employee's backgrounds, Rachel had no reason to believe he wouldn't have pursued Simone's past with great enthusiasm. Added to this was his own personal interest, which Rachel was sure ran deeper than simple employer and employee matters. Yes, Rachel thought, he would have taken the time to carefully investigate Simone's life. Coming to her office, Rachel wasn't surprised to find Jeffery pacing the floor inside.

"Well?" he asked, concern clearly written in his expression.

"I don't know anything yet. The doctor is with her now," Rachel began. "I thought I'd come here and speak to you. . . ." She let the words trail away as she glanced to the floor.

"What is it?" he asked, coming forward to take hold of her shoulders. "You have to tell me."

Rachel looked up and shook her head. "Have you learned anything more about Simone?"

Jeffery's expression contorted. "What do you mean?"

"I mean, did you finish your investigation of her character and background?"

He dropped his hold and shook his head. "No one knows anything about her. I wired your mother's friend in Chicago, but she basically told me the same things your mother said. Simone was already on the train in Cheyenne. She was dirty and unkempt, clearly had been traveling for some time, and didn't seem to have a clue as to where she was headed. The woman spent most of her time explaining things about Chicago and said that Simone said very little about herself. Now, why do you ask me this, unless . . ." It was Jeffery's turn to fall silent.

"Are you . . . I mean, do you believe that she will die? Are you trying to find someone to contact about her condition?"

Rachel shook her head. "I don't know. I have no way of knowing how seriously ill she might be. But something else has come to my attention." She twisted her hands, wondering how much she should say. She didn't want to hurt Simone further by gossiping about the child. The scars on her back had nothing to do with her quality of work, Rachel reasoned.

"Please tell me what it is," Jeffery said.

He looked so troubled and worried that Rachel couldn't help but feel sorry for him. "I undressed Simone and found her back to be a mass of scars."

"Scars? What do you mean? Has she been injured?"

Rachel bit at her lower lip, realizing that she had to continue to tell of Simone's situation. "She's been beaten. And from the looks of it, I believe it's been an ongoing thing for some time."

Jeffery's jaw tightened and his eyes narrowed. "Beaten?" he questioned between clenched teeth.

Rachel nodded. "There are long, ugly scars that crisscross her back. Some are faded and white, indicating to me that some time has passed since they were issued. Others, however, are newer. Maybe given to her just before coming to you in Chicago."

"Who would be animal enough to beat her?" he demanded, anger edging his tone.

"I don't know. I wondered if it might have something to do with her unwillingness to speak of the past. Just the other day I tried to get her to open up about her parents and her childhood, but she closed up faster than a new saloon in Kansas."

"If she has to contend with the idea of someone learning her whereabouts, it might well be the reason she says nothing to us about where she's from."

Rachel nodded. "I wondered if maybe her parents are still alive. Or worse yet, if she's run off from an unreasonable husband."

"A husband!" Jeffery exclaimed. "Surely not that. She hardly looks old enough to be employed here, much less be married."

"You know as well as I do," Rachel countered, "that a good many women marry younger than eighteen. Especially out west where women are still at a premium. Besides, we've both wondered if she's even that old. You know it's true."

Jeffery nodded. "I suppose I do know that. Honestly, I've wondered about many things since she first came to my office. She was clearly upset from the first question I asked regarding her family and background. I suppose I was just a bit overwhelmed by her. She is a beautiful woman," he said, reddening at the neck, as if embarrassed to realize what he'd just admitted.

"Yes, she is," Rachel replied, ignoring his discomfort. "I don't know what your thoughts are on the matter, but, Jeffery, I don't wish to see that child returned to whoever might have done that to her."

"Neither do I," Jeffery answered, seeming to sense an ally in Rachel.

"Perhaps we should protect Simone by inventing her past for her. Give Mr. Harvey the details he needs, and leave the rest between us," Rachel replied. She could tell by the expression on Jeffery's face that he was in complete agreement with her. "I know it's a lie and it goes against all my Christian beliefs, but honestly, Jeffery, wouldn't God prefer we protect one of His own? I remember my grandmother speaking of hiding slaves on the underground railroad. They, too, were escaping inhumane treatment, and my grandmother felt that the lies told to protect them were justified in her Christian duty. I may be totally wrong on this, but I can't help but believe that Simone needs our help."

Jeffery didn't hesitate. "I'll see to it. Until we have reason to believe otherwise, we'll think only the best of her and protect her to our utmost ability."

Rachel nodded, feeling relieved that he'd not condemned her thinking. She would pray it through later and ask God to show her if she'd strayed in her intentions, but for now Simone needed time to heal. With any luck at all, perhaps no one would need to be told anything about Simone. Perhaps Mr. Harvey would simply trust Jeffery's judgment and leave it at that. "I'd best get back up there and see what the doctor's found out."

"I'll keep an eye on things down here, although I'm certain to be no good to anyone," Jeffery muttered, taking a seat at Rachel's desk.

Rachel hurried back upstairs feeling moderate relief at the conspiracy she'd just joined in on. Simone's secret would be safe with them, of this she was sure. She would do whatever she had to in order to see that the child never again faced another beating. Simone might never tell her the truth of the matter, but Rachel no longer cared. She was entitled to her secrets. She'd already paid the price with the marks on her back.

Pushing open the door to Simone's room, Rachel found the doctor just finishing his exam. She frowned at the grave expression on his face. "Is it very bad?"

"I'm afraid it is. I fear she's suffered a heat stroke. We can only hope that the fever won't eat away her brain. You'll have to bathe her constantly in order to bring down the temperature. Also give her a teaspoon of this every four hours," he said, handing Rachel a bottle of liquid. "It should help with the fever." He put his instruments back into the black bag and stood up. "Oh, and try to get some fluids down her. That will help to cool things down on the inside, as well."

Simone moaned, and Rachel immediately went to her side. "When will we know something more?" she asked.

The doctor shrugged. "She could come around right away. Could be a day or two. Just depends on how fast we can get that fever down. She'll be weak afterward, however, and will need additional rest."

"Must you leave?"

"I'm afraid so. I have others who are just as ill. There really is nothing else to be done. I'll return in the morning and check on her condition. Should she seem to take a turn for the worse, you can send for me before then, but good luck in finding me. I've a feeling I'll be out most of the night."

Rachel nodded. "I'll see to it that she has constant care." She turned the bottle of medicine over and over in her hands. "Let me see you out. I need to go downstairs for more ice anyway."

The doctor took up his hat and headed for the door, with Rachel following close behind. She couldn't help but feel great frustration in his noncommittal answers and inability to reassure. It wasn't his fault, she knew, but it would have been so much more comforting to have had him shrug the entire matter off as being nothing more than Simone being overworked and overheated.

After he'd gone, Rachel went to her head waitress, Bethel Anderson. "Simone has possibly suffered a heat stroke, and she's gravely ill. I'll need you to help me by reassigning her station and splitting the work up between the other girls."

"Will she be all right?" Bethel asked.

"I don't know. But it will be my job to see to it that her fever abates. Mine and God's," Rachel added with a hesitant smile. "Remember her in your prayers, Bethel, for only the Lord can truly see her through."

The girl nodded, and Rachel moved toward the kitchen. "I'm putting you in charge, Bethel, but you can always come to me with any problems."

Rachel hurried into the kitchen and sought out Henri. His interpreter, Raymond, was now duly employed as a chef's assistant and seemed to find the work to his liking. Especially given that his handsome, elfish appearance seemed to attract every girl working in the eating establishment. It was difficult to reiterate that Mr. Harvey's rules included no dating between Harvey employees when the girls were busy making calf eyes at Raymond. When Rachel approached them, both men came to attention.

"I'm afraid Miss Irving is quite ill. She has a high fever and the doctor believes her to have succumbed to heat stroke." She paused long enough for Raymond to interpret the message to Henri.

The testy cook grimaced and grabbed his head. "*Non*. This is bad," he managed in heavily accented English. Raymond had been working to teach the older man English, but it came hard to the chef, and he seldom even tried to speak with anyone other than Raymond or Simone.

"Yes, it is," Rachel replied. "I'm taking more ice with me, but I would appreciate it if you would send one of the girls upstairs with a new supply on an hourly basis. It's imperative that we keep Simone cool."

Again Raymond relayed the message, and after Henri shot back a reply in rapid-fire French, the man turned back to Rachel. "He said you may have anything you need, and if you would allow, he will prepare a broth that often helped his mother in treating the family whenever they were ill."

"That would be wonderful," Rachel replied, moving to the icebox.

Henri hurried forward with a large bowl, and before Rachel could even bother, he had opened the box and chipped away a large chunk of ice. He held it up to her like an offering, and with it Rachel took her leave and hurried from the room.

She had just reached the stairs when Jeffery appeared. "How is she? What did the doctor say?"

Rachel paused and tried to smile reassuringly. "It's the heat, just as you feared. I'm to keep her cool by bathing her through the night. I've put Bethel in charge of the House, and between her and the manager, I'm sure everything will run in top order."

"I wish I could do something."

"Pray," Rachel suggested. "That's about all any of us can do." Jeffery nodded but said nothing. "I'll send word to your hotel if anything changes."

"I'd rather stay here," Jeffery answered. "Could I just sleep in your office?"

Rachel knew it was against the rules, but she also knew Jeffery's feelings for Simone. "Just this once, but stay out of sight."

Jeffery nodded. "I will. And, Rachel," he added, causing her to turn once again, "please don't hesitate to send for me if I can do anything to be of assistance."

"I will," she assured. "I promise."

Jeffery sat at Rachel Taylor's desk long into the night. He kept vigil in silent prayer, reminding himself that even though he'd never been given to great shows of faith, he did believe in God's ability to heal the sick. He thought about the times he'd spent in church listening to flowery sermons preached from highly ornate pulpits. His mother felt it very important to be seen in church on Sunday, and the O'Donnell family pew was never without a crowd of well-dressed family and friends, all in order to prove to the good Lord and society the faithfulness of the O'Donnell clan.

But such things did little good in situations like this. Jeffery found it impossible to remember a single verse or idea that had been preached to him. He wanted to pray in a way that would please God—wanted to make sure he included all the right words and acted in just the proper manner, but in truth he wasn't at all sure he knew what the correct manner should be.

"I don't know how to pray," he muttered. "Not truly. I've listened to the words of the ministers with all their *thee*s and *thou*s, and honestly it doesn't mean a whole lot to me." He didn't even realize that he was directing his words to God until he looked upward to the ceiling and sighed. "I suppose I'm doing this all wrong, but I do ask you to make Simone well. I don't know her past, and I don't care. I suppose that sounds improper." He paused and shook his head. "If it is improper, don't hold that against Simone. Punish me for my lack of knowledge and inability to pray, but don't punish her. Obviously she's already endured plenty of that."

He sighed and leaned back in the chair, wishing Rachel might come through the door and announce Simone's full recovery. He had no way of knowing how long these things took. If one prayed and truly believed God would do the deed, did it speed things along more so than when one prayed in an uncertain manner? There were just too many unanswered questions.

Putting his head down on Rachel's desk, Jeffery thought only to rest his eyes for a moment. There was nothing else he could do, he told himself. But it didn't ease his concern. Simone Irving lay close to death just one floor above, and for reasons that defied normal thought, Jeffery couldn't bear the idea of losing her.

EIGHTEEN

FOR A TIME UNA sat in one corner of the room, silently stitching away on Simone's new gingham dress while Rachel continued her bed-side care. The tall Swedish girl had explained that she wanted to finish the dress on Simone's behalf even if the possibilities of her wearing it to the celebration were slim to none. Rachel thought it a lovely idea.

"She'll probably be encouraged by the fact that we continued with plans for Friday. Maybe she'll see that we had every hope that she would recover," Rachel said, trying her best to sound encouraging.

"Ja," Una replied. "My *fader* came down with a sun stroke once. He worked too long in the wheat field and *Moder* found him. He was sick for a good long time."

Rachel nodded and continued to bathe Simone. "Of course, Simone is young and strong. Hopefully, and with God's help, she'll recover quickly."

"Ja," Una whispered softly and continued with her sewing.

Rachel looked back at the restless body of her patient. "No. No," Simone moaned over and over. *At least she's making some signs of life*, Rachel thought. Several long hours had already passed in deathly silence, causing Rachel to fear that she might never again regain consciousness. The moaning and thrashing, however, seemed a good sign. Simone was fighting, and that could only be to her benefit, as far as Rachel was concerned.

"No . . . don't." Simone pushed at imaginary images, then fell silent.

Rachel could only imagine that Simone fought the same creature who had issued the stripes on her back. *What horrors must inhabit the poor child's mind!*

"Shhh," Rachel comforted and stroked Simone's fevered brow with the cloth. "No one can hurt you now. I won't let anyone hurt you."

Simone seemed to settle for a few moments, giving Rachel a feeling of hope and satisfaction. About this time, Una wearied of her sewing and readied herself for bed. She offered to help Rachel through the night, but Rachel admonished her to get some sleep.

"Morning will come soon enough, and you'll have to work doubly hard to help pick up Simone's station."

Una nodded, knelt in prayer, then slipped into her bed. "It's still so hot," she murmured. "I wish we could make it better for Simone."

"I know," Rachel replied. "But God has it all under control. He knows best." She could only pray that God's best included Simone's recovery. She didn't know how she would deal with the death of one of her girls, should Simone prove too weak to endure her ordeal.

All through the night, Rachel bathed Simone with cool water. She longed to offer the unconscious girl comfort, especially when her moaning became more intense. The images had apparently grown more fearsome, and Rachel felt herself moved to tears as Simone pleaded for help.

"Don't go, Mama," she cried out.

"I'm here, Simone," Rachel replied, not knowing how else to help her. She reached a hand up to touch her furrowed brow. The fever didn't seem nearly as high, and Rachel began to hope that Simone's recovery would come soon.

"Didn't mean to," Simone said, thrashing violently to one side. "Didn't kill him."

Rachel physically pulled back, unable to hide her surprise. Grateful that Una slept peacefully, Rachel tried to calm the racing beat of her heart. Kill him? What was she talking about?

Simone continued to moan and twist in the bed until Rachel feared she might hurt herself. Still, every time Rachel tried to restrain

Simone, it only caused her to react more violently.

"No! Don't touch me! Stay away!" Simone cried out, wrestling against Rachel's tender hold.

"God, please help me," Rachel pleaded. "Give this poor child peace of mind so that her body can heal."

Spying the Bible beside Simone's bed, Rachel picked it up and opened the cover. "'Darling Daughter, I love you more dearly than my life, and I would gladly give it to save you from harm. Look for me, I am coming back for you, just as Jesus promised He, too, would come back for us one day. Mama.'" Rachel read the words aloud and wondered at their meaning. Simone had said that her mother was dead. That both parents, in fact, had recently died. What did it mean that she would come back for her? Had her mother gone away only to die before she could make her way back home?

Rachel tried not to think about it overmuch as she leafed through the pages and began to read aloud comforting words from the twenty-seventh chapter of Psalms. "'The LORD is my light and my salvation: whom shall I fear? the LORD is the strength of my life; of whom shall I be afraid?'" Simone seemed to calm at the words, and, feeling encouraged, Rachel continued to read aloud, pausing only when she came to the seventh verse to rinse out the cloth she had placed on Simone's neck and chest.

"'Hear, O LORD, when I cry with my voice: have mercy also upon me, and answer me. When thou saidst, Seek ye my face; my heart said unto thee, Thy face, LORD, will I seek.'" Rachel felt tears come to her eyes and prayed that God might hear Simone's cries of despair.

"'Hide not thy face far from me; put not thy servant away in anger: thou hast been my help; leave me not, neither forsake me, O God of my salvation. When my father and my mother forsake me, then the LORD will take me up.'" Rachel reread the last sentence and thought of all that Simone had told her, and of the words given by Simone's mother inside the cover of the Bible. "Do you hear that, Simone?" she questioned softly, once again bathing the younger woman's body. "Even if the rest of the world has forsaken you, the Lord will take you into His care. You must see that He loves you, Simone. He would not leave you to face this misery by yourself."

Rachel realized that she was rambling on, but even if Simone couldn't hear and understand the words she spoke, they comforted Rachel. In this girl's heart lay hideous and horrible secrets, the likes of which Rachel had never known. Somehow, some way, Rachel wanted to be a help to Simone. She longed to see her healed physically and spiritually. The pain was evident. The need—even more so.

Bowing her head, Rachel began to pray and didn't even realize she'd nodded off until Simone, regaining consciousness, called her name.

"Rachel," the weak voice called.

Rachel jerked awake. "Oh no! I fell asleep!" she exclaimed, meeting Simone's half-opened eyes. "Oh, you're awake!"

Una stirred from her bed but remained silent as Rachel began to question Simone. "Can you understand me?"

"Yes," Simone replied in a barely audible voice. "Where am I?"

"In bed, I'm afraid," Rachel replied, giving her a smile of encouragement. "You've fallen ill due to the heat."

Simone closed her eyes, not seeming to understand. Rachel rinsed the washcloth out in tepid water before speaking again. "I've been bathing you throughout the night. The doctor thought it the best way to bring down your fever. That and some pretty awful-smelling medicine I've been giving you."

Simone nodded and opened her eyes again. "I feel terrible. So weak."

"I don't doubt you feel bad, but it will pass. You overdid things, and the heat made you collapse. It's not all that unusual for Kansas summers. I should have thought better of working you so hard all at once," Rachel replied, rambling along uncomfortably. How could she ever explain to Simone that she knew about her beatings and that in her fever-induced sleep, Simone had shared some rather revealing fears? Trying to ignore her concern, Rachel continued. "But I promise to see to your care, and you'll be back on your feet before you know it. I've also been praying for you. Una too."

This seemed to draw Simone's interest. "Praying for me? Why?"

Rachel smiled. "Because that's where I believe the real power to healing lies. In and of myself, I can do nothing, but with Christ all things are possible."

"You sound like my mother," Simone said, slowly licking her lips. Then, as if she'd made no comment at all, she asked, "Could I have some water?"

"Certainly," Rachel answered, quickly dropping her task with the cloth in order to retrieve a half-full drinking glass. "Here, let me help you." She slipped her arm under Simone's neck and shoulders and helped to lift her up just a bit.

Simone tried to take hold of the water glass but lacked the energy. She allowed Rachel to see to the task and waved her away when she'd had enough. Rachel didn't want to lose the openness Simone had offered in her comment about her mother, and so setting the glass back on the nightstand, she picked up the Bible.

"I hope you don't mind, but I've been reading from your Bible. The Scriptures seemed to help calm you when you were upset."

Simone seemed to struggle to focus on what Rachel was saying. "Upset? Why was I upset?"

Rachel reached out and gently pushed back a strand of black hair. "Why don't you tell me."

Simone shrugged. "I don't know."

"Simone, I'd like to be your friend. I'd like to help you through whatever bad times you're facing. I know you don't know me very well, and maybe it seems hard to believe that anyone would want to be good to you without expecting something else in return. But I care about you. I genuinely care."

Simone shook her head from side to side, and Rachel thought she saw tears in the younger woman's eyes. "Don't care, Rachel. Not about me."

"Why not?"

"I don't deserve it. I'm no good."

"What a thing to say," Rachel replied, totally taken aback by Simone's bluntness. "You're one of God's creation. Of course you deserve to be cared for. Besides, everyone here cares about you. They like you." Simone looked away and said nothing.

Rachel couldn't help but feel inadequate in her attempt to deal with Simone's problems. Her fever-induced rantings revealed all manner of possible trials. "Simone, I hope you won't think me out of line, but I want you to know that you are important to me. Not just because you're one of my Harvey Girls. Not even because we need the extra help. From the first day you came, I knew you were the kind of young woman I'd like to be friends with. You are smart and self-confident, and even though you have said very little about yourself, I can't help but feel that we have much in common."

At this, Simone shook her head and dared a look at Rachel. "No. We have very little in common," she said weakly.

"We are both on our own . . . many miles from the people who love us," Rachel offered.

"There are no people who love me," Simone replied. "That is one of the biggest differences between us."

"I read what your mother wrote inside the cover of this Bible," Rachel countered. "Her love for you is quite clear."

"She's dead!" Simone snapped. "Now, please just go away and leave me be. Either I'll get better or I'll die. One's pretty much the same as the other. Either way I'll be alone."

The bitterness in Simone's words was nearly too much for Rachel. "You don't have to be alone, Simone. God has promised to never leave us or forsake us. He cares, whether you believe in my feelings or not."

"I find all of it hard to believe," Simone replied. "I thought just as you did once. My mother felt that way, too. And now she's dead and I'm nearly that way."

"But the truth is still valid, whether you believe in it or not. God is faithful, even if the people in your life failed to be. His hand is upon you. He sees everything that happens, and it grieves Him when you are hurting."

"Then He must go around grieved an awful lot."

Rachel had no idea how to answer, and it was just as well. Una had awakened and noticed the conversation taking place.

"How is Simone?" she questioned as she sat up.

"Better," Rachel answered. "The fever is down. I'm hopeful for a full recovery."

Una got out of bed and came to Simone's side. "Can I do anything for you, Simone?"

"No," she replied, eyes closed and jaw tightly clenched. "I just want everyone to go away and leave me be."

"That's the sickness talking," Rachel replied. "Una, when you go downstairs to work, will you please get word to Mr. O'Donnell that Simone is much better? He's spent the night in my office."

Simone's eyes snapped open. "He did what?"

"He was worried about you. He wanted to stay close by in case you needed something. I allowed him to sleep in my office. I figure rules can sometimes be broken for extraordinary circumstances like this." She looked hard at Simone, willing her to understand as she added, "Sometimes exceptions are made in order to protect people."

Simone said nothing but quickly looked away.

"I'll tell him she's awake," Una replied. "Do you want me to send for the doctor?"

"No," Rachel replied. "He promised to come by first thing."

Simone shook her head. "I don't need a doctor. I don't want him here." Her tone hinged on fearfulness.

"Dr. Hill is very kind and very attentive. He fears you've suffered a heat stroke, but I think God has lessened the seriousness of your condition. I think perhaps you were just temporarily overcome and soon you'll feel right as rain."

Light was beginning to filter into the room from the dawning of a new morning, and along with the fact that Una had turned on another lamp, Rachel could clearly see that Simone's color was nearly normal. Simone might not believe in miracles, but Rachel did. She was seeing one now—of that she was certain. Somehow, some way, she had to help Simone see it, too. Rachel was also determined to make the younger woman see that she could trust her as a friend. Maybe in doing so she could help Simone to believe that she could trust God, as well.

NINETEEN

"OH, SIMONE, I wish you could come with us to the picnic," Una said, and the genuineness of her concern and desire was evident for all to hear.

"I'll be fine," Simone replied. "Rachel has me all settled here on the sofa, and Henri has supplied me with huge quantities of freshly iced lemonade."

Jeffery O'Donnell watched the scene with intent interest. He'd not yet told Simone of his plan to remain with her while the others went to the festivities. The house would be nearly empty, with the exception of the few Harvey Girls who had volunteered to stay behind and help with the evening meal's preparation. In Rachel's private parlor for "her girls," Jeffery intended to talk to Simone about her past . . . and perhaps even about her future.

"Your new dress looks so pretty," another of the girls added. "I've never seen anything quite so nice."

Simone nodded. "It is lovely, but I have to admit Una did most of the work. I'm still learning how to operate that newfangled sewing machine."

Laughter filled the room as the conversation turned to tales about one mishap after another that some of the girls had experienced with Mr. Singer's machine. Jeffery bided his time patiently until Rachel appeared, bonnet in hand, with the announcement that their transportation had arrived.

As the ladies filed out in animated whispers and giggles, Jeffery watched Simone for any sign of regret. But like a stone statuette, Simone kept all emotions from her face. She had been very quiet and withdrawn since her ordeal, and Jeffery could only hope that it was simply an aftermath of the illness.

"So do you wish you were going along?" he asked casually, coming across the room to where Simone sat.

"No, not really. I had looked forward to the picnic and seeing the boat races," she admitted, "but I'm just as content to stay behind."

Jeffery took a seat opposite her and stretched out his long legs before him. He wondered what she'd think of his actions but didn't have to contemplate it for long.

"Won't you be late?" Simone questioned.

"No," he said, smiling. "I'm not going."

"What?"

He let his smile broaden. "Why would I go along with that passel of giggling geese when I can remain here with the loveliest girl of all?"

Simone blushed and Jeffery knew she was genuinely embarrassed by the flattery. He'd known many a young woman who could blush on command, but with this woman, he knew it was a natural response.

"You should go along with the others," she murmured uncomfortably.

"But I want to be here with you," Jeffery countered, crossing his arms against his chest. "And since I'm in a position to do as I please, while you, my dear Simone, are stuck here recuperating from your illness, I win."

"I could leave and go upstairs," she said defiantly, lifting her chin.

Jeffery studied her face for a moment. Her appearance was like a fine china doll. Her skin, so flawlessly white and smooth, made him long to touch her. Her eyes, dark in their midnight shade of blue, caused him to yearn to know what secrets lay behind their intense gaze. And her lips . . . He shook his head to keep from concentrating too long on the area of her mouth, lest he make a fool of himself by saying the wrong thing.

"Did you hear what I said?" Simone questioned.

Jeffery shrugged and tried to appear nonchalant about the entire matter. "If you think that's best, then I won't stand in your way. However, my fondest wish is that you would stay and allow me the privilege of sharing your company."

Simone rolled her eyes. "My company is hardly something to classify as a privileged event."

"That, my dear Simone, is entirely a matter of perspective."

She stared at him curiously for a moment before smoothing out the folds of her skirt. "Why do you keep calling me that?"

"Calling you what?" Jeffery questioned, genuinely confused.

"My dear. You keep saying 'My dear Simone.'"

"I suppose because I've come to feel that you are dear to me."

She shook her head. "There's no call for that. I'm nobody to you."

"Ah . . . but that, my dear, is where you are wrong." He grinned ever so slowly and watched her discomfort grow.

"I think we should talk about something else. Rachel has rules about getting too familiar with men," Simone offered weakly. "And Mr. Harvey has rules about Harvey employees fraternizing."

"Rachel knows all about my staying here. I'm sure she'll understand my choice of conversation. As for Mr. Harvey, well, I think he'd understand my actions, as well." He watched her look away and toy with her long black braid. Taking pity on her, he added, "But if it makes you feel any better, I'll change the subject."

Simone nodded. "I think that would be a good idea."

"What shall we talk about, then?"

Simone leaned back against the cushioning of pillows Rachel had provided for her comfort and grew thoughtful. "Well, you could tell me about Chicago."

"A harmless enough topic," Jeffery agreed. But before very long he realized that even this subject led him back to better familiarizing himself with Simone, and in turn, making her more familiar with him.

"My family is what you would call 'well-to-do.' I grew up on a monstrous lakeside estate where there were servants for every possible need. We had the best of everything, for my mother was quite concerned that she not be outdone by her neighbors. We entertained regularly, having a dance or dinner party at least once a week—sometimes more. And always, my mother invited unthinkable numbers of people. She had a special dining room table that you could extend to serve up to one hundred people at a time."

"I can't imagine," Simone replied. "There's so much that I have no knowledge of. We lived very far removed from anything of society or big cities."

Jeffery found her sudden openness a hopeful sign, but he hesitated to ask her to continue. From experience, if Simone thought you were focusing on her past, she would clam up. With that in mind, Jeffery shrugged. "Big cities have their merits. You certainly can't give the excuse that you can't find what you're looking for," he offered with a grin. "But on the other hand, there's never any place where you can find true solace or silence."

"I loved the quiet of our mountain. I never realized that until I moved away," Simone said, her expression growing distant. "When I was all alone, it seemed the very best world. When even so much as one other person came to join me, it suddenly felt rather crowded."

Jeffery laughed. "Now I'm the one who can't imagine. A crowd of one? I suppose the cities can feel very intimidating to you. Topeka isn't as bad as Chicago, however. In fact, it is quite lovely. There's plenty of nice places to find some solitude and quiet. Maybe not as quiet as your mountain, but nevertheless, better than a busy rail yard. Maybe one of these days you will permit me to take you for a carriage ride to one of those places."

Simone's brows knit together as if she were thinking very hard on the possibility of such a thing. "I don't think that would meet with anyone's approval. As I mentioned earlier, you know about the rules regarding Harvey employees."

"I know that you aren't to date any of the staff working in this house, if that's what you mean," Jeffery said, watching her closely. "However, I'm not employed by this house and my circumstance is rather unique, even if that were a matter to be considered. I'm under Mr. Harvey's employ, but I'm certainly not a Harvey House staff member."

The silence fell hard between them, and Jeffery, unwilling to lose the closeness Simone had briefly allowed him, quickly continued. "My mother is quite the great lady of Chicago. She's involved in a dozen or more charities and considers herself a matriarch of the city. She has strange ideas for the town, as well as for her son."

"How so?" Simone asked, surprising Jeffery.

"In regards to the city or myself?"

Simone actually looked as though she might smile. "Whichever."

"Well, for the city, Mother sees it as the absolute center of all culture and creation. She chides her friends who insist on making sojourns to New York City and Paris, carefully reminding them that Chicago needs their devotion and allegiance in order to surpass those other places. As for her son . . . well, suffice to say, she has goals and ambitions for me that aren't necessarily in keeping with my own thoughts."

"Such as?"

Jeffery shifted a bit in the seat and stretched his arms casually up before joining his hands together behind his head. "She has plans for me to take my rightful position in society. She believes firmly, however, that in order to do so in a proper manner, I must take a socially acceptable wife. A woman of such high standing and inner grace that she would never for a minute question my mother's guidance or direction."

"A follower of the pack," Simone commented.

"Exactly. Someone who will follow very willingly and not concern herself with the reasonings behind why something was being done a certain way. In other words, someone my mother could boss around."

At this, Simone did smile. "I've known folks like that."

He laughed. "Yes, I suppose we all have. My mother is apparently their queen. You've never seen a more determined woman when it comes to planning out her son's social future. However, I've already fallen well behind her schedule. I'm afraid I've been rather hardheaded about her plans."

"What about the rest of your family?"

"My father is too busy making money to worry about how my mother spends it or who she controls in the process. My older brother, Darius O'Donnell the Third, lives back East, and that's the sum total of the O'Donnell children."

Simone seemed quite interested in his line of conversation, so Jeffery continued. "My brother's wife died a year ago, leaving him without children. My mother is rather desperate to see one of us produce an heir to the O'Donnell lineage."

"Why?" Simone asked curiously.

"Prestige, mostly. But I also think it's a matter of pride. She can have most anything money can buy and flaunts it in the faces of her friends at every opportunity, but she has no grandchildren and can't buy herself one, either. She's pressing me quite hard to marry and reminds Darius in weekly missives that a year of mourning for a young, childless man is more than enough time."

"So why haven't you married?" Simone questioned, glancing away as if realizing how personal her inquiry had become.

Jeffery lowered his arms and thoughtfully stared at his hands. "I suppose because for all the women my mother has paraded past me for my consideration, I've never found one that interested me half so much as you."

He looked up in time to watch the color drain from her face. He'd not intended to simply blurt out his interest, but there it was.

"I think you should listen to your mother's ideas of what's proper for you," Simone finally remarked. "She probably knows better what you need than you know yourself."

"Is that how you felt about your mother? Did she always know your needs better than anyone else?"

Simone's head snapped up and her eyes narrowed angrily. "My mother certainly didn't consider my needs. She was a selfish woman who thought only of herself."

Jeffery hadn't expected the angry retort, and for a moment he did nothing but stare with what he hoped was an open expression of sympathy. But even though words along the same line came to his mind, Jeffery held back from saying anything. Simone despised pity and seemed not to know what to do with sympathy. Better to remain silent and let her set the stage than to plow ahead and undo any newly gained territory.

"I'm sure, Mr. O'Donnell, that your mother has your best interests in mind. She probably knows all about what kind of wife would do you proud."

"How can you be so sure when you don't feel the same quality existed in your own mother?" he asked softly.

Simone looked down at her hands. "I'm only coming to realize just how little I know about the world around me. My mother tried to educate me, but she was a very young woman herself. Still, she knew something of the world and the things that a young person might need to understand in order to get along. However, she left me when I was ten and in her departure failed to leave me with all the elements necessary to take me to adulthood. I could speak and read and write in English and French. I knew how to better conduct myself and my tongue than most folks on the mountain only because my mother had been born a lady. But there was so much more that I didn't know."

"Such as?" Jeffery dared to ask. He could only pray she'd continue to tell him about herself.

"Such as what the rest of the world did while I was asleep at night, or how things were done in other areas of the country. She never bothered to tell me much about anything that wasn't related to our mountain home. Of course, she taught me to speak politely, conduct myself in a proper manner. She came from good breeding, she would tell me, though she scarcely said anything else about her youth or parents. I remember she used to set the table in a very pretty way and then told me how to conduct myself when at a formal dinner. I don't know why she thought I needed that kind of information when she never bothered to teach me how to . . ." Suddenly Simone seemed to realize that she was saying too much.

"How to what?" Jeffery asked casually, hoping against hope that she'd relax and continue. But it wasn't to be.

"Never mind. Regardless of her efforts, I still feel quite the ill-mannered oaf when standing next to some of the girls. They have such different backgrounds and know so much more of the world. A world that goes beyond conducting yourself properly at a dinner party."

"Well, sometime I'll have to take you out to a nice dinner and you can prove to me how good you are with those skills you've learned."

"No," Simone replied. "That wouldn't be appropriate."

"Why not?"

She shook her head. "Because we are clearly from two different worlds. You cannot possibly understand what it is to be from my world, and I can't understand what it is to be from yours."

"But by exposure you would come to better understand," Jeffery suggested.

"No."

At this, Jeffery got up and walked to the window. He didn't want Simone to see the look of frustration that was sure to be on his face. Why couldn't he make her see that he wanted to know her better? That he wasn't ashamed of her social background or her lack of financial status? Deciding it would be his only chance to reach her, Jeffery thought to try honesty.

"I could teach you all that you lack," he said, turning to watch her from across the room.

She stiffened slightly and fixed her stare on the lights overhead. "I think you should listen to your mother, Mr. O'Donnell."

"Jeffery," he stated flatly and came back to where she sat. "Call me Jeffery, and don't think to put that wall of formality between us. I want to know you better, Simone. I want you to know me."

"It will serve no purpose," she said sternly. Swinging her legs off the sofa and onto the floor, she made as if to stand, but Jeffery immediately held up a hand to stop her.

"Wait. Just hear me out." She looked at him doubtfully, then nodded. Jeffery felt a small amount of relief at this reprieve and searched his heart for what he should say. He wanted to ask about the scars on her back. He wanted to know what she was running from and why she couldn't or wouldn't tell him anything but the smallest detail of her life's story. He wanted this and so much more, and he felt so overwhelmingly confused by his need that he feared words would fail him.

"I don't want to live my life under my mother's thumb. I want to be my own man. I've refused to take up my father's work in investments and instead have chosen my own way. I love the railroad and fully plan to work my way into a job with a more substantial role with the Santa Fe line. I hate Chicago, dislike pomp and ceremony, and find you incredibly intriguing. I see the possibility for us to share a companionable friendship."

"Friendship?" Simone questioned simply.

Jeffery frowned, wondering if he should have made a stronger declaration. Neither of them knew each other very well, but he could easily find courtship an acceptable proposition. Courtship would allow him to know whether or not he and Simone would be compatible enough to make a marriage.

Marriage? Where had that thought come from? Yet Jeffery knew very well where it had come from. He'd thought of little else but Simone Irving since he'd first met her. He'd broken one rule after another in order to keep her where he could learn more about her and get to know her better. If Fred Harvey learned the truth, he'd be fired. If his mother learned the truth, he'd be disowned.

Sitting down on the sofa beside Simone, Jeffery reached out to gently touch her hand. He felt her stiffen even more, and as she tried to pull her hand away, he tightened his hold.

"Just listen to me, please. I've come to care about you, Simone. I like your company and I enjoy our conversations. You are so totally different from any other woman I've ever known. You are strong and determined and not afraid to let those qualities show. If you would just allow yourself to forget the past, I know we could have a very bright future together. There's nothing to stand in the way except your own reluctance. Please don't turn me away simply based on your lack of experience and knowledge of such matters."

Simone quickly jerked her hand from his and got to her feet. Jeffery stood just as quickly, but it was Simone's turn to hold up her hand. "No. Don't touch me again and don't try to stop me. I can't stay here any longer. I need to rest."

Jeffery wanted to say something—anything—to ensure that she would remain with him, but instead he watched her go, realizing that there was nothing he could do to offer her comfort or hope. Something had caused Simone to shield her heart from emotion, and from the looks of it, she'd felt this way for a long, long time.

"What do I do now?" he asked aloud. The plan had seemed so

clear in his mind. He had actually felt sure of his direction, but now . . .

Just then a verse from Proverbs came to mind. It had been a part of the Scriptures he'd found himself reading the night before. *"A man's heart deviseth his way: but the Lord directeth his steps."* According to Scripture, the Lord would direct his steps, but now that the moment was upon him, Jeffery wasn't entirely sure how to go about seeking the peace that came from knowing and experiencing God's direction for his steps.

He thought of the great pious prayers prayed in the cathedral of his childhood worship. He thought of his mother and father in their Sunday finery bowing in great shows of prayerful obedience. And he suddenly realized that he knew very little of the comfort of God and of the real understanding of such things. He had great hopes that his nightly studies of the Bible would lead him to a better understanding. A great deal seemed to hinge on better knowing God's plan for his life.

Perhaps that is where I need to start, he thought. Then glancing at the doorway from which Simone had just taken her exit, he added, "Perhaps that's where we both need to start."

TWENTY

SIMONE GUARDED HER HEART much the same way she guarded her memories. If she encased them both in granite, they could neither physically remind her of her needs nor visually remind her of her deeds. Her time at the Harvey House had caused her to become nonchalant about her hidden past, and when Jeffery O'Donnell declared his respectable interest in her, it had nearly been more than Simone could endure.

In the days that followed that declaration, Simone had avoided coming downstairs for any reason. Now that she was ready to work in the dining room once again, she couldn't help but feel a nervous anticipation. Would he seek her out? Would he force her to talk to him—to share his company?

She trembled just thinking of the possibility. Jeffery was unlike the other men she had known. He was thoughtful and kind, where others had been cruel and oppressive. He worried over how she felt and whether she had the things she needed, while the men of her past had cared little for feelings or needs—unless they had been their own. Securing her white hair bow and giving her appearance one final assessment, Simone drew in a deep breath and let it out in a heavy sigh.

"Are you worried about today?" Una asked sweetly.

Simone nodded. "I suppose I am."

"You'll do fine. Just take it easy and don't overdo. If you feel tired, you must tell Rachel immediately and go rest."

"I don't want to shirk my responsibilities any longer. My illness has already made it necessary to extend my training another week."

"Do you have plans for where you want to go when the training is up?" Una asked.

Simone shook her head. "Not really. I suppose I don't much care."

"I would have thought that with Mr. O'Donnell so interested in you, you might want to stay on right here in Topeka. You know they do keep some of the experienced girls on staff to help train the new arrivals."

"No, I don't want to stay." It wasn't entirely true, but for the sake of avoiding romantic entanglements, Simone felt it the only reasonable response. "Mr. O'Donnell is very nice, and I suppose he has shown me great kindness and interest, but there is nothing more than that between us."

Una smiled. "Maybe not on your part."

"Not on anyone's part," Simone murmured, knowing it was a lie.

The girls walked downstairs together, and Una continued to speak. "I'm going to Florence. It's not so very far from here, but it's much closer to Lindsborg. My family and I can see each other more often, and I'll like that much better."

"When will you be going?" Simone questioned, suddenly feeling a pang of regret.

"Next week," Una answered simply.

Simone frowned but said nothing as they stepped into the dining room. Una had been a good companion for the duration of Fred Harvey's training, and to think of her going away made Simone sad. *This is ridiculous*, she told herself. *This is the very reason I didn't want to be close to anyone here. People always go away, and caring about them only causes you to hurt when they've left you behind.*

"You will write to me, won't you?" Una asked in her rhythmic way.

Simone met her hopeful expression and nodded. "Of course."

"Oh, Simone!" Rachel declared as she came into sight. "You look wonderful. How do you feel? Are you up to this?"

"I'm fine. I'm glad to get back to work," Simone answered

honestly. Frankly, having so much leisure time had left Simone nervous and edgy. With so much time on her hands, the memories of the past were doing their best to rise up and remind her that she would never be truly free. It was only then that Simone realized she'd only temporarily exorcised her demons. The past never truly went away—it trailed behind like a faithful dog to his master.

"Simone!" several other girls called out.

A bevy of black-and-white-clad women gathered around. They were all so happy to see her, and for the life of her, Simone couldn't understand why. She'd done nothing to endear herself to any of the other Harvey Girls. She had remained to herself, speaking only when spoken to and never participating in any of the camaraderies Rachel arranged for them. Once, Fred Harvey himself had shown up to lead a Friday night dance, but Simone had quietly slipped to the confines of her room and there she had stayed until morning.

"We were so worried about you," one girl said, giving Simone an impromptu hug.

"I collapsed from the heat last year. I thought I'd never recover, but my ma nursed me back to health," said another.

"Oh, Simone, you've lost weight. We'll have to fatten you up," Bethel teased, taking hold of her arm.

Simone wanted to distance herself, but there was no hope of that now. Neither was there hope of distancing her heart from the growing feelings she had for each of her Harvey sisters. They genuinely seemed to care about her, and standing in the middle of the revelry, Simone could only silently wonder how she might ever reestablish her walls of indifference.

Rachel managed to clear the area. "We have less than an hour before the first train of the morning. I'd suggest you get busy, ladies."

They nodded, wished Simone well, then departed to their various stations. Rachel smiled and put an arm around Simone's shoulders. "I'd like it if you would join me in the office for a moment. There are a couple of things we need to discuss."

Simone felt a moment of panic. "Discuss? What things?"

Rachel was already leading her in the direction of the office. "Well, such as where you'd like to spend your contract agreement." She opened the door and ushered Simone inside. "We have basically concluded your training, and I see no reason to keep you from moving forward with the rest of the girls. You've learned quickly and know the job better than many when they leave here. The sickness may have kept you from serving, but it's only a lack of daily experience that you've missed while ill. And that hardly concerns me given your ability to pick things up so quickly."

Simone breathed a sigh of relief and took a seat opposite Rachel as the older woman sat down to her desk. "I thought perhaps," Rachel said, thumbing through some papers, "that you might like to consider the various places on the line. I know we'd already discussed your staying here in Topeka, but I don't think you're acclimated to working in this kind of heat yet. I'm worried about your health. There are some very nice spots and some others that are not quite so nice, but there is one opening at Raton."

"Raton?" Simone asked, completely unfamiliar with the town.

"It's located in the northern reaches of the New Mexico Territory. I thought of you because the area is mountainous and the climate much drier than Kansas. I've been there twice, and it's a very pretty place. It still gets very warm there, but the humidity isn't a problem. I think it might work quite well for you."

Simone nodded. "I suppose you know better than anyone else."

"There's also a spot in Florence, and I'm sure you know that is the destination Una has picked for herself."

"Yes, she just told me this morning."

"If you'd prefer to consider Florence, there's still time to let me know. I can let you stay on here in Topeka for a short time. Especially given your illness."

Simone saw the concern and compassion in Rachel's eyes and fervently wished that she could somehow remove herself from the feelings that were threatening to overflow from within. She was overwhelmed by the goodness of this woman. She had stayed up all night in order to nurse Simone and keep her from death. What more could Rachel possibly do to prove her friendship? Simone bowed her head and closed her eyes. She had to steady herself.

"Simone, are you sure you're feeling all right?" Rachel asked softly.

Simone nodded but still kept her head bowed. "I'm fine." She glanced back up and gave Rachel the briefest smile. "Honestly, I'll be just fine."

Rachel pushed back the papers she'd been toying with and leaned forward. "Simone, there's something else I'd like to talk to you about."

"What is it?" Simone met Rachel's expression and instantly realized that she'd opened herself up for something much more personal than she'd planned.

"This isn't easy for me, and I'm not usually given to prying," Rachel began. "But there's a concern I have for you that will not be easily dismissed."

"I see," Simone said in a stilted voice that she hoped would discourage Rachel's interrogation.

"Simone, I know this isn't easy for you. I just want to be your friend. I want you to trust me and know that I will help you in any way I can."

"I don't understand," Simone said, a spark of fear igniting her soul.

Rachel bit at her lower lip and looked upward as though seeking help from above. "I cared for you while you were ill—that's something you already know. But perhaps you don't realize how sick you were. You were delirious for several hours. Then, too, it was necessary for me to undress you in order to bathe you through the night." She halted, obviously uncomfortable, perhaps even uncertain as to how she might continue.

Simone shifted uneasily. "I'm grateful for your care, Rachel."

"I know that," she replied. "But that's not why I brought it up."

Simone steeled herself against what Rachel might say next. She couldn't figure out whether Rachel knew something about Garvey Davis and her escape or if she was concerned about something else.

"Simone, you have some very ugly scars on your back." The statement was made so matter-of-factly that Simone could hardly hide her sharp intake of breath. Rachel continued quickly. "Look, I know you must have suffered horribly. I know from the way you fought me during your fever that someone has hurt you greatly. I just want you to know that none of that matters anymore. I want you to feel safe here—safe wherever you work on the Santa Fe line."

Simone hadn't even realized that she'd risen to her feet until Rachel, too, stood and came around from behind the desk. "You don't have to be afraid that I'll think badly of you, Simone. No one should have to endure the misery you have obviously suffered."

"Please don't say any more," Simone murmured, barely able to form the words.

Rachel gently touched her arm. "I just want you to know that I'm your friend. I don't know where you've come from or who you might be running from, but it doesn't matter. God knows all that you've had to endure. He knows and He cares."

"He cared so much that He interceded on my behalf," Simone said sarcastically.

Rachel shook her head. "Simone, I don't know why things happen as they do, but I do know that God cares about His children. He isn't the harsh taskmaster that you make Him out to be. He's a loving father. He cares deeply for you, Simone."

Simone gathered her strength. She knew she had to put an end to Rachel's loving speech about God. She had to push Rachel away and prevent her from trying to get any closer.

"I don't know anything about loving fathers, Rachel. I'm glad that you had one, and even happier that you have pleasant memories from the past. I can't share your image of God because I have no one on which to pattern that image. Please don't pry any further. By what you saw, you should easily realize that it isn't something I wish to talk about. Please respect that."

Rachel nodded, tears welling in her eyes. Simone felt an aching in her chest and fought to ignore it. *I don't want to feel anything for her. I don't want to care.*

Rachel sniffed back tears and smiled. "I suppose I should get back to work. You do know that Jeffery's due in from Chicago, don't you?"

Simone felt her knees go weak. She had tried so hard not to think about Jeffery and the way he felt about her . . . and the way he made her feel about him. She'd worked fervently to dismiss any tempting thought that he just might be right about how things could be between them. She couldn't afford for anyone to be her friend—especially not Jeffery.

"I didn't realize he was coming to Topeka," Simone finally admitted.

Rachel smiled and walked to the door. "I can hardly keep him from coming to Topeka. He's here so much more frequently than he used to be, and I can only guess the reason."

Simone said nothing and waited for several seconds before turning to follow Rachel back to the dining room. Somehow she had to make Jeffery understand that he could no longer care about her. But in the meantime, the northbound train would soon be arriving and she needed to be on duty at her station, as Mr. Harvey required.

The number of passengers requiring breakfast were few. It was a rare moment for the Topeka Harvey House, but Simone was secretly relieved. She found it easy to get back into the routine of servicing the large-portioned meals, but in truth, she was still rather weak from her sickness. Of course, she'd never let Rachel or Henri know the truth. Both had pampered and spoiled her until she could hardly stand it. Henri had fixed special meals and had them brought to her on silver trays with beautiful china dishes. Simone had never known such elegance and beauty. Even Una maintained a special attentiveness and often left her letters unwritten to sit at Simone's bedside.

No, Simone thought, *I mustn't admit to anyone that I'm less than capable of continuing with my duties*. She continued to argue with herself throughout the aftermath of the morning meal. As she polished the silverware, she tried to imagine what she should do with her future. She had no way of knowing how much Rachel actually knew or, for that matter, suspected. If she spoke out in her delirium, it was possible that she could have said almost anything. The idea sent a chill down Simone's spine.

"Simone?" Bethel called from the archway of the hall.

Simone was startled from her quiet reverie. "Yes?"

"Mr. O'Donnell wishes to see you in the manager's office."

Simone swallowed hard and put down her polishing rag. There was no way she could avoid dealing with Jeffery, but nevertheless, it wasn't something she was looking forward to. Jeffery would no doubt restate his interest in their becoming better friends, and there was no way Simone could allow that. Simone firmly believed that when she'd made the choice to hit Garvey Davis over the head, she denied herself the right to any future relationships.

With a sigh, Simone got to her feet and slipped off the white gloves she'd been wearing. Walking down the corridor to the house manager's office, she tried to think of what she would say. Perhaps the best way to approach it would be to announce her departure for Florence or Raton.

Knocking lightly on the closed door, Simone heard Jeffery call out, "Come in."

Pushing aside her fear, Simone turned the handle and entered the room. Jeffery sat looking much the same as he had at his departure some days before. He wore a dark blue suit with a freshly starched shirt and blood red tie. His dark brown hair had been carefully parted and slicked back on either side, but it was his eyes that immediately caught Simone's attention. Locking her gaze with his, she tried to imagine why he stared at her in an almost grieved manner.

"Have a seat," he told her softly.

"I'm in the middle of polishing the silverware, Mr. O'Donnell."

"Yes, I know." He smiled slightly. "I also know we had an agreement that you would call me Jeffery."

"Jeffery, I don't have time for this. Today is my first day back on the floor, and the other girls have been greatly overworked in my absence."

"Sit down, Simone," he insisted, leaning forward.

He appeared gravely concerned about something, so Simone finally did as he told her and sat down on the edge of the nearest chair.

"Simone, you know how I feel about you. I've come to care a great deal about your well-being—"

"Don't, Jeffery," she interrupted, shaking her head. "Please don't."

"Why not, Simone?" he asked her flatly. "Why can't you trust me?"

"There are a great many reasons," Simone said, trying to sound casual.

"Such as?"

"Jeffery, I have to get back to work," she said, getting to her feet. "We can discuss this later."

"I'd like to discuss it now. Along with this," Jeffery replied, pulling out a folded sheet of paper. With slow, methodical care, Jeffery spread the paper open and flattened it out on the desk. "See for yourself. Don't you think there's some sort of explanation due me . . . Miss Dumas?"

Simone started at the use of her real name, but it was the charcoal sketch showing a likeness of her father and a detailed drawing of her own face above the word *WANTED* that caused Simone to nearly faint dead to the floor.

TWENTY-ONE

AFTER MULTIPLE MISHAPS and train delays in cities that he would just as soon forget, Louis Dumas thought Chicago the perfect cover for a man—or for that matter, a woman—trying to hide out from the law. The sheer numbers of people made the job of gaining anonymity a simple task. No one knew him or had any reason to care about him, and this worked greatly to his advantage. The bustling crowd seemed unconcerned with the filthy man, and Louis found this fit perfectly with his plan.

The first thing he'd seen as a necessity wasn't a place to live or even a good stiff drink but rather a bath and change of clothes. Louis realized that should anyone come after him, they'd be looking for a trapper named Louis Dumas. They'd have their sketches and drawings of a burly fellow in roughly fashioned buckskin, with a face full of hair to match the shoulder-length mass on his head. Keeping that in mind, Louis soaked in the tub of a private bathhouse and figured out how he would rearrange his appearance. Only hours ago he'd managed to steal a suitcase from a well-dressed stranger bound for Cleveland. The man had sat opposite Louis on the train and boasted of his wealth and the fact that he owned not one but two very nice suits. Louis figured the man to be too prideful for his own good, and while the man dozed through the stop in Chicago, Louis simply relieved him of his burden and exited the train. It had been so simple. With the case sitting beside the tub, Louis contemplated how he would pull off his charade.

"You gonna want a shave as well as a haircut?" the proprietor called from the doorway.

"I figured on it," Louis replied, climbing out of the now tepid water. He pulled a towel around his body and grabbed his case. "No sense dressing till we get it done."

The proprietor, a short, bald fellow who apparently was used to dealing with Louis's kind, only nodded and pulled back the curtain. "Have a seat in here." Louis followed him into a room off the main area. "This will give you a bit more privacy."

Louis didn't know if the man sensed his desire to remain anonymous or, rather, desired to keep Louis, in his undressed state, out of his main business area. Either way, Louis didn't care. "I want it all cut off. I want the hair short and the beard and mustache gone. No, wait . . . leave a small mustache."

"Sure thing, mister."

Louis sat quietly as the man went to work sharpening his razor. He would have to think through his plans for finding Simone. After all, the same secrecy afforded Louis by the overpopulated city was also afforded his daughter.

"But she don't know what she's doing. She ain't never been alone in a town like this."

"What'd you say, mister?" the barber asked from where he stood.

"Nothin' . . . just thinkin' out loud," Louis muttered.

Louis lost track of time while he contemplated Simone. Over and over he considered his plans for their lives. She would have no other choice but to go wherever he decided to go. She was, after all, his responsibility. She was also a very beautiful young woman, and there was a great deal of wealth to be had in what she could provide. It was simply a matter of replenishing what he'd already spent and then finding Simone.

"Whereabouts you from, stranger?" the barber asked as he clipped Louis's hair.

"Everywhere and nowhere," Louis replied, hating the nosy question. The man needed to keep his questions to himself and leave Louis to think through what was to be done.

"I see you're still carrying your case with you. You need a place to stay?"

Louis realized the man's potential. "Maybe. I'd really like to get in a decent game of poker and have a few drinks. You know a place like that?"

The man leaned close, as if conspiring with Louis. "There's a place just up the street. My sister runs it. I think you'll find she keeps a good room and charges the right price. If you want to know about anything at all that's going on in this city, my sister would be the one to tell you."

Louis nodded. "Sounds good."

Very little was exchanged after that. Louis was too deep in thought to concern himself with what the little man had to tell him. His priorities had to be money and Simone. Nothing else mattered as much as those two things.

After surveying the barber's work, Louis was dumbfounded by the change in his appearance. No one would ever consider him to be a backwoods trapper. His black hair glowed from the application of hair oil and tonic, and his face, a bit pale from the winter months, seemed far more refined than he had recalled. Perhaps it came with age. After all, Louis had worn a beard and moustache for the last thirty years.

He paid the man, obtained directions to his sister's house, and dressed in the stolen clothes. He congratulated himself on sizing up someone who had a reasonably similar build. The only flaw was that his moccasin boots peered out from beneath the trousers. Perhaps he could purchase a pair of shoes after settling up with the barber's sister for a room.

It was a completely different Louis Dumas who stepped from the barber and bath establishment. Should anyone on the street have glanced his way, they would simply have considered him a man of means, down on his luck. The black broadcloth suit had seen some wear but was of quality construction, and therefore it spoke of having come from one of the better tailors. The white shirt, though slightly wrinkled and minorly stained, was scarcely noticeable once Louis buttoned up the vest and coat.

Joining the flow of people on the street, Louis tried to keep his mind clear and his eyes open to anything that might suggest his daughter's whereabouts. It seemed a long shot, he knew, but it was always possible that being without any money other than that which she'd obtained from the sale of Garvey Davis's horse and gear, Simone would have stayed in relatively close proximity to the railroad station. Then again, it was always possible that someone had taken pity on her because of her looks. Who could say? Louis's biggest problem was that enough time had passed between Simone's arrival and his that the girl could literally be anywhere.

Then a bad thought overshadowed the man's thinking. It was very possible that Simone had not gotten off the train in Chicago. Or that if she had, she had merely traded it for another and had headed off again to distance herself from the possibility of Wyoming retribution.

Grumbling and muttering to himself, Louis hardly realized he'd come to the intersection where he was to turn north. Glancing up at the street markers, his eyes were drawn instead to a small, makeshift Wanted poster. Stepping closer, but trying to appear intent on the street's name, Louis saw the remarkable sketch of his daughter and the marginally acceptable rendering of himself.

> WANTED: Louis and Simone Dumas, father and daughter, for questioning in the murder of Garvey Davis, Uniontown, Wyoming. Notify local authorities with information regarding the whereabouts of either party.

Louis quickly calmed his frazzled nerves when he realized that there was no resemblance between him and the man on the poster—even before his shave and haircut. He doubted that even the barber would consider him as the man in the poster. But Simone's sketch was the very image of the girl. If anyone had knowledge of her and saw that poster, there would be no doubt of who she was.

Smiling to himself, Louis thought of how he might use this to his advantage. If the posters were up here in Chicago, the law must believe Simone to still be in the city. That would only prove to aid Louis in his own search.

Glancing around to see who might be watching, Louis pulled down the poster and started to fold it up.

"You know those two?" a voice called out from behind him.

Louis turned to see a rather rough-looking fellow dressed in a brown tweed suit that had seen better days. "Not sure. I was thinkin' my wife might know 'em."

The man nodded. "Well, here." He handed Louis a card. "If it proves to be true and she has any idea where they are, just come around and let me know. I collect scum like those two and turn them into the law."

"A bounty hunter?" Louis questioned.

"The best," the man said, smiling.

Louis nodded. "Ain't promisin' nothin', but iffen she knows 'em, I'll send her over."

"I'm obliged," the man said, tipping his hat to Louis before taking off in the opposite direction.

Louis looked down at the paper and smiled. "Ah, Simone. It's just a matter of time before I find you." Now he clearly had all he needed to persuade Simone to run away with him and do as she was told. All he would have to do upon finding her was show her the poster and threaten to turn her into the law himself if she refused to cooperate.

TWENTY-TWO

JEFFERY WAS TOTALLY UNPREPARED for Simone's reaction to the Wanted poster. He had prayed all the way back from Chicago that the poster was just an odd coincidence. Yet he knew in his heart there were too many things that pointed to it being a perfect explanation of the endless questions surrounding Simone.

Seeing her pale and shaken, Jeffery got to his feet and went to the door. Glancing in the hall to make sure no one else was lingering outside, he closed the door and turned to where Simone sat, her face buried in her hands. What should he say? How should he handle the situation? He didn't want to believe that she was capable of conspiring to commit murder. It hardly seemed to fit her character and nature, yet there had to be some reason for her being this upset.

Taking his seat behind the desk, Jeffery watched her for several moments. She wasn't crying, at least not that he could hear. It seemed almost as if she hoped by hiding her face she could somehow hide the truth, as well.

"Simone, I'm sorry for upsetting you like this," Jeffery began. "I think you know me well enough by now to know that I would never do anything to harm you."

At this, she looked up with her dark eyes. They seemed to search Jeffery's face, as if contemplating the truth of his statement. How he wished he could put her mind at ease.

"I want you to tell me the whole story. Just trust me to understand, Simone."

"It's all true," she murmured, looking away. "I am Simone Dumas, and Garvey Davis is dead because of me."

Jeffery felt his throat constrict. "What happened?"

Simone licked her lips and fell back against the chair as though completely spent. "It's such a long story."

"We have all the time you need. I want to hear it. I need to hear it from you," Jeffery replied, then added, "please."

Simone's face contorted. "I lived with my father in Wyoming, some twelve miles from a run-down place called Uniontown," she began. "My father was a trapper, but the land was played out. One day, he came back from town and announced his decision to sell off everything, including me. He planned to leave Wyoming for the gold mines of Colorado. He sold everything to Garvey Davis."

"How could he include you in on that deal?" Jeffery questioned. He couldn't imagine what Simone was really saying.

"He sold me to Garvey Davis as a wife."

"A wife!" Jeffery exclaimed, louder than he'd meant to. He'd never for a moment imagined that Simone was married to the Davis man.

"Well, we didn't have a preacher in Uniontown. Churches and religion didn't seem overly important to the folks around there. So my father gave me to Mr. Davis to live as his wife until the preacher came around." Simone grew quiet.

Jeffery still found it hard to believe that a father would sell his child to another man. What kind of person would do such a thing? He had a million questions he longed to ask, but it was clear that Simone felt significant pain just in revealing the minimal circumstances to him.

"Did your father leave for Colorado?"

"Yes," Simone managed to say. She took a deep breath, and Jeffery watched as she seemed to will herself to be strong. "He left. I was there alone with Mr. Davis, and when he asked for supper, I fed him. While he ate, I packed, determined that I could never be this man's wife." She paused and looked at Jeffery for the first time since admitting the truth. "I didn't understand then, and I don't understand now, why I felt so strongly that I couldn't do what my father expected." She shuddered and grimaced. "But I couldn't let that man touch me. I just couldn't."

"You could hardly be expected to allow such a thing," Jeffery said, knowing the indignity of the entire matter was clear in his tone.

"But I was expected to allow it," Simone said, closing her eyes as if seeing it all again. "He heard me packing, or maybe he simply realized I was no longer in view. Anyway, he came searching for me. I was in the only other part of the cabin, the sleeping area. He thought that somehow indicated a willingness to . . . to . . ."

"It's all right. I fully understand what he expected," Jeffery said. He felt an angry rage surge inside him. To imagine a poor, defenseless girl such as Simone left to the mercy of a total stranger was one thing. But to imagine that this man intended to take her as his wife, even if it included rape, was more than he could calmly deal with.

"When he grabbed me, I did the only thing I could. I fought back." She opened her eyes but again focused on the ceiling rather than look at Jeffery. "I somehow put my hand on the water pitcher and . . . and I hit him over the head with it. I didn't mean to kill him, I only meant to stop him." Her voice was flat, emotionless, and totally resigned.

Jeffery wondered what comfort he could offer her, but there didn't appear to be anything he could say. She had admitted her guilt and was wanted by the law, but he couldn't just turn her over to be hanged or imprisoned. Not given the circumstances.

"There was blood everywhere," she murmured before he had a chance to speak. "I was terrified. I still am." She shook her head, and Jeffery wished he could clear the vision that most likely haunted her mind. "All I could think of was getting away before someone found out what I'd done. I took Mr. Davis's horse and gear and what little I had that belonged to me, and I fled. I wandered for days, not knowing my way to any place but Uniontown, and of course I couldn't go there."

"Simone, it was self-defense. You didn't mean to kill the man. Therefore, it isn't murder."

Simone gave him a look that almost suggested amusement. "Call it what you will, the man is still dead. The blow came from my hand,

and now I have to live with the consequences. The funny thing is, at least I finally know the truth. I've worried and fretted for months now as to whether or not I'd actually killed the man." She looked away and sorrow edged her voice. "At least I know."

"But, Simone, you're wanted by the law," Jeffery replied. "There's obviously an all-out search for you. If I learned of this so easily, no doubt others will remember you, too. Mrs. Taylor, for one. She'll no doubt see the posters. After all, they're posted at most every street corner in a wide radius of the Chicago train station."

"I think it would be best if I get my things collected," Simone said, starting to get up from the chair. "I should leave here before they come looking for me."

"No!" Jeffery declared, coming around the desk. He took hold of her and gently pushed her back into the chair, then squatted down beside her. "You must give me time to think this out." Simone appeared surprised by his reaction but said nothing. "I can't just let them take you away."

"I'm wanted by the law," Simone replied very frankly, "for a murder I committed. I can't keep running from it. Obviously the only thing to be done is to accept my punishment and deal with the matter. They can only put me to death, and believe me, Jeffery," she said softly, almost sympathetically, "there are worse things than death."

"And well I know it, which is why I won't turn you over to rot in some vile prison cell."

"But I'm already in prison," Simone countered. She appeared to be so greatly relieved by her confession of guilt that she almost seemed to radiate peace. "I've been in prison for most of my life. My father is a hideous monster of a man who thinks nothing of striking down those who dare to question him. Had I refused to stay with Mr. Davis, my father would simply have taken matters into his hands and beat me until I would have been unable to run away."

"Is that how you came by the scars on your back?" Jeffery asked softly.

Simone looked surprised for only a moment. "So Rachel told you about that? Well, I suppose it couldn't be helped. Yes, my father is the one who gave me those scars. He was a harsh and cruel taskmaster."

"Obviously so, if he would give you to a complete stranger." Jeffery reached up to touch Simone's face. She flinched but didn't refuse the touch. "I can't let them take you away. I won't let them. You have come to be much too important to me. Can't you see that my feelings for you are sincere? I have only the very best of intentions toward you."

Where the fright of being faced with confessing Garvey Davis's death had not caused Simone to flee, the declaration of Jeffery's obvious desire for her brought sheer panic. Simone jumped up from the chair, nearly sending Jeffery backward.

"Wait!" he called out as Simone headed for the door. "Please hear me out."

Simone turned, her face pale. "I can't be important to you, Jeffery. If you can't see that now, then there's nothing else I can say to convince you. You would always have this hanging over your head, just as I do now. I can't do that to anyone. It's better that I turn myself in and be done with it."

"Just listen to what I have to say." He took a few hesitant steps toward Simone and held out his arms as if to show himself to be harmless. "I just want to help. Let me figure a way out of this for you."

"I can't put you and Rachel under that kind of pressure. You would no doubt be in all manner of trouble for keeping me from the law."

"Just give me a few days . . . please."

She looked at him with such a sad expression that Jeffery longed only to hold her close. He couldn't bear that she was alone in this, and mindless of what she might think, he crossed the distance between them and pulled her into his arms. Tightening his hold on her as she strained against him, Jeffery hushed her. "I'm not going to hurt you. Please believe me. I would never treat you like your father did or force myself upon you like Mr. Davis."

Simone settled against him. "There are other ways to hurt a person," she whispered.

"Such as?"

"Such as caring too much about having them in your life, only to watch them walk away."

Jeffery loosened his hold with one arm and reached up to lift her face to meet his. "And someone hurt you that way?" he asked gently.

She nodded. "My mother. She took my brother and left to find help and never came back."

"I'm so sorry," he said, stroking her cheek with his thumb. "But you can't judge all people based on the actions of one."

"No, but neither do you have to set yourself up to be hurt that way again. If I don't feel anything for anyone, then I don't have to experience that kind of loss."

"But, my dear, neither do you experience the joy and happiness that can come from such unions."

Simone closed her eyes, as if the matter was too painful to even consider. "It's a price I'm willing to pay."

"Well, I'm not willing to let you," Jeffery replied, gently touching his lips to hers. He kissed her only for a moment, afraid to linger for fear of scaring her off for good. But when he pulled away, there was evidence of a single tear that had escaped her tightly closed eyes. "Don't tell me I mean nothing to you," he said, tracing the wetness on her cheek.

Simone's body relaxed in his arms. "I don't want you to mean anything to me. Can't you understand the difference?"

Jeffery smiled. "It's much too late for that. I think if you search your heart, you'll find me there."

Simone pulled away and opened the door to leave. "My heart is dead, Jeffery. No one can live there."

"Keep telling yourself that, Simone. Maybe one of these days you'll finally believe it," Jeffery called after her.

He stared at her retreating figure until she'd passed into the dining room and out of sight. Closing the door, he gazed at the empty office and felt a sudden pang of loneliness. Jeffery felt at a loss—he didn't know what to do or how to handle the situation.

Running a hand through his hair, Jeffery glanced over to his suitcase. He went immediately to it and opened the lid, searching as he did for what he knew would help. Finding his Bible, he took it to the desk and sat back down.

"Father, you know I'm new to this. At least as far as looking up answers for myself instead of waiting for a Sunday morning service. I don't know how to help Simone, Lord. I don't know what to do next.

You know I care about her. You know I care a great deal."

He paused, looking at the Bible and thinking of his last visit home. He had mentioned Simone to his mother—not by name, but by occupation. She had been livid that he would even dare to suggest that such a woman interested him as a wife. She fell immediately into a vaporous faint, complaining that her children would no doubt be the death of her, before recovering to rant and rave at him throughout his remaining time in Chicago.

Her comments were unending. She knew better than he did who would make a good wife. She had the perfect woman already chosen for him, and Jeffery, she said, was a complete and utter fool to consider anyone else.

"Maybe I am a fool," he thought aloud. "It certainly wouldn't be the first time I had erred in judgment. But, Lord," he resumed his prayer, "I want to be wise. I want to do the right thing—be the man you would have me be."

He leafed through the pages of the Bible, hoping and praying that something might present itself as a help in his confusion. But the pages looked foreign and the messages unclear. How could he possibly hope to gain knowledge from the Bible when he knew so little about truly seeking God? Just then he stopped and looked down at the page, a feeling of complete inadequacy washing over him.

"But rather seek ye the kingdom of God," he read silently, *"and all these things shall be added unto you."* Jeffery pondered the verse for several moments. *But I am seeking God. I see the need and understand my failings.* He closed the Bible, still contemplating the Scripture. Simone said her heart was dead and that no one could live there. Did that include God? Perhaps that was the answer to the problem. If Simone sought God and opened her heart to Him . . .

Oh, how Jeffery wished he better understood spiritual matters. How could a man spend his entire life going to church on Sunday and still not understand what he'd heard?

"Show me, Father," he prayed. "Show me what to do and how to do it. Show me how to help Simone so that she might willingly give her heart to both of us."

TWENTY-THREE

CHICAGO HAD NOT TREATED Louis Dumas kindly. Although he'd managed to keep his head above water by financing his lifestyle through back-street games of poker and blackjack, little else had come to benefit him. He'd seen nothing of Simone. He'd made it a regular habit to visit the Dearborn Station daily, just in case she might magically appear, but day after day it was the same. Simone had simply vanished, and Louis was rapidly losing patience.

"It's been nearly two weeks," he muttered to himself. Two weeks and he'd not had a single clue as to where Simone had gone.

She could be anywhere, he reasoned, the thought driving him crazy. *She should be with me. We should be on our way to Colorado. I could have struck it rich by now*. These thoughts were a constant mockery as they continually coursed through his brain.

He walked past several eating establishments before settling on a shop he'd come to know. The woman who owned the place was overly generous to Louis, heaping big portions of food on his plate and always encouraging him to stay past closing time.

"Ah, I wondered if I'd see you today, Mr. Lewis," a plump blonde called from the counter where she was tending to other customers.

Louis smiled. He'd assumed the name of Mr. Lewis from the first moment he'd laid eyes on the Wanted poster. It suited him well enough, he thought. Sounds important enough without being pretentious.

"Rosie, I see your cooking has brought them in again," Louis laughed, waving an arm past the crowded dining room.

The buxom woman laughed and pushed a stray curl behind her ear. "Nonsense. They come because the prices are cheap and the food doesn't kill them. Can't say the same for all eating establishments in this town." She poured Louis a cup of coffee without even asking if that was his interest. He took a seat on a stool at the counter while Rosie continued her chatter. "I heard down at Ferguson's the fish spoiled and it kilt a man." This brought a strange kind of laughter from the other men at her counter.

"I heard the man was hit over the head with the fish and that's what kilt him, Rosie darlin'," one of the diners called out.

"Yeah, well, it was still Ferguson's fish what kilt him." They all laughed at this, and even Louis enjoyed the chummy camaraderie.

"How about one of those fine beefsteaks you fix up?" Louis asked.

"Sure," Rosie replied, batting her blond lashes seductively. "It'll take a bit of time to fix it up right."

"Take your time," Louis countered, used to the way this woman did business. "I'm in no hurry."

Zack Matthews had just about reached the end of his patience in his search for Simone and Louis Dumas. He had known all along it would be a long shot coming to Chicago, and now, with not one but three wires from his father—all encouraging him to come home and forget the case—Zack felt completely defeated. But he couldn't just walk away from this search. He had to prove to his father that he could finish the job and attain the justice he sought to uphold.

But what bothered him even more was the effect the city had on him. He wanted to sketch it all down and take it back to show his father and mother. He wanted to make a record of every face and establishment that he'd visited. A bit of time had been given over to this, especially when he'd taken his first view of the lake they called Michigan. He could still see the endless shoreline and the wondrous way the water looked when the sun shone down upon it. It sparkled and flickered like a light being turned off and on. He'd done his best to sketch it all out, but his attempt didn't do God's handiwork justice.

Then, too, he had never known such commotion as what went on around the Dearborn Station. There had to be several hundred people coming in and going out of the city on a daily basis. Zack had always presumed Laramie to be a small, albeit busy town, but Chicago made Laramie seem almost insignificant. It also added to his discouragement.

"How can I find a needle in a haystack," he muttered, closing up the local police station's book of *Notorious and Dangerous Criminals*. The only reason he'd hung around to look at the book was in the hopes that someone might come forward with information regarding Simone.

"Hey, are you Matthews?" a man called out to him.

Zack looked up to see a uniformed policeman coming toward him. "What can I do for you?"

"I was told to give you this," he said, handing Zack a piece of paper. "A Mrs. Taylor saw one of your Wanted posters. Thinks she knows where the young woman was headed."

Zack nearly overturned the table trying to get to his feet. "Honestly?" He took up the paper and read the address. "How do I get to this place?"

The officer spent the next few minutes trying to instruct Zack on the proper route to take, only to be interrupted twice by other officers who assured Zack that there were easier ways to get from the station to Mrs. Taylor's boardinghouse. When everyone had exhausted their suggestions, Zack made his way onto the street, donning his out-of-place Stetson with new determination.

He felt as though the weight on his shoulders had been lifted—at least in part. He'd know better after talking to Mrs. Taylor as to whether he could finally put the burden aside altogether and bring in the murderer of Garvey Davis.

"So when I saw the poster, I couldn't help but believe it was the same young woman who'd come to my house a few months back," Mrs. Taylor told Zack.

"Just how long ago would this have been?" he asked, hoping her words would coincide with the time Simone would have left Wyoming. They did.

"She rode in from Cheyenne with a good friend of mine, Grace Masterson is her name. Grace is an honorable woman with a good reputation, but sometimes she doesn't think things through. And obviously she is given over to feeling sorry for strangers. She directed Miss Dumas to my house." Elvira Taylor barely paused to draw breath, and before he could speak a word, she continued. "She meant well, don't you know. She knows I run a respectable place and it was her opinion that Miss Dumas was of a respectable sort. I must say, the woman didn't seem overly complicated. She came directly here from the station upon my friend's recommendation."

Zack jumped in. "And did she stay with you for long?"

"I rented her a room for just one night. It's a right nice room." She leaned forward conspiratorially and added, "We have running water and electricity."

"So why didn't she stay longer with you?"

"She was hired on immediately with the Harvey Company."

"The Harvey Company?"

Mrs. Taylor nodded and poured Zack another cup of coffee before responding. "Fred Harvey runs eating establishments along the Santa Fe Railroad. He calls his places Harvey Houses, and he hires young women of quality to wait the tables." Then without pausing to catch her breath, Elvira Taylor asked, "Is she really wanted for murder?"

"Just questioning," Zack replied, stirring sugar into his coffee. Mrs. Taylor offered him another pastry, and since it'd been a long time since he'd had breakfast, Zack quickly accepted.

"Doesn't hardly seem possible that a little mite like her could have done murder," the old woman said, taking a seat opposite Zack on a well-worn sofa. "She seemed the respectable sort, although she was extremely young. I'm not at all sure that she met the requirement of eighteen for Mr. Harvey's employment. My daughter also shares this opinion."

Zack was puzzled, having no idea what Elvira Taylor's daughter had to do with any of it. Before he could inquire as to what she meant,

Mrs. Taylor began to resume her chatter.

"I saw that poster and I knew right off that it was the same Simone who stayed in my place. I thought there couldn't possibly be another girl with eyes like hers. I don't rightly know how a person could put pen to paper and come up with such a near likeness, but that poster did the job."

"Thank you," Zack replied. "I drew the sketch myself. I'd like to draw another if you think it would help me. I mean, if she changed her appearance for her new job, or maybe even changed it in order to look less like the woman on that poster."

"Oh, she didn't change much, but," Elvira Taylor puffed out her chest, appearing to take on a sense of great importance, "I don't think it would hurt for you to draw another picture of her. After all, she could be doing her hair a lot different by now, and now that I think about it, when she cleaned up to go to her appointment with the Harvey Company, she totally transformed."

Zack nodded, stuffed the last pieces of the pastry in his mouth, and wiped his hands on his jeans before reaching into his back pocket for his small sketch pad. Taking a quick swallow of the steaming coffee, he nodded. "We might as well go ahead with this first."

Elvira rattled on for nearly half an hour. At first she concentrated on Simone's appearance, but it wasn't long before she was fascinated by Zack's ability to draw. She quickly asked if he might do a sketch of her, just so that she could send it to her daughter, and although Zack felt pressed for time, he relented and sketched out the old woman while she talked.

"There always appeared to be something troubling that child," Elvira said. "But I don't believe her to be a killer."

"Why is that?" Zack asked, slanting his pencil stub to shade the area of shadows around Mrs. Taylor's face. The sketched portrait was taking rapid shape.

"It just wasn't in her eyes. Murderers have a look about them, don't you know. I just don't think she had it in her to do murder. She was so quiet and well-behaved. I didn't know her long, but my daughter writes of her and is very fond of her."

Zack nearly dropped his pencil. "What do you mean? Does your daughter know Simone Dumas?"

"I should hope so. She's the poor girl's supervisor in Topeka."

"Topeka?"

"That's right," Elvira responded, trying her best to catch a quick glance at the sketch in Zack's hand. "My daughter trains Harvey Girls in Topeka, Kansas."

Zack nodded, weighing the information carefully. "So Miss Dumas was hired on by the Harvey Company and sent to Topeka, where your daughter is in the process of training her to wait tables for Fred Harvey's restaurants."

"Exactly right."

He sketched a bit longer before asking his next question. "What is your daughter's name?"

"Rachel. Miss Rachel Taylor. She isn't married, but she'll make a fine wife one day. If," Elvira stressed, "she can find the right fellow. A woman can't be too careful these days, and while my Rachel once fell for the wrong sort, she was quickly made aware of the man's compromising nature . . ." she leaned forward and whispered, "before it was too late."

Zack nodded but said nothing. Now he only needed to get the address of the Harvey House in Topeka and the address of Mrs. Taylor's daughter. Putting the final touches on the simple sketch, he tore the page out from his book and handed it to the older woman. He watched as she beamed at the likeness, wondering if she realized he'd left out the better portion of her wrinkled, aged appearance from marring what had most likely once been a very attractive face.

"You do good work," she told him. "Why don't you stay on for lunch as payment?"

"No, I really should get on with investigating this new lead. Can you give me your daughter's address in Topeka, and maybe that of the Harvey restaurant?"

"I can give you both, for they're one and the same," Mrs. Taylor said with a laugh. "Here, lend me that notepaper of yours, and I'll write it down proper for you."

Zack handed over his book and waited patiently while the woman jotted down the address. "Much obliged," he murmured when she had finished.

"You won't have any trouble finding it," she said, getting to her feet as he stood. "Not if you take the Santa Fe to Topeka. Stops right at the depot and that's where all the action takes place."

"Well, I thank you again," Zack said, anxious to make his way to the Dearborn Station.

"Say, would you mind just taking this with you to Topeka?" Elvira asked, handing the sketch back to Zack. "Just give it to my Rachel when you see her. Maybe you could even make a picture of her for me."

"Perhaps," Zack said, taking the paper back in hand. At least it would make for a good way to open the door between himself and the unmarried Miss Taylor. Giving the old woman a nod, Zack pocketed his book and pencil and took up his hat. "Thanks for the coffee and such."

"You're certainly welcome," Elvira replied, following him to the door. "You just come back if you need anything at all."

Zack assured her he would before hurrying down the street in the direction of what he hoped was the train depot. He had spent enough time in the area that he should know it by heart, but it seemed to him the place was constantly changing, and after taking his fourth wrong turn, he hailed a hack and climbed aboard in complete frustration.

After directing the driver to the station, Zack anxiously picked at the material of his jean-clad legs. He was finally on his way! Now he would find Simone Dumas, and perhaps in locating her, he would also locate her father. It was just a matter of time before he had his answers and learned the truth of Garvey Davis's murder.

"Dearborn," the driver soon called back to him, and Zack quickly paid him and made his way into the busy station.

"When's the next train for Topeka, Kansas?" Zack asked ticket agent.

The man looked up at Zack and then to the clock on the wall. "Looks like you made it just in time," he answered in a slow, lazy drawl. "Train leaves in ten minutes."

"What?" Zack asked, finding the news a surprise. He'd not given much thought as to when the next train might take him toward Topeka, but this seemed too providential to be chalked off to mere luck.

"Train leaves from track three in ten minutes. You'll have to change trains in Kansas City."

"That's fine," Zack replied, suddenly realizing that he'd had no time to go back to his boardinghouse to retrieve his change of clothes. "Say," he asked, taking the ticket from the man, "is there someone who could take a message for me?"

"Where to?"

Zack gave the address to the man and added, "If I'm to catch the train, I need to send word about holding my things."

The man nodded. "You can leave the message here, and for ten cents I can send a boy over to deliver it."

Zack thanked the man and crossed through the massive station house to make his way to the right track. He glanced in one direction and then the other. They had certainly made this place big enough.

"You meeting a pretty lady at the station?" an elderly voice called from behind him.

Zack turned to find a woman selling flowers. He shook his head and smiled. "Not exactly, ma'am," he replied. "I'm going to Topeka to meet a pretty lady."

Louis Dumas couldn't believe his eyes when Zack Matthews fairly raced his way into the Dearborn Station. Of all the people in the world, he'd not expected to find the young lawman here. Unable to contain his curiosity, Louis followed at a safe distance and hid behind a pillar while Matthews did business with the ticket agent. He seemed quite animated about something, Louis thought, and the idea that perhaps Matthews had managed to locate Simone crossed his mind in a blaze of excitement.

Maintaining his place behind the pillar, Louis waited as Matthews made his way across the terminal. Then following at a steady pace, Louis found himself alongside a passenger train. He watched the old flower woman approach Matthews and barely heard the exchange between them. But it was enough.

"I'm going to Topeka to meet a pretty lady," Matthews told the old woman.

Louis, upon hearing Matthews' comment, determined he had to be going in search of Simone. He just had to be!

"All 'board!"

The call rang out, shattering Louis's thoughts. Making a mad dash back to the ticket agent, Louis barely was able to pant out the word, "Topeka!"

"Next train leaves in the morning," the agent said in a slow, steady tone.

"No! I want the train that's leaving right now."

The agent looked at him blankly. "I'm sorry, sir, you're too late," the agent replied. He paused, looked around the ticket area as if trying to decide whether he could share the next bit of information with Louis. Finally he spoke. "I can book you on the morning train."

Louis growled in disgust and slapped his money down on the counter. In the distance he heard the mournful cry of steam whistles and growled again. "The morning train, then," he answered sharply. Surely Simone and Matthews would keep that long.

TWENTY-FOUR

SIMONE KNEW SHE SHOULD be polishing the silver downstairs, but instead she paced the small confines of her room and tried to think what was to be done. It was clear that if the Wanted posters had reached Chicago and Jeffery, it would only be a matter of time until Rachel's mother and her friend Grace recognized the sketches and went to the law. And if they did that, then Simone was doomed.

On the other hand, Simone thought, sitting down hard on her bed, *I'm already doomed. I'm a murderess, and I deserve whatever punishment is meted out to me. It won't matter to the authorities in Wyoming that I didn't mean for Garvey Davis to die. It will only matter that by my hand a man is dead*. She shuddered and put her hand to her throat.

"They'll probably hang me," she whispered.

The sudden knock at her door nearly undid Simone's fragile state of mind. "Come in."

Rachel appeared, her expression one of extreme sympathy and kindness. "Are you ill? I saw you rush up here and worried that perhaps you had overdone it today."

"No, it isn't that," Simone said, shaking her head.

Rachel smiled and closed the door behind her. "Then what is it?"

"It's nothing."

Rachel bit her lower lip and took a step forward. "Simone, there's something I want to tell you. Something that you might not care to hear, but . . ." She fell silent for a moment, and to Simone it seemed that she wrestled mentally with the words she was about to say.

Rachel pulled up a chair and positioned it very close to where Simone sat on the bed. She took her seat, chewing thoughtfully on her lip. In Simone's eyes, Rachel looked as if she'd suddenly aged several years.

"Say what you will, Rachel," Simone finally offered. It was killing her to await what might or might not come. Did Rachel already know the truth? Had Jeffery told her? Had she guessed?

Rachel surprised her by reaching out to take hold of her hands. "Simone, I want very much to be a friend to you. I feel a kinship with you that I've not felt with any of the other girls. Oh, I've liked them well enough," she said, pausing with a smile. "But you are different. I knew it from the very start."

As Rachel held her hand, it was easy for Simone to remember Winifred Dumas's gentle voice and touch. But as Simone struggled against the memory, a bigger discomfort grew in its place.

"I know you believe yourself responsible for something quite heinous. You spoke of it when you were delirious," Rachel said matter-of-factly. "You spoke of not meaning to kill him."

Simone felt completely backed into a corner. Not only did Jeffery know her deeds, but now she would have to confess them to Rachel. She shook her head and sighed. If Elvira Taylor saw the Wanted posters, there would be little wasted time in letting her daughter know all about Simone's shaded past.

"I didn't want to say anything," Rachel told her softly. "I had hoped you would trust and confide in me."

Simone looked up and saw a reflection of sincerity in Rachel's green eyes. "I've never had a friend, Rachel. I know nothing of trusting people because people have never availed themselves to me in that manner. I've only known brutality and betrayal . . . and neither leave much room for confidences."

"I'm sure that what you say is true, but I wanted to make a difference. I wanted to be the first. I sensed from your first day that you were very reserved, desiring nothing but to be shut off from the rest of the world. But that's not good for any person."

"Someone else once told me that," Simone remembered. "I knew this old woman, a half-breed Indian named Naniko. After my mother left me, Naniko became the closest thing to a friend I've ever known. She told me it wasn't good to be alone. I guess because she saw me that way so much of the time."

"Why were you left alone?" Rachel gently asked.

Simone shrugged. "I don't suppose I know for sure. My father was a trapper, and he was gone a good part of the time checking his traps and searching for better hunting grounds. When he was home he beat us and railed at us until he fell into a drunken sleep, only to get up and repeat the procedure the next day. My mother decided to leave when I was about ten years old. He had beaten her so badly her arm was broken." Simone remembered the scene as if it were yesterday. "She took my baby brother, and I never saw her again."

"She left you there!" Rachel gasped. "How could she leave you behind?"

"I asked her the same thing," Simone replied, the tightness in her chest threatening to cut off her air supply. "I had just recovered from the measles, but I was still too weak to travel. It was cold and my mother feared for all of us. She said she could go faster and easier if I remained behind."

"And she promised to come back for you," Rachel remembered from the handwritten note in the Bible.

"Yes," Simone said, nodding. "But she never did." She purposely avoided telling Rachel that her father had killed her mother and brother. She didn't want to acknowledge the pain of that final loss.

They fell silent for several moments, and in that time Simone realized how much she had shared with Rachel, how good it felt to unburden her soul. Knowing that Rachel genuinely cared for her was not the encumbering grief that Simone had thought it would be. Instead, it was rather freeing. Just to know that someone else knew her woes and still remained to listen—still held her hand as though she'd not just heard the most offensive thing in the world.

Would Rachel have said how sorry she was, Simone might have ended the conversation then and there. Instead, Rachel patted her hand

and nodded as if the pieces of the puzzle were suddenly falling into place.

"So you grew up under your father's heavy hand, with him no doubt taking out his anger for your mother upon your back. He beat you because he couldn't beat her," Rachel said, her voice barely audible.

"He beat me because he hated me," Simone replied frankly.

"Why? Why should he hate his own child?"

Simone shook her head. "I don't imagine I'll ever know that for sure. I used to think it was because I was a girl and he had wanted a son. But even that shouldn't make a man so angry. I guess he found me wanting, and in that inadequacy he could not reconcile the situation except with violence."

"He was the one to be found inadequate and wanting," Rachel said, suddenly regaining strength in her own anger. "How dare he take out his grief on a helpless child! No wonder you had to defend yourself and kill him."

Simone startled at this and laughed harshly. "I was too much the coward for that."

"But you said—"

"Oh, I'm guilty of murder, but not of my father. The story continues," Simone said, looking beyond Rachel to the open window of her bedroom. Would there be windows in her jail cell? Would the sun be shining when they hanged her? "My father sold our cabin and his traps in order to go to Colorado and make his fortune. In the bargain, he also sold me."

"What?"

Simone returned her gaze to Rachel. "He sold me to a man and left me. Deserted me, just as my mother had. Only this man intended to consider me his wife, and you know what that means." Rachel nodded somberly and Simone continued. "I told him I couldn't be his wife and that I would clear out my things and leave. But Garvey Davis wanted no part of that. He was happy with my father's arrangement. He pressed himself upon me, trying—" Her voice faltered, and she drew a deep breath but no air seemed to enter her lungs. "He intended to have me in his bed," she finally managed. Pulling her hand away from Rachel's grasp, she buried her face in her hands and moaned. "I can still see him and hear him and smell the whiskey on his breath. I can feel his hands upon me, and it's all too unbearable."

She felt Rachel slip onto the bed beside her. Simone sagged against her when Rachel put a supportive arm around her shoulder and pulled her close. "Hush, it's all right. You don't have to talk about it."

Simone's shoulders began to quake and her whole body trembled under the weight of her memories. "I fought him. I tried to get away, but he was too fast for me. I did what I had to do. I picked up a pitcher and hit him over the head. I didn't want to kill him, I just meant for him to leave me alone long enough to escape."

"Of course you didn't mean to kill him," Rachel said, sounding stern and authoritative. "The man was clearly out of line."

Simone shook her head and pushed away. "But he wasn't. My father had made a bargain with him. I was to be his wife, and in the high country, if there was no preacher or justice of the peace to marry folks, they lived on that way until one came along."

"I'm sure that there were others in that area who would have found such practices abominable."

"Perhaps," Simone said, looking Rachel dead in the eye. "But not those who would come to my defense. When the law catches up to me, they won't care that Garvey Davis intended to practice his husbandly rights. They'll only care that my hand took his life."

"But if you ran," Rachel said, suddenly having a thought, "perhaps he didn't die. Maybe you just stunned him and—"

"No," Simone interrupted. "I know he's dead. Mr. O'Donnell just showed me the Wanted posters for myself and my father. Although why they've included him, I cannot say. Mr. O'Donnell found the posters in Chicago, which means if they traced me that far, it'll only be a matter of time until they find me here."

"Then we have to hide you," Rachel said, jumping to her feet. "We can't just give you over. Perhaps we could alter your appearance."

Simone smiled sadly. "Rachel, it won't work. Your own mother will be one of those to recognize me. No, I can't ask you to lie for me. I've already told enough lies. Now I find that I've put you and Jeffery in jeopardy. You must either lie for me or turn me over, and neither case is fair or simple for you."

"I won't let them have you," Rachel stated firmly. "They don't know the truth like I do. And from the way you speak, perhaps they wouldn't even care to know the truth."

"It's not your problem, and I won't let you take it on for yourself. I'll just resign my position and leave. That way no one has to be the wiser. I'll simply get on a train and disappear."

"That's it!" Rachel declared. "We'll send you away. We'll find a place on the Santa Fe line where you can work and no one will know who you are."

"I didn't mean that," Simone protested.

Rachel reached out to pull Simone to her feet. "We have to talk to Jeffery. Does he know this whole story?"

"Yes, I told him."

"Good. He's a fair-minded man and he cares for you. Jeffery will know what to do."

Standing in the shadows of the freight platform, Jeffery and Rachel shielded Simone's body from the view of other passersby. By borrowing clothing from one of the kitchen staff, Jeffery and Rachel had transformed Simone into a shabby-looking boy.

"This will never work," Simone whispered, her possessions clutched tightly in a pillowcase. "Nobody will believe I'm a boy."

"Don't worry," Jeffery answered softly. "You've got a great many friends in the rail yard. We'll put you on a freight train rather than a passenger train and no one will be the wiser."

"You'll go to Florence, and from there you can sneak into the little church that's close by. I've been there before and they never lock it," Rachel admitted. "It's a pleasant little town and folks will treat you right. Just take the letters Jeffery and I have written, and meanwhile Jeffery will wire down to let them know of your arrival. Change your clothes and sleep the night in the church, and when morning comes, along with the southbound passenger train, you can just slip natural-like into the crowd and present yourself to the house manager."

"It seems too much to ask," Simone replied. "You'll both be stuck in the middle of this with me should anyone get wise to our actions. After all, what will you tell the other girls?"

"I'll simply say that you decided to leave us," Rachel said with a shrug of her shoulders. "I don't have to lie to them in order to protect you. In fact, I'm sure it will all work out with very little said. By disguising your appearance to the public, no one will remember seeing you get on a train. No one will be able to share information they don't have."

"But if the law comes looking because they've heard tell I was hired by the Harvey Company, they're going to check out places all along the line," Simone protested once again.

"You leave that to me," Jeffery replied. The train's whistle sounded in the distance. "I'll join you as soon as I can with more details to this plan, but for now, just trust me."

Simone could barely make out his features in the shadows, not to mention that they'd plunked a big straw hat down over her head in order to hide all her hair. The wide brim made it difficult to see, but lifting her face just a bit, she could see the beacon light of the ever-slowing steam engine.

She waited for what seemed an eternity while Jeffery went to speak to someone. Rachel tried to keep up small talk with Simone, but it was clear by the way she kept craning her neck to see behind Simone that conversation was far from her mind. Finally Jeffery returned, motioning them to follow, and Simone found herself carefully stashed on the caboose.

"I should be down to Florence in a couple of days. Until I get there, however," Jeffery told her, "just keep to yourself and do your job. You'll be fine."

"You shouldn't be doing this," Simone said, seeing the fear in his eyes.

Jeffery reached out and touched her dirt-smudged cheek. "I can't imagine doing anything else. All I ask, all I desire, is that you trust me."

The words stung her like a slap across the face. *"Trust me,"* he said. If only he knew how high a price he demanded.

"I'll try," Simone replied weakly. She knew he wanted so much more, but it was impossible to sort through the jumble of thoughts and emotions that were threatening to overwhelm her. "I'll try."

He smiled at her, as if knowing what the words had cost her. "Then all will be well," he assured.

"They're about to leave," Rachel called up from the platform.

Simone caught one last glance from Jeffery. He seemed so regretful, so torn between making her stay and letting her go. "Two days," he whispered.

Simone nodded and then he was gone. She felt the sorrow of his departure wrap around her like an eagle's talons. It ripped at her, tearing chinks in her stony armor. There was no sense in fighting it anymore. She had strong feelings for this man.

She saw the caboose man wave his lantern to signal they were ready for departure. He jumped up on the platform of the caboose and looked down at her. "I don't often get passengers. Do you know how to play cards?" he questioned with a grin.

"No," Simone replied, trying hard to keep her voice low.

"Well, it's four hours to Florence. Guess that's time enough to learn."

TWENTY-FIVE

ZACK'S ANTICIPATION OF catching up with Simone Dumas had kept him awake most of the night. He couldn't bring himself to believe that she was the one responsible for the death of Garvey Davis, but nevertheless, she was the one who had stolen his horse and tack, and she was on the run.

Finding no comfort in the hard leatherback seat, Zack tried to make out the horizon as a new day was born. He found the scenery held little interest for him, however. He'd nearly exhausted his funds and would have to wire his bank in Laramie in order to get more money. He knew his father wouldn't approve or understand, but it no longer mattered. The Davis murder case had become an obsession with him. Zack felt confident that if he could just bring in Davis's killer, his father would finally respect him and hold him in the same regard he held for Zack's siblings.

When the call for Topeka finally sounded, Zack was more than ready to leave the train. He'd had his fill of them and hoped that from this point on he might rent a horse. The riding was easier aback a fine-tempered gelding, he'd decided. And while the train might be faster, it was also dirty, crowded, and too confining for his tastes.

He stepped off the train and onto the platform and read the overhead sign that said Topeka. Taking a deep breath, he straightened his stiff shoulders and headed with the other passengers into the Harvey

House restaurant. It was clear to him that no one was going to have time to talk to him until after the meal was served, so he bided his time and enjoyed a hearty meal.

Keeping a careful watch on the waitresses in the room, Zack tried to study each to determine whether any of them matched Simone Dumas's description. He found no one. There was a dark-headed woman who seemed to be in charge of a great deal, but she was too plain in the face to be the more exotic-looking Simone. He drew out his sketch pad just as the pie was served and the coffee cups were refilled.

"Why, looky here, Martha," an elderly man in simple clothes announced. "They've done cut this pie in quarter shares."

"To be sure," the old woman replied. "I'll bet they made a mistake."

"No mistake," another gentleman at the table told them. "Mr. Harvey cuts his pies this way all along the line. He once caught a fellow trying to cut a pie in sixths and fired him then and there."

"Do say?" the old man replied, appearing to find such news hard to believe.

"Would you like more coffee?" a black-and-white-clad Harvey Girl asked Zack.

"No, thanks. Say, you don't know where I might find Simone Dumas or Rachel Taylor, do you?" Zack felt free to ask since the rush was dying down.

The girl smiled sweetly at him. "I don't know any Simone, but then I just started today. Miss Taylor is that woman over there," she pointed, and Zack followed the direction to a buxom young redheaded woman. "She's in charge. Would you like me to tell her you need to speak with her?"

"Yes. I can wait until everyone clears out."

The girl nodded and took her leave, but before Zack could see whether she'd delivered the message, the man at his right asked him about his background.

"What parts are you from, young man?"

Zack glanced at the man before answering. He was wearing a dark suit coat borrowed from the same rack Zack had taken his. Funny rules this Mr. Harvey had. Hardly seemed sensible to lend clothes out to folks in order to eat. Zack had been more than a little fearful of spilling something on the coat before the meal was finished. Of course, there were linen napkins the size of pillowcases, and that covered a good portion of the coat when a fellow tucked the thing in at the top of his shirt as Zack had.

The announcements were made that the train was departing, and while everyone else got to their feet and departed the station restaurant, Zack remained fixed.

"You'll miss your train, sir," one of the Harvey Girls told him.

"Nope," Zack replied. "I'm staying in Topeka."

"Oh, well, I hope your stay is pleasant," the girl responded. "If you haven't yet found a place to sleep, I recommend The Throop. It's just up from the station several blocks on Fourth and Kansas Avenue."

"Then you know this area well?" Zack questioned, hoping this trim little blonde would be able to give him more information than the other waitress had.

"Miss Mitchell," a deep, masculine voice called from somewhere behind the young woman.

"I have to go," she told Zack with a smile and took off before anything else could be said.

In the young woman's place, however, the owner of the voice appeared. "I understand you wanted to speak with Miss Taylor?"

Zack studied the man for a moment and nodded. "That's right."

"Well, I'm afraid Miss Taylor will be preoccupied for some time to come. She is housemother to all of these young women and this is a mostly new staff. There are many questions to be answered and problems to be solved. Perhaps I could be of help?"

Zack shrugged. "You might be able to, but it won't change the fact that I'll need to speak to Miss Taylor when she's free." He pulled the linen napkin from his shirt and gave it a toss on the table as he got to his feet. "You'll have to excuse my manners. I'm half asleep after that fitful ride down from Chicago. I'm Zack Matthews, Deputy Sheriff out of Laramie, Wyoming."

"You are a far ways from home," the man commented. "I'm Jeffery

O'Donnell. I work for Mr. Fred Harvey, the owner of this establishment."

The men shook hands and Jeffery pointed to a hallway. "I have an office we can speak in. The girls will need us to clear out of here in order for the preparations to begin for the next meal."

Zack nodded and followed Jeffery across the room. "You certainly have it all well organized. I've never seen so many people put together and dealt with in such short order."

"Yes, Mr. Harvey has a system for just about everything. If the system is followed to the letter, then things run smoothly. If not," Jeffery paused beside the office door, "then things fall apart rather quickly."

"I can imagine."

The office was nothing much, but Zack found it offered the privacy that he preferred. He positioned himself in a large leather chair and waited for O'Donnell to seat himself at the desk. O'Donnell, however, seemed in no hurry to do this. He casually walked to the window and spent a few moments opening the drapes a little wider. Then he checked through a stack of papers on the corner of his desk before finally taking his seat.

"Now, what is it that we can do for you, Deputy Matthews?"

"I'm looking for a woman."

Jeffery laughed. "My mother says that I should, as well, but I haven't had the heart to pick just one from a bevy of so many choices."

Zack cleared his throat nervously and started again. "I'm looking for a woman who's wanted for questioning in a murder."

"A murder?"

"That's right."

"And whose murder would this be?" Jeffery questioned.

"A man named Garvey Davis. He lived up the mountain a ways from Laramie. This woman may have information about the killer, since it's presumed she was the last one to see Mr. Davis alive."

"I see. Well, I can assure you that Miss Taylor hasn't left these premises in months. Oh, I've tried to get her to take a vacation—"

"No, it isn't that," Zack interrupted, frustrated by O'Donnell's casual tone. The man was impeccably attired in a three-piece suit and seemed to be in control of far more than Zack was willing to give him.

"But I thought you asked for Miss Taylor?"

"I did . . . but . . . well, not because I believe her to be the woman connected to the murder."

"Connected to the murder? But I thought you said the woman might only have information regarding the murderer."

Zack didn't like the way the talk was going at all. O'Donnell was clearly leading the conversation and leaving Zack to feel like a stuttering child. Finally, in frustration, Zack pulled out a copy of the Chicago Wanted poster. "Have you ever seen this man or woman?"

Jeffery stared at the paper for a moment before reaching into his desk drawer. He carefully pulled out a matching copy of the poster and held it up. "I sure have. I saw this in Chicago and brought it back with me."

"So you know them?"

"Nope. I can't say as I know this Louis Dumas fellow."

Zack let out a breath of exasperation. "But you know Simone Dumas."

"Well, I know I hired a woman named Simone. But she gave her last name as Irving."

"What did she look like?" Zack asked.

O'Donnell thought for a moment. "Well, she wore a black dress and a white apron and she had a white bow for her hair," he paused, as if trying to think of some other feature.

"Mr. O'Donnell, they all dress that way. It's the uniform," Zack reminded him.

Jeffery chuckled. "So it is. But I suppose you can see the problem. Once you get them into the uniform, they look pretty much alike. That's what Mr. Harvey had in mind. Uniformity. He says that—"

"Please, Mr. O'Donnell, I'm running out of time. I need to know where I can find either Simone Irving or Simone Dumas."

"Well, to tell you the truth, I kind of got my own suspicions when I saw this poster," Jeffery said, leaning forward conspiratorially. "I mean, this drawing had some similarities, and the name . . . well, you just don't hear it that often. Sounds French to me, don't you think?"

"Yes," Zack replied in complete exasperation.

Jeffery smiled and nodded. "That's what I figured, too. I mean, not too many people in these parts name their kids by French names. There's a lot of Marys and Margarets, and of course Bible names are quite popular. But—"

"I'm sorry," Zack interrupted, "but I need to know what you think about the woman you hired. Do you believe Simone Irving and Simone Dumas to be one and the same?"

"I think it's very possible."

"Where is she now?" Zack asked, finally feeling that he was getting somewhere with the questioning.

Jeffery surprised him by shrugging. He leaned back casually in his chair and folded his hands together. "I really can't say."

"What do you mean?"

The man looked rather sheepish, and Zack got a sick feeling in his gut that he wasn't going to like whatever it was O'Donnell was going to say.

"I showed her the poster and she ran. Fled the Harvey House altogether. I've not seen her since."

"What!" Zack stood up in surprise. "You just up and confronted her without any kind of lawman here to take her into custody?" The indignity of it was too much for Matthews. "You let her get away?"

"I'm afraid I did," O'Donnell said rather apologetically. "I am sorry, Mr. Matthews. I've never had dealings with criminal types before. I thought maybe it was a silly coincidence. I guess it wasn't."

"And you have no idea where she went?"

"Oh, I have all sorts of ideas. She came here from Chicago and it seems logical that she might want to go back there."

"Why would you say that?" Zack questioned, finally feeling the calm return enough to retake his seat.

Again O'Donnell shrugged. "It's just an idea—a guess, really. You asked me for ideas."

"Yes, but do you have any reason to believe she would return to Chicago? Did she mention it?"

"She wasn't saying much when she left here," Jeffery told him.

"And when exactly did she leave?"

"I couldn't possibly say."

"You have no idea?"

"As I said earlier, I have all kinds of ideas. I've always fancied myself a bit of a sleuth, don't you know. My mother always said—"

"Look, Mr. O'Donnell, I do appreciate the help you've already given me, but I have to have some hard facts to work with. I'm going to have to insist on talking to Miss Taylor. I met with the woman's mother in Chicago, and she believes that Miss Taylor will have plenty of answers to help me."

"You met her mother? In Chicago? Well, isn't that nice. What sort of woman is she?" O'Donnell questioned in a most eager manner.

Zack had pretty well decided that O'Donnell was either too daft to understand the frustration he was causing or too indifferent to care that he was slowing Zack down. Zack had once known a boy in school who was almost too smart for his own good. The simplest things often stumped the boy, but he was a genius in other areas. It could always be possible that this O'Donnell fellow was just the same.

"Could you please send for Miss Taylor?" Zack asked patiently.

O'Donnell seemed to consider this request for several moments, and Zack was just about to repeat the question when Jeffery got to his feet. "I'll call her."

He went to the door, much to Zack's relief and called down the hall.

"Miss Taylor?"

Zack heard a muffled reply from somewhere down the hall.

"Would you be so kind as to join us when time permits?" O'Donnell called out one final time.

Zack wanted to leave Jeffery in the office and go in search of Rachel Taylor on his own, but he decided to wait a few more minutes before insisting on having his own way. He was way out of his own jurisdiction here and therefore totally dependent upon the kindness of these strangers.

O'Donnell had returned to the desk chair, but instead of taking a seat, he waited, hand on the back of his chair, until a light knock sounded on the door.

"Come in," O'Donnell called out.

Zack turned to find the shapely redhead enter the room. Her

expression seemed fearful and her nervousness was evident in the way she twisted her hands. "Yes?"

"Miss Taylor, this gentleman is Deputy Matthews. He's looking for Simone Irving, only her name might be Dumas. I didn't want to show you this, but I saw it in Chicago," Jeffery said, holding up the poster.

"Oh my!" Rachel exclaimed, her hand going to her throat.

"Do you think she looks like the Simone you had working here?"

Rachel nodded ever so slightly.

"Do you know where she is now?"

Rachel looked from Zack to Jeffery and back to the poster. Before she could reply, however, Jeffery spoke up.

"I told Deputy Matthews that she fled when I confronted her with the news. I thought perhaps Chicago might have been a nice destination for her. She had come down to Topeka from there, and it would seem reasonable that she return there."

Rachel nodded, but Matthews could see that she was shaking from head to toe. Her dress quaked as she stood there before him, and for a moment he felt sorry for her. She was a sweet-looking woman, he decided. Her fiery hair and green eyes made him wonder if she had an Irish temper to match. But something seemed amiss between the two Harvey employees. Miss Taylor barely seemed capable of speech, while O'Donnell hardly seemed able to contain himself.

"I think that Chicago would be a truly perfect place to hide," Jeffery was saying as Zack rethought his plan. "It's such a large city. I live there, you know—raised there. My folks have a house—"

"Look, if either of you have any idea where Simone Dumas could be, I'd appreciate your letting me know. I'm going to get a room up at The Throop Hotel. You can reach me there."

Jeffery looked startled at the interruption but nodded. Miss Taylor looked as though she might pass out at any moment, and it was only after studying her face for several seconds that Zack remembered the sketch he had for her.

"Oh, by the way . . ." He pulled the alpaca coat up and reached into his back pocket. "I spoke to your mother in Chicago. While I was talking to her and sketching a new picture of Simone Dumas, she asked if I would sketch one of her to bring to you."

He took out the paper and handed it to Rachel. For a moment, he thought the woman might actually burst into tears. She took the picture, held it up, and studied it with such intensity that Zack didn't know quite what to do or say.

"This is very good," Rachel finally whispered.

"She's mighty proud of you," Zack said, finally deciding it was the safest course. "She asked that I sketch you while I'm down here and bring it to her upon my return."

"Oh, are you returning to Chicago, Mr. Matthews?" Jeffery asked. "I have to return to Chicago and I would be pleased to invite you as my guest."

"No," Zack said, a little more emphatically than he'd intended. "I'm not leaving. Not yet, anyway."

He walked to the door of the office and stopped only long enough to look back at the two. Something was wrong, but for the life of him, Zack's instincts just couldn't nail it.

"I'll be back a little later to see if any of the other girls might have an idea of where Miss Dumas might have gone."

TWENTY-SIX

AFTER DAYS OF TRYING to size up the Topeka depot situation, Louis Dumas clearly had no better idea where his daughter was than when he'd first arrived. Matthews seemed to beat a path back and forth between a nearby hotel and the railroad depot restaurant, but Louis didn't know if this was significant or simply that the man enjoyed the food.

And while Louis knew he looked nothing like the man in the Wanted poster, he could hardly just waltz up to Deputy Matthews and ask what purpose he had in Topeka. Time and a lack of knowledge added straw after straw to the proverbial camel's back while Louis watched and waited. He felt a deep need to distance himself from this pesky young lawman, yet at the same time there was an almost fatal attraction. This man clearly had come to Topeka with Simone in mind, of this Louis was certain. After all, he had dogged their steps all the way from Wyoming. Remembering the determination in his voice when speaking to his father back in Laramie, Louis felt certain the younger man wasn't about to give up the search. No, he'd see this thing through or die trying.

Yawning and stretching from his hiding place in one of the outbuildings near the depot, Louis tried to formulate a plan. For days he'd managed to dodge the rail yard guards, but he knew it couldn't go on indefinitely. He didn't have the kind of funds it would take to stay at a hotel like Matthews, and sooner or later someone would find him—and the issue of his living arrangements would have to be rethought.

He brushed the dirt and debris from his stolen coat and pants and ran his fingers through his black hair as if to comb it into place. Perhaps the time had come, he decided, to question a few people on his own. Of course, businessmen would hardly be inclined to give him the time of day, and neither would the saintly dressed young women of the Harvey Restaurant. His best bet would be the rail yard workers. They would be far more to his liking than anyone he could find inside the Harvey House, and he figured they would come closer to speaking his language than the uppity management of the railroad. Besides, Louis still had no idea what significance the Harvey House held—if any.

Cursing under his breath, he gathered his things together and decided to look like any other passenger when the morning train arrived at the depot. The sound of the whistle made it clear the time for action was upon him.

"I can't give up now," he muttered.

Casting a quick glance around, he darted out from the building and made his way to the depot platform. He easily blended in with the crowd, but when most of the folks went inside for breakfast, Louis waited around the tracks.

"You lost, mister?" a boy who looked to be around fifteen or sixteen questioned.

Louis eyed the young man for a moment. "Ain't exactly lost, but I have lost someone."

"Who'd that be?"

"My daughter. She's about your age."

"Ain't no girls gonna come down here around the tracks. Too dirty and smelly for them female types."

"Well, she ain't exactly your regular girl. She might not mind the dirt or the smells."

"She got a name?"

Louis nodded. "Simone." The boy actually paled at the spoken word, and Louis knew he'd found the right place to start. "Have you seen her?"

"She a passenger?"

"No," Louis said, watching the boy grow more fidgety. "She came here some time ago."

"Why'd she come here?" the boy asked, as if testing Louis's knowledge.

"She ran away," he answered bluntly. It was his only defense. "Her ma died and it made her sad."

The boy seemed to consider this for a minute. "I don't reckon I can tell you anything," he said, then glanced down at the rail, shaking his head. "No, sir, I don't know a thing." He hurried off toward a group of men who were working on a separate line of tracks.

Louis knew the boy was lying, but he couldn't figure out why. What should it matter to the boy whether he told Louis where Simone was? Frustrated, Louis headed down the rails to where the group of men were working on switching out cars. The boy spoke to one of the men, then motioned ever so slightly as Louis approached them.

"Howdy," Louis called in a nonchalant manner.

"Howdy, yorself," an older man replied, stuffing a blue-and-white kerchief in the back pocket of his overalls. "What can I do for ya?"

"I just got into town," Louis lied. "I've come in search of my daughter."

"Your daughter? Why would ya be lookin' for her down here?"

Louis shrugged. "I'm not exactly sure where to start. I'd heard she'd come to Topeka, and other than that I had no idea where I might find her."

"Lots of folks come through and a good enough number stay," the white-haired man related. By this time the other men had moved off down the track to where the engine of one train was being hooked up to the cars of another. "Wish I could help ya."

Louis nodded and feigned a deep sorrow. "We've been parted for ever so long, and I just fear for her safety. She's just a wee thing like her mother, God rest her soul."

The older man removed his cap out of respect. "I'm sorry for your loss."

"Oh, it's been ever so hard on us. Just me and my little Simone."

"Simone? You don't mean Miss Irving, do you?" the man questioned, his face suddenly lighting up.

Louis nodded. "Dark black hair and blue eyes. Stands about this tall."

"Why, shore, I know the filly you're talkin' about. Why, she's one of the best Harvey Girls in town. Works—or I should say, worked—in the restaurant right over there at the depot."

"Worked? You don't mean," Louis paused to give the man a mournful expression, "she's gone?" His voice cracked slightly from the dusty dryness, and Louis thought it lent a poignant air of longing.

"There, now, Father Irving," the man said as though they were the best of friends. "She's not gone far. Just about four hours south of here. Florence, to be exact. She's working at the Harvey House there." The man leaned closer. "Although not many folks know that. I don't rightly know what gives, but they asked me to keep quiet about it."

Louis again changed his expression. This time he beamed the man a smile and hoped he looked as excited and happy as a loving father might be at the thought of reuniting with his long-lost child. "Just four hours away. Oh, what glory!" Then he frowned and looked down at the dirt and rails. "But I've just spent my last dime coming this far. Now I'll never find her."

"Nonsense," the man said with a sympathetic smile. "There's a freighter what'll take you right through to Florence. I work that train tonight. If you can wait that long, I'll see you find a spot on it, although regular passengers ain't allowed to ride on freighters—it's against the rules. But the fact is, Miss Irving herself took a freighter down just a few days back."

"What will I owe you for that?" Louis asked hesitantly.

"Not a penny," the man replied. "I'm right happy to help put the two of you back together. Have you had breakfast yet?"

"No," Louis said, shaking his head. "I figured I'd just wait."

The man dug into his pocket and came out with a handful of change. "It ain't much, but it'll get ya some grub. Now, the Harvey House is good eating, but if you have a mind to see the town, then I can suggest Home Bakery at Eighth and Kansas. They have a great meal for twenty cents. I can guarantee ya won't go away hungry."

"Oh, I couldn't impose," Louis said, trying hard to maintain his role.

The man shoved the change into Louis's hand. "Ain't no imposition. You've raised a right good young woman. She was always kind and good tempered with us workin' folk. Didn't take on any airs. You should be proud."

"Thank you." Louis barely managed to force the words out of his mouth. The man made Simone sound like a pillar of the community—all sweetness and goodness. He didn't need that. What he had in mind for Simone would require a more seductive nature.

"Pleased to help you, mister," the man replied. "I'll see ya back here tonight. Just come on over to that shed about nine," he said, pointing. "I'll be there."

Louis nearly did a dance as he left the train yard. Tonight he would close the final distance between him and Simone! Jiggling the change in his hand, he headed up the street to Kansas Avenue, a path he'd taken in following Matthews. His luck was changing and he felt like celebrating.

"Say," he questioned the first man he came across, "where can a fellow get a drink in this town?"

The man looked at him strangely for a moment. "You aren't from around here, are you?"

"Nope, just came in on the train," Louis admitted.

The man nodded. "Well, that explains it. Kansas is a dry state. We don't have a saloon here."

"What?" Louis asked in surprise. "No liquor?"

"That's right. Not a drop," the man replied, then leaned closer. "Unless, of course, you have a prescription for it."

"A prescription? You mean a fellow has to go to the doctor in order to get a bottle of whiskey?"

The shorter man pulled back and laughed. "That's exactly right. Keeps most of the common folk from having the stuff, but every legislator in town is under a doctor's care. If you get my meaning." He walked off, laughing at his quip, leaving Louis to stare after him as though the man had gone mad.

"No whiskey," he muttered. "What a brutal place."

TWENTY-SEVEN

SOMEHOW KNOWING WITH certainty that she was a wanted woman caused Simone to cling to her freedom like never before. Once again sharing a room with Una at the Florence Harvey House and Clifton Hotel, Simone spent quiet, reflective moments long into the night while her friend jotted letters. It was as if seeing the Wanted posters and considering her own execution had caused a fight for life to rise up in Simone. The significance poured over her in a stunning way. She wanted to live—wanted to grow older, marry, bear children. For the first time in years, Simone yearned to open her heart up to love and happiness. But now it was too late. She felt suffocated at the thought that she would never be able to clear her name . . . and that ultimately she would be found guilty of murder.

During her first week in Florence, Simone had nearly gone to turn herself in to the law on a dozen different occasions. The waiting was killing her. She felt the need to constantly look over her shoulder when she was working, and at night when she was alone it was even worse. Even Una noticed her agitation, but Simone refused to share her secret. Jeffery and Rachel already knew, and that was more than enough. Dragging Una into the situation wouldn't resolve anything.

I can't deal with this anymore, she thought, lying on her bed in pensive silence. Immediately her mother's voice seemed to echo through her mind.

"When all else fails, Simone, don't forget the power of prayer."

The power of prayer? Simone had always wondered about the suggestion that prayer held power. She had prayed so hard as a child that her mother's misery would end—that her own misery could be finished. She thought of the child she'd been, offering up her tearful prayers of repentance, pleading with God to show her forgiveness and give her a happy family. But it had never happened, and it was impossible for Simone to continue believing in a loving God who answered prayers when it was so clear that He wasn't answering hers.

I suppose that was a selfish way to look at things, she surmised. *But it seemed so accurate given the misery I suffered. If God is truly as powerful and loving as Mother always said, then why did He let us suffer so?* She focused her eyes on the ceiling of the dimly lit room. *Why, God? Why did you not hear my prayers? Why couldn't you save me from the circumstance that would lead me to commit murder? You know in my heart I never intended to kill anyone. If you are all-knowing, then you realize even now that I never intended for Garvey Davis to die. I only wanted freedom. I only wanted to save myself from what he had in mind. God, nobody else was fighting for me. I had to fight for myself. Surely you know the truth in this.*

Simone was startled to realize she was praying. After years of declaring it a useless act, and even going so far as to say God didn't exist, here she was crying out to Him for answers.

Una finished her letter and yawned. "I'm ready for bed now. Do you need the candle?"

Simone shook her head. "No. I'm about to fall asleep." This couldn't be further from the truth, but Simone didn't want to encourage her roommate's conversation any further. With a nod, Una blew out the candle, leaving only the light of a nearly full moon to trail in through the window. Simone heard Una kneel beside her bed and could see her shadowy figure spend at least ten minutes in prayer on her knees. How could she be so confident that anyone listened? How could she hold on to the hope that God really cared when it seemed so clearly evident that He might not care at all?

When Una finished she got into her bed without a word, and within a few moments Simone could hear her deep, even breathing—a sure sign that the blond-haired woman had fallen asleep. As if waiting for this cue, Simone sat up in bed and hugged her knees to her chest. At least the heat and humidity had lessened. They were having what Una called a very dry autumn-summer. There was even some concern about drought, although folks were just as inclined to suggest waiting a spell for the weather to change. Kansas, they said, was notorious for such changes. One farmer even teased Simone about the weather, saying that just that morning he'd passed from his house to the barn traveling first in rain. He then left the barn to slop the hogs and found himself in a wind so fierce it nearly took off his clothes. Then leaving the pig shed to go check on his wheat, the farmer found himself in a snowstorm, and by the time he got back to the house, the sun was shining and the heat bearing down on him like a furnace. The other people at her table had laughed at this analogy, swearing it was nearly true. Simone had smiled, even laughed. She'd liked the gentle man and his teasing. How different he was from her father.

Jeffery, too, was different. She hated thinking about him. He had promised to join her in Florence within a couple of days of her departure, but he'd telegrammed her saying that circumstances prevented him from leaving Topeka. It caused Simone to feel anxious, almost hurt, and because of that she didn't know what to say or how to respond. She wanted to guard her heart away from her feelings, but it just wasn't to be. Then a telegram arrived earlier that evening saying that he would see her tomorrow. That he would arrive around noon and they would talk about the future. And while a part of her looked forward to his arrival, another part feared seeing him again.

I don't know what to do, she thought, rocking back and forth, seeking comfort. She remembered a time when her mother would have rocked her. She imagined herself crawling up into her mother's arms and finding the warmth and protection she sought. Tears began to trickle down her cheeks.

"Oh, Mama," she whispered. "I don't really hate you. In fact, I would give my life to have you here just now." Her chest ached with this revelation. She had tried so hard, for so many years, to convince herself that she hated the only human being to ever show her unconditional love. "Why? Why couldn't you have just stayed with me? I was just a little girl. I still feel like a little girl." Simone sobbed softly into the folds of her nightgown.

Unbearable pain tore through her. The misery of the last seven years began to overwhelm her. How hard she had tried to deny her feelings. How hard she had fought to feel nothing. She had convinced herself that her protection was found in not remembering, but now it was clear that this had only led to further grief and suffering.

I'm hopeless, she thought, and a shudder washed over her. There was great truth in that statement. *I am without hope. Nothing could more clearly plead my cause or outline my existence*. She pressed her nightgown against her eyes and willed her tears to stop. *This will not help*, she reminded herself. *It never helped in the past and it surely cannot change things now. I am alone. There is no one to help*.

A verse from the Bible came to mind, but Simone couldn't remember it clearly. Glancing to Una's bed, Simone made certain she was still sleeping before slipping out of her own bed. She located her Bible in her bedstand drawer and took it with her to the open window. She hoped there might be enough light to read by but soon realized the impossibility. Reluctantly, she lit the candle Una had used and sat down at the writing table.

The marker opened the Book to Psalm 27. Simone suddenly remembered the night Rachel had sat at her side, speaking of God. Glancing over the chapter, words—even whole verses—began to sound familiar to her. By the time she reached verse ten, she was crying anew.

"'When my father and my mother forsake me, then the LORD will take me up.'" *Oh, that this would be true*, Simone thought longingly. "'Teach me thy way, O LORD, and lead me in a plain path, because of mine enemies. Deliver me not over unto the will of mine enemies: for false witnesses are risen up against me, and such as breathe out cruelty,'" she whispered the words, barely able to see them for her tears.

"'I had fainted, unless I had believed to see the goodness of the LORD in the land of the living. Wait on the LORD: be of good courage, and he shall strengthen thine heart: wait, I say, on the LORD.'"

She fell upon the open pages and buried her face against her arms. What would it be like to know the goodness of the Lord? To honestly be of good courage because God had heard her cries and had strengthened her?

"I don't know how to wait on you, Lord," she whispered. "I don't know what to do."

Trust me.

The voice wasn't audible, but it rose up from her heart like the faint whistle of an approaching train. Trust me. Such a simple request. Jeffery had asked for her trust. Her mother had made promises based on that trust. God had sent his Son, Jesus, and offered eternal life to those who believed—trusted His promises to be true.

"I want to trust—to believe," Simone said, suddenly so very tired of doing things her own way. She had spent seven, almost eight years in rebellion and anger, and now the time had come to face the consequences of her actions.

"I want to trust you," she said solemnly. Wiping away the last of her tears, Simone realized that there was much to account for. "I was proud and haughty, angry and bitter. I was sure you couldn't care for me because . . ." She fell silent, looking beyond the Bible to the open window. "I thought you left me when my mother went away, but in truth, I was the one who left you. I deserted you, just as I accused Mama of deserting me. Oh, God, how wrong I was."

She sat in silence for several moments, then walked to the window and stared out on the landscape below. Seeing nothing but the years of misery and emptiness, Simone continued her whispered prayer. "I blamed my father for being so cruel. I suffered so much under his hand. But in many ways, I've suffered more under my own.

"You could have stopped it," Simone said as though God might never have thought of such a thing. "You could have done anything, and because of that, I don't understand why you allowed me to suffer like that."

Shaking her head, Simone stepped away from the window and leaned back against the wall. "There seems to be a lot I don't understand."

The only thing Simone did understand at this point was the need to be relieved of her burden. *I must find peace*, she told herself. Despite her lack of knowledge or understanding—despite her fears for tomorrow.

"Forgive me, Lord," she finally whispered. "Please forgive me."

Immediately a sensation of peace washed over her in tiny waves. It was almost like a gentle summer rain washing her clean. Her mother had promised her that God listened to the prayers of His children. Simone hoped that was right—hoped that He was listening to her now. *It feels right*, she thought, breathing out with a sigh. *It must be right*. Tomorrow might bring the lawman to her door, but even if she stood on the gallows facing her death, Simone finally believed with all of her heart that God would stand there with her. Somehow, the future no longer seemed so frightening.

TWENTY-EIGHT

SIMONE AWOKE THE following morning feeling more refreshed and comforted than she'd felt in years. There were still questions in her mind—nagging little doubts about her life and the past—but nevertheless she knew she had chosen the right path. Now she was determined to continue down that course and make the right decisions about her future.

It was her day off, and in spite of her long hours of Bible reading and prayers from the night before, Simone desired nothing more than to go to the nearby church and seek advice from the pastor. There was so much to think about, and by noon Jeffery would be there demanding her to think about him, as well.

Dressing carefully in her blue serge skirt and white shirtwaist, Simone pinned her hair up and made her way downstairs to a late breakfast. The train crowd wouldn't be through again for a few hours, so Simone arranged a quick meal by sandwiching leftover sausage in a biscuit. Taking a bite, Simone gave Una a tiny wave and cleared out before finding herself volunteered to work an extra shift.

She actually hummed as she stepped into the morning sun. Just up the road, the rest of Florence was already well into its day. Wagons maneuvered up and down the dirt road, people called out to each other, anvils rang, and horses whinnied. It all seemed like music to

Simone's ears. This was freedom. This was what she hoped desperately not to lose.

The church stood only a short walking distance away, and Simone had barely finished her biscuit by the time she reached the steps. She gazed upward at the open doorway, wondering if she had the courage to go through with her plan. Una had told her that the preacher, Brother Carlyle, was almost always found inside the building at the first sign of the sun. Simone had counted on this when she'd first made her way to the church, but now a fit of nerves caused her to hesitate.

"Hello there!" a voice called out.

Simone looked but saw no one. Hesitantly she replied, "Hello."

A rather rumpled figure appeared from the shadows of the doorway. The man appeared to be in his mid- to late fifties and sported a balding head over which he had combed wispy bits of hair. He smiled warmly and introduced himself. "I'm Brother Carlyle."

"I'm Simone Irv—" she paused and shook her head. "Simone Dumas. I work at the Harvey House."

"Very nice to meet you. Will you be coming inside today?"

Simone swallowed hard, feeling the last dry crumbs from the biscuit sticking in her throat. "I'd like very much to do just that."

"Then come on ahead. I'm glad to have the company." He stepped back as if to allow her more room. "I come here every morning to start my day. Gives me comfort to face the troubles of life by first spending time with God."

Simone followed him into the simplistic structure. The narrow aisle led forward past rows of wooden pews to a raised platform. It was here, on the edge of the platform rather than the pew, where Brother Carlyle took a seat. "Did you have something in particular that you needed to talk about?"

Simone stood fixed in the aisle, staring at him and trying to decide how much to say. "I suppose I do."

"Then have a seat. You might as well get right to it," he suggested.

Simone nodded, hesitated for a moment longer, then quickly slid into the front pew across from Brother Carlyle. Folding her hands and looking downward, she was at a loss as to how to start.

"So, now," he asked very gently, "how can I help you?"

"I'm not sure you can," Simone admitted. She hoped he could—had even prayed he could, but there was still a great deal of fear in her heart when it came to dealing with people one on one. What if this man was like the others? What if he acted just as cruel and lewdly? She tried not to dwell on these thoughts. Una thought him a very decent sort, and while she'd not had much experience getting to know him, she felt he knew the Bible well and preached a very fine sermon.

"We won't know if you don't tell me what's bothering you," he offered.

Simone looked up and nodded. His face seemed so compassionate. "When I was a little girl, I accepted Jesus as my Savior."

He smiled. "That's a good start."

"My mother taught me about God, and I learned to read from the Bible." Simone bit her lip, knowing that she had to go on. "I fell away from the truth for a long, long time. Last night I made my peace with God. At least in part."

"Only in part?" he asked, still smiling. "What part did you leave undone?"

"Well, I'm not sure. I'm not saying I necessarily left anything undone, but there are things that have come to mind with the morning."

"Such as?"

She took a deep breath. "Such as there are things I've done that I should make right."

"Repentance goes hand in hand with restoration and accepting responsibility for our actions. We all do things we shouldn't—no one is perfect. But when we realize the wrong we've done, we should attempt to put things back in order. We need to turn from our evil ways and walk God's path instead of our own."

Simone nodded. "Yes, I know. But some things can't be undone. Words once said can't be taken back."

"Apologies can be given," he countered.

"Yes, but you can't apologize to the dead."

He nodded. "I see your problem. You said something harsh to someone and now they're gone?"

"Yes. And there's more. I did something . . . something horrible.

I didn't mean to, but it happened nevertheless."

"Can you tell me about it?"

And that was that. With those simple words, Simone found herself laying out the entire story of her childhood and of Garvey Davis's death. After telling him everything, Simone fell silent for a moment, then added, "I never meant to kill him, and if I could do things over again—"

"You'd defend yourself in exactly the same manner," Brother Carlyle interrupted. "Simone, you only protected yourself. God knows the truth of it."

"Yes, but the law doesn't. They're after me even now. I don't want to keep running, but neither do I want to hang for a crime I never meant to commit. I don't know how to deal with this. I'm so angry that my father would sell me to Garvey Davis in the first place, and I'm mad that my mother would go away and leave me in a situation that would allow my father's cruelty."

"Simone, your anger toward your mother and father will not help you now. It might have once given you a false sense of strength, but that's all in the past. You must forgive their errors and let the past stay in the past."

"Forgive them?"

"Doesn't seem quite right or fair, does it?" he asked, the same benevolent expression on his face.

Simone felt her stomach tighten. It didn't seem at all fair. "But what good would it do them now?" she finally managed to ask.

"It might not do *them* any good at all—at least not in the aspect you're probably thinking of." He leaned forward, hands clasped together. "But it would do you a world of good. It would free you from the burden."

"I felt unburdened last night when I came back to God," Simone admitted. "It's just that some of these other things kept creeping in on me this morning. I don't know how to let it go—I'm not sure I can forgive my father."

"Sometimes it isn't easy, but God has already done the hard part."

"The hard part?" Simone asked, still uncertain she was capable of what the man suggested.

"He gave His Son, Jesus, to be a sacrifice for all those sins and wrongs. Before we were even born, Christ went to the cross—paying our price—dying for the evil that would come upon us." He paused and took a deep breath. "Like it or not, Simone, that includes your father's sins.

"Now, I'm not suggesting that what your father did was right. In fact, I feel quite strongly that it was very wrong. But forgiving him isn't saying that you accept what he did as being the right thing. It doesn't make him right by a long shot, but it does free your heart from having to carry his guilt with you for the rest of your life. Do you want your earthly father to have that kind of power over you, or would you rather your heavenly Father have that all-consuming power?"

"I suppose when you put it that way," Simone replied, trying to take it all in, "I would much rather God have the power. It's just so hard."

"I know it is."

"And what about me?" she finally asked, still not certain how to deal with her father. "Do I go throw myself on the mercy of the law and hope they understand the truth? Do I let them hang me, even though it was an accident that Garvey Davis died?"

"You can only answer those questions for yourself, Simone. I can tell you that the Bible says that the truth will set you free. Deception only ensnares and entangles. But I can't force you to turn yourself in, neither will I speak out against you. I will, however, be praying for you to make the right decision."

Simone nodded but said nothing. Her mind was whirling with thoughts of how she might come to terms with forgiving her father. It was easy enough to forgive her mother, and without any hesitation, Simone found herself praying that God might see the openness of her heart.

I know she loved me, Simone thought as her eyes closed in prayer. *I know that if she were alive today, she would still love me—care for me, protect me. I know she did what she thought was best. I saw her tears—her pain. I know the decision to leave did not come without a high price, and I sent her away without ever making it right between us. She died thinking I hated her.*

Oh, God, she believed I hated her. Tears slipped from her closed eyes. *Please forgive me and please let her know that I love her still. That I didn't mean the things I said. I only said them because I was scared. I was so afraid. I still am.*

Simone tried to rein in her emotions. She had no desire to fall apart here in front of the preacher. The image of her father's face came to mind, and for a moment it paralyzed Simone with fear. This was the stuff of her nightmares. Louis Dumas haunted her in a way no one else possibly could.

How can I forgive him? How can I walk away from the matter and call the slate clean? Oh, God, I want to forgive. I want to be free, but this is so hard for me to figure out. I don't think I can do it.

She glanced up and found Brother Carlyle's gaze fixed on her. He seemed to know exactly what she was thinking.

"Much is impossible for us alone, Simone. But with Christ, all things are possible. Even this."

Simone nodded. "I want to believe that."

"Then trust Him."

Simone got to her feet. "I'll try. I want very much to be at peace. I don't know yet when that might be, but I do know that I can't go on running from the law. I'm going to turn myself in." It was funny, but Simone thought it easier to face the consequences of her actions in Wyoming than to think any more on forgiving her father his sins.

"You'll let me know how you're doing, won't you?" Brother Carlyle questioned as he followed her to the door of the church.

Simone smiled ever so slightly. "You may have to check up on me for yourself. Especially if they lock me up."

"You can count on me for a visit as long as needed."

"Thank you."

She left him standing there, knowing that he was watching her as she made her way down the steps. She slipped around the side of the church and made her way toward the path that led to a beautiful woods along the river. Before she turned herself in to the local police, she wanted to spend a few more minutes in prayer.

Barely ten feet from the church, however, Simone found her plans abruptly halted. Someone grabbed her from behind, clamping one hand over her mouth and another around her waist. Her heart raced wildly as the pressure increased and her assailant pulled her tight.

"Don't try anything, or I'll snap your neck like kindlin'."

She froze in place, unable to speak, much less move. The voice belonged to her father.

"I've been watchin' you for nearly a week," Louis Dumas admitted, "and now I have you."

He pushed her forward. "Quick, we're going to go for the cover of those trees," he commanded and half dragged her with him to the shelter.

Once there, Louis quickly tied her hands in front of her and pulled her along with a rope. "We've gotta get downriver a spell before we can have a proper reunion," he told the stunned Simone.

She looked at the man as though he were a stranger. He certainly didn't look like the Louis Dumas she'd known in Wyoming. His clothes were dusty and stained, but they were much nicer than anything she'd ever known her father to dress in. And his face! He was clean-shaven, something Simone had never seen in all her life.

"You don't look happy to see me," Dumas chided, pulling the rope painfully tight. "Don't I even get a greeting of welcome?" But without waiting for an answer, Louis pushed her forward.

Simone couldn't even think rationally. She wanted to cry out, scream for help, but her voice was oddly silent. She felt like she was watching the ordeal happen to someone else. Each jarring step across the uneven ground, each slap of brush against her body . . . Simone's mind refused to accept that her haunted past had returned.

They walked at an increasing pace, pushing ever westward, until Louis finally stopped, glanced around him, then shoved Simone up against a tree. He took the rope that bound her hands and threw it up over a high branch. Pulling this tight, he forced her arms into the air, then tied the thing off at the trunk when he was satisfied Simone was rendered helpless.

Next, he took a handkerchief from his pocket, and without giving Simone a chance to protest, he gagged her with the smelly thing.

This seemed to break the spell of shock momentarily. Simone kicked at him and grunted her protests from the gag.

"So you finally got your wind, did you?" Louis said, sizing her up. "Well, it's no matter. Now, you stay here and protest all you want. We're far enough away that no one's going to hear you. I'm going back to brush out our tracks."

And with that he was gone, leaving Simone to face the situation on her own. Immediately she tried to rid herself of the gag, and even while she worked at rubbing it against her shoulder, Simone tried to make as much noise as possible. She had to get away, and since she was unable to do so on her own, someone would have to come to her rescue.

She began to pray, pleading with God for help. *This*, she thought, *is why I can't forgive him. He's an animal and he doesn't care about me or anyone else. He only cares about himself*. She pulled at the rope, hoping to bring her hands just close enough to her face to release the gag, but it was hopeless.

In the distance she heard the train whistle. At first she thought she'd imagined it. But then it sounded again and she knew without a doubt that it was real. Jeffery would be on that train! She struggled all the harder. Jeffery would go looking for her, and when he didn't find her, he would presume the worst. He would come looking for her, of this Simone was certain. But then a thought came to mind that took all hope from Simone. *What if he thinks I don't want to see him? What if he thinks I've run away in order to avoid him?* It was possible he would see this as the final word in Simone's rejection and leave without giving her another thought. Moaning in despair, Simone tried all the harder to pull the rope loose.

It seemed an eternity before her father returned. He looked at her for a moment and laughed. "I never knew what a real looker you were before hearing the men talk about you in Uniontown. In my mind you were still that stupid, gangly kid who didn't know what a woman's curse was all about. Now I see, however, that you've filled out right nicely. You still a virgin or did Davis get the better of you?"

Simone felt her face flush and knew by that simple action she'd betrayed the truth. Her father laughed. "That's good. You'll play into my plans in good order."

Simone wanted to scream "What plans?" but knew it was impossible. Her father was no fool. He'd not ungag her and risk her crying out for help. Not when they were still so close to Florence.

Louis sat down for a moment, as if contemplating what to do next, and while he did this, Simone took the opportunity to better study him. He looked so completely different from the last time Simone had seen him. She could have easily doubted it was him had his blatant hatred not been the same. Gone was the unruly hair and full beard. In its place was a closely trimmed style that looked very similar to Jeffery's, and a thin moustache. But the cruelty in her father's dark eyes still remained as he let his gaze travel the full length of her.

"Yes, sir, you'll do just fine for what I have in mind." Then, as if he'd heard her voice the question, he grinned. "You don't know what I have in mind, do you? Well, for now that's just as well. See, I know what you did to Garvey Davis."

Simone felt her knees grow weak but knew she couldn't faint now. She forced herself to stand still, to concentrate on breathing deeply while her father continued.

"Yup, you sure did him in. Poor man. All he wanted was a wife and a place of his own." Louis jumped to his feet and dusted off his filthy trousers. "Well, that's the way it goes."

He went to the tree and untied her, reining the rope in tightly as Simone's hands went immediately to her mouth. "I'm not of a mind to let you get rid of that just yet. We've got to position ourselves a ways from town first." Then, as if to prove his point, the train whistle blew in short but very loud bursts to signal its entrance into town.

He pulled her along with him once again, and the pace he kept nearly made Simone ill. They kept out of sight as best they could, following the banks of the Cottonwood River. Simone slipped and nearly lost her footing on more than one occasion, catching her skirt against twigs and exposed roots, but Louis just pulled her up tight and they continued on their way.

Simone's wrists hurt so badly that she struggled to match her father's pace in order to keep from feeling the chafing of the rope against her skin. Surely he would stop soon. They were running out of forest cover, and it would be necessary to take out across open prairie before much longer.

Finally Louis stopped. He glanced behind them and then up ahead. "We'll wait here until dark," he said, dragging Simone back to a tree.

Without waiting for her father to repeat his earlier actions, Simone plopped herself down on the ground in complete exhaustion. Louis stared at her for a moment, then shrugged and tied his end of the rope to the trunk of the nearest tree.

Simone lifted her hands to her mouth, and Louis didn't try to stop her as she pulled at the gag he'd tied around her face. Spitting the hateful thing out, Simone rubbed her tingling face for several moments.

"How did you find me?" she finally questioned.

Louis laughed and sat down on the ground as though it were the finest of furniture. "It was simple. You are dealing with a man who has tracked animals all of his life. Do you suppose tracking one addle-brained female was much more difficult? It wasn't hard with you, nor was it with your mother."

Simone bristled at the reminder but said nothing. "What are you planning? Where are you taking me?"

"Well, you see, I figure what with the law close on your heels for the death of poor Garvey Davis, you'll come willingly with me. We'll head to Colorado where there are plenty of mining towns to lose ourselves in."

"Mining? You? That's hard work," Simone said, realizing she was baiting him.

Louis shrugged. "I don't intend to be the one working, my dear."

Simone shook her head. "Then why the mines?"

"Because the mines need men aplenty to keep them running, and men need female companionship to ease their loneliness and help them forget their lot in life."

Simone felt herself go cold. "You plan to sell me . . . again?"

"Again and again and again," Louis said, eyeing her with contempt. "You'll make me plenty of money before we're through, and if you even think of not cooperating, I'll beat you soundly and hire you out anyway."

Simone felt ill. "You can't be serious."

"Oh, but I am. I got the idea when the fellows in Uniontown told me they would have happily paid to sample your charms. Now, I see us living high on the hog and doin' a banner business. I mean, you are a fetchin' woman, and many a man will be happy to pay the price I'm gonna ask. Especially for your first time around. Why, I heard tell some folks will pay upward of a thousand dollars for someone like you. That would set us up in fine order for a start, and from there we could have a real good life. And if you're extra good about this, I won't beat you. I'll even buy you some doodads to wear and fix yourself up in."

Simone shook her head. "This can't be happening," she moaned, then buried her face in her hands. Surely God wouldn't let this happen again.

TWENTY-NINE

ZACK FOLLOWED O'DONNELL to Florence with relative ease. The man didn't seem to realize that Zack would be so persistent, and Zack couldn't understand himself why it was so impossible to just let this case go. Beyond his desire to impress his father, he simply had a feeling for this case. The signs might point to Simone Dumas as the murderess of Garvey Davis, but Zack's gut instinct told him otherwise.

Still, Topeka had proven infuriating for him. He'd gone on a daily basis to try to talk to the Harvey Girls and Miss Taylor but found that no one had anything much to say to him. Yes, they remembered Simone. No, they didn't realize she was going to run away. No, they didn't know where she'd gone.

But Miss Taylor's nervousness about the entire matter made Zack confident that the truth was otherwise. Whenever he tried to talk to her, Mr. O'Donnell would inevitably intercede and whisk him away. Finally Zack gave up and decided instead to just keep an eye on Jeffery. Just as his gut told him Simone wasn't the killer of Davis, his gut also told him that he would find Simone through O'Donnell. It seemed wise to trust his instincts until they were otherwise proven wrong. And that was why he found himself deboarding the train in Florence, Kansas.

Making certain that he neither expose himself to Jeffery O'Donnell nor appear too out of place with the rest of the passengers, Zack made his way to a place just beyond the Harvey House. It could be that Jeffery would simply share lunch at the restaurant, then reboard and head elsewhere, and for that reason Zack couldn't allow himself the luxury of dinner.

His stomach growled in protest, but Zack stood his ground. He glanced toward the town, finding it smaller than Laramie. It seemed like a nice, quiet town, and Zack certainly couldn't protest against Kansas's refusal to allow open saloons. Surely it kept the crime down and made men more manageable for the law. It was one of the things he hated about his own town. In fact, most towns in Wyoming were the same. Whether or not there was a church or a school, you could pretty much bet there would be a saloon.

Time dragged by as Zack waited for O'Donnell to make some sort of move. The passengers gradually began to gravitate back toward the train, but there was no sign of Jeffery O'Donnell. Zack grew anxious waiting to see what would happen. Leaning up against a large cottonwood tree, Zack thought about his mission. It had become an obsession of sorts, he knew, but he prayed daily about it and still felt inclined to push on. Surely God was bringing him along as He saw fit.

The train whistle sounded, and Zack knew from the routine that the final boarding was only minutes away. He tensed. What if Jeffery made a mad dash for the train at the last minute? But his patience was rewarded when the conductor called the final board and Jeffery O'Donnell remained inside the Harvey House. Zack felt confident that this meant Simone Dumas was near. He couldn't exactly explain why, but he felt it with such assurance that rather than wait to follow O'Donnell around the town, Zack decided to search for the local lawman's office.

The afternoon sun bore down on him, but rather than making him uncomfortable, Zack rather relished the feel of it. Soon enough, winter would come to Wyoming, and by then Zack was sure to be home. The cold winters were enough to give a man thoughts of moving elsewhere, but Zack liked the simplicity of his life, as well as the spaciousness of his brand-new state. They suffered from corruption and conflict, like anyone else, but somehow having the miles between neighbors and even towns gave Zack a feeling of ease.

The sign over the door had been handmade and crudely painted to indicate that this was the destination Zack sought. Opening the door, Zack found himself in a tiny office.

"Can I help you?" a man questioned from where he sat cleaning a rifle.

"I hope so. You the law in these parts?"

"That's right," the man replied. "Who might you be?"

"I'm Deputy Zack Matthews. My father's sheriff up in Albany County, Wyoming."

"You're a long ways from home," the officer said, putting down his rifle. "What can I do for you?"

Zack pulled out the Wanted poster from his pocket. "I'm looking for two people, but in particular, this girl. Have you seen her?"

The man took the poster and instant recognition crossed his face. "Why, sure I have. She's one of the new girls over at the Harvey House. Wanted for questioning, eh? She don't hardly seem the type to be involved in any murder. She's quiet and good-natured. Seems to be a good worker."

Zack nodded. "She's only wanted for questioning."

"I see. Well, she lives over yonder at the Harvey House. I can't tell you much more than that. You could sure talk to the house manager over there. I'm sure they'd arrange for you to talk to her in the parlor. They're pretty protective of their girls, you know."

"I've gathered that," Zack replied, thinking about how his efforts were thwarted in Topeka.

"You want me to go with you? I could sure introduce you to the management."

"I'd like to hold off just a bit. I have my reasons, but I want to see what someone else plans to do before I make my move."

"Who might that be?" the man asked, his curiosity obviously stirred.

"A man who just came in from Topeka. He works for the Harvey line, and I believe he's been protecting Miss Dumas from questioning."

"That this man on the poster—her father?"

"No, he's a much younger man. Probably my age, maybe less. I don't know exactly how he fits into this, but I want to see if he has something else planned. I only intend to watch him for a few hours—that should be more than enough time to see what course he plans to take. Still, if you happen to see Miss Dumas before I do, I'd appreciate it if you would hang on to her. I've chased after her from Laramie to Chicago to Topeka and now here. I'm not of a mind to let her get away from me again."

"Understood. I'll do what I can to help you out."

Zack thanked the man and walked back out into the heat of the day. It wasn't until he was back on the street that he realized he'd never even gotten the man's name. He glanced at the Harvey House and wondered what his best course of action would be.

"God, I just want to do this right," he prayed, feeling torn about bringing Simone Dumas in for questioning. "If she didn't do it, let me find a way to prove it, and if she is guilty . . . well, help me to prove that, too."

THIRTY

JEFFERY WAITED IMPATIENTLY for Simone to return to the Harvey House. He wanted very much to explain Zack Matthews' presence in Topeka and discuss how they might hide her away from him on a permanent basis. But as day faded quickly into evening, Jeffery gradually grew worried that Simone had taken matters into her own hands.

An evening meal was served and still no sign of Simone. Jeffery sat contemplating what he should do when Una appeared, a worried expression on her face.

"I don't know where Simone has gone," she confided. "I asked the other girls and no one else talked to Simone this morning."

"She didn't say anything to you?"

"Not exactly. She asked about the local church. I've only met the preacher a couple of times but he seemed real nice. He preaches straight from the Bible, and I told Simone he appeared to be a good man."

"Why did she want to talk to the preacher?"

"I don't know," Una replied, her Swedish accent a little more evident. "I know she was upset and troubled ever since she'd come to Florence. But she wouldn't talk to me about it. Maybe you will tell me now?"

"I can't," Jeffery said with reluctance. "I would be betraying her confidence. It's not an easy situation, I can tell you that much."

"Do you want some more pie?" she asked softly as another of her co-workers passed close to the table.

"No," Jeffery said, shaking his head. "I've eaten enough to last me a week." Then he lowered his voice and added, "Look, Una, someone has to know where she's gone. This isn't that big of a place. Has she made any friends outside the Harvey House?"

Una shrugged. "I don't think so. She's never mentioned anyone. I've asked the girls, but they had no idea of where she'd gone. That's all I know to do. She should have been here by now. She was supposed to check in nearly half an hour ago. It isn't like her to just up and disappear."

Jeffery considered the situation and thought it would be very understandable if Simone just up and disappeared. A commotion rose up in the front room of the house, and with this commotion Jeffery had some hope that it might include Simone. Getting to his feet, he made his way to the front hall and found the housemother, a stately woman named Nellie, shaking her finger and issuing a warning to one of her girls.

"You've been told about coming in late. You may well have folks nearby, but that's no reason to ignore the rules."

"Sorry, but my ma just had another baby," the girl declared.

This seemed to soften Nellie. "Well, just this once, I suppose. But you'll have to do double the work tomorrow."

"Oh, I promise." The dark-haired girl started to go and then noticed Jeffery and Una.

"Oh, Una, come with me upstairs. I want to tease Simone about her new friend."

Jeffery held his tongue while Una asked, "What new friend?"

"The one I saw her spoonin' with down by the river. I couldn't get a good look at him, but he seemed a bit older than her. Nevertheless, they were mighty close when I spied them. He had his arms wrapped all around her." The girl giggled at this, thinking it all very amusing.

Una's face maintained a look of confusion while Jeffery took over the conversation. "Had you seen the man before?" he asked.

"Not with Simone. I think I saw him, if it was the same one," the girl qualified, "last week at the dry goods, but he never comes in here."

"But you don't know him as being someone from around Florence?"

"Oh no. He isn't from around here. I've lived here all my natural life and he ain't—" she paused to correct herself, "*isn't* from Florence."

Jeffery's sense of urgency doubled. "What did the man look like? I mean, if he was the same one from the store and all."

"He's about this tall," the girl replied, using her hand to indicate the height. "He has a moustache and black hair that he parts in the middle like yours. Other than that, I didn't notice much else about him."

"Was he my age?" Jeffery questioned, hardly imagining that the description she'd just given him was one of Zack Matthews. Nevertheless, he had to be sure.

"Oh, mercy no. He was an older man."

Jeffery thought of the Wanted poster and of Simone's father. The description didn't fit him, either. Stumped as to who the man might be, Jeffery fell silent. Had Simone enlisted the help of someone else?

"I want to see her room," he told Nellie.

"That's hardly fitting with the rules," the woman replied.

"I know, but I have a feeling this might well be an exception to beat all others. I'm afraid Miss Du—Irving might well be in trouble."

"What do you mean?" the girl asked. "Isn't Simone upstairs? Isn't she here?"

"No," Jeffery replied, "and frankly we're very worried about her. I need to see her room and determine if she's taken anything with her."

"I suppose it won't hurt just this once," Nellie replied.

With that, Nellie told a girl to run upstairs and issue an order for all the other Harvey Girls to remain in their rooms. The girl went quickly to the task while Una and Jeffery followed Nellie up the stairs at a slower pace.

"I can't imagine what you hope to find," Nellie muttered.

"I don't know, either. But I'm hoping that maybe something will give me an idea of what she's up to. I've got to talk to Simone. It's absolutely critical. If I see her room, perhaps I can determine if all of her things are still there. Una, you would definitely know if something were missing, wouldn't you?"

"Ja, I'd know it, all right."

"Good. We'll just give it a look over and see what's what."

Nellie made sure that all was clear before allowing Jeffery onto the dormitory floor of the Harvey House. "It appears to be all right," she said, motioning for Jeffery and adding, "Una, you might as well lead the way."

Una opened the room to them and stood back while Jeffery looked around for himself. "Does it appear in order?"

Una went to the closet, counted Simone's uniforms, and took stock of her other things. "She's wearing her blue serge skirt and white blouse," Una told them. She continued looking through Simone's nightstand and dresser drawers, then turned to face Jeffery and Nellie. "Nothing is missing. She didn't even take her coin purse."

Jeffery walked over to the desk and picked up the Bible. "Is this yours?"

"No, it's hers. This is the first time I've ever seen it out," Una replied.

Jeffery leafed through the pages, and when a piece of paper fell to the floor, he quickly retrieved it. It was the telegram he'd sent to her stating that he'd be arriving that day. Perhaps she'd panicked and run away from him. It was a nagging thought, and even though her things were in place around them, Jeffery couldn't help but fear that his words and actions of the past might have something to do with the present.

"I suppose the only thing to do is to wait for curfew and see if she makes it. She had the full day off from work and might just have decided to spend it out away from here. If not, then I don't know what to suggest," Nellie told Jeffery.

"But I thought the curfew was some time ago," Jeffery replied. "I mean, I overheard you with that girl downstairs."

"No, no," Nellie said, shaking her head. "She was late to work on her shift. I had allowed her to go home between shifts because her work was caught up and I knew her ma was in a family way. Curfew is in two hours."

"I suppose we have no other choice but to wait," Jeffery replied in complete frustration. He replaced the telegram in the Bible and placed both back on the desk. "I'll be in the downstairs parlor."

The women nodded and followed him back downstairs. Una went back to work, and Nellie promised to let him know the minute she saw anything of Simone. But two hours later, the circumstance was still the same and no one had seen anything of Simone Dumas.

Jeffery had spent his idle time in prayer and worry. He tried to give the situation over to God as he had heard a good Christian should do. But he seemed equally inclined to take it back as soon as his "Amen" faded and the fears and concerns crept back into his thoughts.

"I'm going to the police," he told the women. Getting to his feet, he realized it was the only choice he had. Going to the police would be exposing Simone to the law, but she might be in danger elsewhere and by keeping silent about her existence in Florence, Jeffery might well be signing her death sentence elsewhere.

"If she shows up, I'll send word to your hotel room," Nellie promised.

Una followed him to the door. "I'll be praying," she told him.

"I would appreciate that," he replied. "I think it may well be our only hope."

After getting quick instructions as to where he would find the local law, Jeffery immediately headed there. He knew Una desired to be reassured that Simone would be found safe and sound, but he couldn't give her that reassurance. In fact, he wanted that same optimism for himself but knew it wasn't to be.

Rounding the corner, his mind steeped in thoughts of Simone, Jeffery failed to see the other person before he slammed into him.

"I'm so sorry," he muttered, then glanced up to see the man's face in the moonlight.

"Matthews? What are you doing here?"

"Hello, O'Donnell. I figured a change of scenery might be nice, so I took the train to Florence. What business do you have here?"

"Look, I don't have time for this."

"Why not?" Matthews asked, crossing his arms against his chest. "You seem to have time enough to sit around this place all day."

Jeffery tried to shrug nonchalantly. "I work for Fred Harvey. I have business all along the line." He frantically tried to think how he might now approach the police without fully exposing Simone's situation. He had hoped only to report her as a missing employee, but with Matthews in town, there would be no other choice but to come clean on the identity of the woman he was seeking.

Matthews seemed to tire of the game. "I know she's here," he said flatly. "I've already talked to the local police officer, and he knows all about her, too."

Jeffery felt his throat grow tight. "Well, that's where you're wrong."

"Don't lie to me," Matthews said indignantly. "I know you've lied all along to me, and while I ought to take some real offense to it, I'm inclined to believe you have a personal affection for this woman. For that reason I'll let the lies from the past slip, but no more. I'm here to take her in and question her about the murder."

"She isn't here," Jeffery declared. And it was then that he realized that perhaps Matthews would be a better ally than adversary. "She's missing. I came into Florence earlier, as you probably already know. I've waited all day for her, but she never came back. I just went through her room, but nothing's missing. Her roommate tells me she took out this morning but never said much about her plans."

Matthews eyed him suspiciously for a moment. "This is the truth?"

"I swear it before God," Jeffery replied. "I was just on my way to the police when I ran into you."

"Come on, then," Matthews nodded with his head. "It's this way."

Jeffery followed in silence. He prayed that he'd done the right thing in telling Matthews about Simone. Zack already knew of her presence in Florence, but Jeffery could have kept him from realizing her disappearance. Or he could have even used her disappearance against him by saying that she had run again and was by now countless miles away.

They reached the office and found it dark. Jeffery tried the door, which opened easily enough, but found the interior devoid of life. "Now what?" he questioned.

"He's probably just making his rounds. I say we light the lamp and wait for his return."

Jeffery nodded and allowed Zack to do the work. They'd no sooner closed the door, however, when it opened and a balding man appeared. "Hello. I'm Brother Carlyle," the man introduced himself. "I don't believe I know either one of you gentlemen. Are you new to Florence?"

"Just here on business," Jeffery answered.

"Me too," Zack replied.

"Well, it's good to have you both. If you are both still here on Sunday, I'd like to invite you to join me in God's house."

"Thanks, but I'll probably be on my way by then," Jeffery said rather indifferently.

"Mac doesn't appear to be in," the preacher stated, glancing around. "Did he ask you to wait here for him?"

"No, we figured he was making rounds," Zack answered for them. "Is there something you were needing?"

"I came to see if Miss Dumas was here."

At this, both Zack and Jeffery were on their feet. "What do you know about Miss Dumas?" they questioned in unison.

Brother Carlyle took a step back. "Whoa, now, I seem to have stirred a bit of excitement."

"Simone is missing," Jeffery replied, eager for information. "When did you see her last?"

"Better yet," Zack interjected, "what makes you think she'd be here?"

"Well, it seems there was a matter she hoped to clear up with the law," Carlyle replied. "I really can't say much more than that."

"We know all about it," Jeffery said, anxious not to let Zack have the upper hand. "She's wanted for questioning in a murder."

"I'm here looking for her," Zack replied.

"She came to talk with me this morning. Well, it was closer to noon, I suppose. But we talked at some length. You do know that she was only defending herself, don't you?" he addressed this question to Zack.

"What do you mean?"

"I mean, the dead man tried to take liberties with her."

"He meant to rape her," Jeffery added more strongly.

Zack seemed to consider the words for a moment. "So she killed him defending her honor, is that it?"

"She never meant to kill him," Jeffery shot back. "She only picked up a pitcher and hit him over the head, hoping to knock him out. Nothing more."

"That's right. That's exactly what she told me. Said she didn't want to hang for a crime she never meant to commit. She only wanted to keep her purity. She hit him and ran."

"That doesn't match up to what I found," Zack replied. "There were broken pieces of a pitcher, but Garvey Davis was bludgeoned to death with something more than a pitcher."

Jeffery got excited at this bit of news. "Then don't you see? She couldn't have killed him. Someone else came in and did the deed."

"I don't see it that way at all," Zack replied. "I hear you saying that she confessed to having hit the man, but that she didn't mean to kill him."

"But Simone has told both this man and myself the same story," Jeffery interjected. "Look, she willingly admitted to hitting him over the head, but then she ran away. She thinks she killed him with a single blow, and according to this man, she intended to come clean about it."

"That's right," Brother Carlyle agreed. "It wasn't that she didn't feel responsible for having killed the man. She wasn't trying to say her blow to the head hadn't caused his death."

Realization dawned in Zack's eyes. "I see your point. She wasn't defending herself of not having killed him, she was merely stating how she did it and why."

"That's right, and if she didn't hit him more than once with a cheap pitcher, she probably wasn't responsible for his death," Jeffery added.

"You may well be right, O'Donnell."

"I know I am. I've never believed her capable of this murder, not even for a minute. Better you look up that father of hers. In fact, I'm afraid we might well be dealing with him now."

"Why do you say that?" Zack asked, eyeing Jeffery suspiciously.

"Because one of the Harvey Girls saw Simone down by the river with an older man. He didn't fit the description on your sketch, but that doesn't mean anything. A man on the run would try to alter his appearance."

"Why do you think it's Dumas?"

"I don't know. I just fear that it is. You have no idea what that man has done to her."

"I can vouch for that," Carlyle said in an almost angry tone. "She told me of his cruelty to her."

"I believe you both. After all, he sold her to Garvey Davis to be a wife. That much I learned from the folks who lived in the area. Any man who would treat his own flesh and blood like that doesn't rate very high in my book."

"If it is Dumas," Jeffery said, unable to hide his fear, "there's no telling what he'll do to her."

"Then we have to find them," Zack answered flatly. "The sooner, the better."

THIRTY-ONE

JEFFERY FELT ENORMOUSLY frustrated by the time the city police officer returned. Mac, as Brother Carlyle continued to call him, suggested they wait until first light to pursue clues as to what had happened to Simone. Jeffery, on the other hand, wanted to head out, even though he knew himself to be incapable of tracking and even less knowledgeable about the land around him. To his surprise, Zack Matthews agreed on the wait, and it wasn't until morning, when Mac rallied them and four other townsmen, that Jeffery fully saw the wisdom in the wait.

"Matthews here will head up the group going west along the river. I'll take the rest of you to the east with me. We need to look for tracks that might indicate a direction taken. We also want to note whether there has been any scuffle. Look for blood, bits of cloth, anything that might let you know which way they went."

Jeffery felt his stomach tighten at the thought of Simone being hurt or bleeding. He wanted to scream that they were wasting time, but no one else—not even Matthews—seemed overly excited about the wait.

"Matthews, O'Donnell, I've secured a couple of horses for you to ride," the officer told them, "but I think the first part of our work will be on foot."

Matthews nodded, so Jeffery felt the need to join in. He didn't want Matthews taking the upper hand. The man was already intimidating him something fierce. Jeffery reminded himself that he'd spent his life in the city, whereas Matthews was clearly country reared. Not only that, but Matthews' background was working as a lawman. He knew what to look for and what to do. That was why Jeffery decided then and there that he would stick with Matthews like a bee to honey. And it wasn't just Matthews' knowledge that made up Jeffery's mind for him. Matthews was determined to find Simone. She'd already caused him to travel thousands of miles, and it was certain he wouldn't stop at this minor inconvenience. And while Jeffery wasn't nearly as worried as he had been that Matthews might try to string Simone up to the nearest tree, he worried that if Matthews found her he'd merely load her up and take her away without giving Jeffery a chance to speak his heart.

And his heart was very full.

Just thinking of all the things he wanted to say to Simone put Jeffery at a disadvantage. His mind wasn't on the details of what they would find on the ground around the Cottonwood, his mind was on Simone and how he had fallen in love with her. He wanted to make her understand that he didn't care what had happened in the past. He wanted her to understand that he believed in her story—believed in her. He wanted to tell her about God and how trusting in Him had given Jeffery new hope for his future . . . their future. So much needed saying, and Jeffery felt a heartache in knowing that he might never get the chance.

"You two go with Matthews," Mac commanded, "and you two come with me. O'Donnell, you—"

"I'm going with Matthews," Jeffery interjected without waiting for any instructions.

Mac nodded. "We'd best get to work, then."

And work it was. Harder than Jeffery had ever imagined. It wasn't physically demanding, but it was painstakingly slow, and it irritated Jeffery in the worst way.

"I can't see tracks of any sort," one of their companions finally said.

"Yes," Matthews replied, the frustration ringing clear. "Whoever Miss Dumas went with, they didn't want anyone to know about it. Someone has come and brushed out all the tracks."

"So follow the brush marks," Jeffery snapped. He pushed back his normally well-placed brown hair and waited for Matthews to contradict his suggestion. Instead, all three men looked at him like he'd lost his senses.

"Whoever brushed out the tracks knew what he was doing. It isn't a matter of following the brush marks. If you'll look for yourself, you'll see there are no brush marks."

"There has to be something there!" Jeffery hated looking like a fool, but he hated even more that Matthews was right.

Matthews looked him square in the eye for just a heartbeat before shaking his head and moving along the river. Anger welled up in Jeffery. Matthews was probably the reason Simone had gone off by herself. He must have exposed his plan to bring her in and Simone probably got wind of it and . . .

No, that didn't make sense, Jeffery had to admit. Simone wasn't stupid. She went to the church to talk to the minister. She planned to talk to the police—to turn herself in. But she never made it.

"Here!" Matthews called out from some five or six yards away. "He missed a spot."

"How can you be sure it's our man?" one of their companions asked.

"It isn't. The footprints are very small and definitely belong to a woman or young girl."

"Could be someone else came this way," the other man commented.

"I suppose so, but this is all we have to work with at this point," Matthew answered and continued moving farther upriver.

Jeffery followed in silent defeat. There seemed very little he could do. *God, I'm so worthless here*, he prayed. *I know nothing about any of this.* He bent down, trying hard to see something that just wasn't there. *Please help us to find a clue. Help us to find Simone. I don't know where she is*, he cried in silent misery, *but you do. You see her even now. You know her every move. Oh, God, keep her safe. Don't let her come to further harm.* Then it dawned on Jeffery that he'd just done the very best thing he could for Simone. He had prayed. He was helpless and worthless in regards to knowing the lay of the land and how to find the right path. But God knew every detail. God would supply his every need.

"Here," Matthews called. He stood a good ten yards away and was eyeing something in his hand like it was gold.

"What is it?" Jeffery asked, rushing to make it to Matthews' side first.

"Do you know what Miss Dumas was wearing?" he asked, closing his hand over whatever he'd found. "Is she wearing one of those uniforms?"

Jeffery tried to remember what Una had said. He thought back to his search through her room. "No," he said, shaking his head. "Her uniforms were all in place. Una said she was wearing a skirt and blouse. I think the blouse was a plain white one. The skirt was blue."

Matthews smiled and opened his hand. There in the middle of his palm was a small piece of blue material. "Found it caught on a piece of root over there. They definitely came this way. My guess is that they'll keep to the river until they're away from town." He turned to one of the other men. "Go get the others and tell them what we've found." The man nodded and took off in the direction of town. "Oh, and now would probably be a good time to bring those horses," he called after the man.

"Will do!" came the reply.

"Now what?" Jeffery questioned. He hated having to ask Matthews for information, but his mind wouldn't accept not knowing.

"We'll keep pushing in this direction. Sooner or later they'll get tired of covering their tracks. They'll figure no one will be able to find them, and they'll get lazy."

"Don't say it like Simone is in on it. She isn't!" Jeffery protested.

Matthews shrugged. "I don't see any signs of a fight, and your eyewitness didn't mention anything about a struggle. I'd say Miss Dumas went very willingly with her companion."

"That's a lie!" Jeffery exclaimed, moving closer to Matthews. The man only had a couple inches on him in height but was probably an additional thirty pounds in muscle. "Simone was terrified of her father, and if she went willingly, then it was because she feared for her life."

"We don't know for sure that it was her father," Matthews reminded him.

"Who else would it be? No one else knows her."

"It could have been a complete stranger with a good time on his mind," the one remaining townsman offered.

Jeffery glared hard at the man, but Matthew only nodded. "Could be."

"No. I feel certain that somehow Louis Dumas has a hand in this," Jeffery replied. "I may not be much good at tracking or figuring out things like this, but I'm certain in my gut that Simone's father has come back to haunt her."

"I'm not saying it isn't a possibility," Matthews replied. "I'm just stating facts here. We don't know who Miss Dumas is with. We only know that someone was seen walking with her along the river."

By this time, the others were coming to join them. "So what did you find?" Mac called out.

Matthews went forward with the material. "This is a piece of material that matches the description of the skirt Miss Dumas was wearing. My guess is that they headed west along the river and eventually they'll break away and head out for other parts. What's the nearest towns?"

"River goes north to Marion. Tracks go south to Newton," Mac replied. "Cottonwood Falls is to the northeast. It wouldn't be too hard to get to. 'Course, if your gal is headed this way, she probably won't backtrack around the town to head that way."

Zack Matthews seemed to take a long time considering this information before posing another question. "What's the lay of farms along the way to Newton?"

"They're scattered. Most of the farms around here were set up as homesteads."

Matthews nodded. "Then this could take some time."

"Well, I can spare the horses but not the time," the officer answered honestly. He shifted in his saddle and gave Jeffery a sympathetic nod. "Wish I could do more, but one wayward female with or without her questionable companion doesn't rate against a payroll shipment. We need to get back to Florence in order to take care of our own business."

"I understand," Matthews replied. "I'm obliged for the loan of the horses. I'll get them back to you as soon as I can."

"Wait!" Jeffery called out as the officer reined his horse around. "You can't mean to just leave her out there."

"I'd like to help, but you're in good hands." He nodded in the direction of Zack. "Matthews seems fully capable of finding the way, and surely the two of you can handle the job."

"We can handle it," Matthews replied, mounting the offered horse. "You coming, O'Donnell?"

Jeffery looked first to Mac and his men and then to Zack. "I suppose I have no choice."

"You can just go back to town and let me do what I came to do," Matthews replied, giving Jeffery a fixed look. After this brief exchange, Matthews turned his horse and headed west.

"Not a chance of that," Jeffery called after him and hurried to his own mount.

Zack wasn't at all pleased to have O'Donnell tagging along. The man was hopeless when it came to tracking and even worse at dealing with the rougher side of life. It seemed clear to Zack that O'Donnell was used to sitting behind a desk and riding in carriages rather than aback a horse on an open prairie. But it wasn't to be helped. The urgency of the matter pressed Zack forward without much time left over to argue with O'Donnell.

As Zack had predicted, once the cover of trees thinned out, there was clear evidence of tracks. "They've headed due west," Zack told Jeffery as he studied the dirt. Remounting, he pointed. "I'm heading for that hill. It's not much, but it might show us something."

Jeffery grunted and wiped his brow. The sun crept ever higher in the sky, bringing with it the August heat. Zack wondered how long O'Donnell could tolerate staying in the saddle. If the heat didn't do him in, no doubt the exercise would.

They rode silently until they'd topped the hill, and it was only after Zack brought his horse to a stop that Jeffery O'Donnell spoke.

"You don't honestly expect them to be anywhere in view, do you? I mean, they've got a good day on us. They could have been picked up by some sympathetic passerby and be almost anywhere by now. Dumas could have even had horses stashed and waiting."

"That's all possible," Zack replied, scanning the horizon. In the distance he could make out the white block form of a farmhouse. "They could have even made their way to that house down there."

"What house?"

Zack watched as O'Donnell nearly unseated himself trying to crane around to see the house. "Do you think they went there? Do you see tracks?"

"No tracks," Zack replied. "Which makes me think that at this point they were still on foot."

"If they even came this way," Jeffery muttered.

Zack didn't reply. Instead, he urged the horse forward in the direction of the farmstead. He wasn't at all sure they were heading in the right direction, but he sure didn't need to hear it from O'Donnell's mouth. His patience with the man was beginning to wear thin. It was obvious that the man felt he had a vested interest in the matter.

They were nearly to the bottom of the hill when Zack finally asked the question that had been nagging him since he'd first met up with O'Donnell in Topeka.

"You have some special connection to Miss Dumas?"

"You might say that," Jeffery replied.

"Well, I figured as much. No man chases after a woman without a reason."

"Like the desire to see her hanged for a murder she didn't commit?" O'Donnell countered.

"I don't want to see her hang if she isn't guilty," Zack replied. "And I never said I thought she was the one who did the murder."

"But you've chased her all the way from Wyoming."

"Yes, but that's because she's wanted for questioning. Just because I think she stands a good chance of being innocent doesn't mean I can let her run off without accounting for the fact that she did steal Davis's horse and gear."

"But she was desperate. She feared for her life and her innocence," O'Donnell argued.

"I'm well aware of what you've told me, but, frankly, I'd like to hear it from Miss Dumas."

Zack felt marginal relief when O'Donnell fell silent. They rode in unison, no sound but the harsh prairie wind blowing and the horses' hooves plodding a path across the open range. Zack had a hunch, and if this hunch rewarded him as others had, he felt certain they'd learn news of Simone and her companion when they stopped at the farmhouse. He was beginning to feel rather excited about the whole thing when O'Donnell started up again.

"What if the people here haven't any news for you? What then?"

Zack shrugged. He honestly wasn't sure what he would do. "I guess we'll cross that bridge when we get to it."

"Can I ask you something else?" Jeffery questioned, and for once his tone wasn't in the same condescending manner to which Zack had grown accustomed.

"What?"

"It seems to me that you are perfectly willing to believe in Simone's innocence. You tell me that you have to pursue her for questioning, and that she might have answers you need."

"That's right."

"But what happens when she tells you what you want to hear? Will you have to take her back with you to Wyoming, even if she tells you the truth?"

"The truth won't be for me to decide," Zack told him, reining back the horse. He stopped and looked Jeffery in the eye. "She'll have to stand trial and let a jury decide. You do understand that, don't you?"

"But I thought—"

"You thought just because I admitted that Davis was bludgeoned to death in a manner that would suggest someone with a whole lot more muscle than the petite Miss Dumas, that I would just let her go once she told her story?"

"But if she's innocent, you can't expect her to just give up her new life and go back to Wyoming."

"I won't go back home without someone to stand trial for Davis's murder."

Jeffery looked away and his shoulders sagged. "I don't want to lose her." His voice was barely audible.

"Neither do I," Zack said frankly, realizing they both wanted Simone Dumas for entirely different reasons. O'Donnell's—for their romantic future together. His—to prove something to his father.

THIRTY-TWO

LOUIS GLANCED OVER at his daughter. She leaned forward, awkwardly positioned atop the horse he'd managed to steal. Her head bobbed up and down with the steady plodding of the horse, and her eyes were closed. She wouldn't last much longer. He'd refused her food and water over the past forty-eight hours, all in hopes of keeping her too weak to fight him. Now, however, she was about to fall off her mount. They'd have to stop in order for her to rest. He glanced around, seeing in the dusky twilight that they were as far removed from civilization as they could get. It gave him a small amount of comfort.

"We'll make camp here," Louis told her. He slid off his mount and walked the beast to a nearby sapling. Tying the reins securely, Louis unfastened the reins to Simone's mount from where he'd tied them to the horn of his own saddle. He pulled the horse up even with his own, then after tying him off, Louis reached up and pulled Simone down.

"Go over there and don't even think of trying to sneak off," he told her, knowing Simone was physically incapable of escaping.

Simone seemed to barely even hear him. She stumbled several paces in the direction her father had pointed, then collapsed onto the hard ground. Louis looked at her for a moment, then shrugged and went back to the business of unsaddling the horses. Better that she sleep, he decided. If she was unconscious, she wouldn't be plotting against him.

He unfastened a bundle he'd secured to the back of his mount, then pulled off the saddle and tethered the horse in such a way that he could feed off the nearby grass. After doing the same for Simone's horse, he built a fire and sat down to satisfy his own needs.

First came a bottle of whiskey. He took a long drink, then congratulated himself for being cunning enough to have found the deserted farmhouse where he stole not only his drink but horses and other supplies, as well. Apparently the family had gone into town, leaving the place completely vulnerable to his needs. There had been a protective farm dog, but Louis's knife had taken care of that matter. It immediately appeared that this farm specialized in breeding horseflesh. It was perfect for their predicament. Six or seven horses were in a nearby corral, and Louis had only to pick out the best looking of the bunch.

Simone had been sick over his treatment of the family pet, so while he searched the house for things they could use, he'd left Simone tied to the porch not ten feet from where the dog lay dying. He had heard her crying the entire time he ransacked the house.

He stared at her unconscious form with indifference. She had no idea what lay ahead for her. No doubt she'd complain about her unfair lot. *Probably cry about everything day and night. Whining female! Just like her mother. Always thinking tears could turn a man's heart*. Louis laughed and took another swig from the bottle.

"Well, you won't be turning a man's heart with tears when I get through with you," he said, continuing to stare at Simone's crumpled form. "They'll line up to pay for what you've got to offer, and it won't be tears. You'll do what you're told, and you'll make me a rich man."

Louis paused long enough to throw some wood on the fire and leaned back once again to cherish the bottle of whiskey. He muttered a curse and took a drink. "Stupid state. Keeping a man from a good drink ought to be against the law, not part of it." He neither knew nor cared why this Florence farm family had managed to secure a bottle for their cabinet—he only thanked the fates for his finding it. He'd taken it, along with a loaf of bread, half a wheel of cheese, and three thick slices of ham that were still sitting on the back of the stove. And now, smirking over his victorious journey to find Simone, Louis helped himself to some of the meat and dreamed of his future.

"You thought you could outrun me," he told the sleeping Simone. "Thought you could run and leave me like your mother. Well, you were a fool."

Louis ate in silence, washing down the dried-out ham with whiskey. They were still several days from the mining camps of Colorado. If the weather held and Simone regained her strength, they could probably be to Denver within a week. Denver would allow Louis a few chances at the poker tables and maybe even a high roller who was willing to pay for Simone's innocence. The idea was thought provoking. Denver was full of moneyed men, and the idea of making a quick buck was enough to warm Louis's blood. That and the whiskey.

Several hours later, the bottle was empty and Louis was drunk. He didn't feel overwhelmingly drunk—after all, he'd spent most of his years imbibing in one form of liquor or another. But it was as if the long wait from Chicago to this prairie field had somehow cleansed his system and allowed the liquor to take a stronger hold. He felt warm and wonderfully relaxed. He could have easily danced a jig or joined in a tavern drinking song, he felt so good.

Simone stirred, and the action caused Louis to take note of her once again.

"Stupid girl. You're slowing me down."

The sound of his voice apparently brought her awake. Sitting up very slowly, Simone stared at him for a moment before taking in the campfire and the scene around them. She looked heavenward at the full moon before rasping out her question.

"Where are we?"

"Can't say," Louis replied. "I ain't never been to this part of the country. It's my guess that we'll make Denver inside of a week. And then you are going to make me a rich man."

Simone shook her head. "You're wrong. I won't do the things you plan for me."

"And how do you propose to stop me? You couldn't even escape me," Louis replied, slurring his words. "I had it all planned. I came back for you that night."

"What are you talking about?" Simone asked, her hand going to her head as if to clear out the haze that kept her from understanding.

Louis laughed. "I came back for you after leavin' you with Davis. Figured on changin' our plans."

"You came back?" she asked and her voice was barely audible. Then, as if forgetting what she had asked, Simone eased up on her knees and asked, "Can I have some water?"

Louis looked at her for a moment. She looked to be in bad shape, and while it had served his purpose to keep her weak, if he was going to get any real money out of her, he was going to have to treat her right. He tossed her a canteen and then begrudgingly cut a chunk of cheese and tossed that at her, as well.

The canteen landed at her right hand, and she'd just managed to sit down when the cheese landed in her lap. She stared dumbly at it for a few minutes before Louis spoke.

"You'd better eat it. We don't have much, but you'll have to keep up your strength." He watched as she drank from the canteen. She looked so much like her mother that to Louis's drunken mind she was very nearly the same woman.

"I told you not to betray me," he muttered. "I warned you good. You shouldn't have left me."

Simone looked up at him. "You gave me away. You sold me to Garvey Davis."

"But I came back."

"You keep saying that," she whispered, nibbling at the cheese.

"I came back to take you with me," he said. "Decided to take you so that you could make me some money."

"I won't," she said flatly, and when she said nothing else, Louis continued.

"They'll like your looks in Denver. They liked your looks in Uniontown. Could've made good money there." He paused and looked past her into the darkness. He could almost see them living it up in Denver. If she would just see things his way.

"I won't go with you," Simone said.

He looked back to her. "You'll go. You don't want me doing to you what I did to him."

"What are you talking about?" she asked, scooting closer to the fire.

"I told you I came back. Saw what you did to Garvey." Louis laughed a deep, throaty laugh. "Didn't know you had it in you."

Simone shuddered. "I'm not proud of what I did. But I was protecting myself. He would have raped me! You left me there and now you suggest—"

"He was to be your husband. That weren't rape. What a man does with his wife ain't rape."

"It is when it's forced," Simone replied.

Louis shrugged. "He was moaning and groaning. Couldn't even get up."

"What are you saying?"

Simone moved closer still, her face blurring before his eyes. He couldn't remember the last time he'd been this tired, and that, on top of the whiskey, was making it hard to remember what he was saying.

But Simone was adamant. "What do you mean he was moaning and groaning? Are you talking about Garvey Davis?"

Louis shrugged again. "Who else would I be talkin' about, you dim-witted girl? I finished the job you started. Took my maul from the tool shed and did the job right." He rubbed his eyes, and when he looked at Simone again, she was crying. "What ails you now?"

She shook her head. "I . . . I thought . . . I killed him."

Louis laughed. "The law thinks that, too. But I don't care. It'll give me control over you. You'll do what you're told, or I'll turn you in."

"But I was going to turn myself in," Simone replied. "All this time I thought I'd killed Garvey Davis." She wiped her eyes. "I didn't kill him. I didn't kill him."

"No, you didn't," Louis replied. "I killed the man. Figured if he was stupid enough to get himself into a fix like that, then he didn't deserve to live."

"But you'd let them hang me for this? For a crime I didn't commit?"

"As far as the law is concerned, you did the deed."

"But I'm your child. Your own flesh and blood."

"You ain't mine. Your ma was already carrying you when I met up with her in Denver."

"What?" Simone got to her feet slowly. "What are you saying?"

Louis, too, struggled to his feet. "I'm saying you ain't my kid."

"Then who is my father?" Simone asked, a look of shock clearly registered on her face.

Louis shook his head. "I don't know and I don't care. I just know that I've done the job all these years and now you're coming with me. You owe me."

Simone shook her head. "No wonder you could do those things to me. No wonder you hated me so much. I couldn't understand how you could just give me to Garvey Davis, but now I know."

"I didn't give you to nobody. Davis bought you fair and square. Just like the others are gonna do."

"No," Simone replied, backing away. "I won't do it."

"You have no choice."

"You can't watch me twenty-four hours a day," Simone replied.

"And there's no place you can run that's far enough to keep me from finding you."

Simone shuddered and Louis laughed. He knew she sensed his power, and it gave him courage. "So unless you want to end up dead like Davis, you'd best get it in your head to cooperate."

"There are worse things than death," she said.

Louis thought about the words for a moment. The girl had a point. He supposed there were a few things worse than death. He staggered back a step before speaking. "It don't matter. You're coming with me. The world thinks you're a murderin' thief. Just remember, it was you—not me, who took Davis's horse and saddle."

"But you killed him," she threw back.

"Yeah, I killed him. I did it. I killed Garvey Davis, but no one 'cept you and me knows that."

The sound of a gun cocking instantly grabbed Louis's attention. He might be drunk, but he wasn't so far gone that he couldn't recognize that sound. He looked at Simone for a moment. The look on her face told him that she'd heard it, too, but it wasn't until she took another step backward that Louis realized he'd been found out.

Two men emerged from behind the trees. One held a gun level with Louis's midsection. The other, too well dressed for this kind of business, clearly had his eyes fixed on Simone.

"Louis Dumas, I'm arresting you for the murder of Garvey Davis."

"Weren't me," Louis protested, his hands flailing. "It was the girl."

"We heard your confession," the man with the gun commented.

The other man moved quickly to where Simone stood. Louis heard him ask if she was all right. "Leave her be. Unless you're paying, you stay away from her."

"Oh, Jeffery, you found me," Simone murmured, her tears flowing anew. "He took me from Florence."

"I know," the man whispered, pulling her into his arms.

Louis pulled a knife from his boot and lunged at Jeffery. "I told you to leave her be."

Simone screamed and Jeffery quickly shielded her behind him. Louis swept the knife through the air. "You aren't going to ruin this for me. You aren't taking her away." He slashed at the air with his knife while Jeffery narrowly escaped by dodging back and forth. The fact that he held Simone behind him slowed his steps, however, and without warning, Louis's blade caught the edge of the man's coat.

Louis knew he'd made contact with the man's flesh, just by the look in his eyes. Louis had seen that look a hundred times before. It was a look of panic—a look that questioned survival.

"I'm gonna kill—" Louis felt the hard blow on his head, and for a moment he stood as though nothing had happened. Then everything went black.

Simone looked down at her father's crumpled form and then to the man who'd struck him with the butt of his revolver. The man with the gun came forward and stood not two feet away while Jeffery tried to bind his cut with his handkerchief.

"I didn't kill him." Simone looked into the man's face, shadows from the fire dancing around him. "I didn't kill Garvey Davis."

"I know," the man with the gun replied. "I heard everything he said."

Jeffery turned to her. "We were out there for most of the time you were sleeping. We were going to come in then, but we were afraid of what might have happened if you awoke in a start."

"Jeffery," she gasped, looking at the red-stained handkerchief.

"You're bleeding pretty good," the other man said, holstering his gun. "You'd best let me see if I can get it stopped."

Simone watched as he unwrapped the handkerchief and inspected the bleeding wound. It was more than she could take. With the knowledge of her innocence, Simone followed her father's example and passed out cold on the hard prairie ground.

THIRTY-THREE

"WELL, IF YOU AREN'T the popular one," Nellie said, bringing in not one but two bouquets of flowers for Simone's inspection. The Harvey House mother beamed a smile at Simone. "I'm glad to see you up and dressed. You look so much better. These ought to perk you up even more."

Simone shook her head and finished securing a pin into her hair. "Where in the world did those come from?"

"The two gents who are awaiting your arrival in our downstairs parlor," Nellie replied. "Same two gents who brought you here in the first place. That nice Mr. O'Donnell and his friend Mr. Matthews."

Simone nodded. She had known without asking that this would be the case. Una had told her the night before that both men seemed very concerned for her welfare. She had teased Simone about keeping a stable of beaus, but Simone hadn't taken the matter seriously. Zack Matthews had his heart set on one thing alone, and that was solving the Davis murder case. In speaking with him on the long ride back to Florence, Simone had been amazed to learn that Matthews had followed her from Wyoming, all on the chance that he could solve the case and bring in the murderer of Garvey Davis.

He had also confided that he'd never really believed Simone to be the murderer. He did worry that she'd been a pawn in her father's schemes but was happy to be proven wrong on that matter. Jeffery, ever attentive and concerned for her well-being, had said practically nothing as they'd ridden across the windy prairie. He seemed greatly preoccupied with something else, but he gave Simone no indication of what that might be. She supposed he was anxious to get back to work and to Chicago.

"You'd best go down and speak with those boys," Nellie said, interrupting Simone's reflections and placing the flowers on the desk. "They've been here constantly nagging me for information. Poor Una was stuck answering questions all morning. They aren't likely to go away until they've talked to you and seen for themselves that you've survived your ordeal."

Simone discarded her thoughts and nodded. "I know you're probably right." She gave her appearance a hasty assessment and smoothed down the form-fitting bodice of the red gingham gown. "I suppose I'm as ready as I'll ever be."

"You look mighty pretty in that dress. I'm sure you'll have both of those men eating out of your hand."

Simone laughed. "I'll point them to Mr. Harvey's dining room if they so much as attempt such an act. Nowhere in my line of duty am I required to hand-feed customers."

Nellie laughed at this and stepped into the hallway. "You could probably make those two do anything you suggested."

Still smiling, she followed Nellie downstairs and into the parlor. Both Zack and Jeffery stood in welcome to greet her. Jeffery grinned from ear to ear, while Zack looked rather embarrassed by the entire matter. Simone understood Zack's reaction. She felt rather embarrassed herself.

"Simone, come sit here," Jeffery said, coming forward. "We don't want you to wear yourself out."

Unused to anyone pampering her like this, Simone stiffened slightly. "Jeffery, I assure you I am fine. Nellie took good care of me these past two days, and there is nothing more that need be done for me."

She turned to Zack, who was twisting his hat in his hands. What a contrast between the two men. Zack in his faded jeans and broadcloth shirt. Zack with his tanned face and windblown hair. He seemed to be a deep thinker and a man of few words. He didn't mind that his appearance was less than orderly. As she looked at Jeffery she saw nothing but perfection. He was impeccably dressed in his brown serge suit, his hair had been carefully parted down the middle and slicked back on either side with tonic water. She could smell his cologne from where she stood, while Zack smelled of nothing more than soap and summer air.

"I . . . uh . . . just wanted to let you know," Zack began awkwardly, "I'll be taking your father . . . uh . . . Mr. Dumas back to Wyoming today. We leave on the afternoon train."

"I see." Simone looked at the floor and tried to feel something other than relief that this man she'd called Father would soon be far away from her. "Forgive me if I sound harsh. I really don't mean to be, but I'm glad you're taking him away." She looked up hesitantly. "I just don't think I could go through the trial."

"I don't think there'll be much of a trial. I mean, I heard his confession and I have both yours and Mr. O'Donnell's sworn statements. I figure given the circumstances, the charges against you for theft will be dropped, and there should be no need for you to come back to Wyoming."

"Thank you." Her voice betrayed her obvious relief.

"I think you should know that given the situation," Zack continued, "and the violent nature of Mr. Davis's demise, your . . . Mr. Dumas will probably face death for his actions."

Simone nodded and lifted her eyes to meet Zack's compassionate gaze. "I know. I've thought of nothing else for some time." She paused and looked at Jeffery. "It could have been me. And because of the horror of what I'd experienced, I thought I wanted him dead. Now I realize taking his life won't change what he's done. When I think of how close I came to . . ." She paused and shuddered. "It could have been me. He could have killed me or left me to hang for Garvey Davis's death."

"Shhh," Jeffery interjected. "God interceded. He knew the truth of the matter and didn't allow an innocent person to be blamed for something they didn't do."

"It's more than I can begin to understand," Simone said softly. "I stand amazed that such a miracle could take place on my behalf. God really heard my prayers."

"I don't suppose you want to see him before we leave," Zack said as if to introduce the idea to Simone.

"No, I don't want to see him. I never want to see him again. He's caused me nothing but heartache. I really want to forgive that man for all he's done to me, especially for taking away my mother and brother."

"I thought you said they deserted you," Jeffery interjected.

Simone shook her head. "My mother left to bring the law back with her. She intended to return, but Louis Dumas killed her and my baby brother."

"What!" Zack and Jeffery declared in unison.

"It's true," Simone replied, looking from man to man. "He used to taunt me with that fact. He came home and found they were gone and he went off in search of them. When he returned, he told me how he'd killed them and how my mother would never come back to help me again."

"Did he ever tell you where he put their bodies?" Zack questioned, then realized the delicacy of the situation. "My pardon."

Simone shook her head. "No, he never said a single word about what he had done with them afterward." She felt a heavy sadness overwhelm her. "I wish I knew where they were."

"But you do know," Jeffery replied. "You told me yourself that your mother had accepted Christ as her Savior. You'll see her again one day in heaven."

Simone realized he was right, but it didn't lessen the sense of loss. "I've spent a lot of time being angry over things I couldn't control. Now I feel God has finally given me hope for the future."

Zack smiled. "He's good to do that."

She nodded. "I guess I'm just starting to see that for myself. It's a wondrous thing."

"Perhaps your earthly father is still living," Zack offered. "You might find out one day who he is and where he lives."

"Perhaps," Simone replied, "but I'm sure a search like that would take a great deal of time and money." She sighed and smiled. "Besides, I have a job with Mr. Harvey's company. I have a contract that I must see through, and I'm thankfully no longer a wanted woman."

"Oh, you're wanted," Jeffery whispered, leaning very close.

He seemed not to mind that Zack could hear his words, but Simone felt her face grow hot.

"Well, I'd best be going," Zack said, finally breaking the silence. "I have to collect my things before I head out."

"Thank you again," Simone said, stepping forward to offer her hand. "I'm still overwhelmed to realize that God brought you here. I thought for a time it was His curse that you should be able to track me down, but now I understand that what I saw as harmful, God meant for good."

Zack smiled and shook her hand very gently. "I'll send you a letter and let you know what happens."

"Thank you. I think that would be most helpful."

He nodded first to her, then to Jeffery. "If you folks get up Wyoming way, look me up."

With that said, he took his leave. Simone had no time to think about Zack Matthews' departure because no sooner had the screen door closed behind him than Jeffery pulled her into his arms and surprised her with a kiss. His lips were warm against hers, and Simone felt a sensation of heat spread out from the union.

"I've wanted to do that since you first came into the room," he told her.

Simone pushed him away. Her head was swimming dizzily from the contact. She couldn't understand why this man had such control over her emotions. When Jeffery was near, rational thought fled.

"Don't do that," she admonished. "Someone will see you."

"I don't care," Jeffery replied. "I intend to do it quite often." He moved toward her, but Simone sidestepped him and positioned herself behind a chair.

"Stop it, now, and listen to me."

Jeffery laughed. "All right. But if you'd honestly rather talk than kiss, I can see I have much to teach you."

Simone nodded. "That's along the lines of what I'm trying to say. I have a lot to learn. I've scarcely seen much of life, unless you count my seventeen years of torment in a mountain cabin in Wyoming."

"You're only seventeen?" Jeffery questioned with a grin. "You know that goes against Fred Harvey's rules."

"So does hiring a woman without a thorough background check," Simone countered. "I'll be eighteen come spring and that isn't that far off. Fire me if you must, but it won't change anything."

"But you care for me," Jeffery replied.

Simone bit at her lower lip. It was hard to know how to deal with her emotions and Jeffery at the same time. "Yes, I suppose I do."

"Ah-ha!" Jeffery said, jumping on her words. "I knew it!"

"But I also care about Rachel and Una and my job," Simone replied.

"But you care about me more, now, admit it," he countered, his face smug with assurance.

"I'm just starting to care about a great deal. You have to understand, Jeffery, that I've buried my feelings for so long that I don't know quite how to deal with this storm that's raging inside of me." Tears welled in her eyes. "It's all so new to me. For so long no one cared about me, and now so many people seem to want only my happiness."

"Now, Mr. O'Donnell," Nellie said, sweeping into the room unannounced, "you can't be wearing this poor girl out. We've just got her back on her feet."

Jeffery gave Simone one final look of longing before turning to Nellie. "Yes, I know. However, I want to let Miss Dumas know that her old job is open and waiting for her in Topeka."

Nellie shooed him toward the door. "Nonsense. We need the girl here. Now, you go on about your business. The noon meal is on the table, and if you don't get in there, you won't get fed."

Jeffery laughed. "Then I would have to report you to Mr. Harvey, and you know the customer is always right."

Nellie laughed and followed him from the room, leaving Simone to stare after them. Her heart felt full with emotions she couldn't even begin to put into words.

"I'm really free," she whispered to herself. "I don't have to go back to that cabin and way of life. I don't have to worry about being hunted down."

She gripped the back of the chair and looked across the room to the lacy curtained windows that opened out to give vision to the world beyond the Harvey House. She had hope for her future . . . and freedom to live her life as she chose. To ask for anything more seemed utterly and completely selfish.

"But I do need more," she whispered and glanced heavenward.

"I need direction on where to go and . . ." She fell silent, thinking of Jeffery. How did he fit into all of this?

"I need to know what to do with him, Lord," she prayed aloud. "I don't want to hurt him, but neither do I want to get hurt again. I'm just so afraid to open myself up to what he has in mind."

THIRTY-FOUR

SIMONE SAT UNDER the shade of a large elm and stared at the idle, muddy waters of the Cottonwood River. Soon she would be needed in the dining room, but for these few cherished moments, she simply intended to enjoy the quiet of the day.

Overhead, cottonball clouds drifted lazily across the blue prairie skies, and Simone thought how perfect life seemed. It would be so easy to sit back and allow the rest of the world to go about its business without her. But in her heart Simone knew that God had other plans for her.

"I thought I might find you here," Jeffery announced, coming up behind her.

Simone sighed. "And I figured you would eventually seek me out."

"Try not to sound so enthusiastic," Jeffery replied, sitting down on the dead brown grass of the riverbank.

"I'm sorry." She glanced up to meet Jeffery's face. "I'm not trying to be difficult."

Jeffery smiled. "I'd say since I met you, you've been nothing but difficult."

Simone shook her head and looked back at the river. "You've not been exactly the easiest company in the world to contend with."

"You've had my undying devotion from the start." His words were offered in a most serious manner. "In fact, I've come here now to speak my mind."

"Don't."

The word was offered simply yet firmly, surprising Jeffery into silence. For several moments Simone thought—even prayed—that Jeffery might drop the subject and prepare for his departure. It wasn't that she longed to see him return to Topeka, but she needed time to think things through, and with Jeffery continually popping up unannounced, considering matters for very long was impossible.

"I won't be kept from speaking my mind," Jeffery finally said. "I've come to care a great deal for you, Simone. I am quite determined to talk about our future together, and I think you know very well what I have in mind."

Simone tried to make light of the matter and chuckled. "You are only trying to win your bet that I would marry before my contract time is up."

Jeffery jumped to his feet. "Don't laugh at me, Simone."

She looked up at the hurt expression and knew she'd gone too far. Getting to her feet, Simone faced Jeffery. "I wasn't laughing at you, Jeffery. I only wanted to make this situation easier to deal with. I'm so confused. Surely you can understand that."

Jeffery reached out to take hold of her arms. "I only understand that I love you. That I hold you more dear than anything else in this world. I cannot bear that you might not return those feelings. Please tell me you feel something more than amusement for me."

"Of course I feel something more," Simone replied, refusing to elaborate. "You are a dear friend to me."

"I don't want to be just a friend."

Simone turned sharply. "But you don't understand. I never had a friend before coming to you in Chicago. At least not a male friend. My whole life has been filled with pain and misery. Even my mother's love was stripped away from me at an early age. I'm not even sure I know how to be a friend in return. I don't want to hurt you."

"Let me worry about that," Jeffery replied, pulling her against him. "I want you for my wife."

Simone felt her heart pound wildly as her breathing quickened.

Jeffery's eyes seemed to burn holes into her soul. It was as if he could clearly see all of her feelings, the worry and fear . . . the doubts.

"Please try to understand," she murmured. "I've only come to know what it is to be free. I don't know how to give my feelings. I don't even know for sure what those feelings are."

"Then let me help you understand them."

He reached up to gently touch her hair. His fingers trailed down to her cheek, and Simone closed her eyes to keep from betraying her emotions. Tears came to her eyes, and when they escaped her tightly closed lids and trickled down her cheeks, Jeffery's fingers stopped their motion. Simone opened her eyes to meet Jeffery's confused expression.

"This is very difficult for me. For so long I truly believed that hope was nonexistent. I had no hope, no faith—and to trust others was unthinkable." Simone looked at him, praying that he might understand. "I have hope again. I know what it is to look forward to tomorrow. And after a lifetime of fear, I'm just coming to understand that I can trust people and not pay for it with my life.

"But I have to seek what God wants me to do," she whispered. "I've only just allowed myself to listen to Him again. I can't and won't make choices without paying the strictest attention to what He wants for me. I've isolated myself from everyone and everything for so long, and now you want me to just forget my past and head into a new, joyful future. And, Jeffery, I can't do that."

Jeffery released her and stepped back. "I see." His voice was flat, almost harsh.

"No, you don't see," Simone replied. "Most of my life people have betrayed me in one manner or another. That isn't something you just up and decide doesn't matter anymore."

He stared at her, as if longing to say something that would change her mind, but instead he remained silent. The sorrow and disappointment in his expression were almost more than Simone could bear. Stepping forward, she gently put her hand on his cheek.

"Please try to understand what I'm saying. It isn't you—it's me. I don't know who I am or what I'm supposed to do. I don't know what to feel or think. I need time to know my heart."

"I think you already know your heart," Jeffery replied. "I think you know it, but you're too afraid to trust your feelings, and—" He paused to make certain she was listening. "You're too afraid to trust me."

"It isn't that simple."

"Oh no?" he questioned, pulling her back against him. He lowered his mouth to hers and kissed her with a fiery passion that left Simone stunned and unable to speak when he finally let her go.

"I think you're trying to make this harder than it has to be. I'm leaving for Topeka in a few hours. You have a job there if you want it, and you have me there—at least for a short time. The choice is yours."

He didn't wait for an answer but instead turned and walked back toward town. Simone watched him go. A part of her longed to call out after him, while another equally determined part refused to allow her a single word.

He's leaving. He's going away and I could stop him. Unlike the others in her life, Simone knew with confidence that if she but issued the request, Jeffery would turn in his tracks and return to her. But she didn't stop him. Not then, nor two hours later when the passenger train bound for Emporia and Topeka pulled away from the Florence depot.

"Are you going back to Topeka?" Una asked her later that night.

Simone sat brushing her long ebony hair, and with each stroke she considered her plight. "I don't know. Rachel sent me a telegram and begged me to return. She told me how lonely she'd been since I'd come to Florence. But I just don't know what to do." She put her brush on the nightstand and sighed. "I wish the answers were easy and clear."

Una smiled. "I think they're more clear than you realize. But I think, too, that you're scared. You're afraid to feel things for folks, especially someone like Mr. O'Donnell, no?"

Simone nodded. "I'm very much afraid. I mean, I know I don't have to worry about the things I lived with in the past. It would seem very few people act like Louis Dumas and Garvey Davis. There are geniunely good people in this world, and I want to believe that I'll never have to contend with those who are less than honest. But, Una, I'm afraid my ignorance will be the ruin of me."

"God understands your fears, Simone. He knows about them even before you take them to Him."

"I thought I'd been through the worst possible of fears," Simone admitted. "My life had so much to be afraid of. But this . . . this is something so completely overwhelming. My head hurts from thinking so long and hard about it."

"Is it so bad to accept that you care for him? That you have love for him?"

Simone shook her head. "It's not bad to accept the idea, but it's what to do with it after that."

Una sat down beside Simone. "God will guide your steps, but you can't move ahead unless you are willing to step out in faith that He will be there."

"It's so hard."

"Ja. Nothing good ever comes easy."

"Have you ever been in love, Una?"

The blond-haired girl shook her head. "No. I've been too busy. My moder needed me to work at her side, and when I left home to work for Mr. Harvey, I was too busy with my job to think about such things." She grinned and added, "However, there is a nice man here in town who has asked me to come with him to the opera. Imagine me at the opera!"

Simone smiled. "Are you going?"

Una shrugged her shoulders. "Don't know yet. I told him I'd think on it."

"I think you should go," Simone replied conspiratorially. "I think you'd have a great time."

"I think you should go to Topeka," Una countered. "You can't just keep running away from your problems. Sooner or later you're going to have to stand up to them face-to-face."

Simone realized the truth in her words. "I'd not thought about it as running away. I suppose it is just one more way I've avoided dealing with my feelings."

Una nodded. "Ja, I think so."

"It's just that . . ." Simone paused and shuddered. How could she explain all the things that came to mind whenever she considered a future with Jeffery? She knew it was foolish, but awful thoughts came to mind when she thought about becoming anyone's wife.

Una took hold of her hand. "What is it?"

"I'm just so afraid, Una. When Jeffery kisses me I feel all weak and overwhelmed. I can hardly even speak. Then I think about what he really wants from me. How he wants me for his wife and what all that means. I think back to my mother and father and the horror and ugliness that existed between them. They fought constantly and the pain my mother suffered—"

"You don't think for one minute that Jeffery would treat you that way, do you?" Una interrupted.

Simone met Una's expression of disbelief. "I don't know what to think. I can't imagine that my father—and for all purposes he was the only father I knew—I can't imagine that he was cruel in the beginning. Otherwise my mother would never have married him. He probably acted in some charming way, assuring her that he was good and kind. He probably bought her gifts and showed her a wonderful time. Why else would my mother have ever agreed to marry him?"

"You told me your mother was already expecting you. Maybe she was desperate to be away from her parents and took up with the first man who offered her an honorable solution. Maybe he had his obvious faults even then, and she didn't care. Or if she cared, maybe what she had to contend with in dealing with her folks was worse than what your father had in mind for her."

"I'd never thought of it that way," Simone replied.

"I don't think you should judge your own situation on what happened with them, Simone. My parents have been happily married for over thirty-five years. They've shared many good times and a few bad times, but they have never treated each other with anything but love and respect. Marriage can be a real blessing when the right people are joined together."

"But what if Jeffery and I aren't meant to be together? What if his interest has only been stimulated by the mystery surrounding my life?

What if we married and found ourselves totally wrong together?"

Una seemed unconcerned. "I can't help but think Jeffery would understand all of this, if you would just tell him how you feel. He is, after all, a reasonable and intelligent man. Just tell him your fears—tell him the truth."

Simone bit at her lower lip. "He deserves that much and more. But I need time."

Una patted her lovingly. "He doesn't seem the type to let a good thing get away from him based on impatience. Give him a reason to wait, and I think you'll find him most cooperative."

"But what if he's not the right one for me? I mean, just because his kisses leave me weak is hardly a reason to plan a wedding."

"True enough, but I think there is so much more. You trust Jeffery, don't you?"

"Yes," Simone admitted. "I trust him."

"Then that's the very best place to start. You have something special in that trust. You know he will keep your secrets, and that no matter how ill the rest of the world thinks about you, Jeffery will think only the best. He's proven it to be so."

"I suppose you're right in that."

"Pray about it. Take it to God, then listen to your heart. Trust Jeffery to understand. Be honest with him, and I think you'd be surprised by his reaction."

"But he wants a wife now, and I know I can't be that for him. Not yet."

"Then tell him that," Una urged. "You have nothing to lose."

"Nothing but his friendship."

"If he withdraws his friendship because you were honest, then he wasn't much of a friend at all." Una stood and looked at Simone. "But I think he will stand by you. I think friendship is important to him as well as to you. I think Mr. O'Donnell will do whatever he must in order to keep you close to him."

"I suppose I should go back to Topeka," Simone said flatly.

"It would be the best way to deal with the matter and maintain your job with Fred Harvey's company. Besides, Jeffery will be returning to Chicago. You heard yourself from Miss Taylor that he made far more trips to Topeka than he used to. There's bound to be times when he has to be away in order to properly do his job."

"I know you're right," Simone replied, smiling sadly. "But it also means leaving you."

"We won't be that far away. You'll come to visit me, and I'll come to visit you. You'll see. Now, go to sleep, and in the morning it will all be more clear. God will give you a peace about it if you seek to know peace. Some folks prefer the turmoil because it's the most familiar element in their life. They get so used to wallowing in it that they start to seek it out. Don't be like them, Simone. You've known a lot of strife and heartache. Don't reject peace and happiness just because it's different."

"I won't," Simone promised, wondering if she was truly already on the road to such actions.

Long after Una had fallen asleep, Simone lay awake trying to decide what she would do. Rachel very much wanted her back in Topeka. Jeffery wanted her to be his wife. "And what do you want of me, Lord?" she prayed softly. "What shall I do that would be pleasing to you?" After years of telling herself that God's desires were unimportant to her, Simone felt a deep longing to know the truth of His choice for her in this matter. It was the last conscious thought she had before falling into a deep, consuming sleep.

THIRTY-FIVE

TWO WEEKS LATER, Simone wandered into the Topeka Harvey dining room feeling very much like she'd been away for years. She smiled, sniffing the air to catch Henri's famous Chicken a la Marengo with its pungent garlic and red wine calling-card aromas. She had missed her good friend and their quiet talks in French. She had also missed his cooking. She nearly laughed aloud as Rachel entered from the kitchen, three totally engrossed trainees on her heel. The animated discussion reminded Simone of her early days with the Harvey House.

"There is never to be a linen tablecloth put on a single table without thoroughly inspecting it for signs of wear and tear," Rachel told the girls. "Mr. Harvey would strip the table bare should he find a single blemish, and believe me, he has done just that on more than one occasion. We have no desire to be that careless again." The three uniformed girls nodded seriously.

"Mr. Harvey has also been known to send chipped china plates flying across the room to prove his point that they are not of a high enough standard to grace the tables of Fred Harvey's establishments," Simone added very softly.

Rachel turned and met her words with an enthusiastic smile. "Simone!" She left the stunned girls and rushed to embrace Simone. "Why didn't you let me know you were coming?"

"I wanted it to be a surprise."

"Well, it certainly is that. I mean, after you didn't reply to my first two telegrams, I presumed you'd given up thoughts of returning to Topeka," Rachel said, squeezing Simone's arm. "I can't believe you're here. Are you going to stay? Where are your bags?"

Simone laughed. "Still the same old Miss Taylor, I see." She nodded to the quizzical girls. "She's a tough taskmaster, but she's fair-minded and a good friend in times of need."

Rachel laughed. "Don't go getting them all soft on me. I've just managed to put some fear into them."

The girls grinned timidly at this, and Rachel shooed them off. "Go into the kitchen and help Bethel." The girls scurried off, leaving Rachel and Simone alone in the dining room. "When did you get in? I didn't see you on the morning train."

"No, I wasn't here. I came in last night, but I went to the hotel up the street. In all my life I'd never stayed at a fancy hotel, and I thought I deserved at least one night on my own."

"Did you enjoy it?" Rachel questioned, leading Simone past the tables and down the hall to her office.

"No," Simone admitted. "I was lonely." She laughed. "It's so funny. I used to enjoy being alone. It was all that I longed for, but now I find that the company I've kept these past months is something of an addiction. I crave the voices and the camaraderie. As hard as it is to admit it, I need people."

Rachel nodded. "I completely understand. I feel the same way. I suppose it might be different if I ever met the right man and settled down. Perhaps a family of my own would be enough to keep me entertained."

She opened the door to her office and led the way into the room. "Come sit with me and tell me everything that's happened while you were away. I mean, I heard it from Jeffery, but I want to know the rest from you."

Simone sighed, brushed off her blue serge skirt, and sat down on the soft red upholstery of a wing-backed chair. "Is this new?" she asked, running her hand along the arm.

"Yes. Jeffery thought my office needed a bit of a feminine touch. I didn't argue. He hasn't been himself at all. I know that you're all he's thinking of."

At the second reference to Jeffery, Simone bowed her head. She knew she loved him, and she fully intended to talk to Rachel about it, but she didn't quite know how to broach the subject. Perhaps she should just jump in with both feet and declare her feelings. After all, Rachel would be sympathetic and understand, and perhaps she could even suggest what Simone should do.

"I'd like to believe that it was missing me that brought you back to Topeka, but I think I know better," Rachel's voice called through her thoughts.

Simone raised her face to meet Rachel's sympathetic expression. "Is it that obvious?"

Rachel laughed. "It always has been."

Simone shook her head. "I just don't know what to do about my feelings, Rachel. I have no one but you and Una to talk them over with. Una thinks me mad for not throwing myself into Jeffery's arms to happily become his wife, but I don't know what to do. I mean, Jeffery has always been good to me. He's been protective and remarkably patient, but is that enough to plan a life on? What do you think?"

Rachel eased back in her chair. "It doesn't really matter what I think. You have to live with your choices. Are you ready to say that you want to spend the rest of your life with Jeffery O'Donnell?"

"I can't imagine my life without him," Simone admitted. "But, Rachel, I'm only seventeen. I know a great many women marry younger than seventeen—my own mother married at fifteen. But I know, too, that I'm not ready." Simone got to her feet and paced a few steps, covering the width of the tiny office. "There's so much that I have to deal with. Betrayal and pain that is only now starting to fade. When I think of all that I've been through and all that I have yet to deal with, I fear that I would be much too preoccupied with myself to be any good to anyone else. Then, too, I love my job. I like being independent and I like making new friends."

"Would that all have to end if you agreed to become Jeffery's wife?"

"I don't know. I suppose it's something that would need to be addressed with Jeffery. But honestly, Rachel, there are already so many other things I need to consider that keeping Jeffery's marriage proposal out of the center of things seems the only intelligent resolution."

"Have you prayed about these things?" Rachel asked gently.

"Absolutely," Simone replied emphatically. "I pray and pray and I know that God hears me, but it isn't like it's all fixed the minute I say 'Amen.'"

"Of course not. God doesn't always work like that. There are times when you'll find things dealt with that easily, but it isn't always so. In fact, it's usually not done that way at all. Most of life seems to be a process of peaks and valleys, and the path isn't always well defined. But I wouldn't want you to alienate Jeffery just because your life has been difficult. You should just be honest with him. Tell him that you love him and tell him that you need time. I'm willing to bet he'll understand."

"Una said the same thing. I suppose I'm afraid."

"Of what?"

Simone came back to the chair and sat down on the edge. "Afraid that he'll tell me good-bye. Afraid that he's not willing to wait and that I'll have to swallow my own fears and concerns and marry him right away or risk losing him forever."

"Simone, you should never, ever feel that you must hurry into any lifelong decision. God wants you to take the time to pray and consider His will. If it's right for you to marry Jeffery, God will help you to put the past in order and feel comfortable with planning out a future. Trust Him."

"I suppose you're right." She paused, then shook her head again. "No, I know you're right." With new determination, Simone got to her feet. "I know I can trust God! I won't give in to my fears. I've allowed fear to run my life in the past, and it's time to put it to an end!"

"Good girl. Now, why don't you go down the hall to the house manager's office and tell Jeffery."

"He's here?" Simone said, sinking back into the chair. Gone was all sign of her bravado. Her voice sounded weak and uncertain. "He's really here?"

"He's here, all right. He stormed off to Chicago when you didn't show up the day after he arrived here in Topeka. I really think he figured you'd follow him."

"I wanted to," Simone admitted. "But I just couldn't."

"I understand, but now that you've had some time, I think you should talk to him. He's getting ready to go south again. I don't know if you're familiar with the new Harvey House resort that's being planned for New Mexico, but it's going to be the largest and finest establishment Mr. Harvey has yet to put into place. Jeffery has been trying to put together the necessary staff."

"I see." Simone felt a tightening in her chest.

"I don't think you should let him go off to New Mexico Territory without at least talking to him about your feelings."

Simone nodded. She felt desperate to see Jeffery. After watching him walk away nearly two weeks earlier, she knew she had to see him—had to explain. Getting up very slowly, she moved toward the door and smiled weakly over her shoulder at Rachel and said, "I suppose I'll go see him."

"Tell him the truth, Simone. Lay your cards out on the table, so to speak." Rachel, too, got to her feet. "And when you're done . . ."

Simone stopped and turned. "Yes?"

"Get your things out of that hotel and get back here to help me with the lunch crowd."

Simone grinned. "Yes, ma'am."

Jeffery shrugged out of his jacket and tried once again to focus on the ledgers in front of him. He wanted to lose himself in his work, but every time he tried he thought only of how his work separated him from pursuing Simone in Florence. Perhaps a change of jobs was in order. After all, hadn't he thought of working for the Santa Fe Railroad in a capacity that would completely remove him from the Harvey House? He liked the idea of purchasing, and the railroad was always in need of innovative and intelligent people when it came to keeping the line running at a profitable cost. But the papers in front of him reminded Jeffery that he still had a job to do for Fred Harvey.

Pounding his fists on the desk, he nearly jumped when a knock sounded at the door. "Yes, what is it?" he shouted back.

The door opened slowly to admit the one person he'd never dared to even hope would be standing on the other side. "Simone." He breathed her name in a quiet hush and got to his feet.

"I'm sorry if I'm bothering you," she apologized.

He regretted yelling. She looked so timid and unsure of herself. Her eyes seemed huge as they searched his face. "You know better," he said, letting out a heavy sigh. He tried to protect himself by feigning nonchalance, but all the time he longed to rush to her side and take her in his arms. "What do you want?"

Simone stared at him a moment longer before answering him. "I've come back to Topeka. Rachel asked me to work here for a time longer, and I thought it would be a good idea."

Jeffery refused to look away, afraid she might vanish into thin air. "I see," he replied curtly. "I suppose I shall be seeing the papers of transfer." He forced himself to sit back down at the desk, but still he watched her.

She took a hesitant step forward, then another. Her eyes searched his face as if hoping to find something. Biting her lower lip she glanced back at the door for a quick moment before returning her gaze to Jeffery.

Afraid that his indifference would cause her to bolt and run, Jeffery gave up his pride. "Sit down and tell me what you've come to say."

She twisted her gloved hands together. "I . . . I . . . oh, I can't do this!" she suddenly exclaimed and moved back to the door.

Jeffery had never known himself capable of such speed, but when he saw Simone preparing to leave, he jumped up from the desk and beat her to the door. "No! Don't go! You came all this way, now tell me what you're thinking." He put himself between her and the door and waited for her to speak.

"It's just that . . ." She hesitated and shook her head. "This is so hard for me."

"It's been no picnic for me," he countered. "I think you owe me some kind of explanation. Some word on why you refused to answer my telegrams—or even Rachel's."

"I needed time," Simone snapped back. "You've never understood that, but I need time. I can't just rush headlong into things, and I won't be pushed around as if my feelings aren't important."

"I'd just like to know what those feelings are," Jeffery replied, his voice edged with obvious irritation.

Simone bristled. "So would I."

"Ha!" Jeffery stepped toward her. "You know exactly how you feel, but you won't admit it."

"That isn't true!" Simone moved back a step.

"Yes, it is." Jeffery took another step forward. This wasn't how he'd envisioned their reunion, but he wasn't about to back down. "You wouldn't be here if you didn't know exactly what you were feeling. I think you owe me the common courtesy of sharing those feelings. Is that too much to ask?"

"It didn't seem so a few minutes ago," Simone muttered.

"What?" He stopped short of touching her, but there were only mere inches separating their bodies.

"Oh, bother!" she declared, putting her hands on her hips. "I love you! There! Are you satisfied?"

The declaration was given with such an air of frustration and despair that Jeffery couldn't help but be taken aback. But when the initial shock wore off, he began to chuckle, and then to laugh. Simone stared at him in total confusion.

"You're laughing? I bare my soul and you laugh at me?" She started to sidestep him, but Jeffery would have no part of it.

"Oh no, you don't. You aren't going anywhere. At least not until we sort this thing out. You make it sound as though loving me is a loathsome thing. How can you imagine that I would allow you to just waltz out the door without any further explanation?" He felt her tremble beneath his hands and sobered. Instantly he knew that this wasn't the way to handle Simone Dumas. People had been asserting authority over her all of her life. No, he needed to be gentle, giving, yielding . . . even though he didn't feel like yielding. Humbling himself, he lowered his voice. "Please don't go. Please. I promise to hear you out."

Simone nodded. "I'm sorry. It's just that this doesn't come easy for me."

"It's not easy for either of us." He reached up to touch her cheek. Oh, but her skin was soft, and her eyes were like a deep blue velvet. He wanted to never let her go from his sight, and yet he knew—instinctively he knew—she had not come here to accept his proposal of marriage. The thought sobered him even more. "I know you can't marry me."

Her expression registered surprise. "Not yet," she finally whispered.

Hope surged anew in his heart. "Not yet?"

She smiled ever so slightly and reached a hand up to touch his face. "I need time. It isn't that I don't want to marry you. I do." He watched her battle with her emotions as tears came to her eyes. "There's just so much I need to put behind me. Can you understand?"

Jeffery nodded. "Yes, I think I can. And if not, then I respect your need."

Silence hung heavy between them, and for several moments they did nothing but gaze into each other's eyes and touch each other's faces. Jeffery wanted to reassure Simone, yet he knew she had to control this situation. He waited impatiently for her to speak, praying that she'd be willing to make some form of commitment to him.

"I do love you," she finally whispered. "And it's such a foreign feeling to me that I almost didn't recognize it for what it was. But I can't marry you without giving myself some time to grow up. That may sound silly, but I feel as though I've been that scared little ten-year-old girl for the past seven years. I need to find a way to put her at rest in order to mature into the woman I want to be."

He let his fingers trail up the side of her face. Gently caressing her hair, he nodded. "I do understand, but I love you so very much . . . and I'm so afraid of losing you."

"That's exactly how I feel about you," she admitted. "In fact, I just told Rachel that very thing."

"And what did the good Miss Taylor tell you?" he asked, smiling.

"To be honest with you."

He nodded. "I'm glad I hired that woman."

Simone giggled. "Me too."

"So what do we do about this?" he questioned.

Simone bit at her lip and lowered her eyes. "Would it be so awful to wait for me?"

He pulled her against him tightly, relishing the softness of her, her willingness to be held by him. "I would wait forever—if you only ask."

She pulled back just enough to look into his eyes. "Please wait."

He smiled and nodded. "Forever."

"No," she said, shaking her head. "Just a little while."

Jeffery felt his heart nearly burst with joy and pride. She loved him! She loved him and she was willing to pledge herself to him—to ask him to wait for her. She put her hand behind his head and pulled him down to meet her lips. The surprise of her actions affected him in a way he'd not expected. He almost felt as timid and uncertain as she had looked earlier when first arriving in his office.

He let her lead the action, dictating how deep the kiss, how long the touch. When she pulled back, Jeffery tightened his hold and she put her head against his shoulder and sighed.

"You sure don't kiss like a ten-year-old," he teased.

Simone began to giggle and then to laugh. Her joy was like music to his heart. After seeing her so terrified and miserable for as long as he'd known her, Jeffery thought there could be no better sound in all the world. But he was wrong. The very best came when she finally regained control and with an expression of elation reaffirmed her feelings.

"I love you, Mr. O'Donnell."

THIRTY-SIX

April 1891

"HAPPY BIRTHDAY!" a chorus of Harvey Girls cried as Simone came into the dining room on Jeffery's arm.

Rachel came forward with a large hatbox. "We all pitched in and thought you should have this."

Simone looked to Jeffery, who just shrugged his shoulders and moved away to allow her to take hold of the package.

"We know you might not need it today, but I have a feeling it won't be so very long until you will need it," Rachel added.

Simone took the box and allowed herself to be led to the table where a beautiful two-tiered birthday cake awaited her.

"Happy Birthday, Simone," said Henri with great gusto. His English had improved much over the months he'd been under Fred Harvey's employment.

"Oh, Henri, what a creation," Simone replied in French. She loved the sound of her mother's tongue. The way the words seemed to come forth almost in song. "I feel so honored that you would go to so much trouble." She touched her free hand to a pale pink icing rose.

"Only the best for my dear friend," he replied.

"Now sit down and open your gift," Rachel commanded.

Simone took her gaze from the white-haired Henri and looked back to the expectant expressions of her fellow workers. "I've never had a birthday party."

"This shall be the first of many," Jeffery declared, pulling an envelope from his pocket. "Here, I believe I owe you this."

Simone looked up. "Owe me what?"

"Just look inside," he said, laughing. "You'll understand."

Simone opened the envelope and counted out seventeen dollars and fifty cents. She smiled, nodding. "I had nearly forgotten."

"It's the results of our bet," Jeffery told Rachel and the other girls. "I told her I bet she couldn't stay single for the duration of her contract with Mr. Harvey." He put his hands to his chest in a melodramatic manner. "But, alas, she has proven me wrong and taken my last dime." The girls giggled, and even Henri snorted a laugh.

"The day that seventeen dollars and fifty cents takes Mr. O'Donnell to his last dime will be the day pigs fly," Rachel said.

"Well, my good woman, that is where you are wrong. I have this day given up my position with the Harvey office in Chicago and it is my intention to take over the running of the purchasing and shipping offices for the Santa Fe Railroad in New Mexico. Leastwise, in the town of Morita, where Mr. Harvey's newest and finest resort hotel will feature our own Miss Taylor as house manager."

"Rachel! Why didn't you tell us?" the girls all clamored in unison.

Rachel looked at Jeffery and Simone in stunned surprise. "I suppose because I didn't know about it. Is this true?"

"It is. You've been approved to become a house manager. Not an easy feat for any man, let alone any woman. But I told Mr. Harvey you were more than capable of dealing with the responsibility, and we both agreed it would be impossible to find a more trustworthy person for the position."

"I . . . don't know what to say," Rachel replied. "Me, a house manager? And for a resort the size of Morita!"

"You'll be perfect for it," Simone said, putting aside Jeffery's envelope of money and the hatbox. She came to take hold of Rachel's hands. "I only hope you will hire me on as one of your staff members."

"Of course! Oh, my dear, I wouldn't even want to consider going if you weren't going to be nearby."

"It's my hope she'll be nearby for both of us," Jeffery replied.

Simone threw him what she hoped was a loving look of affirmation. She loved him more every day, although she had no idea how it was possible. "I'll be there for you both. You can count on me for that."

"Open your present," Bethel exclaimed. "Open it now, or I shall start crying at the thought of you both going away."

Simone nodded and, after giving Rachel's hands a squeeze, went back to the table where she'd left her hatbox. Opening the lid, she gasped at the sight of the wedding veil inside. Lifting it tenderly from the box, Simone could only stare in appreciation of the white Brussels lace and netting.

"It's exquisite," she finally managed to say. The lump in her throat refused to be swallowed down, and looking up, she met Jeffery's eyes and the unspoken question that came from their depths. He had been so very patient with her and now seemed the perfect moment to honor his loving care. Smiling, she looked back to Rachel and the girls. "I'm sure I'll be needing this very soon."

The girls cheered and Rachel moved forward to hug Simone in a motherly fashion. "Oh, Simone, I'm so happy for you."

Simone looked over Rachel's shoulder to where Jeffery stood with a smug expression of contentment upon his face. He raised a questioning brow but never said a word.

The party passed all too quickly and soon the dining room was once again converted back into the Harvey dining hall. Simone took her things back to her room, including a big piece of birthday cake that Henri had insisted she keep for later. She had the rest of the day off, and Jeffery had promised to take her to a fine restaurant before escorting her to her very first opera at the Grand Opera House.

She dressed carefully for the evening in her very first store-bought gown of burgundy crepe de chine. This was Jeffery's birthday gift to her, and he'd brought it all the way from Chicago. She had thought to refuse such a personal gift, but Rachel quickly assured her that under the circumstances, Jeffery would no doubt soon be buying all of her clothes.

Glancing at her reflection in the mirror, Simone paused a moment to look for any flaw. She appeared quite grown-up and fashionable, something she'd never thought to see herself as. The material was icy and smooth against her skin, and Simone reveled in an opulence she'd never before known.

Seeing by the clock that Jeffery would soon begin to worry about her, Simone quickly pulled on gloves and found the small beaded purse that Rachel had lent her. With one final glance in the mirror, Simone lifted her chin and squared her shoulders. Tonight she would accept Jeffery's proposal of marriage. There was now no doubt about it, and for the first time since he'd mentioned the idea, Simone felt at peace. She longed to become his wife and felt that with Zack Matthews' brief missive explaining her father's incarceration in a Wyoming prison, the past was now firmly behind her.

She left the room and found Jeffery waiting for her at the bottom of the stairs. The sharp intake of his breath gave her little doubt that he approved of her appearance. His expression of complete adoration and unspoken love made Simone feel flushed and warm.

"You, my dear Simone, are a vision to behold," Jeffery said, taking her hand in his.

"I hardly feel at all like myself," she confided.

"Well, you are just as you should be. Stunningly beautiful." He ushered her through the dining room, where the other Harvey Girls gave her their hearty approval.

"You look divine!" Bethel proclaimed.

"I've never seen a gown like that," another declared. "I suppose Chicago has all manner of mysteries I might not ever know."

The girls laughed and teased each other, wondering aloud if Jeffery had any brothers or friends he might send their way. Rachel finally appeared, issued her own approval, then hustled the girls back to their stations so that Simone and Jeffery might be free to go.

"I thought we might never be alone," Jeffery whispered in Simone's ear just before handing her up into his awaiting carriage.

Simone shivered as she took her seat on the rich leather upholstery. Jeffery signaled the driver, then joined her inside the covered carriage, taking great pleasure in positioning himself at her side.

"And now it is just as it should be. You are here with me, and there is no one else in the entire world but us."

Simone swallowed the lump in her throat. She felt a trembling begin in her toes that worked its way up her body. Somehow things had changed between them. With her very public announcement that she would soon be married, Jeffery seemed more handsome, his shoulders more broad, his eyes more penetrating.

He put his arm around her and pulled her close. "I have something else to give to you. I had prayed that you might accept it tonight, and now, well . . ." He fell silent, but with his free hand he produced a shimmering ring of sapphires and gold.

"Oh my," Simone barely whispered. She looked at him, hoping his expression would reassure her.

Jeffery smiled as if reading her mind. "I love you, Simone. Please do me the honor of being my wife. Please tell me that the waiting is over."

Simone glanced down at the ring, then removed her glove and extended her hand. "The waiting is over," she assured him.

Slipping the ring on her finger, Jeffery clasped her fingers in his hand and pulled her closer. "Let's just skip the opera and dinner and find a preacher."

Simone giggled. "I don't think the Harvey Girls would understand. They are very much looking forward to making our wedding quite the affair of the year."

Jeffery rolled his eyes and shook his head. "You lied. You said the waiting was over."

Simone leaned forward, her lips only a breath away from his. "I'm sure they could plan something rather quickly. After all, Fred Harvey prides himself on the fact that his girls are quick and efficient."

"So true," Jeffery whispered, pressing a light kiss upon her lips.

Simone sighed and put her arms around his neck. "According to Rachel," she told him, "this is very scandalous behavior for an unchaperoned young woman."

"If Mr. Harvey saw you, you would be fired for such a public display."

Simone grinned. "Good old Mr. Harvey. I suppose we have him to thank for our coming together."

"Him and God," Jeffery replied.

Laughter filled the carriage, and Simone nestled herself against her intended. Her life felt transformed from the despair of her childhood. She thought back to her cabin home in the Wyoming mountains. Only a year before, she had thought nothing good could ever come to her. Only a year before, she had given up on life, keeping her heart carefully protected from any harm. But God had worked a miracle. He had given her a shelter of hope. He had taken the despair from her heart and left love and joy in its place.

NOTE TO THE READER

Fred Harvey's line of restaurants was famous throughout the nation from the late 1870s and well into the twentieth century. The locations varied along the Santa Fe Rail line, and a few examples of the restaurants, hotels, and resorts are still in existence to this day.

I have taken liberty with the description of the Topeka Harvey House in order to better fit my story. The description used in this book with the dining room on the ground floor and the girls' dormitories on the second floor was a typical arrangement in many of the Harvey Houses, but in 1890s Topeka, the restaurant was in fact on the second floor of the depot. Very little has been recorded of this, the first of the Harvey Houses, but it was the start of a very successful career for Fred Harvey.

I would also like to add that the managing personnel for the Harvey Houses have been completely fictionalized for all locations, with the exception to references about Fred Harvey. Also, the location of Morita, mentioned toward the end of the book, is a fictional town and resort.

As in any work of fiction, names and places, people and events have been created to serve the purpose of the story. However, I have worked hard to keep the details as close as possible to the actual historical accounts of the times.

Tracie Peterson